MESSIEURS

by Robert Rahula

ALSO BY ROBERT RAHULA

NOVELS:
Panamaniac
Island of Misfits
Day Another Paradise In
One Last Fling
Bathhouse Stories
Conversation in a Belgian Bar
All the Yage in Reno
Exigent Circumstances
Uninvited Guest

POETRY:
Trigger Points
Dentro Del Corazón Bloqueada
Camino
Migration
I Sing the Body Politic
Wonderland
From Whose Bourn
Poemas Españoles
Expat Poems

ANTHOLOGIES:
Half Life
The Essential Dan Landes

Translated by Joseph Wambatten.

ISBN 978-0-9994736-9-6

Alma-gator Press
Barcelona • Madrid • La Chorrera

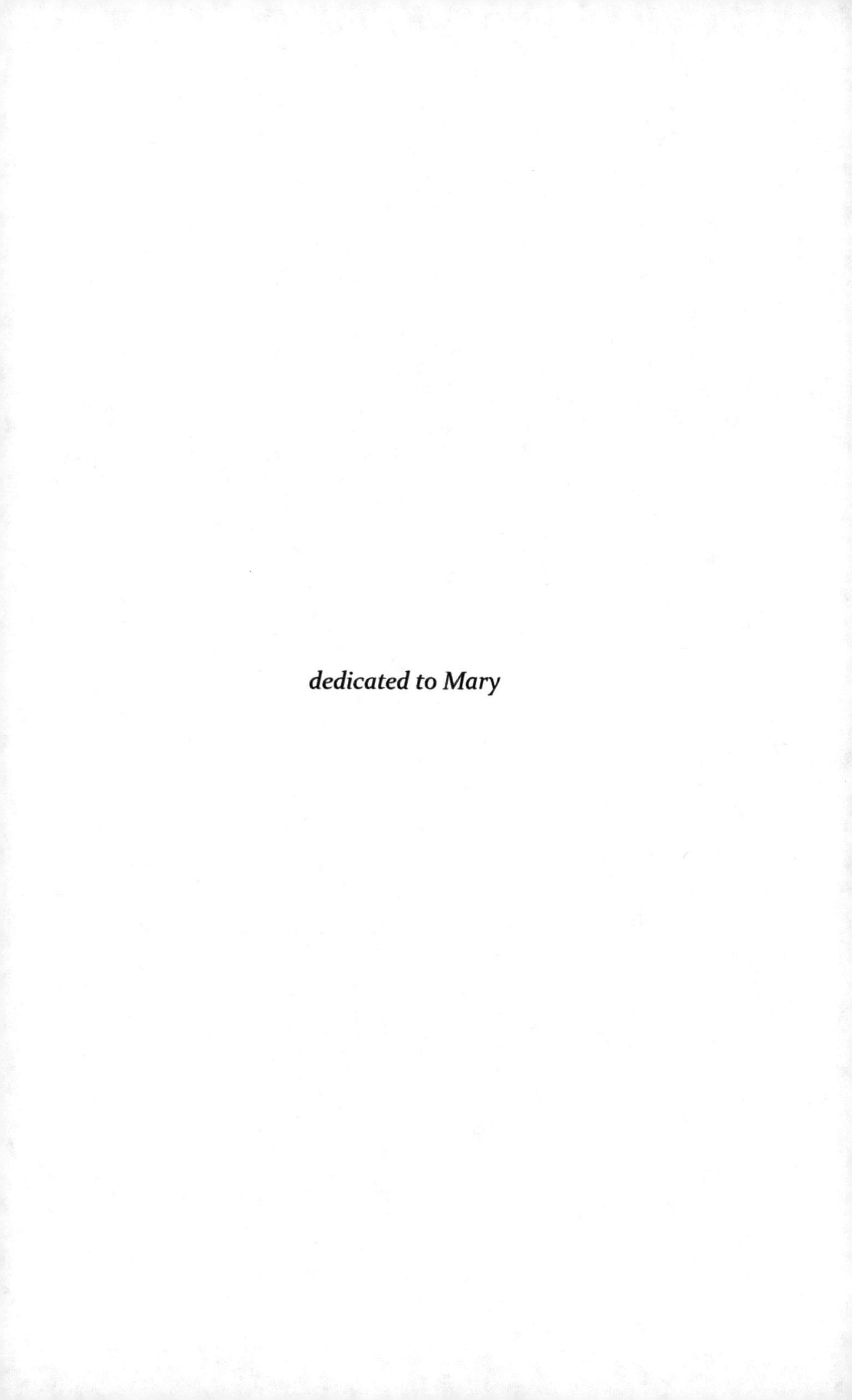

dedicated to Mary

Nobody realizes that some people
expend tremendous energy
merely to be normal.

-Albert Camus

PART 1:   MONSIEUR

When the heart attack came, time just stopped. Monsieur knew instantly that he was in deep, deep trouble. The first wave of pain was more like a jolt. The second wave of pain was actually painful, and Monsieur went to his knees. His brain assessed the situation and told him that he could not bargain this away. But somehow, oddly, Monsieur didn't care...

·   ·   ·   ·

Two years earlier:

It all started with an itch. Monsieur was in the shower. The door to the bathroom was closed but not locked. The water was hot. He lathered up under his arms, then his chest and stomach, and then, almost absent mindedly, he took the bar of soap and lathered up his pubic hair. He ran his right hand down over his stomach, through his hair, and pulling the suds onto his penis, stretched it out slightly, and then released it. He took the soap and made another lather in his hands and then grabbed his penis again and pulled it straight out away from his body and let it flop back down between his legs.

He felt the itch in his asshole.

You could wash your asshole, his brain said. *That would be clean because you'd be using soap.*

He made a lather in his hands again, scooped up the lather in his right hand, and reached around his back, felt between his buttocks, and located his asshole. It was slightly lower than where he thought it would be. Even with his hand full of suds, Monsieur felt grit around his asshole. He rubbed the suds in, circling his asshole with his first two fingers. He circled round the mouth of his asshole without actually touching his asshole. Then he turned around in the shower and let the water fall down the small of his back, over his buttocks, and run down between his butt cheeks. He took the bar of soap and washed his hands, turned around and rinsed them in the showerfall.

The itch was worse.

Try again, his brain said.

He lathered up again and reached around. This time he touched the center of his asshole. The skin was all crinkly around the actual hole, which felt small and tight. He felt a small hemorrhoid, on the circumference of his asshole nearest his balls. He rubbed the suds around the hemorrhoid. That felt good. He glanced through the glazed glass shower door to the dark red door of the bathroom. It was still closed. Not that his wife would come in. After all, it was his bathroom. But if she did, could she see through the steam and the wet shower door? Could she see him leaning slightly forward, with his right arm wrapped around his right side, reaching, reaching back, down around his thigh, his hand hidden, his wrist bent inward, his fingers curled except for his index finger which was extended, reaching in and up?

His brain spoke up again. *You're safe. She won't come in, and even if she did, she wouldn't be able to see what you're doing.*

He made more lather and reached back again, this time running a little circle over the mouth of his asshole. The itch felt better. He pressed harder. He made fast small circles around his asshole, each time hitting the speed bump of the hemorrhoid. He pressed even harder. The suds made his fingers slide quickly over the puckered tight mouth, but it was difficult pressing so hard. His wrist began to hurt. He stopped and washed his hands under the hot water. The itch was still there, but not as bad. His asshole felt something—

not hurt, but not bad. But it wanted more. Monsieur checked his fingernails to see if they were clean. He scraped four lines in the soap bar with his fingers, curling up four strings of soap underneath his nails, and then lathered his hands again. Then he sniffed his fingers.

You'd better stop here, his brain said.

He washed his hair, rinsed, added some conditioner, rinsed his head again, rinsed his whole body twice, turning around and around in the shower, and then turned the shower off and grabbed a towel.

•　•　•　•

He had felt the itch before. He remembered back in Paris when he was living with his first wife, how the itch would torment him. Not always. Sometimes he wouldn't notice it for months. But then it would begin. He would slowly become aware of it during the day. He would try to ignore it. But eventually, he would end up sitting on the toilet, using a wad of toilet paper to rub his asshole. The rubbing was pleasurable. The itch would grow with each stroke. Back and forth. Monsieur would drop the wad of toilet paper into the toilet and get a fresh wad. Then he would rub even harder. He knew he wasn't rubbing to get clean— he was rubbing to scratch the itch. Harder and harder. Then his ass would start to hurt. Monsieur would look at the toilet paper. There were no shit stains, just tiny lines of red blood, as if drawn by a red felt-tip pen. He imagined pin pricks of tiny holes on his asshole, each exuding blood, so that when the wad of toilet paper passed over them, they left a thin straight line of blood.

He could never satisfy the itch with toilet paper. He would rub and rub, using up five or six wads of paper. Eventually the pain would get so bad he'd have to stop.

He bought various creams, all containing benzocaine. He'd rub them in to kill the itch. But sometimes the cream would stimulate the itch, and he'd end up using more toilet paper with cream on it to rub harder and harder, to try and reach the itch.

Sometimes he would put a glob of cream on his finger and push it ever so slightly up into his asshole. Maybe the itch was inside. Then he would wash his hands several times.

• • • •

Paris was many years ago. Monsieur did not know where his first wife was anymore. He had heard that she had moved back to Lille. His brain told him to not think about her. He had moved south, found a new job, and had gotten married again.

• • • •

Monsieur divorced his second wife. He did not know whether he was numb or just experienced from his first divorce, but he felt no grief. He was glad to be divorced. There had been no sex for at least a year, and the things she always complained about to him seemed to be in a foreign language. His brain told him to listen quietly, nod his head, say he was sorry at the appropriate moments, and just wait for her to stop complaining.

He did notice that after the divorce, the itch seemed to go away. He missed it. Sometimes in the shower, he would lather up and rub his asshole in hopes of reawakening it. But nothing happened. He didn't think he was losing his sex drive, because he thought about sex all the time.

• • • •

After the divorce from his second wife was finalized, Monsieur moved again, to a different city, and found a new job. Although he had lived for many years in some cities, it seemed to him that he was always moving. He liked new cities. He liked exploring them when he first arrived, when no one knew him. He liked being invisible.

He especially liked finding himself in cities with gay bathhouses. He would research them on the internet before he actually got to the city. He would memorize the addresses and try and find an apartment to rent near them. He anticipated his first visit to each one.

The gay bathhouses were all oddly similar. There would be a solid door to the street with a very discreet sign near the door. Once inside the first door, there was usually a long hallway up to what always seemed like a bullet-proof window with a slot open at the bottom for money. For a first-timer, there was always a membership form to fill out disclaiming this or that. Monsieur never read them—he just signed them with an illegible signature and handed them back. Then there was the inevitable question of whether he wanted just a locker, or a room, or a room with a TV, or a room with a sling. He always took the room with a TV. Then the man behind the glass window would take Monsieur's money and buzz him in through another solid door. Inside, there would be another window under which the man would pass Monsieur two towels and a key to the room. Condoms were free, but tubes of lubricant were one euro each. Finding his room usually involved walking down long dimly lit hallways. On the way to his room he would pass other rooms, some with the doors closed, others with the doors open and naked men lying on their beds, usually stroking their erect cocks, waiting for someone to come in and take them.

Monsieur would find his room and go inside. The door would always lock automatically behind him. He would turn the TV on but keep the sound off. It was almost always all male gay porn, young men with huge cocks, sucking each other or fucking each other in the ass. He would flip through the channels before he got undressed. Occasionally he would find bisexual porn.

Monsieur would then undress and lock his clothes in a locker inside the room. Then he would wrap a towel around himself and head for the showers.

· · · ·

Monsieur did not think of himself as gay. No one would describe him as gay. He had no effeminate gestures that ignorant people use to designate gayness. Actually, Monsieur preferred women. But they required so much effort. He had to meet them, talk to them, and develop a relationship before he could have sex with them. And then he had to be careful to walk that line between developing a relationship and being committed to a relationship. Monsieur found it hard to muster up the energy. He wanted the sex, the touching, the passion, the love and the surrender... but he did not want the planning, the decision-making, the long conversations, the compromising, the arguments, the endless analysis of where the relationship stood. He certainly did not want to get married again. Twice was enough.

Over the years, he had developed a method for parsing out the little energy he had. For example, he never tried to pick up women in bars or anywhere else. There would be no point. He simply did not have enough energy. His only technique was to wait for women to pick him up. He knew that if he remained in the right spot long enough, eventually some woman would come along—some woman just out of a relationship, someone just lonely enough, or scared of aging, or just horny enough to let him know she was interested and available. Then he just had to say hello and be a good listener. Usually the woman did the rest.

It wasn't the best technique in the world, but it was the only one which fit his energy pattern. He would keep himself well-groomed, well-dressed. He paid attention to every woman in whatever job he had. He was a very good listener. He paid equal attention to the heavy girls and the unattractive girls, because he knew they all had girlfriends. He would listen and offer consolation, perhaps a word of advice. He would rarely reveal much about himself, just enough to establish camaraderie, but still with a slight formal touch, a little distance. Women found him comforting, yet hidden. They thought him shy perhaps. They did not understand why he was unattached. They would invite him to various social get-togethers. Oftentimes he would hear them say to each other, "We have to find a girlfriend for Monsieur." Oftentimes there would be a group of three or four women from work going for a drink after work and they would invite him along. That was perfect.

And if he did find himself on what amounted to a date with a woman, he never made the first move. He was a gentleman the entire time, paying attention to her, making sure she had a good evening. Not that he was being manipulative—he was enjoying himself too. He would be enjoying looking at her, listening to her, making her laugh with a little joke, engaging in some serious discussion, being silly—he enjoyed every minute. But he would never try and kiss her goodnight. He would, of course, try and see her again. Usually by the third date, the woman couldn't stand it anymore, and would ask, "Are you going to fuck me or what?" Not so directly, but basically that was always the question. Then of course, he would.

•　　•　　•　　•

He had been to better bathhouses than this one, but this city only had two bathhouses, and this one was the better of the two. Monsieur paid and went in. By now he had a membership card and there were no forms to sign. He found his room and changed.

In the shower room, he lathered up good. He always

hated it when he met someone in the bathhouse who didn't take advantage of the showers. He didn't want to kiss a man's nipples and smell the man's scent. He wanted a clean soapy smell.

He noticed a muscular stocky fellow with a huge thick semi-erect cock showering nearby. Monsieur caught the glint of a metal cock ring around the base of the man's penis. *He's not your type,* his brain said, although Monsieur liked big cocks as well as anyone. He remembered one night in a Bilbao bathhouse giving a blowjob to a man with a huge cock. There is something erotic about a big cock, about touching such a huge organ. But Monsieur's brain told him that this man in the shower would be too aggressive.

The stocky man finished showering, dried off, and walked down the hall to the darkrooms. Monsieur finished showering, wrapped his towel around him, and went into the sauna.

Every gay bathhouse has a different design for their saunas. Some are so steamy it's impossible to see who's sucking who, which is the point. Others are warm with dark corners. Some are lined in redwood. Some are tile. This one was tile, built in a vague figure-eight shape, big enough to hold twenty people, with different levels to sit on, and many dark corners. Monsieur found a place to sit and undraped his towel from around his waist and started to discretely play with himself. He looked around. About ten feet from him in a dark corner was a man stretched out on his back. Someone was hunched over the man's middle, sucking his cock up and down. Monsieur watched this for a moment and started to get hard. Two other men were standing by this couple. One of the standing men reached over to the sucking man and started to rub his balls, and then began to finger his asshole. The sucking man didn't stop sucking, didn't even look around, but climbed onto the level where the prone man was, got on his knees and continued sucking, and raised his ass in the air toward the man who was fingering his ass. The standing man grabbed a condom package from a shelf, opened it and quickly snapped it onto his cock.

This should be interesting, Monsieur's brain said. The standing man continued to finger the sucking man but did not try to fuck him. Then the standing man just walked away. *Well, maybe not,* Monsieur's brain commented. A fat man with a stoned look in his eye walked near Monsieur and ran his hand on Monsieur's knee. Monsieur pulled his towel over his lap and gently shook his head no without making eye contact. The fat man walked away. The sucking man apparently finished too, for he got up and walked away. Monsieur looked around. There was an Hispanic man sitting across the way. Two Asians walked by, cruising together. Monsieur got up and walked out of the sauna.

Walking around is the main activity in most bathhouses—walking around until one is just in exactly the right corner with the right person. Monsieur walked down a hallway with many doors to rooms. Some doors were open. These were invitations. Monsieur looked inside one room. Here was a skinny young man lying on his bed stroking a huge cock. *Too skinny, but interesting,* Monsieur's brain said. He walked on. The room encounters were tricky because once inside, one had to decide to close the door, do something, or leave. Monsieur approached another open door. Here the light was turned off and a man was lying naked on his stomach. Monsieur knew this was a signal that the man wanted to be fucked in the ass. Monsieur had never tried this in a bathhouse. He did have an encounter once in a gay hotel where he was lying face up on the bed of an older man and the man put a condom on Monsieur's cock and lower himself onto Monsieur's cock. It was interesting but not as good as pussy, Monsieur's brain had decided. With pussy, there was warm wet snug contact the entire length of the cock. With this guy, there was only the ring of tightness at the asshole and not much inside. However, later the guy jerked Monsieur off and while he was doing so, stuck his finger slightly up Monsieur's ass, and that was strangely exciting to Monsieur.

Monsieur had also been rimmed by a girlfriend once, years ago, and he had found that also very exciting, in a forbidden dark way that he could not explain. They had been seeing each other a while, and sleeping together a lot, and one morning as he was waking up, as he was lying on his stomach, she climbed over him, got between his legs, pushed his legs apart and began to tongue his asshole. There had been no indication that she was going to do this, no prior discussion. She just did it. Monsieur was surprised, startled, but then arched his ass slightly up to make it easier for her to run her tongue all around his asshole and to probe into the center of his asshole. He found himself moaning until he couldn't stand it anymore and turned over and fucked her. Later he tried to talk with her about it, but she did not want to discuss it. A few days later, he fucked her in the ass. She did not refuse. She seemed to like it. He used some K-Y jelly. It wasn't like making love, where he would be concerned about her cumming. It was more animal-like. She was submitting. He fucked her until he came. When he pulled out, he looked down, and his cock looked black. It was dark in the room, so he couldn't be sure, so he got up and wordlessly went to the bathroom and turned the light on. His cock was covered with dark shit. Shit mixed with K-Y. He washed it off thoroughly in the sink. He washed his hands thoroughly too. This seemed a messy business.

Monsieur had been rimmed once or twice by men too. He remembered an older man that he met in a bathhouse once in Frankfurt. They had hit it off and took turns sucking each other in the sauna and resting and talking. Sometimes the object is not to cum. They ended up in the man's room where the man rimmed Monsieur while Monsieur lay on his back with his knees up and masturbated. It was very exciting. Monsieur came in several pulsating moments.

However, this particular night as Monsieur walked around, he was not having much luck. He walked through the darkrooms—twisting corridors designed to be dark with many corners for encounters—and did not find any options that excited him. Here was a very fat man; here was a very tattooed man; here was a young man who averted his eyes when Monsieur approached which was a sure sign of non-interest. Monsieur walked back through the sauna. A very muscular man was sitting in the corner sucking a man who stood straddled over him. Monsieur walked back to his room, closed the door behind him, lay on the bed, watched the porn on the TV, masturbated, and came.

•   •   •   •

Monsieur's new job was in a small government office. It was a provincial government probation office that reported to the courts. However, the actual probation officers were in another building downtown. This office just collected and filed reports. Monsieur would scour arrests reports through hundreds of websites from other provinces, match up arrests with "clients" and then send violation reports to the probation officers, who would in turn attempt to revoke the clients' probation and send them to jail. Monsieur liked the work because it was meaningless. He just handled reports. He didn't have to even pretend to care. As long as the reports got filed, the managers were happy and left Monsieur alone.

Monsieur often wondered at the unspoken agenda of this office. They were not paid on any type of quota, but clearly the worker who uncovered the most offenses committed by parolees were held in high esteem and rewarded by the managers. It was assumed that parolees were always out there committing new crimes, and each new uncovered offense was received as an affirmation of this belief. Particularly brazen offenses were posted on a bulletin board along with the name of the worker who uncovered it.

There were mostly women in the office. Monsieur, as usual, was equally nice to all of them, although he found it particularly difficult to remain gracious with a few of them. One was older, almost as old as Monsieur, but quite gray-haired, and overweight, and with the type of facial wrinkles that only years of smoking can bring, and a raspy smoker's laugh. She was very lonely and often came to Monsieur's cubicle to talk, usually interrupting him when he was trying to concentrate on his job. Monsieur tried to modify her behavior by only paying her compliments when he went to her cubicle yet withholding any positive reinforcement when she came to his cubicle. This did not deter her. Apparently, just a male presence was enough of a reward for her loneliness.

There was another overweight older woman there, not as lonely, but with a loud irritating voice. Fortunately, she did not interact much with Monsieur. The rest of the woman there were average, some almost pleasant.

Except there was one woman there who was younger, much younger than he, who was obviously a free spirit. Monsieur found himself attracted to her. She had dark eyes, some strange tattoos on her arms, a dark curly head of hair, and most alluring, dark hair on her arms. Monsieur visualized a bushy hairy pubic area. He loved bushy pussies. She was bright and had a quick sense of humor.

Unfortunately, she ignored Monsieur.

It's probably the age difference, his brain said. *You don't notice it, but she probably does. You look old to her, and younger women don't like old guys hitting on them. Plus, you work with her, on the same floor! This is not a good idea.*

It was true that Monsieur had a prohibition against fucking someone he worked with. The secret to his success on the job was his impeccable discretion. Employers always trusted him. Fellow workers never suspected him of any dalliance.

But Monsieur argued back to his brain. *Look at those hairy arms,* he said, *those beautiful soft long dark hairs on those white arms. You know what that means.*

Monsieur's brain could never win any battle where sex was concerned. It was as if he had cut a deal with his brain years ago. His brain could direct every aspect of his life and Monsieur would obey—every aspect except sex. Sex was the only time when Monsieur could make his brain shut up.

And so, Monsieur prepared for a long campaign. Over the weeks, he paid attention whenever she spoke at meetings. He would agree with her suggestions. He would support her position on issues. He made little jokes with her at coffee breaks. He avoided obvious out-and-out compliments or any obviously flirty comments. He did not want to be seen as a suitor. He never went to her cubicle, but if he passed her in the hall, he would often have a little clipping in his pocket that was pertinent to the cases that she was assigned to, and he would offhandedly give it to her, saying "Oh I happened to stumble on this the other day; I thought it might interest you." Of course, he might have secretly photocopied the list of clients she had to research that week, and he might have spent a few hours the night before studying websites to find some misdemeanor that one of her clients committed recently in a remote province... His only goal was to make her comfortable around him, at ease in his presence, perhaps at ease enough that she would open up, treat him as a confidant. The he would wait hopefully for some crisis in her life to occur. He knew it would be a long campaign, but he was patient.

Her name was Enid.

•　•　•　•

Monsieur had his down days. They would descend upon him like a soft fog. On those days he felt dull, out of focus. He had difficulty making decisions. Sometimes he would just sit for long periods of time in his apartment.

If it was a weekday, the need to get to work and to be seen as productive always prevailed, and he would get out of bed, wash, dress, and drive to work. On those days he was simply quiet and kept to himself. Because he was never loud or gregarious on his up days, his co-workers never noticed Monsieur's quiet days. He would do his work, get through the day, and quietly go home. Usually, after a couple of days, the fog would lift.

During the weekdays, the fog was not debilitating. But if it came on a weekend, he suffered. It would take enormous effort to leave his apartment. Routine errands seemed meaningless. Even breathing took effort. He would look forward to Monday and the work week. Therefore, Monsieur always tried to have a weekend activity lined up— something he had to do no matter his mood, something that would force him out of the apartment. He joined a gym and would schedule a work-out session. He would put off a specific purchase until the weekend, just to have a required activity. If he was lucky enough to have an invitation to a social event, that would be enough to keep the fog away. But if he failed to plan ahead, and the fog coincided with an empty schedule, he simply had to endure it. Once the fog hit, he was powerless to do anything but endure it until Monday.

He drank every night, usually a whole bottle of wine. He looked forward to the wine as the five o'clock hour approached. But if he was out with people, he never drank. He would never risk a DUI. Office mates assumed that he simply did not drink. They did not know that he got quietly drunk every night. He preferred drinking alone.

• • • •

The seduction of Enid was not going particularly well. In fact, it wasn't even getting off the ground. She obviously enjoyed his "witty repartee" as she put it, but there were no small unveilings of her soul from her. Monsieur knew that if a woman was interested in a man, she would, slowly at first, begin to reveal things about herself, her interests, her dreams, her past, her fears. It was some part of "forming a relationship" that women did, but he got none of that from Enid. They found a sense of humor in common, puns and double entendres and the like, but that's as far as it went. About a month into the job, he overheard her discussing something with a co-worker in which she mentioned her age, and Monsieur was shocked to realize that she was half his age.

See—this is an exercise in futility, his brain said.

No, he answered, *I'm being very discrete. No one can accuse me of hitting on her. And even it never leads to anything, I enjoy talking with her.*

It was true. Monsieur was genuinely fond of Enid. He liked her tattoos, her small breasts, the way she wore her black curly hair tied back, her smart-alecky take on the world, her intellectual references, and her Jewish accent.

She's kind of neurotic, his brain pointed out, *and self-centered.*

That's not my problem, he answered, *and if nothing develops between us, it will never be my problem.*

Monsieur did consider his other work options. There were other women in the building with whom he had exchanged pleasantries, but no real leads, no strong indications. Monsieur knew that the world is full of people who want to fuck but who hid this from the world. After all, he was one of them.

Be patient, his brain advised. *You're still the new kid in town. Just wait.*

·   ·   ·   ·

In the meantime, there were the gay options. On this particular night, Monsieur wanted to try a gay bar. He had purchased an underground guidebook to the gay scene in this particular city and had identified several bars that seemed interesting. This evening he picked one that was near the gay bathhouse, which was his back-up plan.

It was a rainy night, dark and drizzly, which Monsieur found to his liking. He always liked the dark. He had a map in his car and drove until he found the general neighborhood. He parked his car, checked the address on his post-it note, checked the map and got out of his car.

The bar was unmarked, except for the number on the door. He went in. It smelled good. Another door led him inside to a bar area that immediately felt inviting. The bar was square, with two bartenders in the middle, surrounded by four sides of bar, six to eight barstools on each side, TVs in the corner, pinball machines and video machines off to the side, tables all around. It did not feel threatening, like some gay bars did. Monsieur walked up to the bar and sat down. A bartender came over. Monsieur ordered a beer. It appeared quickly.

As he drank, Monsieur looked around. There was a man with a large beard across the way, talking with a younger man. There was another man sitting at the bar dressed in a lot of leather stylings. Shaved heads seemed to be in. It was not crowded, but everyone seemed to be talking to someone. In other words, everyone was there with someone. It could have been a neighborhood bar in Dublin with factory mates having a beer before returning home to their wives. Nobody was cruising.

Still, Monsieur felt comfortable. He drank his beer and leafed through a gay neighborhood newspaper. There were various articles about community issues, ads for upcoming drag shows, advice columns, warnings about disease, tirades against the police, the usual mix for such a newspaper. Monsieur wasn't sure why he wanted to come to this bar. The guidebook made it sound friendly, but Monsieur knew he had never had any real success in gay bars, or in any bar for that matter. And so it was this night. He finished his beer, left a tip and walked back into the rain.

Luckily the gay bathhouse was just four blocks away.

A soft drizzle was still falling. He got to the bathhouse. He showed his membership card, asked for a room with a TV, paid his money, and went in.

• • • •

As usual, one of the secretaries asked Monsieur to join her and her husband and other friends at a bar after work. This was a variation of "let's find a girlfriend for Monsieur", a pastime that Monsieur particularly liked. When he arrived at the bar, it was conveniently suggested that he sit at the open seat at the table which happened to be next to Amanda. Amanda, it turned out, was American. She was a friend of the secretary and she was unattached, having recently broken up with a boyfriend whom she referred to as a "Larry the Cable Guy" kind of person... Amanda had large breasts, and she accented them by her choice of bra and blouse, which Monsieur enjoyed. There were about ten people at the table, which was just about right.

There were margaritas all around, along with chitchat and a lot of bawdy jokes. Monsieur drank club soda, remained polite and respectful, as was his style. He engaged Amanda in light conversation. As usual, he hardly had to ask a single question. She provided all the questions and responses. He merely had to be a good listener, something he was skilled at. He learned that she had one child at home (pregnancy by accident), and one other pregnancy which didn't result in a child (either by abortion or miscarriage, he did not determine), that the father of her child was not paying child support but she was getting ready to charge him with contempt of court, that she hated her job, that she liked to drink, that she would marry a guy for the money, and would mess around, and had just gotten a raise, but was trying to find a new job. Monsieur always found it amazing what people would tell him if he just listened to them. Monsieur didn't have to tell her anything about his life. He just had to maintain eye contact, nod his head, and occasionally say, "Yes, I understand."

If this had been twenty years ago, ten years ago, even five years ago, Monsieur would have made a move to separate this girl from the herd, would have made some excuse to get alone with her, drive her home, or take her somewhere else, get her alone, make a proposition, and try and fuck her. But tonight, he simply did not have the energy. After about three hours of drinking and appetizers, he made his excuses, said a gracious goodbye to everyone, especially the secretary who had invited him, and left. He knew that this was not a wasted evening. He knew that if Amanda liked him, she would tell the secretary, and the secretary would let it slip to him, and that if he found himself situated with Amanda again, and if he was in the right mood, that he would encounter no resistance. Monsieur knew the mathematics of playing hard to get.

．　．　．　．

Yet Monsieur also knew the cold side of mathematics. Life was a bell curve. And in the median area, there was a lot of sex, a lot of women, a lot of men. But at the right-hand side, the supply dropped.

Monsieur had to admit he was past his prime. On one hand he was glad of that, because he had the patience and wisdom that only experience and time provide, but on the other hand, he was older. And age, in this game, was everything.

Monsieur was now in his fifties. He didn't look it. He could pass for late thirties or early forties, but that was only because he got a good haircut every two weeks and touch up his beard with dye every other day. And he kept in shape, going to the gym regularly.

．　．　．　．

It was a quiet weekend, but Monsieur had succeeded in keeping the walls from caving in. He had done his laundry, picked up his dry cleaning, cleaned his apartment, driven into town and done some shopping, stopped by the office to finish working on some files, found a tiny out-of-the-way restaurant to eat in, and generally managed to get through the weekend. On Sunday night, he drove to a remote convenience store that he had previously discovered was the only one around that carried X-rated magazines in the back. But tonight, a young woman was working the counter, and

Monsieur did not have the courage to buy a magazine from her. She looked eighteen. Instead, he bought some beer, made small talk with her while he paid, pretending to be a regular citizen, and then slithered out to his car.

He hoped that the next weekend would be better.

·   ·   ·   ·

Monsieur was settling into this new city. He now had his favorite grocery store, his favorite restaurant, his favorite drycleaner. He did not know how long he would stay—it might be years. It depended on what happened. That's the way things always were with him. He understood that he did not determine his fate—his fate determined him.

Monsieur counted the months since his divorce. Then he tried to remember the last time he had fucked a woman. Even counting his ex-wife, he thought it might have been as long as two years ago. He remembered fucking her in January, but he couldn't remember which year that had been.

Monsieur had prescriptions for Viagra and for Levitra, of course. He had originally gotten these medicines because he was on blood pressure medicine and had trouble maintaining an erection with his second wife. But secretly he wondered if that was more due to being married than to the blood pressure medicine. He noticed that if he went to the bathhouses, and forgot to take either Levitra or Viagra, it didn't seem to affect his ability to get an erection.

·   ·   ·   ·

The next weekend, Monsieur headed uptown. It was a beautiful Saturday afternoon, with the sun streaming down through the high buildings. But the brightness seemed to hurry him all the more quickly to the bathhouse. As he walked along, he found himself wondering if he would ever get ass-fucked. He knew it would only happen if he found a man with a very small dick. The last time he was at the bathhouse, a fat older man walked up to him while he was sitting in the sauna. Wordlessly, the man reached under Monsieur's towel and began to rub the head of Monsieur's cock. Monsieur reached under the man's towel and gently grabbed the man's cock. It was very big. The man leaned forward and whispered, "Do you have a room? Take me to your room and I will fuck you hard." The man was very fat, and something in the urgency of the man's voice scared Monsieur. Monsieur's brain made him lie and say he did not have a room. Then he got up and walked away.

Monsieur knew it would take a lot of practice before he could ever be fucked. He had heard of young men taking dildos of different sizes and practicing for months inserting them in their asses. Being fucked in the ass required relaxing the sphincter muscles. And this, Monsieur knew, meant practice. He had tried inserting the small rounded handle of his hairbrush, with a condom around the handle of course, into his ass. Using some lubricant, he managed to get it in, but it was only the thickness of his little finger. He moved it in and out of his ass, while he stroked his cock. It felt interesting, but not really pleasurable. It didn't seem worth the mess that it made. But perhaps a person's cock would be different. Not so much the cock but being wanted by a man. He often imagined what a woman must feel like the first time she goes to bed with a man she's been dating. Monsieur imagined that the physical pleasure of sex would almost be secondary to the feeling of being taken, being stripped naked, lying down, legs apart, to have someone entering you insistently and deeply. He wondered if that's what gay men liked about being fucked too.

Monsieur got to the corner near the bathhouse. He knew that if he walked straight two more blocks, there was a small sex shop where he could buy some latex dildos. He knew he would have to someday, if he ever wanted to really be fucked by someone. But today, he was eager to get to the bathhouse. He turned left and walked towards it.

He arrived at the door and went in. He showed his membership card to the man behind the glass window, purchased a small tube of lubricant just in case, got a room key and two towels, and went to find his room.

For a Saturday afternoon, the place was crowded. Maybe Saturday afternoons were the time to come here. He passed a room with an open door. A man was lying down, his cock fully erect. Another man was sitting on the bed slowly running his hand around the man's cock, as if to tease him. A few doors ahead, a young man was sucking an older man. Techno-pop music played over the loudspeakers.

Monsieur found his room, went inside, and closed the door behind him. He turned the TV on. On the TV, a man was being aggressively fucked in the ass while he stroked himself. Then the other man pulled out and masturbated and both men came at the same time. Monsieur took his clothes off and locked them in the little metal locker. He wrapped a towel around himself and headed for the shower.

He washed himself well and made sure he cleaned his ass and cock. Then he went into the dry sauna. The lights were down very low. One man was lying down in the darkest corner. Monsieur could not see what he looked like. A middle-aged man sat up on the upper ledge, rubbing his cock. Another man appeared to be sleeping on another ledge. Monsieur found the warmest spot—a low ledge near the heating unit—so that he could let the heat dry him out from the shower. A fat man walked by Monsieur and paused. Following the unspoken bathhouse rules, Monsieur simply avoided eye-contact and the man walked on. An older man with sagging skin walked by. Monsieur did not look at him either.

As he began to dry off, Monsieur reached underneath his towel and began stroking himself. He could feel the Levitra he had taken earlier starting to kick in. After a minute, he felt his cock thicken up. He got up, left the dry sauna, and walked around. He walked through the "sling room". Monsieur remembered the first time he had ever seen such a room. It was at an Antwerp bathhouse. He walked in and there was a naked man in a sling. The sling placed the man's ass just waist high, so that anyone could just stand there, insert himself into the man's ass and swing the man back and forth instead of thrusting in and out. Monsieur remembered looking at the man in the sling. His dick was soft, but lubricant was oozing out of his asshole. Monsieur had heard that it was hard to maintain an erection while being fucked. He wanted to ask the man questions, but he knew that would be inappropriate, so he simply left.

However, there was no one in this sling room today. Monsieur walked down the hallway of rooms, but this time all the doors were closed. He walked back to the sauna. There were less people there this time. He walked past the sitting ledges. A very fat hairy man was sitting on one of the lower ledges. Monsieur walked by, but as he did, the man reached out and ran his hand across the front of Monsieur's towel. Monsieur stopped and looked at the man. He was very hairy and fat, but what the hell. Monsieur sat down beside him and reached in under the man's towel. He was surprised to find a very small dick. It was soft and no more than an inch in length. Meanwhile, the man had reached under Monsieur's towel and was stroking Monsieur's cock, which was semi-erect.

As Monsieur massaged the man's dick, it began to harden, but still, it was no more than two inches long. Monsieur looked at the man's belly. It was obesely fat and covered with coarse thick hair. Monsieur wondered what it would be like being fucked by this man. The dick would certainly fit, he knew, but he found the idea of being fucked by such a slob repulsive. Monsieur got up and walked out of the sauna.

Monsieur walked down the hall, past the showers, and went into another dark room, a twisting hallway with dark corners. He passed an older man. As he walked passed, he sensed the man turning. Monsieur stopped and turned around. This man looked about 65 but he was not fat.

Monsieur reached under the man's towel and felt his soft cock. The man reached under Monsieur's towel as well. Monsieur turned and walked toward one of the darkened corners, intending to do some mutual masturbation. The man followed him. But on the way to the corner, another man appeared. Monsieur liked the look of this man immediately—older and kind looking. Monsieur let his hand drape along this man towel. He felt a bulge.

Monsieur stepped into the corner. The first man stepped in and started touching Monsieur's cock. Monsieur was feeling this man's cock with his right hand. The other man walked into the corner too, and Monsieur reached in under his towel with his left hand. He had been correct—the man's cock was rather large. Monsieur stood there, a cock in each hand. He preferred the larger one.

The first man must have instinctively felt slighted, because he walked out. Monsieur continued to play with the larger cock, while the man stroked Monsieur's cock.

Then the man said, "Come to my room and let me fuck you." Monsieur was not sure he heard him right. "What?"

The man repeated, "Come to my room and let me fuck you."

Monsieur let go of the man's cock. The man walked out. Monsieur followed him down a dark hallway.

When they got to the man's room, Monsieur undraped his towel and sat on the bed, but said, "I'm not sure this will work. You're so big."

"It'll be fine," the man said, and grabbed a condom off the table and began putting it on himself.

"I've never done this before," Monsieur said.

"Never?"

"No, never. I don't think you will fit."

"Well, it'll hurt." the man said.

Monsieur laughed and said, "Well that'll be bad."

"Well, let's see," the man said. "You'll have to put a pillow under your ass." The man placed a pillow on the edge of the bed. "But first, help get me hard," the man said.

The man was standing by the bed, and Monsieur was sitting on the bed, so the man's cock was right at Monsieur's mouth level, semi-erect, with a condom on. Monsieur began sucking him, tasting the latex of the condom. Monsieur liked that the man practiced safe sex. The man began getting harder and thrusting himself deeper into Monsieur's mouth.

Monsieur liked giving head. He tried to take the man deeper into his mouth. The man began to moan. He held the back of Monsieur's head with both his hands while he thrust himself even deeper. Monsieur did not want to gag—he thought it made him look inexperienced, but he was at the point of gagging. However, the man's cock was erect now, and he stopped thrusting.

"Here, put your ass on the pillows." the man said.

Monsieur did as he was told. The man stayed standing by the bed and grabbed both of Monsieur's ankles and placed them on this shoulder. Then he grabbed a tube of lubricant from the table hand, squeezed some on his fingers, and massaged Monsieur's asshole. Monsieur liked this. He liked this a lot. Then the man thrust one lubricated finger all the way into Monsieur's asshole. It was a tight fit. The man moved it in and out. Monsieur lifted his head and looked at the man's cock.

"I don't think this is going to work," Monsieur said.

"I'll go slow." the man said and squeezed lubricant onto his cock.

Monsieur let his head fall back as the man began to enter Monsieur.

What happened next, Monsieur later realized, was a beautiful balanced dance. Monsieur had reached his hands down to the man's pelvis so that his fingertips could push against the man's pelvis and keep him from pushing too hard. And Monsieur's feet were now flat against the top of the man's shoulders, so that Monsieur could push against the man with his legs. And the man had his hands on Monsieur's thighs near Monsieur's pelvis, so he could pull Monsieur into him, and he was gently thrusting into

Monsieur.

It did hurt. Monsieur could feel the ring of his sphincter stretched around the man's cock.

"Relax," the man said.

Monsieur tried to relax. The man thrust harder. Monsieur pushed his hands against the man's pelvis.

It hurt. Monsieur pushed his legs and hands back, keeping the man from pushing into him.

"Relax." the man said, "I almost had the head in. Just relax. I'll go slow."

Monsieur concentrated on relaxing. The man pushed in again. Monsieur liked the pressure, but he didn't like the pain.

"Relax," the man said again, and continue thrusting.

"Here," the man said, "jerk yourself off."

"I'll come," Monsieur said.

"That's okay," the man said, "it'll relax you."

So, Monsieur stroked himself with his right hand, his legs high in the air, and his left hand still pressing against the man's thigh, keeping him from pushing too hard.

It was impossible to tell how far the man had gotten into Monsieur. It may have only been the head of his cock, maybe a bit more. Monsieur was sure it was not far. It was hurting, but not in a bad way.

Monsieur came. It was not a lot of cum, and he did not feel a huge orgasm, but he did come and cum oozed down his cock.

The man stopped thrusting and squeezed some lubricant into his hands and began stroking Monsieur's cock, as if to squeeze out the last bit of cum.

"I'm sorry," Monsieur said, "I've just never done this before."

"That's okay," the man said, "I've got a big cock. You just need to find someone with a small cock to fuck you."

Monsieur stood up, grabbed his towel and wrapped it around himself. The man said, "Come here," and gave Monsieur a hug.

"Thank you." Monsieur said, and then he walked out of the room.

He walked to the showers and showered extensively. He checked for blood from his ass and was glad to find none. He lathered up several times and washed his ass and his cock. He dried off and went back to his room.

In his room, he finished drying off and got dressed. His mind was calm, without thoughts. The TV continued to play porn, but Monsieur did not pay any attention to it. He felt completely at ease.

Once dressed, he walked down the corridor and checked out. He stepped back into the sunlit day and started walking to where he had parked his car several blocks away. He considered again going to the sex store to buy some dildos, but did not want to interact with anyone, and so he continued to his car.

Once in his car and driving home, he reflected on what had happened and noted that his ass felt good. There was no itch, no pain, just a calm quiet feeling. He wondered if this would cure the itch.

But the next day, in the shower, the itch was back.

• • • •

In fact, it was back with a vengeance. When he woke up, Monsieur could not wait to get into the shower. He would lather up his left hand, reach around, bending over slightly, and began to massage all around his asshole. After all these years, he could still never pinpoint the actual location of the itch. Sometimes he would start two or three inches away from his asshole, pressing up hard into his ass cheeks. Other times, he would make circles on the outside of his asshole, again, pushing up as hard as he could. The problem was the hemorrhoids on the edge of his ass. If he rubbed those hard enough, they would bleed, and his ass would sting painfully all day long. The trick was to satisfy the itch without creating pain throughout the day. He tried to ameliorate the situation by rubbing in antibiotic cream around his asshole at night before he went to bed, and again after his morning shower.

Still, the mystery of that itch was overwhelming. The alarm clock would go off, and he would, zombie like, walk to the kitchen and pour a cup of coffee (the coffee maker being on automatic setting), and walk into the bathroom, sipping coffee and trying to focus his eyes. He would turn the shower water on and step into the shower, lather up and start working on his asshole. Suddenly he was awake and would find himself hunched over in the pouring water, bent in half, his hand pushing around his ass as hard as he could. It was a strange way to wake up.

•   •   •   •

Monsieur considered his face in his bathroom mirror. The gray in his beard needed fixing. He reached for the small plastic tray on the shelf and placed it on the sink. He carefully squeezed a blob of beard dye into the tray and rubbed a Q-tip in it. Holding his face a few inches from the mirror, he touched up his beard. The trick was not to hide the gray—that would look fake—but to make his beard look "salt and pepper". By carefully touching individual hairs with the Q-tip, Monsieur could create the impression of a darker beard without denying the traces of gray. One by one he selected individual hairs to touch. Five minutes to apply the dye, and five minutes to let it set. Every other day.

•   •   •   •

Monsieur was asked out for drinks by some of the women in the office. Just a friendly after-work drink. He considered turning the offer down, not only because he was tired after a long day, but because it was three of the older women in the office, but Monsieur's rule was never to turn down a social event from women. Plus, a female friend of one of them was supposed to join them. So, Monsieur met them at the bar.

The female friend turned out to be Monsieur's age. Her name was Carole. The "just a friendly after-work drink" was obviously a variation of "let's find a girlfriend for Monsieur". However, Carole was not to Monsieur's personal taste. She was bright, but overweight. Her face, like most middle-aged faces, had settled into "a face", i.e., a carefully defined look after decades of trying to look a certain way. She looked hardened. Her lips were thin. She had large breasts, but they looked like they would fall low once unhooked from her bra. Her tummy was round and protruded. She was about thirty pounds overweight. But she was definitely on the make. Before the evening was over, she asked Monsieur no less than five times to spend the weekend with her. This was a lonely girl, Monsieur thought. This would be an easy lay. He knew he could get her back to his apartment in twenty minutes. There would be no games, no bantering, just flesh and more flesh.

He even considered it. He tried to picture her naked. It was not a pretty sight. Large floppy breasts, hanging low over a distended belly and a fat ass. Somewhere there would be pussy hair and under that, a pussy. Monsieur did not like what he saw.

With men, he could overlook extra pounds; he could overlook age; he could overlook wrinkles. It was the cock and the kindness that beckoned him. But with women, it had to be the whole package: the slenderness, the mouth, the voice, the chance of perky breasts, the slender hips, the flat belly, the burst of pubic hair, then the pussy. Add some perfume and thick head of hair and he would be in love instantly.

It wasn't the woman's age. He had fucked a sixty-five year old woman when he was twenty-five. But she had style, and was in good shape, and had enthusiasm. And it wasn't the weight. He had fucked fat women with huge breasts and enjoyed it immensely. But they were big without being flabby. And, Monsieur had to admit, they had also been young. Young and fat is always different than old and fat. With women, it was always the whole package. And this particular woman did not have anywhere near the whole package. *Still*, Monsieur's brain said, *one mustn't burn bridges.* He was gracious. He listened. He chatted. He didn't answer yes or no. He was evasive without being negative. Who knew if a day might come when fucking a fat unattractive woman his own age might be his only option. He paid for their drinks and, at the appropriate time, made his exit.

•　•　•　•

Monsieur had given up hope of landing Enid. He continued to banter with her at work, continued to give her arrest reports that pertained to her clients, continued to support her in office meetings, but he knew his chances of getting her alone were nil.

He did not believe in unrequited love. He thought it was stupid to pine over someone who was too stupid to reciprocate. But that philosophy did not stop him from feeling sad that someone might not know how he felt, or rather, that someone might not know how he might feel them... should he be given the chance to run his hands up their leg to that moist compartment. And he did feel sad about Enid. Sad may not have been the right word. He felt regret, an emptiness, a hollowness when he saw her in the hallway and realized that he would never kiss those lips, never experience being wanted by her. She was oblivious to his secret desire. She obviously enjoyed the banter. Monsieur wondered what she did think of him. Did she think he was a middle-aged raconteur? An older mentor? An extra in the play of her life? One never knows how another perceives one, and the other will never tell the truth, because the other is only perceiving on the fly, without really thinking about what they are perceiving.

Still, it made Monsieur sad. He felt he was running

37

out of options for exciting female companions. Would he have to resort to fucking middle aged fat women? Would his only other option be spending every weekend in the gay bathhouse? Would he end up one of those older men who prowl the bathhouse looking for lost souls like him to suck off?

Monsieur just wanted love, whatever that was.

•   •   •   •

Monsieur did not exactly believe in God, but he talked to God every day. Literally and out loud. When he drove his car to work on the weekdays, or when he woke up in the morning on the weekend and lay in bed thinking of why he should bother getting up, or when he lay in bed at night reviewing the day's activities, Monsieur would speak to God.

Hello... again. It's me. How are you doing? Monsieur would begin. He felt it was a good idea to always be polite to God.

On this particular day, as he did every day, Monsieur was reviewing his situation with women.

You know, he said, addressing God, *I know that Enid is out of the question. She's too fucked up; she's too young; and there is that minor point that she's not interested... but who else do I have to consider? I'm not going to call Carole... what would be the point? She's too fat to fuck...* Monsieur grimaced at the image of her naked. Then he listed the names of the other women at work with reasons why he would never fuck them: too old... married... not interested... and of course, he worked with them. He then thought about all the other women whom he encountered at his job who worked for outside venders or other government agencies. Aside from his own prohibition about never becoming involved with anyone whom he remotely worked with, he noted that he simply wasn't attracted to any of them.

Monsieur reflected for a moment. *I know, Lord, that*

I've always been, well, I've always been reticent. I know this. I prefer the shadows. I'm not your dominant male... I'm passive, I know this. But I am what I am. I can't change. I have to wait until the moment draws me into action, like a swimmer pulled into the current... Monsieur's paused. He hated thinking of himself as passive. His work with women took immense amounts of energy and planning. It was no easy task to position himself and other people into a situation where events seemed natural, and where the natural turn of events led to sex. Such positioning took immense patience and meticulous planning. But the fact was, Monsieur was tired of it. He had been attentive to Enid for several months now, and nothing was happening. He also had been listening politely to the whining and gossiping of the other women at work for several months, and although they had tried on a couple occasions to connect him to one of their friends, Monsieur had to admit that the intensity of their efforts was not what it would have been ten or twenty years ago. When he was thirty, women were trying to fix him up every week, as if there were a door prize awarded every time Monsieur scored. It was a wonderful time.

Am I past my prime, Lord?... Okay, I know I am... but I think I've got a few more years here before anyone else knows. What exactly should I do?

Of course, God never answered Monsieur, but Monsieur always felt better after these conversations, as if God had been listening to him. And he felt that in these conversations, answers did come to him. With Enid, he simply had to continue doing what he had been doing. Being nice, mentor-like, concerned but not intruding, humorous with a hint of flirting but never enough to call it flirting, and above all, available for any spontaneous conversation. If Enid were to decide that she was interested in Monsieur, if she ever were to make a move, and give *him* an opening, then Monsieur could, ever so delicately, move in. Until that time, if it ever came, he simply was prohibited from doing anything else. At twice her age, he could not risk even being thought of as creating a "hostile work environment" by being direct with his desire.

•　•　•　•

It had been another tough weekend for Monsieur. It was one of those weekends where he simply did not interact with anyone. His tongue felt thick. He simply had not spoken to anyone except short exchanges with service persons. Depression fell on him like soft snow. He made a feeble attempt to go shopping at the mall... pretended to look at clothes while watching all the women walk by. Half of them were with guys, and the other half were unapproachable. He found some blue jeans that were in his size, but he simply wasn't interested in buying anything. He wandered through electronic stores, specialty stores, department stores... and bought nothing. He wondered if some bored loss-prevention person was up in his booth watching him shop, following him through the ceiling cameras as he walked through the aisles, stopping at this rack to examine a tag, then moving to another rack to examine the material. Monsieur was sure he looked like a bored husband killing time while his wife shopped. No one would notice him.

As he drove home, he passed a casino. He considered stopping by to gamble but the parking lot was full of cars, and Monsieur hated crowds. He did not stop. He was hungry. He passed a Greek restaurant that looked inviting, but he could see people seated inside, and he drove on by. Further up the road, there was a new restaurant that he had read about. Monsieur made up his mind to stop and eat there.

He did not mind eating alone at a restaurant, but the situation had to be right. It could not be filled with couples. The tables could not be too close together. Booths were great. Other people eating alone were great. Anything to avoid standing out.

The "open" sign was on, but the parking lot of the restaurant was empty. That was a good sign. Still, Monsieur

40

parked his car about two blocks away and walked up to the building. He read the menu in the window. It looked good. He stepped inside. The place was empty. Each table had a white table cloth, and carefully laid out silverware. It was obviously a bit upscale. There was a bottle of wine on each table. Someone was approaching.

"Are you open?" Monsieur asked.

"Yes, sir, we just opened."

Monsieur glanced around again and felt a bit of panic. The tables were very close together, and the place had gotten a good review in the paper. If people began to pour in, he would be trapped.

"Could I see the menu?" he asked.

"Yes, of course," the man answered, and handed Monsieur a menu.

He pretended to study it, even though he had just read it in the window outside.

"Yes, very nice." Monsieur said. "I have some friends down the street. Let me go and get them. I'll be right back."

"Very good, sir."

Monsieur left and walked towards his car. As he did, two couples were walking into the restaurant. Monsieur felt that he had made the right decision. His hunger would have to wait. He got into his car and drove home. He would eat at home this weekend.

• • • •

Monsieur was filing a report on one of the office's "clients", Carlos Vids. Carlos was on parole for a sex offense conviction, living under house arrest in his parents' house. His conviction was for being twenty-three and having consensual sex with a thirteen-year-old girl, but it was clear from the case file that Carlos was retarded, that he was the same age as the girl emotionally. He was on "treatment parole" which meant that Monsieur had to read and file the weekly therapist treatment reports. Monsieur stamped them "received", forwarded a copy to the court, forwarded another copy to Carlos' probation officer, and put the original in the file. This report read:

> Carlos Vids continues to attend his weekly individual sessions in a timely fashion.
>
> This week we developed rules and guidelines for masturbation. We created an appropriate sexual fantasy involving the fictional "Stella". Carlos is limited to masturbating twice in any given week. He is not to use any pictures or masturbate to television. He is to remain behind a locked door, either his bedroom or the bathroom. He is required to document the day he masturbates in a diary, labeling it as "exercise."
>
> Carlos has been completing a chapter per week from *Sexual Addiction Workbook:* by Psychologists Szabo and Donabu. I am pleased with his progress, and his written assignments. Carlos has limited academic skills, but he applies himself to the work. Although his spelling is poor, he writes legibly in complete sentences. His responses to workbook questions indicate he grasps the general thrust of the material. We review the material in each session and attempt to apply it to his experience.
>
> As referenced above, Carlos is documenting his day in his diary. The

intent here is to heighten his awareness that he needs to structure his day and accomplish something in spite of being bored with his house arrest.

Carlos reports that he has a polygraph scheduled for next week. He says he is confident he will pass.

Carlos now comprehends the laws relating to minors and society's strict prohibitions from engaging them in sex. He mentions often his desire to have a girlfriend, although he has no female friends in his life at this time. He admits he has pushed past relationships too quickly, and probably put off age-appropriate females who might otherwise be candidates for intimacy. He has been told that there will be no dating or promoting of a romantic relationship until he has been able to demonstrate an ability to comply with his parole conditions. From a therapeutic position, he will need to learn and practice living skills that include internal and self-imposed external controls of self-regulation.

Carlos' sessions have been productive, and I have been pleased with his efforts to comply with treatment assignments and exercises. In session, he is often tangential, engages in loose-associations, is orally impulsive, and easily distracted. On the other hand, his strength appears to be his dedication to working on his workbook. There are, however, deficits in memory and retention in new information. He admits being confined to home and boredom helps him focus on his assignments.

What a crock of shit, Monsieur thought. *They're telling this boy that he can't jerk off more than twice a week and that he can't have a girlfriend. But they give him an imaginary girlfriend named Stella.*

Monsieur shook his head. He thought of Marlon Brando screaming "Stella" in the rain, then he thought of Carlos silently visualizing Stella while he jerked off in his parents' bathroom twice a week, making sure afterwards to document his "exercise" in his little diary. He imagined the polygraph examiner grilling Carlos, "Admit it, you masturbated three times this week in defiance of the court order, didn't you Carlos?"

There but for the grace of God, Monsieur thought, *go I.* He was pretty sure that there had not been a time since he was age fourteen that, if he wasn't having sex, he hadn't jerk off at least four times a week. *Poor Carlos, poor stupid Carlos.*

Monsieur slipped the report into the file. Monsieur's "clients" included forty-four sexual offenders on parole in the province. He probably handled ten to twelve such "treatment parole" reports each week, all written in the same style: pedantic, uptight, controlling psycho-babble in the guise of therapy for lost souls who got caught in the criminal justice system.

However, Monsieur had learned long ago that he worked in an insane system. He could not help Carlos, or any of the others. He could not make any difference in their lives. They were all on a one-way course to whatever their destiny was. Monsieur's job was simply to stamp the reports "received", make copies, forward copies, and put the files back in the filing cabinet.

•　•　•　•

Monsieur went to see his doctor. "Dr. Mengele" Monsieur called him—but not to his face. He had been having pain in his abdomen, on the right side for several weeks. Mengele, who had no bedside manner, quickly ruled out appendicitis.

"Could be cancer." said Mengele, ever the upbeat advisor, "Let's take an x-ray." Monsieur let himself be led down the hall for the disrobing and the lying on the cold table. Thirty minutes later, back in the exam room, Mengele said, "I don't see anything on the x-ray except a lot of feces. We'll take blood and check your stool for blood. If either of those are irregular, we'll do a barium x-ray and a colonoscopy.

"As long as you're taking blood, can you check my liver?"

Mengele knew that Monsieur drank, so the request did not seem to surprise him.

"Okay, we'll check your liver."

"And could you do an HIV test, too?"

"Why? Have you been exposed to HIV?" Mengele asked.

This question took Monsieur by surprise.

"No... I just think it's a good idea to check, and it's been several years since I had one."

"Well, the only reason to do that is if you've been exposed. Since you haven't been exposed, there's no point in doing it."

What a dick, Monsieur thought. He would just have to wait until there was a HIV testing day at the bathhouse.

A couple of days later, Mengele left a message on Monsieur's home phone saying that the blood and stool tests came back negative. Mengele suggested that he try laxatives and call him if the pain continued.

Monsieur tried a variety of laxatives for the next

several weeks. The dull pain on his right side continued. He did not call Mengele back.

• • • •

Monsieur took a couple of vacation days and flew over to Genoa. He felt he needed to get away, and he had found a cheap flight/hotel combination on one of those "last minute deals" sites on the internet. He hoped that a few days in Italy would rejuvenate him.

Because the trip was last minute, Monsieur did not have much time to research the city. He did locate the names and addresses of the gay bathhouses and noted their location on a city map that he printed out from the internet. He also noted the location of several strip clubs.

His hotel was in the center of downtown, so once the cab dropped him off there, he did not need to rent a car—he could walk most everywhere. After he dropped his luggage off at the hotel, he walked around with his map, and found two of the bathhouses and one of the strip clubs within eight blocks of his hotel.

But first, he was hungry. He stopped into an open-air Pakistani restaurant that had tables on the sidewalk. He ordered some type of chicken plate with falafel and a bottled water. While he ate, he flipped through a "local scene" type newspaper. He noticed many ads for escorts and a few ads for what appeared to be brothels. He wondered if prostitution was legal here. One of the ads listed an address. He checked his map. It was close by. He finished his falafel and started walking.

The Celebrity Club had a sign out front indicating "massage". He walked up the concrete steps and rang the bell. An older lady quickly answered and ushered him in. The place was large and well furnished. Two young girls in scanty outfits came out from behind a curtain and sat on the couch. The older woman explained that it was fifty-five

46

euros for the room, but that paying the girls for "massage" was extra. Monsieur paid her fifty-five euros. She then asked him which girl he wanted. They both looked the same. He indicated the one on the left. The older lady showed him upstairs to the room.

It must have been a stately townhouse at one point. Spacious, tall ceilings, large rooms. The room that Monsieur was in was nicely furnished with a queen-size bed and a clean bathrobe laid out on the bed. Monsieur undressed, put the bathrobe on and lay down on the bed. After a few minutes, there was a knock on the door and the girl he had selected came in.

"You can dispense with the robe." she said.

He took the robe off and lay back down, naked, on the bed. She was wearing a bikini.

She told him her name. He didn't quite catch it. Then she told him the rates for sex. They were very expensive, starting at three hundred euros. Monsieur was horny, but he did not want to spend that amount of money. He wished he had known downstairs what the prices were going to be. He remembered how he liked the prostitutes in Amsterdam, where they would tell you at the door exactly how much each act cost. "One hundred euros to suck; one hundred fifty euros to fuck." Now he was stuck upstairs naked with some girl who wanted to empty his wallet. She was running her fingernails over his chest.

"I didn't bring that much money." Monsieur said.

She had heard that before. She ran through the litany: Credit cards discretely billed. Nearby ATM machine. But Monsieur shook his head and repeated that he did not have that much money. Then she put forth the story how she had to pay the madam twenty euros for the use of the room and couldn't she and he work something out.

"What's the cheapest service you have?" Monsieur asked.

She told him a topless massage for fifty euros. It

seemed to be the only way out. Monsieur agreed. She took off her top and then almost as an afterthought, slipped off her bikini bottoms. Her breasts were not bad but had obviously been augmented. Small nipples but the implants caused them to ride too high.

Her massage abilities were horrid. Monsieur endured it for a few minutes and then sat up and made profuse apologies for being poor and paid her, being careful not to show her how much money he actually had in his wallet. He got dressed, and she he walked him downstairs. He made a beeline for the gay bathhouse. This was exactly why he couldn't deal with women. The enticement, the promise of one price but the extortion of much more, the guilt-trip, as if he had created her situation, the money paid out, the letdown, the leaving, the anger. It was always the same story.

The bathhouse fee was fifteen euros. Monsieur paid it willingly. He got his towels, found his room, and undressed. This was better. He found the shower and lathered up, washing the memory of the girl from his face and chest. The water was hot and plentiful. He wrapped the towel around him and found the steam room, went inside and sat down. He liked this place. Wooden benches in the steam room. Lots of steam. He could make out a very skinny Asian locked in a rhythmic embrace with an older man. They were just hugging and rocking back and forth. The oriental had a boy's ass. Monsieur wished he could hold him. Someone came in and sat next to the couple. The older man reached out and grabbed the newcomer's cock. Monsieur felt at home watching this. The steam felt good. He began to relax.

•　•　•　•

The pain in Monsieur's side did not go away. He woke up with it. It stayed with him all morning. It seemed to abate in the early afternoon and only occasionally flared at night. Monsieur, of course, assumed the worst. It had to be some type of intestinal cancer, some type of tumor impeding the flow of shit down the bowels. That would explain his irregular shits. He knew he was doomed to die.

Some days were worse than others. He could struggle through the mornings, but when Enid would come by his office, Monsieur would realize how impaired he was. It was hard to make jokes with her, hard to focus on the chit-chat. He decided to increase the use of laxative. He started taking them every night, which of course, caused major colon blow-outs each morning. He would sit on the toilet while large quantities of shit blew out his ass like a whale's blowhole. The noise was loud. Monsieur wondered if his neighbors could hear it through the apartment walls. Even so, Monsieur doubled the dosage. He noticed that after he was emptied of shit, he felt better. The pain seemed to lift. If only he could find a laxative that didn't involve making a wind tunnel out of his ass. He tried various fiber drinks, Metamucil, and special diet teas. All seem to create the same blow-out.

In the meantime, Enid seemed to be acting friendlier. She would come by his office every day. She started emailing him. She loaned him some books. Once she even asked him to join her and one of her girlfriends for drinks after work, but then later recanted, saying her girlfriend made other plans. Still, it pleased him that she was paying attention to him. She revealed that she had broken up with yet another boyfriend. Evidently, he couldn't put up with her compulsive habits. Monsieur would sympathize and assure her that she would find someone. But secretly he felt she would not. She was too neurotic. Ironically, he thought, he was the only one who really understood her. She was always forgetting her purse, forgetting to put gas in the car, forgetting to pay tickets, etc. She took everything personally. She was all emotion. Quick to judge others, quick to react, slow to look at herself. Monsieur felt such a tenderness toward her. She reminded him of all his lovers. Still, he did not know how to proceed. She was a woman, with tits and pussy, and lips, but there was the insurmountable fact that she worked in the same office as him. He saw her at work every day. It would be insane to get involved with her. She couldn't keep a secret. Every woman in the office knew all the details of her love life. Even he got the lowdown on her lovers, for example, how her last lover was uncircumcised, and she couldn't deal with it.

Monsieur tried to imagine bedding her down. He couldn't seem to picture her kissing him, wanting him, loving him. No image came up.

• • • •

Monsieur noticed that the hairs in his beard were getting whiter. Now he had to add dye to them every day. Soon he would have to consider shaving his beard altogether. He could still pass for early forties, but he knew that it was just a matter of time before that would no longer be the case. He felt that he was Dorian Grey, except that his portrait was locked inside his heart. One day, the portrait would simply explode on his face for all the world to see. He was old.

• • • •

But the following week was better. Enid mentioned she was going to a pot-luck dinner party on the following Friday and perhaps Monsieur would like to meet her there. There would be many people that Monsieur would like, she explained. Monsieur wondered if perhaps she was simply being kind and trying to hook him up with others, but he did not care why she asked him. He was simply elated that she asked him at all. He pretended to check his calendar and then told her yes, yes, he could make that. It would be interesting to see the age group of these people. Were they friends of Enid? Her age? Or were they work-mates from a previous job, all of different ages? Or perhaps it was a function that Enid had to attend, full of geriatric friends of her parents, and she thought Monsieur would fit in. This dinner would perhaps reveal what she thought of him. Perhaps she would have a glass of wine. Perhaps she would talk to him in less inhibited ways. Monsieur wondered if people still danced at parties. He realized, sadly, that it had been many, many years since he had been at a dinner party.

Monsieur chided himself for being so romantic, but he still looked forward all week to this event. She emailed him directions on Thursday. That Thursday night he prepared a little pasta salad to take to the party. Monsieur didn't usually cook much but the idea of spending time with Enid seemed to energize him. He only hoped his abdomen pain would not flair up Friday.

He noted that the address was downtown, not too many kilometers from a gay bathhouse. In the worst case, if the party turned out dismal, he could still console himself in the arms of men. He wondered how he would cope at the party. Other than Enid, he would know no one there. He would have to interact with complete strangers. Worse, he was showing up alone. He rehearsed possible lines. Hello, he would say, I hope I'm at the right place. I'm a friend of Enid's, he would say. She asked me to meet her here, he would say. I brought a side-dish... Would he be looking at cold strangers, hostile because there was a stranger in their midst? He would have to quickly remember names, make small talk, try and appear harmless, interested, and interesting. It would require a tremendous effort. Many times, in the past, faced with such a group of strangers, he had simply disappeared, walked out to "check something he'd left in the car" and simply driven away. He hoped he wouldn't do that. He hoped Enid would spend time with him, introduce him to the people. He hoped he would find a comfortable way to be. He waited for Friday.

. . . .

Friday evening came. As he was getting ready to leave,

Enid called him and said she was running an hour late. She had gotten "distracted" and lost track of time. Not a problem, Monsieur assured her, he would adjust his leave time. He did not want to arrive before she did, since he knew no one there. He sat in his apartment, reread the paper, drank another cup of tea, and wondered how one became "distracted". After an hour, he left, and arrived at the party address. Enid was there and, thankfully, introduced him to the host and hostess. It was a standard backyard potluck. Monsieur brought the pasta salad he had made the night before. He was glad to see that there were all ages there. He would not stand out as the only older person there.

Enid was sitting at a table in the back yard. There was an empty seat next to her. She beckoned for him to join her. The hostess handed him a beer. He thanked her, and he sat down beside Enid.

The next half-hour was magical. They were talking. The night was cool. They were not at work. The sun was setting. They were sitting together chatting about things. The night seemed full of promise.

They talked some about work, but more about her life before work, where she had lived, adventures she had had, and about how long she knew the hostess of this party. Monsieur, as always, was the consummate listener. Only this time he was enthralled. Yet, as the time moved by, and she finished her beer, and had another beer, and finished that one, and opened another, while Monsieur was still nursing his first beer, he noticed that she began to become slightly detached, out of focus, almost twitchy. Her laugh started to sound artificial. The hostess joined them, and Enid and the hostess started telling stories and laughing loudly. Something was wrong. After an hour, Enid seemed drunk. She and the hostess were talking loudly, laughing loudly, spilling beer.

Monsieur stared down at the top of the beer can—still his first beer—in his hand. Why was it people always missed the point? Monsieur now knew why Enid had gotten distracted. She was one of "them". People. People always are distracted. That's their main state of awareness. Monsieur could walk down any street and look into the faces of everyone walking his way. Never a real face. Always distracted faces. Concerned with something. Thinking about something. Stuck in their personality. Stuck in their stories. Fixed to one inextricable point. Never anyone who would look him directly in the eye and see anything. Enid was one of them and they were all the same.

However, an old memory came back to him. Monsieur had been walking in Genoa and saw a young man coming towards him, wearing a backpack. As the young man reached into his pocket for something, Monsieur saw something fall from his pocket. It glittered in the sunlight. The young man did not notice. He walked past Monsieur. Monsieur walked a few more steps and picked up the card that the young man had dropped. It was some type of laminated bus pass. Monsieur turned around and caught up with the young man. "Is this yours?" Monsieur said. "You dropped it a minute ago." The young man seemed started, immediately suspicious of Monsieur, but looked at the card that he was holding out to him. Then a flash of recognition. It was a valuable card. The man took it. "Thank you, thank you." he said. "No problem." Monsieur said. And then the young man, just for the briefest of microseconds, looked like he was trying to say something. A complete stranger had just saved him a major inconvenience and who knows how much money. The young man looked at the card and looked at Monsieur and looked back at the card and opened his mouth, but no words came out. Monsieur smiled and said, "Have a nice day." and walked away. At least that was a real moment. The man was struggling with trying to connect, trying to say something. There was the possibility of something real in that briefest of moments.

Monsieur looked at Enid. Her legs were crossed. Her arms were crossed. She was staring into space. She was on her fifth or sixth beer. He got up and went to the table where the food was. He might as well eat something before he drove home. He got a plate of food and made small talk with an older woman who was standing next to him. The food was good. The woman he was talking to made no sense to him. He nodded and smiled. She was glad to have someone to talk to.

After another hour, Monsieur made his excuses, thanked the host and hostess, thanked Enid for inviting him, and left. The party was in full swing. Perhaps there were other women there that he could meet. But he did not care. He had expended enough energy for the evening. He did not even want to go to the bathhouse. He drove home. He was glad to be alone. This may be the way it's going to be, he said to himself. Maybe he just had to vacation in Amsterdam once a year and pay for prostitutes there, and simply accept that he was not going to have a girlfriend like he used to have in his youth. Maybe he would try the internet online dating racket. Maybe his lust for women would pass. Maybe he would buy a dildo at the adult toy store and stretch out his rectum so that he could be fucked by older men in the bathhouse. He did not know. He was sad that women never seemed to fit the fantasy. But they never did. He did not know if the fantasy was delusional or real. He only knew that women always kept talking, and the endless words, and endless history, and endless stories eventually became boring beyond belief.

•　　•　　•　　•

Several weeks passed. Perhaps Monsieur was not paying as much attention to Enid as he previously had. Maybe she felt him withdrawing. Or perhaps she was curious. He wasn't trying to lure her. He just felt detached. But suddenly, one Friday, she asked if he wanted to come over Saturday and drink some beers and "just hang out". Monsieur was taken back, but he quickly accepted. He told her he would bring some snacks and they could have a little picnic.

That night in his apartment, Monsieur felt very disconcerted. On one hand, he now had something to do on the weekend. And a female had invited him. But invited him to what? Perhaps she just wanted to drink some beers. Perhaps she interpreted his recent aloofness for depression (which it was) and was merely trying to help. Or maybe she wanted romance or sex. Women never come out and tell the truth. Maybe they don't know themselves.

Monsieur had stopped by the store on the way home and purchased snacks, ice, beer, and condoms. He pulled an old ice chest out from the closet so he could pack it in the morning with food and beer. He placed several condoms inside the leather jacket he planned to wear. He also wrapped several Levitra pills in Kleenex and put them in the same pocket of his jacket. He considered the time table. He was supposed to meet Enid at her house at noon. It takes Levitra forty-five minutes to take effect, and the effect lasts about four hours. He decided to wait until he arrived at her house before deciding when to take the Levitra. If he got there and she wanted to take a hike or go shopping or to a movie, there would be no sense in taking the Levitra too early. But if they started into the beer and snacks right away, he might have a chance at getting her in bed that afternoon.

After everything was packed, Monsieur went to bed. He was nervous and kept turning images over in his head. Should he try and simply touch her and see how she responded? Should he just come out and tell her how he felt? Should he avoid the subject altogether because it would be incredibly stupid to get involve with someone he worked with? Should he avoid the subject because she might laugh at the thought that a man his age even thought he had a chance with her? Should he let her call the shots? Monsieur simply did not know. He decided not to masturbate. Eventually he fell asleep.

The next morning, he packed the ice chest and drove to her house, following a map she had drawn out for him. She was living in a nice little rented house with a yard and a view. She was already drinking a beer when he pulled into the drive. Monsieur got out of his car, waved hello, and got the ice chest from the trunk.

He was hyper-aware of everything, but none of it

gave him a clear message. She did not hug him or touch his arm when he approached her, but she seemed happy to see him. It was only noon, yet she had started drinking without him. The day was beautiful, and she suggested they sit on her porch and snack and enjoy the view. She quickly got him a beer. The talk was easy. They nibbled on the snacks he had brought. They gossiped about people at work. They made fun of co-workers they did not like. They laughed together. An outsider would think they were a romantic couple, but there was something missing. There was no emotional revealing, so discussion of personal issues. The conversation stayed light and breezy. On one hand, this was not difficult for Monsieur. He was most adept at light and breezy conversation. But he wanted a real connection to Enid. Or rather, he wanted a real connection to a woman. Enid just happened to be the one who was beside him.

Time slipped by. The sun was hot. They drank several more beers. Monsieur excused himself, found the bathroom, pissed, and then took one of his Levitras. He grabbed two more beers from the refrigerator on his way back to the porch. They moved their chairs to the shade under a tree and continued talking. It was easy talking to Enid, and the talk was becoming more risqué. She told him of several sexual adventures she had had—how she had woken up a year ago in a man's bedroom after getting very drunk and having sex with him, and then waking up to find she detested him, grabbing her clothes and running out of his apartment. Monsieur had to reach way back in his memory to find a heterosexual story to tell. They laughed as they made up stories of how ridiculous their coworkers must look naked and making love. They made up things that each coworker might utter as they came to orgasm.

After several more beers, Monsieur lost his inhibition. He reached over, grabbed her hand and lightly held it. Enid looked at his hand and then at him, then continued talking. She did not squeeze her hand, yet she did not pull away. Monsieur wasn't sure what this meant. They continued talking about something else.

After five or six minutes of conversation had passed, Monsieur looked at Enid and said, "Kiss me."

She seemed startled. "What did you say?"

"I said, kiss me."

A dark look came over her face. "No," she said. "That would be a bad idea."

"Why?"

"Because we work together."

Reason seemed to come back to Monsieur, but he did not let go of her hand. "Well, that's true, Enid. It would be a bad idea." He paused, then said, "Work relationships never work... they never work... I know that. But I am torn, Enid, because I like you a lot, and I am attracted to you." Monsieur did not know what else to say.

"I value our friendship so much, Monsieur. I just don't want to lose that. I look forward to coming to work just to talk with you. And if I have a rough day, I know you can always brighten my mood."

Monsieur smiled, squeezed her hand, and then let go of her hand.

Later that night, he played the memory of that conversation over in his head. How they spent the next thirty minutes talking about the dangers of work relationship, how they told each other how important and special their relationship was to each other, how they promised they would just try and be good friends to each other, spend time together outside of work without calling it dating, get to know each other. How they drank more beers and talked and laughed more, and how they later ordered a pizza and watched TV before Monsieur drove home. Yes, it had been a great discussion. But Monsieur knew it was all a crock of shit. Enid wasn't lying to him, but Monsieur had been down this road before. Their relationship had plateaued. There was not going to be any more growth or change. It was going to remain status quo. Oh, they might get together for dinner after work once and a while, but there were going to be no pseudo-dates, no change of heart, no love, and no sex.

Monsieur knew the truth. Relationship either spark or they don't. Yes, one has to remove the wrapper of presentation. Getting past the front that the other presents to the world can take some time. But once you are past that, the heart either quickens its pace, or it doesn't. And all the talk in the world, all the plans and good intentions are bullshit.

However, he was very glad they had not made love. That would have been disastrous. Now they could pretend Monsieur's attempt at seduction never happened; now they could carry on with their wry exchanges at work, knowing that their relationship was safe from sex, safe from rejection, safe from pain, safe from growth.

Monsieur thought about these things as he lay in bed that night. Luckily the Levitra seemed to have some small effect remaining. He began to masturbate. He tried to think of Enid, but images of naked men in bathhouses entered his mind. He fantasized a faceless man with a towel wrapped around him walking up as Monsieur was sitting in the steam room. The man opened his towel to show his erection. Monsieur leaned forward and took the man's cock in his mouth. As this image filled his mind, he came.

•   •   •   •

Monsieur was right about Enid. Their relationship at work remained exactly the same: fun, friendly, but shallow. He continued to help her on projects, and they would email each other little jokes. The next weekend she asked if he wanted to get together for a hike in a nearby state park. He accepted, but when the weekend came, she bowed out, with some excuse or other. He knew it wasn't her fault. She just didn't know herself, didn't recognized that the currents of relationships buffeted her around like they do all persons. No doubt she thought that she wanted to see Monsieur. No doubt she thought she wanted to spend time with him. No doubt she thought her excuse was a good and understandable one. She simply did not know. Most people are like this, Monsieur believed. Like the fat lady walking slowly down the middle of the aisle, completely oblivious to the number of people she is blocking behind her. If only she would walk on one side or the other, but no, humankind lumbers up the middle, dull and slow.

Monsieur found himself alone the entire weekend. He had failed to plan an activity, even though he had anticipated that Enid would cancel. Depression enveloped him, as usual. He posted a picture of himself on one of the online dating sites but took it down after a few hours. He did get one email from a Hindu lady who lived four hours south of him. Slender, not unpretty, although he couldn't tell much from the small photo of her. She had sent a nice enough email, but Monsieur didn't respond. Four hours is a long drive, but he knew the real reason was that he wasn't really ready to be involved... or perhaps he wasn't really able to be involved.

•　•　•　•

But the following week, Monsieur had a certain feeling he couldn't explain, a certain optimism. He emailed Enid. He asked her if she wanted to have dinner with him at a certain restaurant that he knew was expensive but was near her house. She emailed him back and accepted. Even though their offices were on the same floor in the building, he coordinated the details of this "date" via email. He had first suggested that they meet at the restaurant, but she suggested that he pick her up at her place. That pleased Monsieur because he knew that he would then have to drive her back to her place after they ate.

The day arrived. He drove to her house. She met him at the door, already ready to go. *Hard to interpret that,* he thought. He drove her to the restaurant. They talked and laughed. He enjoyed talking with her. He did not have to work at trying to make small talk with her. He talked—she talked—they laughed. He liked that.

The restaurant was nearly empty. He liked that too. They were escorted to a table and given menus. Monsieur ordered wine. They laughed about the eyebrows on the waiter. They perused the menus. Enid expressed reservations about ordering both appetizers and a salad and dinner, but Monsieur reassured her he had money and that she could order what she liked. They toasted each other and made gossip about people at work. The wine hit them both fast.

The food arrived, and luckily, it was exquisite. They talked and ate and drank and talked. Time simply went away. Mostly they made fun of their mutual difficulties at work, but occasionally bits of biographical information seeped in, where she grew up, what her parents were like, where she went to school. Monsieur tried to listen, but he kept losing himself in her hazel eyes and the soft curve of her breasts as she talked.

When the waiter came with the dessert menu, Enid offered to share a chocolate dessert. Monsieur agreed. Before it arrived, he excused himself and went to the men's room and swallowed a Levitra tablet. Chocolate, he knew, was an aphrodisiac.

And it was good chocolate, drizzled with raspberry sauce. He picked up the last piece with his fork and offered it to her mouth. She opened her mouth and took it in gently and smiled.

The check came. Monsieur insisted on paying. She relented. As they walked to his car, he took her hand. She did not pull her hand away.

"Enid," he said, "I know it's crazy, but I really like you."

She hesitated, then held his hand tighter.

"I like you too, Monsieur."

They were quiet all the way to the car.

When they got back to her place, he stopped the car with the motor running, looked at her and laughed. "This is where you say goodnight or you invite me," he said in a fake British accent.

"Well," she responded, in her own fake British accent,

"would you like to come in?"

"Well, just for a moment." he said.

Inside, she poured him a glass of wine. They went to sit on the porch. He commented on what a beautiful night it was, and what a good dinner they had.

"Yes," she said, "I had a lovely time."

They made fun of their boss. They talked about the stupid reports they were both forced to write. They talked about how cheap the province was to buy inexpensive computers for them to work on. They laughed about office politics.

The talk about office politics made Monsieur think a little bit.

"You know, Enid," he said, "you and I ought to have rules. I mean, we work together and, well, I don't want to create a situation that makes you uncomfortable... I, I enjoy our time together at work so much..."

"Yes," she said, "we do need to have rules... rules and clear boundaries..."

Then quickly, she leaned forward and kissed him, and she did not pull away when he kissed her back.

•　•　•　•

Three months and more went by.

Monsieur felt at the end of his rope. He felt like a walking amnesiac. He and Enid had become lovers, had hidden it from everyone at work. The affair went on for months. They would meet at her apartment and jump straight into bed, then go out to eat and come back and climb into bed again. Her body was everything he had imagined it would be. She had strong legs, muscular arms, pouty breasts with small nipples, massive amounts of hair: armpit hair, a thin line of curly black hair starting at her belly button and running south until it exploded in a dark jungle of wonderful thick black public hair. Her pussy was plump, with big pink lips, and a large delicious clitoris.

Monsieur spent as much time as he could eating her out every time they were in bed. He would make her come two to three times before he fucked her. Part of that was he just enjoyed pleasing her so much; Part of that was that he had to wait until the Levitra took effect. He never told her he was taking Levitra—he just kept extra pills in his pocket with the condoms. Sometimes he would excuse himself to pee and swallow another Levitra. Finally, he had his doctor prescribe Cialis, which lasted longer. He liked Cialis especially because he would often wake up the next morning with a stiff erection and he would fuck Enid again.

She turned out to be quite feral. She liked to bite and grab, and she especially liked to be fucked hard. He could not believe his good fortune to find a lover twenty-five years his junior.

Then it all crashed.

In retrospect, Monsieur realized he should have seen it coming. Little comments she started to make as the weeks went by. Some unpredictable mood swings. The occasional dig about his age or something he said. But he was too wrapped up in her body. She had told him details about her last very recent breakup. A reasonable man would have considered that she was on the rebound, but Monsieur was on his own private rebound too, so he never saw the end coming. And it came fast. A little disagreement one day that led to a fight the next day followed by an exchange of angry emails.

Then one day she simply quit her job and left without saying anything to Monsieur. When he called her at home, she told him that she had found another job in a nearby city and did not want to see him again. She accused him of crowding her, of not understanding her... but Monsieur had stopped listening. He just waited for her to finish ranting and said "Okay" and hung up.

•   •   •   •

Going to the job wasn't the same anymore without

Enid. The work, although meaningless before, now made him feel heavy and dead. Nothing mattered. The hallway that led to her old office seemed to close in on him. The air was hard to breath. He lasted about three weeks and then gave his notice. He took some comfort in the fact that he at least gave notice. Unlike Enid who simply quit the job without notice leaving the office in a bind, Monsieur knew he would get a good referral from his boss. He made up some excuse about a family emergency back in Paris. Everyone felt sorry for him. After his two weeks were up, he said his goodbyes and left the office.

•   •   •   •

Now he had to find a job. Every day he got up, scoured the various cities and towns online within one hundred kilometers of him, looked up the employment websites of each province, each city, each municipality. He sent out cover letters, emails, resumes, and filled out dozens of online applications. Then he waited.

•   •   •   •

The weeks went by. The Christmas holidays were approaching. It was a bad time to be job searching. The ads were there, hovering in the online ether, but Monsieur was not getting any response, only the occasional rejection letter. Still, he had some money left. He remained undaunted.

He tried to structure each day, so he kept busy. He had the routine down. He would sleep as late as he could, but that usually meant only as late as nine. Then he would rise, make coffee, and while the coffee was brewing, he would examine his face in the bathroom mirror. And each morning, he would make the decision anew to add just a little dye to his beard. He had gotten adept at creating the salt and pepper beard look by using a Q-tip to only touch every other beard hair with a drop of dye. The problem was that each morning, when he trimmed the beard back, it became mostly white again.

He knew that it was only a matter of time before he would have to shave it off completely. But he figured that day was at least a year off. And in the meantime, the short stubble style suited him and, he believed, made him appear younger, or at least, more hip.

After his shower, he would dry himself, and put on deodorant and cologne. Then he would dress, always selecting a nice dry-cleaned shirt to wear with jeans. Even though these days he rarely left his apartment, he knew that it was important to look presentable.

Then he would spend the next two to three hours at his computer, scouring the employment ads at the twenty or thirty select websites. His goal was to send out at least two resumes with cover letters a day. Lately, however, it was becoming difficult to find even one interesting job to respond to. He had done government work most all of his adult life, and his resume certainly showed a qualified, reliable worker. The problem was, there were few openings. He knew that most of the jobs he wanted opened up at the first of the year, when the new year's budgets kicked in. He simply had to wait, survive the holidays. He knew he had left his job at the worst time, but he did not regret that. Without Enid there, he simply could not bear being there.

Sometimes he would drift off into private thoughts in the middle of a web search. He would see Enid lying in bed, naked except with her glasses on. And then, like a silent movie unfolding, he would see himself kissing her breasts, her nipples. She even had tiny black hairs on her areolas. He liked that. He would kiss and suck her nipples and she would moan. Then he would put both hands on her breasts and play with her nipples while he inched his way down to that dark hairy beautiful crotch. He would part her hair with his lips and let his tongue lick up and down that wet pussy.

He loved teasing her with his tongue, always going around the outer banks of her pussy lips with his tongue, and then slowly circling in towards her clit. Then he would take one hand off her breasts and, using just one finger, gentle insert it into her pussy about an inch or so, and while he gently tongued her clit, he would move his finger back and forth at the very top of her pussy. He could never feel that pea sized G-spot, but he knew it was there. Enid knew it was there too. She would begin to moan louder and squeeze his hand that was still on her breast, squeeze it tight against her breast.

Monsieur would have to shake his head to stop these thoughts. They would just sneak up on him when he wasn't paying attention.

He considered whether he should go to the bathhouse on the following weekend. If he could find a good anonymous sex partner maybe he would stop reliving those moments with Enid. He debated going late at night on a Saturday. He knew that the bathhouse would be very crowded after eleven at night. Crowded with a wide age-range of men. He just didn't like staying out that late. But if he went in the afternoon, there were usually only a few old fat men there. The last time he went in the afternoon, there were no one there who interested him, and after a few hours of walking back and forth between the steam room and the empty maze rooms, he finally went home without any sex. He decided that when the weekend came, he would treat himself, maybe have a late dinner downtown, and get to the bathhouse as late as possible.

•   •   •   •

It had been at least a month since he and Enid split up. However, that Friday morning, he discovered that she had sent him an email. His heart started pounding immediately. He was afraid to open it, but his fingers clicked it open anyway. The message was short—she was asking him what he wanted her to do with the various things he had left at her apartment: a bathrobe, some clothing, toiletries, etc. It was phrased in such a way as to not reveal any emotion. Two can play that game, he thought. He emailed her back, and tersely said to throw them away. Then he turned his computer off. *How could love come to this*, he thought, but of course, he knew better.

But seeing her name, thinking of her, upset him. He couldn't sit in his apartment. He felt trapped. He got his coat and went outside to walk around the block, but the cold air and the gauze-like blue of the sky seemed even more oppressive than the walls of his apartment, and he turned around and went back inside. He sat on the couch. He moved to the desk chair. He looked at porn on his computer for a while. Then he got out a stack of index cards from the desk drawer and picked out five of them. He labeled each card "N.F.G." which he knew meant "Notes From God" but if he were to suddenly die and someone inventoried his apartment, they would not know what it meant. On the first three cards he wrote D. P. which stood for don't panic. He placed one in the bedroom on his dresser, one in the kitchen on the refrigerator, and the third one he placed by his computer.

He looked at the calendar and then wrote the date for the following week on the fourth card. If he could just survive another week, surely something, or someone, good would come along. He placed that card in the bedroom, next to his alarm clock.

On the fifth card, he wrote T.I.S.O.T.F.Y, which stood for There is someone out there for you. Then he crossed that out and wrote S.I.W. which meant someone is waiting. He didn't like that either, so he crossed that out, and rewrote T.I.S.O.T.F.Y.

He placed that card on his bookshelf.

He felt a bit better.

•   •   •   •

He did go to the bathhouse late one Saturday, but much to Monsieur's surprise, the bathhouse was quite empty. He showered, he steamed, he walked around, but there were only two or three old men in the place. He wasn't interested in any of them, and they didn't seem interested in him. He had rented a room with a TV, so he went back to his room and watched porn for a while. Usually there was something on one of the channels that was entertaining, but tonight, nothing seemed to interest him. Even the men on the screen didn't seem to care. On each channel, someone would be fucking someone else in the ass or in the mouth. But there was no passion, no moaning, no drooling, no rolling of eyes. At least with straight porn, the girls pretend to be excited.

After about thirty minutes of flipping through the channels, Monsieur got off his bed and walked around the bathhouse again. Down the hall, he passed one room with the door open, and a fully clothed young man sitting on the bed with a large leather bag. Monsieur looked at the note taped to the door. "Free HIV testing—ten to midnight"

Monsieur looked at the young man, looked back at the sign, then said,

"How does this work? Do you draw blood then mail me the results?"

"Nope. We just take a swab from inside your mouth. We have the results in twenty minutes. It's all anonymous."

Monsieur still stood by the door. "And who sponsors you?"

"The Registry of Health. We're here every Saturday night."

"Anonymous?"

"Absolutely."

"Free?"

"Completely"

Monsieur walked inside the room, closed the door and sat down on the bed. He felt a little odd, sitting there with only a towel on, talking to this fully clothed young man.

"My name is Tim." the young man said and extended

his hand. Monsieur took his hand and shook it.

"Hello, Tim. My name is Monsieur. Glad to meet you, although these are weird circumstances."

Tim chuckled, "I understand," he said.

Monsieur looked at Tim. He liked him. He didn't seem gay, or straight. Maybe bi.

"So, when was the last time you were tested, Monsieur?"

"Hmm, it's been a while."

Tim pulled out some papers and a small plastic pouch from his leather bag. He opened the pouch and took out a small plastic bottle. He twisted the cap of the bottle open and pulled out what looked to Monsieur to be a miniature dipstick. He handed the dipstick to Monsieur.

"Just scrape the end of the stick inside your upper lip and place it back inside the bottle."

Monsieur did as he was told.

Tim explained that the test measured HIV antibodies and that after twenty minutes of sitting in the solution in the bottle, either one or two lines would appear on the top of the dipstick. One line meant that there was enough scraping on the stick to be used for testing and no HIV antibodies were detected; but two lines meant that HIV antibodies were detected. Monsieur said he understood. Tim started to explain about the three-month time window that existed with the creation of antibodies—that someone could be exposed to HIV recently but not have any antibodies for several months, but Monsieur stopped him and said he understood all that.

"In that case, I just have a few questions, all anonymous, but we do this for research purposes." Tim started reading from his papers.

"Do you think that you have been exposed to HIV recently?"

"I hope not."

"Do you engage in anal sex?"

"No." Monsieur lied. He didn't want to explain about

the one guy who tried to fuck him many months ago but was too big. And besides, that guy had worn a condom and had not even come close to coming.

Then Tim had a number of questions about crystal meth, poppers, needles, all of which Monsieur could honestly answer no.

"What about oral sex? Do you engage in that?"

"Well, yes, but I never let anyone cum in my mouth." Actually, it had been over year since Monsieur had even had another man's cock in his mouth that wasn't covered by a condom. Tim started talking about the statistical odds of catching HIV from sucking cock, but Monsieur was trying to think back to the last time he had actually sucked a guy without a condom. It had been about a year before, at some bathhouse up north. A nice fellow that Monsieur got along with, had actually talked with. At some point in their mutual masturbation, Monsieur had sucked the guy's cock for a short while. But the guy had not cum. Monsieur realized what his sexual behavior had been this past year just as Tim was summarizing it.

"So, it sounds like you've been relatively safe. You do go to the bathhouses but you either engage in mutual masturbation or you let someone suck you off."

Tim then went on discussing the impossibly low odds of catching HIV by coming in someone else's mouth. Monsieur understood that, but he was still compulsive—he would always shower right away, washing his cock and balls good, and he would always try and piss right after coming. Still, hearing Tim summarize his behavior made Monsieur feel like a fraud, that he only came here to squirt semen in one of two rigid ways, either by getting jerked off or by getting sucked off.

"So, when was the last time you had an ongoing gay relationship?"

Monsieur had to think. It had been at least ten years since he had spent time with the same guy. His name was Bill. Monsieur couldn't remember his last name. It was between his first and second marriage. He would go over to Bill's house and they would jerk each other off. It really wasn't a relationship. They didn't date or anything, but it was a pattern they maintained for two to three months. Before that, Monsieur would have to go back another twenty or thirty years.

"It's been a long, long time, Tim."

"What about relationships with women? When was the last time you had sex with a woman?"

Of course, that would be Enid. Monsieur took a deep breath. He felt heavy. "Well, I *did* date this one girl for a while this year."

"Did you practice safe sex with her?"

Monsieur remembered the many times he ate Enid out, even when she was on her period. One time he rimmed her ass. And Enid didn't like condoms, so they often fucked without them, with Monsieur pulling out at the last minute. He knew at the time that was crazy, but he was so intoxicated with fucking her that he didn't care.

"Hmm, relatively safe," he lied.

"And do you see yourself ending up in a long-term relationship with a man or a woman?"

That question took Monsieur by surprise.

"I don't know, Tim. That's a topic for a more... a more philosophic moment... I just don't know."

Monsieur was quiet. Tim said nothing. Then a little timer bell went off on Tim's watch.

"Well, it's been twenty minutes, Monsieur. Turn the bottle around and tell me what it says."

Monsieur turned the bottle around. His hand was trembling. There was one line on the top of the dipstick.

"Well, that's good, Monsieur. Although, based on our discussion, I would have been surprised if there had been two lines."

"Yeah, me too, but it had been so long since I had been tested... and you never know."

"Well, that's it then, Monsieur."

"Oh, okay, thanks, Tim. Thanks a lot. I appreciate you being here. You do a good job."

Monsieur got up and walked out of the room. He knew he had been more scared about HIV than he had let on. Now he felt relieved, yet still upset. He was glad he did not have HIV, but Tim's question about whether he saw himself in another long-term relationship with either a man or a woman bothered him. It bothered him because he didn't see himself in another long-term relationship with anyone.

There were more people in the hallway now. The place had filled up while he had been talking with Tim. Monsieur went inside the steam room and sat in an unoccupied corner to think about Tim's question. But after a few minutes, he looked up to see a young man standing over in the doorway, looking at him and rubbing his cock through the outside of the towel wrapped around his waist. Monsieur opened his towel up and started masturbating while staring back at the man. The man walked over to where Monsieur was sitting, bent down, and took Monsieur's cock into his mouth. Monsieur's cock got harder. The man kept working at it. After a few minutes, Monsieur came. The man stopped, spit Monsieur's cum out onto the tile floor and walked out. Monsieur got up and walked to the showers.

·   ·   ·   ·

Several more weeks went by. Monsieur was dreaming. He dreamed he was lying on a bed in a bedroom which opened up into another living area. He saw Enid walking in the living room. Monsieur tried to get out of the bed, but his legs did not seem to work. He fell to the ground and pulled himself to the doorway to the living area. He reached the doorway and looked around for Enid. She was not there. He began to sob.

Then he woke up. The sun was coming through the curtain. His real bedroom did not open up onto some living area. He knew it was just a dream, but he marveled at the memory of him sobbing uncontrollably, gasping painfully for air, as if his rib cage would break, just a few minutes ago, lying there in agony over Enid. He wondered where the real Enid was.

Christmas had come and gone, but no job offers had come his way. He had a lead at a probation office in the next town north, but it depended on whether one of their employees was going to announce her retirement between Christmas and New Year's day. She had been there a zillion years and everyone wanted her to retire, and he was told that he would be first choice to replace her if she did retire, but then again, she was supposed to retire a year ago, and didn't. So Monsieur had to wait a few more days to learn his fate. If that job fell through, he wasn't sure what he was going to do. He had never had such a difficult time finding a job. His money was about to run out. He rationed what funds he had left. He had stopped eating out at restaurants and had reduced his choices of wines to the boxed variety, all in an effort to remain solvent.

He thought of suicide, of course. There a nearby bridge. Cold water far below. Thinking about suicide was nothing new. He had toyed with the idea of suicide all his life. He knew that suicide was not a choice—it was just a last resort, a non-choice that life sometimes dealt out. He knew, for example, that had his HIV test come back positive, he would have killed himself. It was a simple calculation. It would have meant that either he gave HIV to Enid or she gave it to him, but in either case, he could not afford medication, and even if he could afford it, medication would have doomed him to the outskirts of relationships. Despite all his dark sojourns to the bathhouses, Monsieur longed for a deep committed relationship with a woman... a deeply sexual, amoral, experiential relationship to be sure, but a committed one. But even as an HIV negative single man, he couldn't even manage to date. How could he cope as a HIV-positive? Life arranged the path—you had no choice but to follow. Monsieur had always visualized the gods in some pre-Christian gathering around a viewing pool, up in heaven, placing bets on the earthlings below.

"Look, Zeus, I'll give him AIDS and bet you two hundred drackles that he hangs himself in a week."

Or...

"Look, Apollo, I'll create a feral female creature to drive him sexually mad, and I'll bet twenty gold pieces he quits his job and goes insane."

Nothing else ever explained the variety of human behavior like Monsieur's belief of betting demonic gods. Why would the Hollywood star, rich beyond Monsieur's dreams, blow his girlfriend's brains out? Why would the handsome politician with a wife and child get caught in a male prostitution ring? Why would the young minister's wife, beloved by the congregation, drown her own children? Why the gym coach caught with the eleven-year-old student? Why the sixty-year-old esteemed senator sentenced to five years in prison for embezzlement? None of it made any sense unless you assumed that the gods had arranged for an irresistible temptation to be placed in each of their paths, all for betting purposes. Monsieur had seen many men in the bathhouses fuck complete strangers in the ass without a condom. How insane, he would think as he would watch them and stroked his own cock. Yet he fucked Enid without a condom many times, because she "did not like how condoms felt". Free will is a joke, Monsieur thought, just another over-intellectualized concept like personal change or forgiveness. The gods could create hundreds of irresistible temptations. Monsieur knew that he was so lonely that he would fuck the next female that showed any interest in him, no matter how fat or stupid she was. He also knew he would take the next job that was offered to him. Where did free will come into the picture?

Nonetheless, he decided to get out of bed and shower.

• • • •

The days and weeks moved through Monsieur's life like molasses, slow, thick, but steady. He'd get up each day,

73

later and later it seemed, trim his beard and check it for gray, touch it up with dye, shower, dress, and spend a few hours at his computer looking for jobs. If he found an opening, he would prepare a cover letter, a resume, print out any forms they needed completed, and then drive to the post office to mail the letter. There he would also check his P.O. box for mail. He was always amazed that there were only bills and no rejection letters. Of the hundred jobs he had sent letters to, only ten percent had responded with rejection letters. The others were simply silent. Then he would return home to spend the afternoon back online, although his afternoon sessions were less dedicated than his morning sessions. He would often deviate to the porn websites for an hour or more. Then, somewhere between the hours of four and five he would open a box of wine. Many days went by where he did not speak to anyone, except maybe the clerk at the grocery store where he would buy his wine. "How are you today?" they would say, without looking at him. "Fine." He would answer, "How are you?" They never did answer that. "Thanks for shopping with us," would be the response, again with no eye contact.

As the days went by, he had to geographically expand his job hunt. He originally wanted to stay in the same city, to save the expense of another move. But now, he was looking at cities two to three hundred kilometers away. He had maps of all the provinces and he would check each province's website and each city's website every day, stretching his search a few kilometers further and further out. He would check the government websites. He would check the job hotlines. He would check the employment agency websites. He even subscribed to a few search websites that claimed they would turn up every job available, which of course they never did. But he felt he had to cover all the bases.

• • • •

Monsieur was waking up from a nap. The late

afternoon sun, low in the sky, was turning the white curtain golden yellow. Monsieur stared at the color. It made him sad somehow. Late winter afternoons always seemed sad to him. Monsieur was thinking about goodness.

All my life, he heard himself think, *I have tried to do good, tried not to hurt anyone. Why can't a little of that goodness come back to me? A good job... maybe winning the lottery?*

He heard a voice in his head laugh at him. It was a new voice, meaner than the other ones. It said, *Why, you haven't been any different than any other man. You haven't done anything good. You just haven't done that much harm. You've divorced two wives, fathered no children, made no radical difference to anyone's life, made no improvement in society. You spend your time thinking about sex and slinking into bathhouses. And even there, you're not gay—you don't suck anyone off, you don't fuck anyone in the ass, no one fucks you in the ass. You just wait for someone to jerk you off or suck you off. You're incapable of forming a relationship with a man or a woman. And besides, your sexuality, your ability—or inability—to love, all that has nothing to do with getting a job or winning the lottery. Those things are not things you get because you deserve them. They just happen.*

This sequence of thoughts upset Monsieur.

But I have been good, he answered. *Goodness isn't necessarily grandiose achievements. I do listen to others. I do care. The fact that I haven't found love may be a fault of mine, or may be fate, but it doesn't mean I'm not good. In fact, I have loved, maybe too much, and maybe that's been my downfall. I've always honored love—always followed it.*

The voice in his head laughed and said, *It's not love you've been following; it's lust.*

There's no difference, Monsieur countered, *no real difference. The man who waits for hours on the corner for a certain woman looks, acts, and feels the same, no matter whether he is waiting for the wife he loves or a prostitute he can't turn away from. The world makes fun of the john, but honors the devoted husband. Yet their desires, their motives, and their chains are exactly the same.*

Really? said the voice. *Is that why you only pursue your "love" under the cover of night, like a lizard darting under rocks, or a rat in the shadows?*

It was true—Monsieur preferred shadows. When it came to walking down the street from his parked car to the gay bathhouses, he preferred dark rainy nights. He craved and demanded anonymity.

That's only because the world does not want to acknowledge that a man could simply go into a bathhouse, get a blow job from another man, shower, and go home a better person, he answered back.

Really? said the voice. *Is that why you used to go to whorehouses when your first wife was out of town—to be a better person?*

That was true too—he used to do that. He felt bad remembering that. They were motley places, old houses with a couple of girls. But it was the same lust that drove him there. Society would not approve of that either. Society simply did not approve of lust, of desire, of simple carnal pleasure. The voice was right—it was lust that drove him there.

He could sense the voice laughing at him. But then he heard his brain talking to the voice: *Maybe Monsieur is seeking love but simply settling for lust.*

The voice didn't answer that, and Monsieur thought about this for a moment. Maybe it was not simple pleasure that he sought. Maybe his brain was right—that he yearned for a true lover's touch, but he would settle for an anonymous hand job. At least it was a human touch. A flesh-and-blood hand. That's why it never mattered to Monsieur whether the hand was male or female—because it was always a substitute for a true lover's touch. In truth, if there existed bathhouses of all women where he could go and get hand jobs, it would never occur to him to go to a gay bathhouse. It wasn't the fact that there were men there—it was the fact that there was flesh, human flesh, human touch, human warmth, and even an occasional kind and loving human touch. That's why the loss of Enid had hurt him so deeply, because she was a woman who, for a brief while, desired him, touched him, loved him or at least loved him in a physical way. She wasn't just an anonymous hand job. There was for a brief period, something more...

The voice in his head laughed and started talking directly to his brain instead of to Monsieur. *It still comes back to love. If he had loved his first wife, he wouldn't have had to go to whorehouses.*

Bullshit, Monsieur thought, *that's just total fucking bullshit.* He had loved his first wife. He wanted to say that what drives a man to other women is not that they don't love their wives, it's that something is unfulfilled in them. He wanted to say that if any man is completely satisfied, completely absorbed and fulfilled by one woman, he will not cheat. But when he considered that, Monsieur had to admit to himself that he did not know if it was possible for any man to be completely satisfied, completely absorbed and fulfilled by any one woman, and most of all, Monsieur didn't care whether it was true or not, because he knew that it was not true for him. He had never been, except for only brief moments, ever completely fulfilled by one woman. Even with Enid, even when he was totally engaged with her, he still was going to gay bathhouses.

He felt horribly confused. He couldn't stand it when the voices in his head argued. He knew that none of what he did made any consistent sense. He wanted love from one beloved person but did nothing to achieve that. He loved women but sought men. He espoused love but engaged in anonymous sex. He didn't think he was two-faced, but he obviously maintained a secret lifestyle. He flirted with women but never asked them out. He didn't want to think about this anymore. He had to survive. Any debate about love meant nothing if he wasn't employed. If he could only find a job, then he could drive these voices out of his head. If he could find a job, he wouldn't feel like a failure. He just wanted all the voices to shut up!

Monsieur took a deep breath and slowly let it out. There was quiet. He looked at the clock. It was four-thirty in the afternoon. He could get up and go to the store and buy another box of wine, come home and make some dinner and drink wine. He resolved to do just that. Even though there would be other people at the store at this hour, he would not talk to them. Monsieur accepted his inability to make contact. Goodness had nothing to do with that, either. Meeting someone was all fate, all propinquity. He simply had to wait for the right set of events. He knew that. He resented it, but he knew it. When he found a job, then he would meet someone. Somehow, it would happen.

He tried to tell himself that despite the voices it had been a productive morning. He had found two new positions in nearby provinces and mailed out applications. Perhaps in a week or so... In the meantime, he simply had to survive, not cave in, not let the voices talk, not think about what would happen if he got no job and his money ran out... The image of the nearby bridge with the cold rushing water below came to his mind.

He shook his head, as if to shake the image of the bridge out of his thoughts. He got up and went to the store.

• • • •

Monsieur finally found a job. Like every job he'd ever found, it happened in the blink of an eye. At least that's the way it felt to him. One day he was unemployed, thinking of suicide, and the next day he was employed. It didn't really happen like that, of course. Among many other applications, he had sent in one to a job to a city almost two hundred kilometers away, a small city of about nineteen thousand people, and they called and wanted to interview him the following week. He accepted the interview, but wished it were sooner. The days until the interview just dragged on in misery.

When it finally came, the interview started in a rather routine way. The three persons interviewing him went over his resume in detail, and asked questions about each of his jobs. But, to his shock, at the very end of the interview, they offered him the job. He knew that there had to be undisclosed problems at the office, since they needed someone so fast, but he gladly accepted. He had been unemployed for almost four months and needed the job.

They wanted him to start the following week. He'd done this before, so he knew the drill. Not that he owned much anyway, but it still all needed to be boxed up. And he needed to find a place to live, and there were notices to give, and it was all the usual headache and back strain, but he'd done it a million times, so he boxed up his belongings, marked each box according to his system, went and looked at a half-dozen apartments, found a new place to live, signed the lease, gave notice to his old landlord, packed his car, and moved.

However, in the middle of the move, Enid emailed him.

He was dumbstruck to see her name in his email inbox. She wrote that she had moved, but of course he knew that. She had had some tough times, had thought about a lot of things, and was writing to apologize to him, and ask him if he still wanted to be friends. He sat at his apartment table, staring at his laptop, reading and rereading the message. It took him multiple readings, in fact, he finally had to read the email out loud, to discern that she was not asking to restart the relationship. She had moved beyond that, or so she said, but she did want to be friends, to start a new relationship. Although there was some ambiguity in the message, she clearly wanted some kind of contact. So he wrote back, saying that of course he would want to be friends, that he had always treasured his relationship with her, and that he would be honored to reconnect. Of course, he was not sure he wanted to reconnect in a way that left him as vulnerable as he had been, but he would try to be more discerning this time.

Of course, he was moving further away from her with this new job—almost two hundred kilometers further away in fact. And it turned out that this new job was going to be more difficult than his previous jobs. This was a much bigger office than ones he'd been used to, and they were giving him more responsibilities. He tried to act like he could handle it, but of course, he had his doubts. After the interview, they had introduced him to all the staff. They were a blur of faces except for Alice and Michelle. Alice was a young girl, maybe a few years older than Enid, big boned, high cheekbones, who was an assistant to one of the other employees. Michelle was a receptionist, maybe thirty-seven years old, sassy and funny. Of course, it was much too early to tell, but Monsieur had to analyze the situation. Enid had been his equal in the office, but Alice and Michelle were different. Technically speaking, both Alice and Michelle would be considered as subordinate to his position, so the legal issue of sexual harassment was a consideration. He would wait and see how things developed.

Of course, he also got on the internet and checked out the gay bathhouse possibilities. Unfortunately, there were none in this particular city. He would have to research alternatives.

. . . .

The first week at the new job was a blur. There were many more files to handle on a daily basis than Monsieur was used to, but he managed. There were many more staff to interact with than he was used to, but, again, he managed. There were many older women in the office and he knew how to use charm to get them to help him with his cases. He felt that he was being successful in fitting in. He always tried to be the model employee—quiet, but efficient.

He did not see Alice or Michelle during his first week, but he was so busy with the files that he had no time to think about them. Actually, he had thought about them, but he had assumed that he should not approach them because of the legal landmines.

In fact, during the first week, he had not even spent much time thinking about sex. He didn't even have time to connect to his favorite porn websites at night. He brought work home with him each night, made dinner, and worked on his files until it was time for bed. He was so tired each night that he slept without masturbating, without dreams, just deep sleep. One thing that that Monsieur hated worse than no sex was being seen as incompetent. He threw himself into the work, trying to figure out not just the office procedures but also their politics, how things got done, who did them, and why things were done in a certain way. Although it was a strange syllogism, he told himself, that if he could master this larger office, he would be able to then to find a girlfriend.

•　•　•　•

He was dreaming of Enid. She had invited him to some sort of lesbian fashion show, where half-naked women were writhing in the corner of a large store. Enid was busy greeting all the women as they came into the store. He stayed by the buffet table, watching her. He felt that he should not interfere with her networking with the women. Then the scene shifted. They had left the party and were in either her or his house. They started kissing and caressing each other. But there was someone else there. It was a young girl about four years old that Enid was supposed to take care of. She was in the same room, playing in the corner. Monsieur felt that was wrong to make love to Enid in front of this girl. So, he continued kissing Enid but did not run his hands over her body the way he wanted to.

When he woke, he lay in bed and thought about this

81

dream. It made no sense to him. It didn't fit any interpretation. Did he want Enid or not? Who was this child? What was the lesbian fashion show?

After he took his morning shower and dressed for work, he looked at his cell phone. He had taken some pictures of Enid last year with the built-in camera. She was not that attractive in an objective sense. Still, when he saw the pictures, he felt an aching... but it was a detached aching, like a memory about something that used to matter.

None of this made sense to him. Later that day, he saw that she had emailed him at work. He answered, but it was only out of a sense of politeness. He was starting not to care.

• • • •

Monsieur was on his third week on the new job. Although he felt that he was still struggling to keep his head above water, he was the only one who felt that way. Everyone else was pleased with how well he was fitting in, how hard he worked, his attention to detail, how he would pitch in to help with projects without taking control of them or even taking credit for them. Monsieur's biggest skill was getting along with others. During the second week, the new boss even took Monsieur aside to tell him how happy he was with Monsieur's work. Of course, the boss phrased it to be self-congratulatory ("I'm so glad I was intuitive enough to hire you....") but it was sufficient to Monsieur that the boss had been lulled into approval.

On the negative side, Monsieur learned that both Michelle and Alice were married. With Michelle, he didn't mind so much. Michelle was older, and Monsieur wasn't that interested. But Alice was younger with dark hair and large tits. She had broad cheekbones and eyes set wide apart. But her husband was a toad of a man. Monsieur never could figure out why some women married some men. The image of this naked flabby hirsute man reaching for Alice in bed in the middle of the night was repulsive. His only conclusion was that she must be stupid to marry such a toad. He had never really engaged her in conversation, and after seeing her husband, he chose not to engage her in any more than perfunctory work talk. Still, he had to admit that he felt, or imagined, that when she walked by him, she was sensing him, somehow looking at him. Perhaps she was just looking, or just curious, or perhaps she was unhappy with her hirsute man. Maybe she married young and was wondering what else was out there. Many an American country-and-western song was based on just such a situation. As were many murders. Monsieur did not need such complications.

Slowly, as time from work permitted, Monsieur began to explore the city. There wasn't much to explore— no downtown to speak of, just the standard grocery stories, a few bars, and a handful of antique shops. Nonetheless, Monsieur was glad to have a job.

· · · ·

Out of the blue, Enid called Monsieur. Actually, she left a message on his phone, and after a few anxious hours, Monsieur called her back. He got her voicemail, so he left a vague but cheerful message, saying he was glad she had called. The next day she called him back. They chatted like old friends who hadn't spoken in a while, updating each other with current events, but both being careful not to discuss their relationship or to mention the break-up or the months that had passed. Her job was going well. She regaled him with stories at work. She listened to his travails at the new job. They gossiped about people they had known at the old job. No mention was made, no hint was given, no reference was even implied of their history, of the late dinners in out-of-the-way restaurants, of the nights at her little apartment, of the drinking on her balcony, the falling into her bed wrapped in each other arms, of the tearing off of clothes, of the frantic hungry kisses, the meeting of tongues, the sucking of nipples, the fingers reaching up inside her, the sex, the sex the sex... No mention at all. They might as well have been pen pals talking on the phone.

How odd, Monsieur though. *What creatures we are that can devour each other's most private parts and then pretend it never happened.* He remembered one time he was eating her pussy and then put both hands under her round ass and lifted it up and began to rim her asshole with his tongue. *You can't get more intimate than that,* he thought. A woman can keep her pussy fresh, or a man can keep his cock and balls clean, but one never know what one's own asshole tastes like. Hers was remarkably clean. It seemed to Monsieur that once you ate someone's asshole, you should be bonded to them forever. Evidently, such was not the case.

They chatted for about ten minutes and then she had to go. Neither one of them suggested getting together at any point in the future.

Maybe that's why people pretend that certain intimacies never happened, Monsieur thought, *so they are not bonded forever, so that they can move on.* Monsieur knew that he felt a deep sexual bond that bordered on love for Enid, but it wasn't love.

How could it have been love? he asked himself. He thought about this. Enid had not known him at all. How could she? He was the chameleon of men. None of Monsieur's wives ever knew him. He knew, in the darkest part of his heart, that he never revealed himself to anyone. His skill at relationships—the intuition of what the other person wanted—was also his greatest weakness: he was so good at intuiting what the other wanted that he never could stop and tell them what he wanted. The fact was, he never knew what he wanted. He was a fake man, a ghost in a man's body, not evil, but mutilated somehow, lacking some organ, some connection to humanness. Only his sexual desire connected him to others.

He shook his head sadly and stared at the floor.

•　•　•　•

Monsieur continued to work hard at the new job, coming in early and staying late. The new boss seemed pleased with him. He had the knack of fitting it even if the work was meaningless and boring.

At night he retreated to his new little apartment and drank. Although he was immensely polite to all those in the office, he socialized with no one. He kept his privacy wrapped around him. He felt he was entering a cocoon stage, hibernating in a soft cotton shroud while time passed and the seasons changed. He knew that at a certain point in time, he would emerge, and things would be different.

Monsieur had been in this cocoon state before. It was like hibernation, where he only did simple things because simple things were all he had the energy for. Weeks went by. Spring came slowly, hesitantly to this city, but the afternoons were warmer and sunnier each day. Enid continued to email him, long emails explaining all the dramatic and often horrible things that she was going through. Monsieur began to see how angry she was much of the time. Things were always happening to her that weren't her fault. He would email back a sympathetic line or two but stopped giving advice, stopped responding to every email. It wasn't that he didn't have memories. He did. But he knew there was no future with Enid. He knew that, in their line of work, at some point in the future he would run into her at some conference somewhere. He did not look forward to that, but he knew he could handle it. He hoped it would be later rather than sooner.

The days continued to move past him. He had his routine and it gave him great comfort. The pain in his side had disappeared some time ago. The itch had disappeared as well.

Blessed be the mysterious cocoon, he thought, *for in*

it we are transformed... although we don't know how, we are transformed.

    •   •   •   •

Two more months went by. Monsieur had become an accepted and regular part of the office. But he was beginning to feel hemmed in by his cocoon. He had not been to a bathhouse since he started this job. He thought about the upcoming weekend. He had discovered online that there was a bathhouse in a resort city about two-hundred fifty kilometers south of him. He decided it was time to venture out and made up his mind to drive south, to get a hotel room for the night, to splurge on a nice meal in a quiet restaurant, and to spend a few hours at this new bathhouse. He made a reservation online at a hotel about ten blocks from the bathhouse.

As the weekend approached, Monsieur began to feel anticipation. He mapped out the route he would drive. He had researched online the various restaurants in that city that weekend and, in a moment of courage, called a very expensive one, and ended-up having a long conversation with the maitre d', who convinced him to book a reservation. Monsieur began to look forward to a rare exquisite meal. He was going to have a mini-vacation. A mini-vacation with a variety of cocks, he hoped. He pictured men standing in a group naked, some large cocks, some small cocks, some erect, some just thick and flaccid, balls hanging down under dark pubic hair, men standing around a dark steam room while he perused the group, trying to decide which one or one to pick. It was a nice fantasy. It helped him pass the time at work. It even helped him ignore the silly email that Enid sent him that week where she was complaining about some problem she had created. He deleted it and went back to his fantasy.

    •   •   •   •

The trip to the southern city ended up taking Monsieur more than four hours. It was raining hard the entire way. There was so much rain, he felt that he was crossing a sea. The windshield wipers cast a hypnotic spell of rhythm and sound. In that spell, Monsieur saw himself as a submarine, propelling south, across of sea of rain, blind but for the next one hundred meters in his headlights, trusting only in the white lines of the road. Monsieur alternately imagined himself on a boat, on a raft, on a sea-plane, on a sea-jet, shooting through over and under water. The sea seemed cold. He was sailing south, sailing toward the unknown. He thought of Lethe, the river of forgetfulness that separates the land of the living from the land of the dead. Driving through the rain toward the possibility of anonymous gay sex in some dark bathhouse was like a sailing on a black sea of forgetfulness. Sex numbed everything else. The journey toward sex numbed the rest of the world. The rain was gray, oily gray. It smeared his windshield. It obliterated the scenery. He felt in a bubble. He drove on.

Once he arrived at the city, however, the rain seemed to lift. He found his hotel. It was a contemporary place in the heart of the city. He obtained his room key, went upstairs, got into his room, locked the door, and without unpacking, climbed into bed and fell into a deep dreamless sleep.

When he awoke, it was almost dinner time. He must have slept for several hours. It was time to head to the restaurant.

Part of the reason he had selected this hotel was because it was in walking distance of the restaurant and the bathhouse. His plan was to simply walk to the bathhouse after enjoying a fine meal. However, on his way to the restaurant, he was beset by the strangest feeling.

It was a feeling of déjà-vu. He felt had been here before, but in some past life. He kept having a memory of staying in an old wooden hotel, not the steel and glass modern hotel he was now staying in. And the city was different, older, decayed, mossy-feeling somehow, like Prague when it rains.

And his clothing was different. He kept imagining himself descending a steep wooden staircase dressed in formal clothes from a hundred years ago. But the feeling was the same, the walking, the sense of going somewhere before heading somewhere else for some debauchery. His thoughts were the same, as if he had thought them all before.

With every step towards the restaurant, the déjà-vu grew stronger. Was it a dream he had once had? A premonition? It couldn't be a premonition because it felt like it had happened in some other century. It felt more like a dream—like smoke just beyond Monsieur's grasp. Was there a wooden staircase? Was he wearing a white suit? A white hat with a broad brim? If he was descending a staircase, where was he heading? Was he going to a restaurant? He certainly felt an eerie familiarity with walking to this restaurant. He thought back. Had he been in this city before? He could not remember when.

When he arrived at the door to the restaurant, the feeling only increased, despite the fact that Monsieur was absolutely sure he had never been in this city nor at any similar restaurant. This restaurant was not a part of any chain—it was a very fancy and distinguished restaurant. Monsieur examined the door. Large, wooden, carved with an intricate pattern, framed by large steel bands. He had never seen such a door before. Yet it was hauntingly familiar. Monsieur opened it and went inside.

True to his word, the maitre d' escorted Monsieur to a very private table on the upper floor away from the other diners. Monsieur felt very comfortable here. From his table he could view the street below and the people walking along the sidewalk, but they could not see him. He enjoyed, as always, watching other people. He could even make out some faces, beset with concerns, happy or sad, intent on getting somewhere, or lost in thought. Every face gave a hint of some story.

The waiter came, and Monsieur ordered wine while he perused the menu. The feeling of being here before came back. Monsieur struggled to catch an image. If he could only recall a single image, it would tell him of some dream he had had. And if he could recall what dream he had had, perhaps the anxiety would dissipate. But, alas, no single image was retrievable. It was simply a feeling of being here before, of having done every single act exactly the same, before.

The waiter came back, and Monsieur asked him what he might suggest. Since Monsieur was on "vacation", he did not care about the cost. He wanted to have a good meal. The waiter understood, and over the next two hours, brought Monsieur a variety of small plates: scallops simmered in a lentil sauce, grilled octopus with olives in a green salad, grilled flounder and clams over a potato base, pork bellies with mint and sweet sauce. Finally, sorbet and coffee. With the last sip of coffee, Monsieur took a Cialis pill, in preparation for the night ahead.

It had been an exquisite meal. Monsieur was sure he had never eaten a meal like this. But he could not shake the feeling that even though he could not remember such food, he was reliving a past moment, or perhaps a future moment. This feeling tempered his enjoyment of the meal. He had tried to focus on enjoying the food and tried to drive the feeling out of his head. He told himself that the feeling of déjà-vu was just a trick of the mind, a "skip" in the record of memory triggered by a synapse misfiring, or triggered by a smell or a repressed memory that the unconscious was forbidden to review and so had to code into a feeling of "being here before".

Monsieur paid his bill and tipped the waiter forty euros. It had been worth every penny. He left the restaurant and stepped out into the street.

It was dark now, but there were people still out walking in the warm spring night. Monsieur strolled toward the bathhouse. He was glad that this bathhouse was in a good section of town, not like some he had been to in decades past, hidden in dangerous parts of town.

But as he walked along, he couldn't shake the feeling

of familiarity. He looked around. Clearly, he was in a new city. These were street lights he had never seen. Stores he had never seen. Everything was new. And yet, and yet, he couldn't shake the feeling that he had been here before. He began to feel heavy. Not sad. But somehow burdened.

He arrived at the bathhouse. There was, as often is the case, no name or number on the door. He entered. There was the familiar hallway. The thick glass window with a cashier at the end of the hallway. He paid for his room and was buzzed into the establishment. Once inside, he was given a room key and two towels. This particular place also gave him two complimentary tubes of lubricant along with some condoms.

Monsieur found his room. It had a TV with gay porn. He stripped down, wrapped a towel around him and went to find the shower.

But all the while, the feeling of déjà-vu grew stronger and stronger. At the shower, Monsieur let the hot water spray over his head and face. He tried to wash the feeling away. But when he opened his eyes, everything looked familiar. He dried off and walked into the sauna. There were several men sitting on the wooden levels. They were all fat. Monsieur couldn't look at their faces. He found it hard to focus his eyes. He found a place to sit down. A fat man walked by. Another fat man walked by. Monsieur got up and walked around. He walked down the corridors of rooms. Some of the doors were open. But in each one, a fat man lay on the bed. He couldn't understand why there were so many fat men at this bathhouse. He walked back to the sauna. There was a young man, almost a boy, lying face down on one of the wooden levels of the sauna. Monsieur couldn't see his face. But the shape of his body, his young buttocks, beckoned him. The young man had a skinny young girl's body. Monsieur stopped beside him and stared. Monsieur wanted to fuck him, to get behind him and spread his legs apart, to run his hands over those round buttocks, to push his fingers up into that asshole. Monsieur reached out and touched the man/boy's buttocks. The young man pulled away.

Monsieur understood and walked away. He never thought of himself as a top, as someone who would fuck another man, but he had to admit, he was attracted to young men who looked like women. He had often fantasized about fucking a man who was in the process of transgendering into a woman... a man who acted like a woman, who looked like a woman, who had small breasts like a woman, but who still had a cock.

Monsieur walked around. In addition to the déjà-vu, he began to feel oppressed with a new feeling, a feeling of pointlessness. If he simply repeated all these actions over and over, through lifetimes, through time, over centuries, what was the point?

He began to feel dazed. Was it the wine from dinner kicking in? The stress of being in a new city? Some side effect of the Cialis? He walked along the corridors. He couldn't look at anyone's face. Everybody he passed seemed inhuman. Flesh wrapped in towels. Another open door. Another fat man.

He went up and down the corridors. He wasn't sure what he was looking for. Finally, he walked back into the sauna. There in the corner was a man, sitting on one of the levels, towel open, masturbating. Monsieur walked up and sat next to him. Monsieur opened his towel and began to stroke his own cock. The man next to him stroked faster. He had a nice-looking cock, thick and erect. Monsieur kept working his cock, trying to get an erection.

But things were not responding. After a few minutes, it was clear to Monsieur that he was not going to get an erection. The feeling was just not there. Maybe the Cialis had failed him. Maybe he was dead. Maybe he just wasn't in the mood. But his dick remained limp and unresponsive, no matter how much he pumped it. This was the final straw. If he was unable to get hard, then there was no sex. And if there was no sex, there was no reason to exist. Without the ability to get a hard-on, there was no Monsieur.

The man must have noticed, because after a moment, he got up and left. Monsieur sat there wondering what was going on. Another fat man walked by and stood over in the corner where he could watch Monsieur. The fat man began to stroke himself. Monsieur had no interest. He got up and walked out.

Monsieur thought that he might as well go back to the hotel. Something was clearly wrong. He showered again, letting the hot water wash over his face and body. Then he started to walk back to his room to change clothes. But before he got to his room, he decided to take one last look in the maze, a dark hallway that twisted and turned, creating many dark secluded corners. At various points in the maze there were monitors showing porn. Monsieur wasn't sure why he went into the maze, but when he got near its end, he saw a man with a shaved head, sanding there watching one of the monitors, and stroking himself. It was dark, but Monsieur could tell that the man was very white, as if covered in talcum powder. Monsieur slid into a corner near him and undraped his towel and started to stroke his flaccid cock, and as he did, he studied the man. The man had his back turned to Monsieur, so Monsieur couldn't see his face. But the man was very muscular, balding with a shaved head, maybe about thirty years old. The initial white luminescence that Monsieur had noticed must have been a trick of the light from the TV monitor, although it did appear to Monsieur that what hair he could see on the man's head looked silver or white. Monsieur wondered if he dyed it that color, or if it was another trick of the light.

The man moved into the darker part of the corner and sat down. Monsieur still could not see his face or see what he was doing. Monsieur stepped forward still stroking his limp cock. The man then, without standing up, turned toward Monsieur and took Monsieur's limp cock in his mouth and started sucking him. Monsieur could only see the top of the man's head and the back of his neck and shoulders. But Monsieur held the man's head gently while the man sucked him. Slowly, Monsieur began to get hard. The man held Monsieur's balls in one hand and moved his mouth the length of Monsieur's cock up and down with his mouth. Monsieur felt the man's teeth gently bite him at the base of his cock.

Yet, even during this blow job, even while he was holding the man's head and moaning, even during this, Monsieur had stopped caring. It had all happened before. It was just a blow job. Another blow job. In another bathhouse. By someone who didn't even have a face. It simply didn't mean anything. Finding someone who would physically satisfy him wasn't enough anymore. He felt the man's tongue wrap around his cock. He felt the man's hand stroke his balls. Monsieur felt completely separated from the experience.

Yet he was getting close to climax. He leaned over and said, "I'm gonna cum." The man grunted and continued to suck him. Monsieur came, thrusting in and out of the man's mouth, squirting his cum into the man's throat. He could feel the man swallow.

Monsieur hunched over and pulled his cock out of the man's mouth. He was glad to finally cum and be done with this nonsense.

"Thank you," he said to the man.

The man said nothing and just turned away.

Monsieur pulled his towel around him and walked away. He never did see the man's face. While he did understand liking to suck another man's cock, Monsieur never could understand why someone wanted to swallow a stranger's cum. Some men, he knew, would swallow five or ten men's cum in a single night in a gay bathhouse. This was beyond Monsieur's understanding.

Monsieur found his way back to the showers again, and took another long hot shower, being sure to wash his cock well. Then he went to the urinal and made sure to pee a little bit, to wash any bacteria away. Then he made his way back to his room and got dressed.

The check-out of the bathhouse happened in a blur, and Monsieur found himself back on the street, walking to his hotel. It was much darker now, and there were fewer people out on the street. Monsieur glided back toward his hotel as if he knew the way by heart. His head had begun to hurt. He knew now that he had walked these streets before. It didn't matter that he could not remember or explain it. He had done this before. He had spent his life and all his past lives and all his future lives on dark streets, going to or coming from gay bathhouses or whore houses, or dark corners, or dark bars. He had spent his whole life dreaming of undoing a holy lover's blouse but settling for blow jobs by unknown men and prostitutes. He felt worse than alone, worse than dead. He felt used.

The streets where he walked seemed narrower than before. The sidewalk seemed to be turning black. The buildings were taller and seemed to be leaning toward the street. Monsieur felt hemmed in. It was hard to breathe. But he kept walking. Down this street, up another street. Turning left. Walking. Turning right. He kept going on. That's what he had always been good at, he thought to himself... going on, enduring. He could always count on his ability to hunker down and survive, to wait out the storm, to keep going on, to survive the cocoon, to survive the bad marriages, to survive the loneliness, to survive the lack of women. But now, he felt that strength faltering. A feeling of panic seemed to burst from his gut. Bleak and horrid images rose up before him, but he couldn't get them out of his mind. Everything was diseased. Cocks with cankers sores. Fat women with pussies stinking of fish and oozing foul pus. Diseased old men stumbling towards him, wanting to have their cocks sucked. Old fat women crying in bed. Assholes leaking shit. He saw himself falling out of the nursing home bed, shitting himself, breaking hips and bones and teeth. Gums bleeding, hands shaking with palsy, blue lips slack and drooling. He felt his head swirling. He stopped walking. "I can't go on," he thought. He felt tears welling up in his eyes. He looked down. He couldn't see his hands. He blinked and wiped at his eyes. He felt like he was going to faint, or vomit, or both. He looked up. There, on the next block, was his hotel.

• • • •

More than a month had gone by since "that incident", as Monsieur called it, had happened in that southern city. He had made it back to the hotel, back to his room for the night, where he spent a horrible night fighting some unknown panic. The next morning, he quickly left the city and headed north. He drove, beset with an anxiousness that seemed to emanate from his belly. He vowed to return to a disciplined routine in his daily life. He vowed to enter a period of celibacy. He knew that only a rigorous routine would restore a sense of normalcy to his life. He had lost control and he had to get it back via the only method he knew: an unalterable routine. He made a religion out of a daily routine. He got up at the same time every morning. He ate a banana every morning for breakfast. He made the same sandwich every day for work. On Mondays, Wednesdays, and Fridays, he would wear a white shirt. On Tuesdays and Thursday, he would wear a light blue shirt. He went to the gym every other evening after work and he followed the exact same exercise routine. He did his laundry at the laundromat every Saturday morning at seven when it opened, when no one else would be there. He used the same washer and dryer on those Saturday mornings. He would sit in the same seat in the laundromat while he waited for his laundry to go through the cycles. He did not go to any bathhouses. He spent as much of his workday in his office as he could. He even avoided going to the court to file reports. He would send his reports over with other workers who went there. The few times that he had to make the trip to the courthouse, he did so quickly, and never lingered. He did not socialize with people unless he had to at work out of politeness, and then he would excuse himself as quickly as possible. He made sure his reports were completed on time and that they were accurate. In fact, his work output seemed even better to his bosses, and they continued to be pleased with this dutiful employee.

At night he stayed in his apartment and drank. He knew drinking so regularly was not healthy, but it numbed the anxiety and gave him something to do.

•　•　•　•

Slowly, over the next several months, he felt like he was gaining control over his life again. His rigid routine provided safety. The anxiety that had been a constant companion seemed to be slowly dissipating. He no longer dreaded another attack. He no longer had horrible images well up in his mind. He allowed his routine to expand so he would file his reports at the courthouse himself and sometimes even chat with the court clerks. He stopped dying his beard. The white hairs dominated the few dark hairs, but it didn't bother him anymore. He didn't think looking gray was so bad.

It was only when he was drinking at night, that he allowed himself to think about his life. He wondered what he would do about sex, if he would go back to bathhouses or go back to trying to find a girlfriend? He knew that the sex in the bathhouses was empty sex, anonymous sex, but it was, after all, at least some sex, that is, some type of human contact, but he also realized that it was the accumulation of that emptiness that probably created his panic attack.

He tried to access his situation: He was fifty-six years old, and he looked it. He lived in a small apartment. He had no family, no children, no safety net, and no actual future. But he was at least employed, relatively attractive, deferential, and had the appearance of being available for a relationship, despite having no energy for one. He knew he lived a dual life. He was straight and he was gay. He loved women and he wanted men. He talked with God but knew there was no relief from God. He was gracious toward people and couldn't stand them. He worked hard and did not believe his work made any difference.

Only at night would he let himself muse on these things.

•   •   •   •

Another month went by. It was a Friday night. Monsieur had stopped by the liquor store and brought two bottles of pinot noir.

The occasion was no particular one. It was just that Monsieur felt like getting drunk. Enid had emailed him with one of her annoying "how r u?" queries that told him nothing about how she was doing or why she would be inquiring into his state of affairs. *Bad phrase that*, he thought, as he filled his glass. Since he was having no affairs, his "state of affairs" was zero. Other than the one blow job the night of the incident, he had not had sex since he moved to this city. He had deleted Enid's email without responding before he left work and headed for the liquor store.

He examined his glass of wine. He loved pinot noir. He liked the color, the taste, but most of all, he loved the way it softly numbed everything. He looked about his little room. The book shelves, the table, the chairs...it all was meaningless to him. He was numb.

Drink had been his faithful companion for almost four decades, always faithful, always there. He raised his glass to the God of drink.

•   •   •   •

The weeks passed by. Summer faded into fall. Monsieur received no more emails from Enid. He would chat with the women at work or ones at the courthouse, but the conversations never seemed to get above the superficial level. Monsieur was convinced they simply saw him as a nice old man.

Work had become numbingly routine. He was glad to get through each day so he could return to his apartment and drink.

Monsieur had now been at the job long enough to have earned some vacation time. Although he was not particularly interested in going anywhere, he knew that if he did not take a vacation he would lose the time. He thought that perhaps a vacation might shake him out of the rut he was in. So, after several days of thinking about where to go, he made plane reservations to fly to Paris the following month. He remembered the bathhouses there, the ones he used to frequent years ago. He thought he could risk going back to bathhouses now, especially ones he knew. He realized that going to any bathhouse was going to be disappointing, but what other choice did he have? Like that old joke about attending a crooked card game because it's the only game in town, Monsieur knew he had to return to the bathhouses. It was a hollow release, true, but it was a release. It was only sex, but it was the closest he could get to love. Monsieur knew he was not going to change his ways. Enid had been his last hurrah as a heterosexual. He never had been the aggressive pick-up man, never been able to approach strange women and engage them in conversation. He had always relied on fate and circumstance to bring women into his life, and into his bed. He loved women, loved their bodies, loved making them come. Monsieur felt that there was nothing more magical on earth than bringing a woman to orgasm with his mouth on her pussy. Monsieur missed that. But fate had stopped bringing women to Monsieur. It had been almost a year since he had last fucked Enid. But it seemed more like a century. He felt old. Monsieur now felt sympathy for the old white-haired men, paunchy and hunched over, who sat alone in the steam rooms. He used to watch them disappear into the dark rooms or into the glory hole corridors to suck off some younger man who didn't realize that his cock was being sucked by someone three times his age. Monsieur no longer pitied these old men. He felt he understood their fate.

In the meantime, he got online and located the address, phone numbers, and hours of operations of several bathhouses in Paris. He marked the dates of his vacation in his calendar and waited. Who knew, perhaps tomorrow would be better.

• • • •

When the heart attack came, time just stopped. Monsieur knew instantly that he was in deep, deep trouble. The first wave of pain was more like a jolt. The second wave of pain was actually painful, and Monsieur went to his knees. His brain assessed the situation and told him that he could not bargain this away. But somehow, oddly, Monsieur didn't care.

Events seemed to speed up and slow down at the same time. His eyes were tightly closed yet he could see so many different things. He felt a sharp intake of air. Then there was a popping sound. He stopped hearing what people were saying and just observed how the past and present and future were colliding. It was as if his brain was split into a hundred brains each thinking thoughts independently, yet he could see and hear each thought.

He saw himself as a baby crawling in the grass and felt the sun on his back. At the same time, he heard himself calling out in pain. At the same time, he saw himself hard at work at his desk. At the same time, he saw a giant wave overcoming him. At the same time, he saw himself on the floor. He felt his face grimacing. Then he saw mountains. At the same time, he saw himself naked in the bathhouse too weak to resist being groped by a dozen old fat men. At the same time, he saw himself signing his decree of divorce with his first wife. At the same time, he saw himself hanging up the phone angrily on his second wife. At the same time, he saw Enid glaring at him before vanishing.

There was a rush of sound, like wind in a tunnel. At first, he ignored it. But then he realized it was a combination of a thousand sounds and voices. There were too many voices to decipher, a million sounds threading together. It rose up and enveloped him.

He stood up and moved away from himself. He drifted outside and watched the ambulance come. He drifted across the street and into an office building. At last he was truly invisible. He looked at himself and saw nothing, felt nothing.

At his funeral, there was a nice gathering. Monsieur thought it odd that he could see himself still lying on the floor and the paramedics trying to talk to him at the same time that he could see his funeral. Time had simply stopped, or rather, everything was happening at the same time. He could turn to his left and see himself in real time walking in the rainy nighttime toward the bathhouse; he could look to his right and see himself in bed with a woman licking her nipples while he reached his hand between her legs; he could look again and see himself in a hot shower, letting the steam lift his spirit. These were not visions, they were real, they were unfolding before him, he was experiencing them as they actually happened, all happening at the same time, all happening at different times, all real, all real, all real.

He looked over to his left and saw a park and drifted into it. It was quiet, late afternoon. The sun sent yellow shafts of light through the trees. He thought he must be sitting on a park bench. No one was around.

All his life, he had tried to live on the outside. He sought experience. He had sucked off boys when he was eleven. He had eaten pussies of women twice his age and pussies of girls half his age. Sex was the only thing that made him feel alive. He wanted love but never found it. He needed the experience of sex. He had decided at an early age that one simply had to wait between experiences, wait for something to happen. He had been good at waiting. He had turned it into an art form. Now he was waiting again.

He wondered what he was waiting for. There didn't seem to be any point in hanging around here. He wondered if he could just dissipate, just evaporate. He closed eyes that did not exist. He let out the breath that did not exist. He felt the molecules of his soul expanding, spreading apart and expanding out into the universe. He couldn't control his thoughts anymore. He couldn't remember. He was expanding... flowing... and then... and then... Monsieur no longer existed.

PART 2:   THE BOOK OF PAUL

<u>Chapter 1</u>

They had published Paul's first book. It had taken a few months for the exhilaration to wear off. But his first few royalty checks helped him come back to earth. He did the math and realized that being a published author was just another way to make a living, and maybe not such a good way to make a living. He made an appointment with his life coach and was telling her about it.

"I thought I had it made, but I'm only going to make around ten thousand on this book."

"Is that normal?"

"Well, my agent says that unless a book gets on a New York Times best-seller list, or gets picked up by Oprah, that ten thousand is about average."

"You have an agent now?"

"Yeah, I just got one."

"Paul, why did you get an agent *after* the book was published? I thought the point of an agent was to get a book published in the first place."

"Oh no, I could never have gotten an agent before the first book was published, when I was unknown. The agent is going to help me get my second book published."

"You've written a second book?"

"Well... no, not yet. But now I have to. If I can get another manuscript done in three months, my agent says she can get it sold."

Paul's life coach frowned.

"Wait a minute Paul, I'm confused. It took you two years to write the first book, and six months more to get a publishing contract. And you're going to try to write another book in three months?"

Paul squirmed a bit in the chair.

"Well, my agent says that if I can have another book ready, while my first one is still selling, it will be much easier to get it placed with a publisher, even if it's not that good."

"Not that good?"

"Well, I didn't mean it that way. I just meant that she says we need to capitalize on the fact that the first book is selling."

"Okay, I see. And how much are you paying this agent?"

Paul got defensive.

"I don't pay her anything... She just gets a commission on the second book... but that's worthwhile to me. You remember how hard it was for me."

"I remember. Okay, so what's the second book about?"

"Well, I haven't decided yet... I'm still working on that."

And he was working on it. He kept a little notebook with him and he would jot down every idea that came to him.

"Hamlet from Ophelia's point of view."

"Sci-fi sex—a creature comes to earth and has sex with everyone it can."

"Detective genre?—a bi-sexual amoral detective a la Sam Spade... who sleeps with all his clients."

"Vampire, guilt-ridden, in therapy... conversations with his therapist. Tony Soprano meets Lestat."

But nothing struck a chord in him. The first book had been a work of love... No, that's not correct. It had been a work of lust looking for love. Lots of graphic sex scenes. Lots of repressed homosexual angst. Fortunately for Paul, it had struck a positive nerve with the tenth publisher he sent it to. And even though the publisher was a small independent one, it had a good web presence, and then the book stirred some controversy because of the sex scenes, and that generated some publicity, which resulted in a spike in sales, and then it got a good mention in Rolling Stone and sales really took off because Rolling Stone was gracious enough to mention the publisher's website. The publisher even flew him to New York, Chicago, and San Francisco for book signings. For a few weeks, Paul felt like a rock star.

But the book signings ended, and even though there was a second printing, and even though the publisher still always took his phone calls, and treated him well, the royalty checks started to become smaller each month.

When he first met his agent, she told him this was normal.

"Paul, there are over twenty-thousand books published each month. Each month! Most never make it anywhere. Most end up in cut-out bins in dollar stores, or worse, stay in boxes in the author's basement, or are given to the author's family and friends. You are one of the lucky ones. You sold copies of your first book. You don't know how rare that is. Do you know how many authors I turn down each month? When I read your book, I knew you had a future as a writer. It was cutting edge stuff. A bit raw, but the next five or six books will mature. In two or three years, you'll be a household name."

Four or five books?... In two or three years?... Paul worried about this. His life coach had been right. It had taken him two years to write his first book. And he had struggled with it. How could he turn out five more in two to three years? But he didn't want to imply any hesitation to his agent. He liked having an agent. She was going to be his business partner. All he had to do was write. She would do the rest. All he had to do was write.

Chapter 2

Paul's first book was titled *The Man Who Mistook his Hemorrhoid for a Clitoris*. Rolling Stone called it "a cross between *Naked Lunch* and Camus' *The Stranger*"—a quote Paul loved. He knew that his publisher had given that line to the Rolling Stone reviewer, but he loved it anyway. Paul had the article framed, and it hung in his "writing room", which was the living room of his apartment. Next to it hung a photograph of Bob Dylan which years ago he had cut out, ironically enough, from an article in Rolling Stone. Paul was so proud when he first hung his book review on the wall, proud to be in the same magazine that published articles about Bob Dylan, proud to see his name in print. It was a type of validation he had never felt before, not even from his life coach. He imagined dinner guests pausing as they wandered through the apartment to read the article. In truth, he did not have any dinner guests in his two room apartment, but he thought if he did have them, and if they did wander through the place, they could stop and read the article.

Chapter 3

"How's that second book coming along?" His life coach asked him as soon as he sat down.

"I'm working on it," Paul said.

"Do you have a topic yet?"

There were times Paul hated his life coach. It wasn't a "topic". It was a story, or a theme, or an idea. But even when he hated her, he knew that it was her hard prodding that kept him writing the first book, got him to finish it, and cajoled him into submitting it to publishers.

"No, not yet."

"Well, I've been thinking about our last session, Paul. And I've been thinking that, knowing you, the pressure of having to come up with a topic and getting it written in a few months, would be rather overwhelming. Is it?"

"No, I don't feel it as pressure," Paul lied. "It feels more like an opportunity."

"I see."

Paul knew from her tone of voice that she knew he was lying. He did feel it as pressure. But he couldn't change his situation. He had to take advantage of the fact that he was a published author. He had to write a second book.

Chapter 4

Paul was conversing with himself, which he often did.

"It can't be forced. It has to be an idea that lets me write freely", he thought.

He knew that the reason it was possible for him to write *The Man Who Mistook his Hemorrhoid for a Clitoris* was because it was written in a stream of consciousness style, which allowed him to simply sit at his writing desk, pour a glass of wine, and start to write.

"I need to find a structure that lets me write that easily," he thought. He ruled out a sequel because, unfortunately, he had killed off his protagonist in the first book. Whatever story the second book told, it had to be better than the first book. And probably totally different from his first book.

"What was it Nietzsche said?" he thought, "a critic is someone who thinks he's doing you a favor by saying your second book is better than your first book?"

Paul had tried to make his first book a combination of black humor and serious inquiry into the meaning of personal destiny. Some of the reviews didn't quite get the latter half, but as long as they praised the book, Paul hadn't minded. One reviewer had even called it "camp" and "high satire" which Paul had never intended. But his publisher, which tracked sales after each review, noted that the book had a good spike in sales after that particular review. The publisher asked Paul to write the reviewer a personal thank-you note, which Paul had done, even though he thought the review was idiotic. He justified the letter as "good business."

Paul reviewed his notebook for recent book ideas:

"Transgendered male-to-female who then becomes a lesbian—her thoughts and feelings... maybe have her seduce the female doctor who did the transgender surgery... or perhaps have him/her not be a lesbian but be a successful male-to-female operation, have her be normal, and have the doctor be male, and then "she" falls in love with the doctor but have the doctor reject her because the doctor's gay."

Paul liked that idea. He told himself he could explore the concepts of happiness and psycho-sexual identity. He liked the idea of someone finally achieving the identity they always wanted, the identity they thought would bring them happiness, but still having happiness be elusive. But Paul also knew he would have to do a lot of research on transgender issues and surgery procedures to make the book real. And above all, Paul secretly knew he was a lazy writer. He needed a subject that was interesting enough for him to want to write without having to do a lot of research.

He read through the other recent ideas in his notebook:

"Online predators. Not predators but an emerging personality type. Twenty-something men who have only known social interaction via the internet. Maybe a loner who would have been a social outcast twenty years ago, but now has an active social life via the internet, but still can't relate to people. Can only get first dates but has an endless supply of first dates because he's always online."

Paul disregarded that idea. He read on.

"Professional sperm donor who discovers that, through mismanagement at the sperm bank, he is the father to hundreds/thousands of children. His identity becomes known after an investigation of the sperm bank and the newspaper publishes his name. He gets sued for child support by hundreds of mothers... maybe he discovers that his young lover is actually his daughter... or perhaps he discovers his lover's identity first and then the investigation ensues..."

Paul liked that idea because he thought he could explore the whole issue of how important the biological connection to one's past is. At the same time, he could deal with some of the issues in his first book: how people, especially men, are disconnected from family and history.

But Paul also had darker, terser, entries in his journal:

"One day in the life of a homeless man... can't get money or food... cold rain... No shelter... kills self or another..."

"Cripple/wheelchair or some type of impediment... goes online... ala match.com and tries to find partner... ends up soliciting hooker on craigslist."

"Botched suicide attempt, then the state charges man with attempted murder of himself, and he spends the rest of his life in prison."

And there were brighter entries:

"Blessings... dialogue of angels that hover around two people during one day in their lives."

"A dog born human... he goes to karma court and

because he was such a good dog, he gets to be born human this time, but through some quirk, he retains his dog-like perceptions—his views on humans and human behavior."

"All things alive. A man can suddenly hear the thoughts of all animate and inanimate objects around him. He thinks he's going mad but comes to understand that everything is holy."

But still, nothing grabbed his soul like *The Man Who Mistook his Hemorrhoid for a Clitoris*. But Paul was optimistic. The ideas were coming freely. It was just a matter of time before he came upon the perfect idea.

Chapter 5

Marv was Paul's agent. Marv was a female. At least, she looked like a female. And to Paul, she looked like an attractive female. But she insisted on being called Marv, and Paul didn't question her on this.

She called him and told him to meet her at Vagabond's Bistro at 7 p.m. sharp. He debated eating something before he went there. But then he called Vagabond's and learned that the kitchen stayed open until nine. Maybe Marv would pay for his dinner. So he arrived exactly at seven with an empty stomach. He didn't see Marv there, so he grabbed a table near the bar. He texted her. She responded quickly. She was running late.

Paul was hungry. He waved down a waitress and asked for a menu.

"Oh, I'm sorry sir, the kitchen closed at six today."

"What? I just called before I got here and was told it'd be open until nine!"

"I'm sorry, but the cook burned his hand and had to leave."

"Oh man, I'm starved. Do you have anything to nibble

on?"

"I'll see what I can find."

The waitress came back a minute later with a bowl of some kind of snack mix: pretzels, peanuts, crunchy things. Paul thanked her and ordered a glass of wine. He was halfway through the glass and the crunchy things when Marv arrived.

"Oh *Paul,* you wouldn't believe what a day it's been. I've been inundated with writers since Wilson Concord's book got such good reviews. I've had to turn down so *many* promising young men."

Marv always had a way of making him feel insecure. Wilson Concord had just published *Fag or Gag—Memoir of a Transgendered Truck Stop Prostitute.* Paul had tried to read it, but it was horrible. Still, he had told Marv how much he liked it. Paul didn't want to lose the only agent he'd ever had.

"They closed the kitchen early, Marv. We can go somewhere else if you want to get something to eat."

Paul wanted to go somewhere else. He was very hungry, and he hated drinking on an empty stomach.

"No, no," Marv said, "I ate earlier. I need a drink."

She summoned a waitress, waving her long arms, bracelets clanking in the air.

"I'll have a dirty martini. What are you drinking Paul? Wine? And another glass of wine for my friend."

Paul didn't want another glass of wine. But he did not dare protest. He munched on his snack mix.

"I'm trying to set up a panel discussion of new writers for PBS in a month or two. You're going to be on it."

Paul was aghast. "What?"

"It'll be on their local affiliate radio station. You'll be there along with Wilson Concord, Michael Serrell, and Amy Pearson. The subject is the new beaten generation."

"The *what*?"

"The beaten generation. It's a term I came up with myself. I've tried to assimilate the current trend of writers

I've seen, their style, their position in the world, their anguish, their sexuality, their rage, and their defeatism... and I've coined the term "the beaten generation." If it catches on, if the media picks up on it, you could be as famous as Ginsberg."

Paul was taken aback. First of all, he was just a writer. He was not part of any group or ideology. He didn't feel he was beaten. Nor did he think his book had made any cultural dent. He only felt that he had been lucky. He was terrified that if he was promoted as any kind of spokesperson for a generation of anything, he would be exposed as a fraud. He had been to book signings—that he could handle. But a panel? To discuss literary issues? He didn't know what the current trends were, and he didn't care. He just wanted to make a living.

"That's sounds good, Marv."

"The time is right, Paul, for gay and transgendered writers to claim their place in the literary world, to be recognized for their contributions, to take their place on the podium with every other writer."

Paul was not gay, nor was he transgendered, at least not the last time he looked. He felt very straight. His book had explored some gay themes with some graphic erotic fantasies, and Paul certainly was well-informed from his publisher how well the book was selling in the gay community, so he never disavowed the rumors that circulated, or the ones that his publisher circulated, about him. No one ever asked him, and he never said. But the truth was, he very much preferred women. He had worried that when his book got published whether someone would ever ask him about his sexual orientation. But no one ever asked. He did admit that when he was sent to book signings in San Francisco, that he wore a little hat and acted a bit more effeminate at the book signing than he normally acted, but that was just marketing.

The waitress brought their drinks. Paul hadn't finished his first glass of wine yet so he moved the new glass to the side. Marv gulped half her martini down immediately.

"I tell you, Paul. This is a brutal business. You remember Bruno Streeter? I got Nozolla Books to publish that sweet little book of his, *Knock-Eternal Emissions.* And it did pretty well! But then he wrote that ghastly sequel, what was it called? Oh yes, *A Series of Dreams,* and *The New Yorker* just trashed it, and all his sales went into the toilet. Well, I just saw him last week, working at a HoJo's. Isn't that ironic? It was so embarrassing, having him wait on me. I left him a big tip. Anyway, he told me he's working on another book called *Fluid Days.* He wants me to rep him, but I can't, I just can't. I told him to send me a copy though, just to be sure. How's your sequel coming along?"

Paul wasn't sure what to say. "Well, it's not a sequel, Marv, since the protagonist died in the first book. But it's coming along fine."

"That's good, darling. I think you're such a strong writer. Where did that waitress go?"

Marv was waiving her arm at the waitress for a refill. Paul checked his watch. He hated the feeling of anxiety and empty-stomach drinking. It reminded him of high school dating. He did the only thing he knew how to do in those situations—He asked Marv questions to get her talking about herself.

"Who would say was the best writer you've represented, Marv? I don't mean necessarily the most successful, but the person who was the best writer."

"Oh Lord, Paul, that would be Amy Pearson. Her book *Innocent until Guilty* was the perfect blend of hip lesbian language, post-modern love, and Jewish guilt. I couldn't put it down. It was pure panache. People thought it was too flippant about relationships, but it wasn't flippant— it was *sassy.* It was as if Oscar Wilde was a lesbian on meth."

Oscar Wilde probably *was* on meth, Paul thought, or at least whatever stimulant was around back then. But he didn't say anything. He hadn't read Amy Pearson's book.

"You'll get to meet her at that PBS show, Paul. She'll be there. I'll introduce you."

Paul made a mental note to read her book.

"Where did you meet her, Marv?"

Marv started on a story about how she met her at some open mic poetry reading. Paul couldn't picture Marv sitting still long enough at an open mic coffee shop to listen to anyone. He could more picture her at some fancy cocktail party, mixing and mingling with a drink in her hand. But he maintained eye contact with Marv and nodded his head and tried to appear interested. It was going to be a long evening.

Chapter 6

A week later Paul returned by himself to Vagabond's. Even though his last visit there with Marv had been stressful, he noticed that the restaurant had gotten a good write-up in the weekend edition of the paper. The reviewer had especially raved about their appetizers. And besides, the place was close to where he lived. Paul had had a late lunch, so he wasn't that hungry, but he was looking forward to nibbling on something and thinking about his next novel.

However, when he got there, the waitress informed him that the kitchen was closed. They had some jazz-dance trio playing and they closed the kitchen early because of that, she told him. That made no sense to Paul. Why close the kitchen early when you have a musical act that brings people in? And why close the kitchen early when you just got a good review in the paper? But he ordered a glass of wine and sat in a corner booth. The jazz trio was not that bad, and better yet, they weren't that loud. They were playing a jazz standard that people could dance to. Paul looked around while he waited for his wine. One old couple was dancing. The man was at least seventy and bald, with his pants hiked up too high. Why do old men do that? Paul wondered. The man was grinning and had both hands in the air now, index fingers pointed straight up. What kind of dance move was this? Paul looked at his partner. She was approaching seventy as well, wearing some type of spandex pants that clung to a paunch that stuck out under her sagging breasts. Her hair was bleached blond and very scraggly but tied up on the top of her head like a buoy. She was bumping her hips against the old man, as he twirled around. It was almost pornographic to watch them. How do old people make love? Paul wondered. Do they feel lust? Do they each fantasize of young partners as they ply the winkled flesh of their partners? Does he suck on her sagging teats? Can he get it up? Is her public hair all gray? Does he use a lot of lubricant? Is she dry as sandpaper? Does she come? Does she come as strong as she did when she was twenty? Does he shoot out jism or just trickle out a drop? Was there a novel in this? Could he work this into a story about something? He didn't think so. His wine arrived. The song ended, thankfully, and the old couple carefully made their way back to their table. What was he going to write about? He pulled out his pocket journal and reviewed his book ideas of the day:

"Therapist who leads double life. Helps people during the day but engages in hard-core bondage sessions at night. Struggles with his identity. Has to fight urges to seduce his patients."

"Series of stories told to gay hairdresser by his straight women clients... who all complain that they're not getting enough sex... How he handles their problems... Contrasting his sex life with theirs..."

"Something like Eliot Spitzer... prosecutor who acts morally superior during the day but is tormented by his demons at night... Running for office, he has to prosecute gays but then gets outed himself... Or caught with prostitutes..."

"Bad-seed sixteen-year-old (male or female?) who seduces older man. He/she has no conscience, but then local D.A. gets involved in the prosecution of the older man... has to present child as "victim" but in reality he/she is the aggressor... eventually he/she seduces the D.A. but he gets re-elected anyway and what happens to child? He/she kills him or herself or just goes on?"

Paul knew that all his ideas had sex as a theme. And conflict. After all, that was the basis of *The Man Who Mistook his Hemorrhoid for a Clitoris*. And Paul had to acknowledge that it was the basis of much of his mental activity as well. But it certainly helped that it was the basis of the buying public's interest too. He loved the idea that sex always involved repression and repression always involved sex. It was as if the evolution gods had a twisted sense of humor, making the object of everyone's intention so impossible to reach.

Paul looked around the bar. He liked this place. Lots of pine and colored lights. Green tiki lights above the bar. Red neon beer signs on the wall. Blue Christmas lights on the ceiling. It was a comfortable place to drink. The band started another song. It was a classic Fleetwood Mac number done with a jazz style. Many people started for the dance floor. Paul sipped at his wine and watched what he couldn't quite understand.

Here were three women dancing together, two of them about two hundred fifty pounds each while the third woman was slender and hot, with large breasts. Yet all three were dancing close and making a lot of eye contact. Were they just friends or lovers? Did the two fat girls do the slender girl at once? What was the deal? The old couple also made it back to the dance floor. He was flashing his big denture smile and waving his hands in the air again, and she was shimmying her torso against his. Fucking weird, Paul thought. Here was another couple, older but doing a very elegant jitterbug dance. His beard was grey, but he moved well. She was older too, but in good shape. Obviously, they had taken some dance classes somewhere, because every move was choreographed together. Step, step, twirl, spin, step, step, repeat. But they seemed to be having a good time.

He did notice that there was one woman who was dancing with someone that she obviously did not know well. She kept glancing over at Paul. He looked back. She had dark hair, and a nice figure. Seemed about forty, maybe older. But Paul was no spring chicken himself. He had been though a bad divorce a few years ago, had avoided bankruptcy, and had just climbed out of the debt pit when *The Man Who Mistook his Hemorrhoid for a Clitoris* was published. For the first time in years, he felt he had a little money. Not much, but after being debt-ridden for so long, even a few dollars in his wallet made him feel rich.

He missed being married, but he liked being free. Another inevitable conflict of life. The dark-haired girl seemed to be looking at him again. He couldn't tell for sure. But he smiled back, just in case she was. He could feel the wine kicking in. He noticed the other dancers. Here was a tattooed man dancing with a fat woman. He was wearing a shirt with the sleeves cut off, to show his tattoos, Paul thought. His woman was fat but dancing close to him. He seemed in a trance. Here was a black man dancing with a white woman. Paul watched him. The black man danced so smoothly, so easily, so confidently. How do they do it? Paul wondered. How do they look so good? The black man's woman was a bit overweight, but danced okay, but also seemed so happy to dance with this man. It was pleasant to watch them. Maybe he could write something about a man who watches dancers dance. But what kind of plot would that be?

The waitress came by and asked if he wanted another glass of wine. Paul knew that if he did, he'd be in trouble. Even though he wasn't that hungry, he knew he had to eat before he drank more. Plus, if he stayed, he might find himself asking someone to dance. It was that kind of place, obviously. But Paul pushed down those options. He wasn't ready to handle rejection. He asked for his bill.

<u>Chapter 7</u>

The next morning Paul got up early and made the coffee extra strong. He sat at his computer in his bathrobe drinking coffee and nibbling on peanuts. He had to get started on this second book. He needed an idea. Some idea that would take over his thinking, that would become a mission, a passion. He started free-associating.

"The gods, the gods are sitting around Mount Olympus, and they decide to create a world, a playground where they can take a form that is totally devoted to pleasure, but just to make it interesting, they devise a game whereby the moment they take a human form, they totally forget that they are gods, and they take turns becoming human and the rest of the gods make wagers on whether the ones on earth can ever remember that they are gods while they're in a human form."

He rejected that idea. He liked the idea of playing with concepts of destiny and purpose, but he didn't think he could write convincing god dialogue.

"Maybe a Frankenstein theme. A man's brain is transplanted into a dog's... no, a dog's brain is placed... no, *fused*, with a man's brain, so that the man is both a man and yet thinks like a dog... no, wait, that's a werewolf... okay, no... maybe something like that *Monster* movie, a prostitute who kills, but she always gets away with it. Never gets caught. Just gets better and richer, and older, and more successful. Putting up with fucking strangers, the smell of a john's breath, the bodies, the requests, the techniques for making them cum quickly. What is a whore's perspective? Does she detach while having sex, or is she always detached?"

Paul toyed with this idea for a moment or two. Could he write from a woman's point of view? From a hooker's point of view? Maybe he could pay some hooker to talk to him. Of course, he would want to fuck her, too. Could he research a book about how much hookers hated men while he fucked them... while he became the very thing she detested?

"Maybe a version of Hitchcock's Psycho... a fellow is the night clerk at a hotel, and he's a loner, but he's been there forever, so the hotel owners trust him, and he puts electronic bugs in all the rooms, and listens in on the lives of the guests, writes down their stories, but never gets involved with them... Then what?... Something has to go wrong. A woman in trouble... someone he starts feeling compassion for, but then she starts to commit suicide, and he has to decide whether to break his shell and save her, which risks exposing his eavesdropping, or let her die."

Paul liked that idea. He liked the idea of the loner who spends his time observing others but can never connect with them. *The Man Who Mistook his Hemorrhoid for a Clitoris* was basically a story about an outsider but with a gay theme. He could call this new book *The Zero Hotel*. He liked the title. A good title was motivating. *The Zero Hotel*. He poured himself another cup of coffee and began to hum. Words formed in his head, and he began to compose a little song.
"I was sitting in the Zero Hotel.
I was thinking of your wishing well.
We can't go on like this. How do I feel?
Well, my heart's just a fist. My love is real."
Paul liked his little song. Maybe this was just the idea he needed. Maybe he could start writing now. He created a new folder on his computer, labeled "Zero Hotel" and started writing:

Chapter One:
It was dusk when the little man arrived at work. He

entered the hotel through a side door, walked down a hallway, and went through a door marked "employees only." He took off his raincoat and draped it over the back of a chair. It had not been raining, but the coat was the closest thing to a light jacket that the little man owned, and the nights were just starting to turn cool now. He checked his watch. He was a few minutes early. He opened his locker and took out a wrinkled maroon vest with a nametag and put it on. The tag said "Night Manager" and below that title his name was embossed. "Alfredo," it said. "Alfredo Hurtado".

Paul thought about the man's name for a moment. At first, the name "Carlos" had come to him. But he wanted a name that was not as strong. "Alfredo" kind of sounded like "I'm afraid" and "Hurtado" had the syllable "hurt" in it. He liked both names. He might change them, but for the moment, they worked. And he liked the Spanish feel. The foreigner, the displaced person, the exile. These were themes Paul liked.

Alfredo pulled at his vest to stretch some of the wrinkles out. He knew that it needed washing and ironing. He knew that a week ago, but he had neglected it. Perhaps this week he would wash and iron it. He hated his vest, and ironing it to make it look nice was, to Alfredo, an emasculating capitulation to authority. Why did they make all the clerks wear these stupid vests? But he knew there was no use in complaining. The hotel was owned by a large hotel chain. The bosses did not care.

Alfredo walked out of the locker room and into the "office." The "office" was an old closet that had been converted into a room with a computer and a telephone, where the day manager and the night manager would meet to tabulate reports on the money earned and to exchange information on the day-to-day running of the hotel. Mamood was already in the office, sitting at the only desk there, studying a printout of daily income.

"Good evening, Mamood," Alfredo said.

Mamood looked up. "Hallo, mon ami."

"What's new?"

"Not much. We caught Cecile trying to sneak into a guest's room again. The police took her away. I'm sure they won't keep her. Had one bad credit card, but we caught that before they left. Got a whining couple in 305, and a loose cannon in 402. But it's been a quiet day."

Alfredo liked Mamood. He was all business, but casual about it. Cecile was a local hooker. Both Alfredo and Mamood had spent time with her in the past. But she liked to come back to a guest's room after they had left. Alfredo and Mamood would look the other way if a guest brought her in, but when she came back alone, they would watch her like a hawk. Alfredo could always count on Mamood to keep track of all the comings and goings in the hotel.

"When does 305 check out?" Alfredo asked.

"Not until Tuesday, but they've already complained about the room service, the towels, the air-conditioning, and their shower. I'm sure they will ask for a discount."

"Tuesday," Alfredo said. "That will be Tony's shift. Let's be sure to leave him a note."

"I've already started to draft it, mon ami. It's saved on the desktop under "Tony-Warning-305""

Alfredo admired how on top of things Mamood was.

"Who's the loose cannon?"

"Some loner attending the gun show at the convention. I checked out his room while he was gone. He didn't have any guns but had a lot of anti-government literature. I think he's okay but watch out if he brings any packages into the place."

"Is he in or out now?"

"He's out, but I think you're okay for the evening. He asked for directions to the strip clubs. I predict he'll wander back in by himself around one o'clock. You're probably in for a quiet night."

"That would be good, Mamood. I could use a quiet night."

Paul read what he had written. He liked it. He felt connected to both Alfredo and Mamood. Paul liked the metaphor of the hotel. He felt he could write this story. He got up and went into the kitchen and refilled his coffee cup and then walked back to his computer.

"Is the coffee fresh, Mamood?" Alfredo asked.

"No, it's pretty old. You might want to make a fresh pot."

Alfredo went to the table and took the coffee pot over to the sink to wash it out. The bottom was black from years of use. It occurred to Alfredo that it looked like the bottom of his soul.

"One of these days we need to get a new coffee pot," he said.

Mamood laughed. "Not in zzzbudget." He said, in a voice imitating the lisp of their district manager. Alfredo smiled. The owners of this hotel were tightwads, and he and Mamood often complained about it. But the fact was, Alfredo was glad to have this job. He had worked for the hotel for six years, which is a long time in the hotel business. The owners might be tightwads, but they knew a reliable employee when they had one, and they felt they had one in Alfredo. As long as there were no problems with the hotel and the numbers were consistent, they left him alone. And he and Mamood made sure there were no problems with the hotel and that the numbers were consistent. Mamood could not afford problems. He was in the country illegally and didn't have the documentation now required for new jobs. As long as he kept this job, he could support his wife and children and continue sending money home to his parents in Morocco.

Alfredo put a new paper filter into the basket and filled it with coffee. The managers did budget for coffee for the night manager, but it was cheap coffee. Alfredo remembered the coffee he had at Mamood's apartment once—thick as syrup, sweet, but strong enough to make him feel like he was on meth all day. That was coffee.

Alfredo went back to the desk and looked over the report of the daily income figures. Everything looked good.

"Is the till full?" he asked.

"Yeah, it's okay." Mamood said.

"Any babes check in?"

"No, not really. There's a lesbian couple in 220, both not cute. Tony said a pharmaceutical rep checked in this morning. He put her in 222, next to the lesbians just to mess with her. He said she was about 40 and not bad. I haven't seen her."

Mamood signed off on the daily report.

"Okay, mon ami, I am outta here."

"See you tomorrow night, Mamood."

"Have a quiet night, mon ami."

"Hope so."

Mamood grabbed his jacket from his locker and left. Alfredo moved over to the chair in front of the computer. Alfredo needed a quiet night. His nerves had been bad lately, and he knew why. But he tried to keep those feelings down. He typed his password into the computer and asked for the security cameras. The screen divided into eight cells. Each of the four floors of the hotel had five security cameras, one by the elevator, two at the midway point in the hallway, and one at each end. The first screen with the eight cells showed the elevator of each floor and a long shot down each floor's hallway. No one was about. With the push of a button, Alfredo could go to any camera, or any series of cameras. There were also cameras in the elevator, two in the lobby, one at the outside entrance, and one in the parking lot. The security system allowed him to, if he wanted, follow a guest, or anyone, from the moment they left their car to the moment they entered their room. In the hotel business, nothing was the kiss of death like crime inside the hotel, and the owners knew this, and they bought the best equipment available. One of the reasons that Alfredo, Mamood and Tony had job security was the fact that the hotel had a zero-crime rate. Even though it was an older hotel, and not located in the best *part of the city, it had the best crime-free rating of all the hotels in the owners' chain of hotels. However, only Alfredo and Mamood knew why they were able to achieve that status. He and Mamood had agreed, years ago (when Mamood confided his immigration status to Alfredo) that they would do whatever it would take to ensure their mutual job security. And if that meant entering guest's room to check for guns, or skimming cash from the register for a fund to pay the local gang to keep their boys away from the hotel, well, that simply was the price one paid for good business. Mamood and Alfredo even had a little slush fund for the taxi cab drivers, to keep abreast of tips about guests and local events. Taxi drivers were the pulse of the city and had a better grasp on crime trends than the cops. Three days earlier, Eric Mitchell, who drove for Yellow, had told Mamood that because the cops were doing sweeps of the Belltown area, the crack trade had moved over to Fourth Avenue. There was a restaurant, Tantoni's, that was within walking distance of the hotel, but that walk crossed Fourth Avenue. Now, both Mamood and Alfredo would simply omit Tantoni's from recommendations to out-of-town guests. But for returning guests who were venturing out for dinner, Mamood and Alfredo would engage them in conversation in order to learn their dinner plans, and then advise them to take a cab or perhaps walk south to another equally-good restaurant. Alfredo also put a call into the owner of Tantoni's, advising him to pressure the police to stop the sweeps on Belltown. Alfredo also made a small donation to the local cops to make extra patrols near the hotel. His donations to cops usually consisted of free dinner coupons to some very nice local restaurants. He bought these coupons from the slush fund.*

Alfredo and Mamood made a good team. They had figured out years ago that people would pay extra for a room if either they needed it now and could afford it, or if they thought they were getting a good deal. So, when they got a "walk-in" (someone who just walked in and needed a room) both Mamood and Alfredo would charge ten to twenty dollars more a night than the room normally rented for. This of course, depended on when the person walked in. Mid-day walk-ins had time to shop around. Evening walk-ins didn't. Late-night walk-ins had to have a room immediately. If one of the guests was stupid enough to have Cecile or one of her friends with him, Alfredo would often charge him fifty dollars over the regular rate. Alfredo and Mamood also devised a script when someone called in trying to get a price. Usually such people were looking for the lowest price. If the hotel down the street had a room for ten dollars less, they would go there. But Alfredo knew that people would pay more if they thought they were getting a special deal. So, he and Mamood actually sat down and wrote a script whereby they claimed that the Executive Suite had a sudden cancellation and they would offer it to the caller at a discount of fifty dollars off. What they didn't tell the caller was that even with the "discount", the price was still twenty dollars higher than the regular rate for the Executive Suite. Nor did they tell the caller that the Executive Suite rarely rented at all. It was Mamood's idea to put mirrors on the ceiling and a vibrating bed into the room. They would always mention the mirrors on the ceiling and the vibrating bed to a caller. Selling the Executive Suite was an art—one had to determine who the caller was. Women never bought it. Families never bought it. But a single man shopping around, a single man with illusions of what the business trip might bring him, that's the man whom Mamood and Alfredo would pitch the Executive Suite to. Even if they had cheaper rooms available, they would say:

"I'm afraid we're all booked up this weekend, sir."

"All booked up?" the caller would say. This was the artful part. Mamood or Alfredo had to do a microsecond decision based on the tone of voice of the caller. Did they have money? If not, Mamood or Alfredo might suddenly realize that they had one room still available at a cheap rate. But if the tone of voice had a certain sound to it, they would say:

"Yes, all sold out. Are you here for the conference?"

The script called for never identifying which

conference.

"Yes, I thought so. City is completely full because of that conference and the other conventions. The only thing we have available, well, we had a sudden cancellation on the Executive Suite, which is our VIP suite with mirrors on the ceiling, a hot tub and the vibrating bed, and at this late hour, we could offer it to you at a special rate. With a fifty dollars discount, your price would be ..."

Nine times out of ten, the client would book it at the over-charged rate. And after all, it was a nice room.

Mamood had devised a computer program that allowed them to charge the inflated rate, print out a bill and a receipt, but then discount the rate to the regular rate before it got entered into the hotel's database. The difference in rates got put into a credit account called the VIP account. It had been Alfredo's brilliant idea years ago to get the previous owners of the hotel to approve a VIP account to allow Alfredo to obtain cash for theatre tickets and special consideration for guests. When the hotel got bought out years ago, the new owners never learned about the VIP account, and Alfredo was still able to retrieve cash from it. Mamood had massaged the audit program so that all the owners saw in the report was that the guest paid the going rate. They never saw that some guests' credit cards were billed for more and the difference went to the VIP account, and the VIP account was then cashed out of the till. This showed up on the owner's audit as guests using their credit cards for cash advances, so no red flags were ever raised. Mamood even found a way to add five dollars to every x-rated film that a guest watched in the privacy of their room. A film like "Homo Hard-on" would normally cost ten dollars and would appear discretely on a guest's bill as "misc. charges", but Mamood altered the program to charge the guest fifteen dollars and put the difference to the VIP fund. In the six years since they had instituted the program, no guest had ever complained. After all, who would complain? "Look, I rented "Homo Hard-on" and the TV said it would only cost ten, and my bill says fifteen..." No, people were quiet and paid their bill.

One thing that Mamood and Alfredo had agreed on early: they would never personally take money from the VIP fund. The success of their program depended on using the money only for the stated purpose, which was to ultimately protect the guests, keep the crime rate at zero, and thus protect Mamood's (and Alfredo's) job. There had been times when the VIP fund topped several thousand dollars, but neither Mamood or Alfredo ever took a dime for it for personal gain. After all, they had their ethics.

They would usually meet once a week to talk about payments made. Which taxi driver got what amount. Which cop had received a "free" dinner. Which gang leader got some "treat money." Which hooker got warned to stay away. Which hooker got told it was okay to hang around the nearby bar. And if the hotel bookings were down, they would "rent" rooms using the slush fund to pay for the rooms, so that their occupancy rate continued to look good. As long as the hotel had a good occupancy rate and crime was zero, the owners never bothered them. It was a good arrangement.

However, there was one part of that arrangement that only Alfredo knew about. And that was the hidden camera part.

Paul sat back and read what he had written. He liked it. However, Alfredo was turning out to be a stronger, more intelligent, person than Paul had first envisioned. Perhaps the name Alfredo was not right for him.

Paul did not believe in the craft of writing. For him, one simply wrote. The stories wrote themselves. There was no point in doing a chapter outline or trying in any way to pre-plan a story once the initial plot had been established. For Paul, it was almost like automatic writing. He was simply the connection, the fingers on the keyboard. Nothing more. The story wrote itself.

But he liked what he had written. It felt real. He felt relaxed for the first time in weeks. He had the beginning of his second book.

<u>Chapter 8</u>

Paul's good mood continued. The next day, he went to his session with his life coach.

"I'm feeling good. I'm writing again."

"You do seem happy. Are you working on the new book?"

"Yes."

"What's it about?"

"Well, I'd rather not say much until I get further into it."

"Okay. I understand. What else is going on?"

"Not much."

"Are you seeing anyone?"

Paul hesitated. "No."

"What's going on with that?"

"Well, I've been busy."

"Uh huh... What about that bar you told me about? The one where people dance?"

"Vagabonds? Well, yeah, I was there the other night."

"Did you dance with anyone?"

"No."

"Did you talk with anyone?"

"No."

"Well, Paul, you know that you have to practice the things we talked about every day. That's how the system works. We break these behaviors down to the smallest component, and you practice just the components. Saying hello. Small talk. Dancing. Nothing more. What did you do at the club?"

"I just watched people."

"Well, you can't do that. We've talked about this. Observation leads to isolation. You have to interact. When will you go there again?"

"I don't know. I could go this Friday night."

"Okay, let's go back to the basics. This Friday take your three coins. You know how this works. Put them in your left pocket. I want you to dance with three people, that's all. Move each coin from your left pocket to your right pocket after each new person. No asking for dates. No asking for phone numbers. Just ask them to dance. That's the only goal. Don't leave the club until you dance with three women. And try not to drink so much."

"Okay."

Yeah, okay, Paul thought to himself, I will go there, unless I'm involved with writing.

Sometimes the writing did carry him away.

Chapter Two:

The camera was Mamood's idea originally. It was several years ago, and they knew that a local dealer was using the hotel for some drug deals. They had to stop it. They couldn't wait for the police. The police only got involved if there was a bust or if someone got hurt, and they couldn't afford that bad publicity. They had to get this guy out their own way. But how?

Mamood had an idea.

"What if we video-taped him doing a deal and showed him the video-tape and threatened to turn it over to the police unless he left and never returned?"

"How would you video-tape him?" Alfredo asked.

"That would be easy. Remember how we modified the smoke detector for a camera for that lawyer? We'd just do that again."

"But how would you know which room he would rent?"

"Well, it would take some time, but I could wire each smoke detector in every room to accept a wireless transmitter. Whatever room he rented, while he was signing in, one of us could stick the camera into the smoke detector. If we wire every room in the hotel, whatever room he rents, it would only take a few minutes to snap in the camera."

Alfredo thought about it for a moment. A local divorce lawyer had approached them with a deal some months before. All they had to do was provide a video-tape of the husband leaving a hotel room with his lover.

Mamood was good with electronics and computers and he altered the hallway smoke detectors so that he could fit a small digital camera into each one. A transmitter then sent the images to a receiver and VCR in their small office. No matter which floor the husband took his paramour to, they could get a picture. And no one would know they were involved. The lawyer told his client his private investigator followed the husband and took the pictures. Mamood and Alfredo collected one thousand dollars for their VIP fund for their efforts. And the lawyer let them keep the VCR.

Mamood and Alfredo spent the next three days altering every smoke detector in every room so that it could power a USB. Then they rented a micro-digital camera with wireless transmitter from a local "spy" shop. The next time the dealer checked in, Alfredo made sure he had problems with the hotel computerized check-in system so that Mamood had enough time to run upstairs and install the camera in the room the dealer had rented. The dealer had brought a girl with him, so Mamood and Alfredo were treated to a view of their fucking before the girl left and the stream of visitors came by to buy drugs.

"This guy's dealing big time," Mamood said as they watched the monitor.

"Yeah, I know. Maybe we'd better rethink this confrontation."

"I've been thinking the same thing. Isn't this Zagota's territory? Isn't this guy poaching on Zagota's turf? What if we give the tape to Zagota and let him deal with this guy?"

"Zagota might kill him."

"Yeah, he might."

"Hmmm. I think that's a good idea."

Alfredo had done Jorge Zagota a favor in the past by printing out a phony receipt that Zagota could use as an alibi, so Mamood and Alfredo decided that Alfredo should deliver the tape to Zagota, as a favor, to let him know that this guy was poaching on Zagota's territory. Plus, that had the advantage of letting Zagota know never to use their hotel for similar transactions because, obviously, everything was being taped.

Mamood and Alfredo never learned what happened to this particular dealer, but they never saw him again.

Mamood had rented the digital camera and transmitter, but he asked Alfredo to return it. However, when Alfredo got to the spy shop, he had formulated a new plan, and he talked the shop into selling him the camera instead. It cost seven hundred fifty dollars of his own money, but he thought it was worth it. He had been hooked by the grainy images of the dealer fucking the girl doggy-style on the bed. He wanted to see more.

Chapter Three:

Over the next several years, Alfredo experimented with the camera. He would install it in one of the nicer rooms and then make sure he rented that room to a romantic-looking couple. Working late into the evening, things slowed down after midnight, and he could often tune in that room and watch them make love. He enjoyed it. It was like he was participating as an equal. The man would kiss the woman's nipples and Alfredo felt like he was kissing her nipples. The man would take the woman from behind and Alfredo would feel like he was fucking the woman. He particularly loved the look on their faces as they contorted with ecstasy. He only wished he could zoom the camera in closer, but alas, he could not.

Alfredo never recorded the images he saw. There was no evidence that would incriminate him. Even when he installed the camera, he made sure he wiped it clean of fingerprints. He kept the receiver in his pocket and would insert it into the USB port of the office computer where it would transmit directly to the monitor screen. Certain rooms provided better angles. Once he discovered that a lesbian couple regularly rented a fourth floor room, and he moved the camera there to watch them. Over the years he watched gay men fucking each other in the ass; he watched businessmen fuck hookers; he watched lesbian couples kissing tenderly and fingering each other beneath the sheets; he watched married couples trying to rekindle romance; he watched prom night kids awkwardly struggling with bras and zippers; he watched many a drunken lovemaking between two people who had picked each other up at the local bar; once he thought he witnessed a rape, where the woman didn't seem all that willing. It was oddly exciting to him. After the man was finished, they slept together the rest of the night.

He had never told Mamood about his little camera. It was his little secret. It helped him get through many a long lonely winter night at the hotel.

It was not that Alfredo was homely or too poor to find a woman. It was just that he was of a disposition that made it next to impossible to find someone in the American active young singles world. It was all too hyper-aggressive for him. Alfredo was fifty-six. His parents had immigrated to the States from Nicaragua. He was born a few years later, a full-fledged citizen, but his birthright was that of an exile. His parents had worked hard for him and his brothers and sisters, but like most immigrants, they never fully understood American society. Alfredo, like most children of immigrants, grew up fully saturated with American culture but never really fit in. He never developed the ambition or the anger of most children of immigrants. As a teenager, he had been committed twice to the local psychiatric ward for observation. After the second commitment, he learned to say what others wanted to hear. Yes, he was fine. No, he didn't hear voices. Yes, things were good. Still, he had strange dreams. There was music just out of hearing, a memory just out of remembering, a metallic taste in his mouth, a feeling of other invisible beings just out of his perception. Sometimes in the early morning half-

wakefulness, he could feel the yellow dust of a dirt road and smell cooking over an open fire. The feeling made him shiver. It was as his blood yearned for dark shadows under banana leaves. He always wanted to visit Nicaragua, to see if there was something there that would make him feel like he had come home. But he never had the time or the money. He grew up to be a quiet man, and now, a quiet middle-aged man.

However, Alfredo was not without strengths. People found him reliable. The hotel trade was a good fit for him. He was responsive to others, knowledgeable about the city he had lived in all his life, articulate, yet just distant enough so that guests didn't impose for longer than necessary in order to get the information they needed. He always got good reviews from guests. He had job security.

Chapter 9

Paul was feeling good about his writing. He decided to go to Vagabonds again. This time he was going to put his life coach's plan into action. He would try not to drink so much. He would try to engage women in small talk. He would try and ask someone to dance. Nothing more. He and his life coach had agreed that step one only involved making small talk and dancing. He and his life coach had drafted very specific rules. If some woman wanted more and asked him back to her place or asked to see him again, that was okay. He could accept if he wanted to. But he was prohibited from being the one to ask her back to his place. His life coach's theory was that Paul had to master all the basic steps of forming a relationship first, without the pressure of trying to pick someone up. If he could just talk with a woman, even just making meaningless conversation at the bar... If he could just dance with a woman, well, it would be a breakthrough.

Paul hadn't dated anyone for almost three years. After his divorce, he had just fallen apart and never could reconnect with women. He didn't think he had had a nervous breakdown, but certainly he had been profoundly depressed and rarely left his apartment. Plus, the world of dating had changed. And his circumstances had changed. He was older. The institutions that generally promote easy dating, such as college or post-graduate school or the busy workplace, were no longer part of Paul's world. And now, as a writer, he lived a solitary life and simply didn't interact with a lot of people. Worse, as an older, self-employed person, it was simply mathematically more difficult to date, and the more he didn't date, the more out of practice he became. If it hadn't been for finding his life coach, well, Paul knew he would have been extremely lost. She had worked with him for the past two and a half years. Sometimes there were weeks when she was the only woman he even interacted with.

What he liked about her was that she was practical.

"Look," she would say, "this isn't rocket science. You're out of practice. If you don't exercise a muscle, it will atrophy. The same is true for dating. Your dating muscles need toning. But you don't start off an exercise program by running the Olympics. You start slow. You build skills. You build confidence. We're going to break these behaviors down to their basic components and start with the very basic skills. As soon as you master each skill, we'll increase the tasks."

For an entire week, she made him just make eye contact with women wherever he went. Eye contact and smile. He was forbidden to speak unless they spoke to him. She made him keep a log of who he smiled at. She made him change his shopping habits so that he had to go to the grocery store every day to buy that day's groceries, just so he'd be in places where women would be. He would write in his log "Thursday, Safeway, made eye contact with two women, smiled at both, one smiled back".

For the second week, the task was the same, but he had to write down something he noticed about each woman, the color of her hair, what she wore, what she had put into her shopping cart.

For the third and fourth week, he had to make eye contact and smile, and if they made eye contact back, he had to say hello. His life coach forbade him from engaging in any more conversation unless the woman initiated it, but he had to say hello to every woman who returned his eye contact.

For months Paul and his life coach worked to build up his skills. He felt he was making good progress. Just the fact that he had weeks go by without feeling extremely depressed was a joy to Paul. And he did feel like he was able to talk more easily with women. But he still had not found anyone to date. This life coach started to pressure him to join an online dating service, but Paul kept refusing. It was just too scary.

Then he had his lucky break. He had submitted a small piece to the New Yorker and they had published it in their "Shouts and Murmurs" humor section. The New Yorker only paid five-hundred dollars for unsolicited humorous pieces, but to Paul, the fact that he was now published was worth millions. Maybe he wasn't a crazy loser. Maybe he was a writer. He felt as if he had been given a reprieve on life. He finally found the courage to show his life coach the beginning of his manuscript for *The Man Who Mistook his Hemorrhoid for a Clitoris*. It had a gay theme that Paul didn't quite understand but had written anyway. It was his life coach who encouraged him to finish the manuscript and to try and get it published. Perhaps she sensed that finding some success in his writing was more important than increasing his skills at dating. In any event, she put the dating skills on the back burner for almost a year while she worked with him on his writing, encouraged him to maintain a writing routine, made him bring his work to her sessions and read her each new chapter, and made him send out sample chapters to publishers. When *The Man Who Mistook his Hemorrhoid for a Clitoris* finally did get published, Paul felt that he should have dedicated the book to his life coach, because it wouldn't have happened without her.

Maybe he would dedicate the second book to her, he thought. But tonight, he was not going to think about that. He was going to think only about meeting women. He decided that it would be better if he went to Vagabonds around ten. He had been going around nine, but the dancing crowd (and the women) did not seem to arrive there until around ten, when the band was starting their second set. And the problem with his getting there at nine was that he would sit in a booth and drink, so by the time ten rolled around, he had already had three or four glasses of wine, and was too inebriated to start conversations with women, or to dance with them, so he always ended up leaving, catching a cab home, and feeling depressed. So tonight, he would prevent that outcome by not getting there until ten. He took a hot shower at nine, shaved, and put on a clean shirt and a clean pair of blue jeans.

But the fates were not with Paul tonight. When he arrived at ten, the place was packed. The band was playing. People were dancing. Paul didn't see a single table available where he could sit. He just stood there looking around. Krystal the barmaid recognized him, and came up to him. He asked her to get him a glass of wine and find a place where he could sit. She said she would.

She came back with a glass of wine and signaled him to follow her. He did, as she wove her way through the crowded tables, heading for a back corner of the bar. But when she got there, the tables were full. She looked around, but there were simply no tables available.

"It's alright," Paul said, "I'll find a place."

He took the wine from her tray and gave her a ten dollar bill and made his way back to the bar. He found what looked to be an empty seat next to two women. Maybe this wouldn't be so bad.

"Is this seat taken?" He asked.

"I don't think so." one of the women said.

He sat down and started sipping his wine. He glanced at the two women. They both were young, slightly overweight yet pretty. But they were engaged in conversation with each other.

The woman sitting next to him turned to him and said, "Would you make sure no one takes our seats?"

"Sure," Paul said.

The two women got up and made their way to the dance floor and started dancing with each other. It was that kind of place. People came there to dance—it didn't matter with whom. That's why Paul and his life coach thought it would be a safe environment for him to practice interacting with women.

Paul continued sipping his wine. More people came in. The place was getting crowded. Very crowded. And noisy. He hated noise. Maybe it was just a function of being older, but when a place was noisy, he had such a hard time talking to people. It was as if the background noise drowned out all words. He glanced again at the two women dancing with each other. He could see now that they were much younger than him. If one of them had been interested in him, they wouldn't have left so quickly, he thought. He looked around. People were still streaming into the bar. It was a busy night. He sipped at his wine.

The song ended. The two women came back to their seats and continued talking to each other. They didn't seem to notice Paul.

This wasn't going to work, he thought. The band was good, but loud. There were many people dancing, but too many people. There were lots of women, but tonight they all seemed younger than him. He felt out of place. Normally, when he arrived at Vagabonds earlier in the evening, he could find a safe table to sit at and watch people, but tonight, sitting at the bar, with his back to the band and to the dance floor, he felt exposed, vulnerable. This just wasn't his night. The woman next to him had her back to him. He finished his drink and walked out.

There were lots of taxis available. He took one home.

<u>Chapter 10</u>

But Paul was persistent. It was his greatest strength. He often felt defeated; he often felt at the end of his rope; but he did persevere. He went back to Vagabonds the next night.

This time he made sure he got there at nine, before it got crowded. He found a small booth with a good view of the dance floor and yet back far enough where he could see any women who came in and found places to sit. Krystal brought him a white wine. He also ordered water, so that he could slow the alcohol intake down by drinking a glass of water with every glass of wine.

The band was pretty good, and the place started getting crowded around nine thirty. Vagabonds was such a strange place, Paul thought. There were always women dancing with women, one or two old couples doing very choreographed dance steps, bikers with fat women...just a very strange bar.

Paul looked around. About ten feet away, a group of six women sat at a table, but they were large women. They huddled tightly around the table like a wagon train pulling the wagons into a circle. It was as if they wanted to make sure no one could approach them to ask one of them to dance. And no one did. And they didn't dance with each other. They just stayed huddled tightly together, song after song. Paul didn't understand that.

To his right, there was a table with a man who was obviously with a woman, but the woman had another woman friend along with her. The woman friend was heavy, with a big ass. They must be regulars, Paul thought, because various old and fat men came over and asked the friend to dance. And she danced with each one, no matter how fat or old they were. Paul wondered, does she do that because she figures that no one else will ask her to dance? Does she yearn for a slim, gentle young lover? Paul couldn't quite see her face, so he had no idea how young she was. He considered going over and asking her to dance but ruled it out.

Paul turned his gaze to the dance floor. He wasn't sure why he liked this bar, but he did. The dance floor was filled with such a variety of characters. There was one hugely obese woman dancing with another woman. There were older couples. Krystal came by and brought him another glass of wine. Paul noticed one old coot, with a full gray beard, wearing a ball cap, and what looked to be work clothes from a gas station, but he danced with everyone, young or old, thin or fat. He must be a character, Paul thought. Paul watched him as he went to one old lady in a wheel chair and got her out on the dance floor. If he was forty, she must have been at least sixty-five or seventy. Paul took another sip of wine. That guy may be crazy, but at least he's dancing. Here I am sane, he thought, but unable to dance with anyone.

The song ended. People returned to their tables. The band started another song. People made their way to the dance floor. Paul watched as various fat old men approached various women, some fat and old but some young, and asked them to dance and they would step out onto the dance floor.

Paul began to feel depressed. He looked over at the wagon train table. They were still tightly pulled into a circle, intensely talking about something. He looked up at the dance floor. The old coot was now dancing with a woman in a short dress. She was dancing very provocatively, rubbing up against the old coot. He was smiling and enjoying it. When the song ended, they both walked back to their respective tables, but the woman's path took her by Paul's booth. She didn't make any eye contact with Paul, but he was able to get a better look at her face. Even though she was wearing what was almost a mini-skirt, she had to be at least fifty, maybe older. She had a Playboy bunny tattoo on her shoulder. What kind of woman has a Playboy bunny tattoo? He watched as she walked back toward her table, but before she got there, a fat man in a denim work shirt and leather vest stopped her and spoke. Then they both headed back out to the dance floor. Paul watched them. She danced just as provocatively with the fat man as she had done with the old coot, rubbing up and down his body. Maybe everyone knew each other. Maybe this is what happens to young barflies when they hit fifty. Maybe this is just what every blue-collar dance bar looks like.

The band was playing "Southern Man." That would fit this age group. But then Paul realized that this was his age group. Paul knew that every bar had its own inner circle of regulars. Hell, every business and every group did too. Maybe if he came here every weekend for six or seven months, he would be eventually accepted as a regular. But Paul was pretty sure he couldn't stand the agony of spending every weekend there, sitting alone. He dug into his wallet to find a tip to leave for Krystal, so he could leave.

Chapter 11

"Well, Paul, obviously, we need to get back to the basic issues," his life coach was saying. "You're just a little out of practice, and some unrealistic expectations have crept back in. You're in a stressful environment, thinking that you're going to find a perfect woman, and then expecting that you'll feel comfortable interacting with her. Let's just back up a bit and remaster the basic steps."

Paul nodded his head.

She went on. "For the next week, wherever you go, I only want you to make eye contact with women, smile at them and say hello. That's all. Do not try to engage in small talk. If small talk happens, that's okay, but that's not the assignment. The assignment is only to make eye contact, smile and say hello. In order to have a conversation with someone, you have to appear accessible to them, safe to them, friendly and non-threatening to them. You just sitting by yourself at a booth in a bar doesn't make them want to talk with you. You have to smile to let them relax, maintain eye contact to show that you're interested in them, and say hello to let them know you're accessible to them. You have to master this basic component before you can move on. Do you understand?"

Paul let out a sigh. "Yes, I do."

"I want you to carry your pocket notebook, or even just a piece of paper, and I want you to write down every time you complete this component. Don't try to remember it to write down later. After each and every time that you, one, make eye contact, two, smile, and three say hello, as soon as that woman is out of sight, I want you to write down the time and location and something about her. It can be as easy as writing Safeway, brunette, five p.m. Stopping and writing it down will reinforce that it's only an exercise, an exercise that you can master with more practice. But you've got to practice this basic behavior. Until this becomes second nature, you'll never be able to initiate conversations. I know you. You sit and watch people. All writers do that. Which is why most writers are not good at relationships. But you can have both, but you have to practice this skill every day. Do you understand?

Paul understood.

"And since you spend a lot of time in your apartment writing, which is, by definition, a solitary activity, we've got to get you out into the world every day. Go back to buying just enough groceries for dinner each day. But don't make lunch at home. Always go out for lunch. And I want you to go to a different restaurant each day until you find one that you feel comfortable in, then stay with that one. If you can't afford to each lunch out every day, then I want you to go out for coffee each day. If the restaurant or the Starbucks has an outside patio area and the weather is nice, sit out outside. Don't take a magazine to read. Don't take your book notes to work on. I want to you sit there and make eye contact and smile and say hello if the other person makes eye contact with you. And I want you to take a walk, a thirty-minute walk, every day. It's a healthy way to practice these skills. Look at every woman you see, smile, and say hello if she makes eye contact with you. It doesn't matter how phony or silly it feels. Just do it. Are you writing all this down?"

"Yes." He was scribbling fast.

"Taking these breaks will help you concentrate on your writing when you get back to the apartment. So, it's a double benefit. And I want you to keep a diary, a log of every walk, of every trip to the grocery, to the post office, every meal out. Just a simple log. Try and notice something nice about each woman you see. Is she wearing a pretty blouse? Nice jewelry? Training your observation skills will be a good exercise when we move to the later step of paying them a compliment. Got it?"

"I got it."

And secretively, Paul was relieved. Now he didn't have to talk with women. He only had to say hello. He could handle this.

Chapter 12

Paul liked to write early in the day, while drinking lots of black coffee.

Chapter Four:

Alfredo was glad the couple wanted a suite. He was able to rent them room 320, the Executive Suite with a mini bar, leather couch, mirrors on the ceiling, a hot tub, and the small camera conveniently hidden in the smoke detector. They seemed like the perfect couple for the camera. He was older, with a thick heavy body, and thick almost pure white hair, wearing an expensive suit, while she was young and petite, short black hair and large eyes. She was way too beautiful to be with this older man except for his money or his power. The woman did not return Alfredo's glance. The man was trying too hard to act casual, making too much small talk, moving his stance so as to block Alfredo's view of the woman. He asked for a quiet room with no neighbors. Alfredo was sure

Paul sat back and read what he had written. He wasn't sure where he was going with this. Was Alfredo going to intervene? If so, how? Was Alfredo going to end up in a relationship with the woman? Is the woman good or bad? A willing participant, a bondage hooker, or a battered victim? Where was this scene going? Paul wasn't sure. He liked Alfredo. He wanted Alfredo to persevere. But he also knew that Alfredo was riddled with conflict about American women and sexuality.

Paul decided to take a break and let his unconscious percolate for a bit. He didn't want to go to Starbucks—he had already had enough coffee, so he decided to take his morning walk. He would go down Pine Street where there were a lot of boutiques and a lot of women shopping. He would practice his mantra: eye contact, smile, hello.

It was a sunny day, warm but not hot. A good day to be out walking. But Paul had trouble getting the image out of his mind. The woman had short black hair. The gag across her mouth was black, maybe leather, but the ball in the middle of the gag was bright red. Her mouth was obviously held open by the ball. She must only be able to breathe through her nose. Her eyes were wide with fear, and the black eye make-up she wore only made her eyes look bigger. She looked to be in genuine pain. But that made no sense. She had come there willingly. What was her name? What was her relationship with the man? Why was he wearing a dildo? Was he going to hurt her, even kill her?

Paul had gotten all the way to Third Street before he realized that he had been so deep in thought that he had not looked at a single person. He turned left on Third and tried to make eye contact with women as he walked along. He realized that his face was tense from thinking. He tried to relax his face and the muscles around his mouth, so he could be ready to smile.

What if she's a willing slave, he thought. Slaves voluntarily enter into the master-slave relationship, but they are held captive by their need to be subjugated. They are controlled by their need to be controlled. They don't have a choice. But the bigger question was what this would do to

Alfredo. He's locked up so tight, and the key to unlocking him has to fit the lock. The fact that she's in trouble might not be enough to force him to act. Is she foreign? Slave traffic? No, that's too stereotyped. What if she disappears? Disappears? Maybe. Yes, maybe.

Paul turned around and walked back to his apartment.

The man took a step forward. He turned the whip around in his hand and started using the butt end to probe the woman's pubic area. He wasn't inserting it, just pushing it into the fleshy sides of her vagina, jabbing her flesh. Then he reached over and squeezed one of her nipples. Alfredo could see the woman eyes shut tight in pain.

Then the man took the whip and started to snap it so that it hit the woman's breasts. He aimed right at her nipples. He was not being gentle. She twisted against the ropes and rocked her head back and forth. He reached over and grabbed her head and stopped it from moving. Then he slapped her, hard enough that it knocked her head over to the side. Then he grabbed her head by the jaw and straightened it out and used his thumb and first finger to pry open each eye. It looked to Alfredo as if tears were coming out of her eyes. The man then took the butt end of his whip and started to tap her on the top of her head. He was saying something to her. She nodded yes.

Alfredo yanked the receiver out of the USB port, and the image of the man and woman disappeared from the screen. This was not a good situation. Alfredo didn't want to panic, but he was feeling very scared. He couldn't call Mamood without telling him how he knew the woman was being abused. He couldn't call the police. He couldn't tell anyone. What if the man hurt her bad? What if he killed her? He put the receiver in his pocket and stepped out into the lobby and walked out the front door.

The night air was cool. Alfredo realized he was breathing fast. He forced himself to slow his breathing down. He had to interrupt them, find some ruse to interrupt them. Maybe claim that he had to change rooms due to some electrical problem. Maybe call their room and say that someone had complained about the noise? He'd have to think of some excuse.

He walked back into the hotel and into the office and reinserted the receiver into the USB port. After a second or two, the camera image came back to the screen.

But now, the woman was untied. She was getting up from the bed and turning around. Now she was climbing back onto the bed on her hands and knees, with her butt raised in the air towards the man. He walked around the bed and reattached the left wrist restraint. Then he walked around to the other side and reattached the right wrist restraint. Then he got behind the woman and began to insert the black dildo into her ass.

Alfredo thought maybe he had overreacted. The woman seemed to be a willing participant. She had gotten up from the bed and had turned over and offered her ass to the man. She may be a slave, she may be abused, but she was not being forced.

The man was now reaching forward and pulling on the woman's hair. He was pulling hard enough to force her whole head back. It looked like he had the whole dildo up her rectum and was shoving it in and out hard.

Alfredo pulled the receiver out of the USB port. He didn't want to see anymore. He had decided that his best course of action would be to do nothing. This woman came to the hotel voluntarily. She was participating in this sex voluntarily. She may be psychologically fucked up, but that was her problem. In all probability, they would finish their session and leave in the morning, and he would never see either of them again. That was the best scenario after all. Alfredo wanted to believe that. He didn't want to watch any more of their mating. He never had understood the American fascination with bondage and sex, anyway. It all seemed too cruel to be sexy. But more importantly, he didn't want any *more information about the woman that might make him change his mind and wonder if he should intervene. The odds were that it was going to be okay.*

He had other reports to complete before the morning, and he was glad that he did. They would keep his mind off the couple in room 320. He had to tabulate the gross income and occupancy figures for the week and compare the year-to-date figures for the monthly report that was due tomorrow. He poured himself a cup of coffee and started working on the report.

About an hour or so later, however, the lobby buzzer when off. Alfredo stepped out of the office to the front desk. Before him stood the man from 320. The woman was not with him.

Chapter Five :
"Yes, sir?" Alfredo asked.
"Just checking out. I have a very early flight to catch."
Alfredo didn't believe him. It wasn't quite three a.m., and Alfredo knew that the earliest flight out of the airport was at six. There were no traffic delays getting to the airport at this hour—he would be there in fifteen minutes.
"Very good, sir. Will you be leaving the room charge on your credit card?"
"No, I'll pay cash." The man handed Alfredo three one hundred-dollar bills. The Executive Suite usually rented for one hundred eighty but Alfredo had told the man it was two hundred fifty when they checked in. Alfredo handed the man back fifty dollars.
"Did you need a receipt, sir?"
"No, not really. Would you call me a cab?"
"Yes sir, right away. Let me just get their number."
Alfredo didn't need to get their number—he knew it by heart. He wanted an excuse to make the call from the back office. He dialed the cab dispatch.
"Hello, Billy, it's Alfredo. Is Eric working downtown

tonight? Good. Would you send him over to us right away. Great. Thanks, Billy."

Alfredo stepped out to the front desk.

"The taxi should be in two minutes, sir."

"Thanks, I'll wait outside."

"Yes, sir."

Alfredo stayed at the front desk and pretended to be busy. He wanted to keep an eye on the man, to make sure he really took a cab, to make sure he took Eric's cab. That way he could find out where the man went. The man was standing just outside the front door, talking on his cell phone. He finished his call and then lit a cigarette.

What was bothering Alfredo was, where was the woman? Other than this man standing outside calmly smoking a cigarette, no one had left hotel since Alfredo had unplugged the camera receiver. Every exit door was programmed to ring a small buzzer in the office, so that the manager could use the security cameras to see who was leaving, or who might be secretly letting someone into the hotel. If the woman had left the hotel before the man, some door would have been opened, and the buzzer in the office would have sounded. Therefore, she had to still be in the hotel, still in the room. And the big question was, was she okay?

Eric's cab pulled up. Alfredo watched the man put out his cigarette and get in the cab. Then Alfredo quickly stepped back into the office and plugged the receiver into the USB port. His heart was pounding. He hoped she was alright. He hoped that he had not made a terrible error in not intervening earlier.

The image of the room came onto the screen. There was the bed, with the blankets and sheets strewn on the floor. But the bed was empty. She was not there. Where then? Was she in the bathroom? Tied up in the closet? God, he wished he could remotely swivel the camera around to see every angle of the room. He waited. Perhaps she was okay, just finishing up in the bathroom, putting on some makeup to hide the bruising, or counting her money. He would just wait a bit to *see if she appeared on camera. He waited two minutes. Five minutes. Time was agonizing slow. Ten minutes. Nothing.*

I should give her thirty minutes, he thought. It's not unusual for a woman to take thirty minutes in the bathroom. If I don't see her in thirty minutes, I will go up and check.

Alfredo picked up the phone and dialed the taxi company.

"Billy, hey, it's Alfredo again. Hey, tell me, that guy that Eric picked up from here, where did Eric take him? The San Juan Hotel? He went from here to another hotel? No, it's just weird, Billy. He told me that he was going to the airport. Yeah, I know. Did the guy ask Eric to wait, to take him somewhere else? No, hmmm. Okay, thanks, Billy. Thanks. Bye."

Alfredo looked at the screen again. He noticed two glasses on the table by the bed. The straps that had held the wrist and leg restraints were gone, of course. And on one corner of the bed, there was a small dark spot. Alfredo stared at it. Could it be blood? Or maybe a shit stain from the dildo. After all, the man had it up her ass. Where was she?!

Alfredo couldn't stand it anymore. He unplugged the receiver and punched up the security cameras for all the exits. The computer screen divided into four quarters: one showing the front door, and the other three showing the other three exits from the hotel. Alfredo hit the record button. If she left while he was walking up to her room, it would be recorded.

He left the office, crossed the lobby to the elevator. It was still on the lobby level from when the man had come down. He punched the number three button, and the door closed.

As he walked down the hallway to room 320, he wondered what he would say. He seemed silly to knock and say "Housekeeping" at this hour of the night. And he didn't want to alarm her by announcing "Security". He decided the safest phrase to use was "Hotel Manager". Official, but not threatening. And his excuse would be that he was required to do a room check after every guest had checked out. And the man had checked out. If she was offended, he would be blameless. The man had not told him that she was still there. He could apologize and be blameless. The perfect combination.

He got to 320 and knocked.

"Hotel Manager"

There was no response.

He waited a moment, then knocked again.

"Manager"

Still nothing. Alfredo took out his master room card. He noticed his hands were trembling. He slid the card down the slot and the door clicked open. As the door opened, he knocked on it again and said,

"Hello, excuse me, hello, hotel management."

He stepped into the room. He could see the bathroom door was open. No sound came from anywhere in the room.

"Hello, is anyone here? Hello?"

He didn't see anyone. He checked behind the door. He checked the front closet. He walked into the bathroom. Empty. The kitchen area was empty. He got down on his hands and knees and looked under the bed. There was no one there.

As he stood up his eyes saw the stain on the corner of the bed. It was a dark smear about five inches long and three inches wide. It looked like blood.

Alfredo went over to the window and looked out towards the ground. Since all the rooms were climate controlled, none of the windows opened. Still, Alfredo had to look to reassure himself she wasn't lying on the sidewalk.

This made no sense. He checked the bathroom and the closets again. He opened every drawer of the dresser. He opened the TV cabinet. He looked behind the couch. There was simply no one there.

Alfredo walked out of the room and closed the door behind him. He took the elevator down to the lobby, went into the office, and rewound the four digital security cameras and had them play back, in fast motion, what they had recorded since he had left the office ten minutes earlier. The images of the four doors flickered. No one had left the hotel.

Surely, he was missing something. The couple had checked in together. Alfredo had seen them on the camera in their room sometime after one o'clock. No exit door buzzer had gone off from that point until the man left. She had to be in the hotel. Unless one of the exit door's electronic sensor was faulty. Unless she had left earlier, and he just didn't hear the buzzer. Unless the man had carried her body and left it somewhere else in the hotel.

He called Mamood.

"Mamood, man I am sorry to wake you. Can you come down to the hotel now? I'm not totally sure, but we may have a problem."

Alfredo went back to room 320. After he checked the bathroom and the closets again, he locked the door, and placed the desk chair underneath the smoke detector. He removed the cover and then popped out the wireless camera from its holding clip. He slipped the camera into his pocket and placed the cover back on the smoke detector. He then moved the chair back to the desk and went downstairs to wait for Mamood.

Chapter 13

Paul showed what he had written to his life coach.

"This bondage stuff is something new for you, Paul. Tell me about it."

"I don't think it's me. I mean, I don't feel attracted to it when I write it."

"You're not involved in anything like that now?"

"No"

"Ever been?"

"No, not really. It just came out as I was writing."

"Okay, tell me about Mamood."

"About Mamood?"

"Yeah, I'm wondering if he's your alter-ego."

"I don't know. He just came to me, like all the characters do. But he is the least twisted. I mean, Alfredo is complicated, whereas Mamood has integrity... That's not right, because Alfredo has integrity too. But Mamood is simpler. He just wants to send money to his family."

"What's going to happen to Mamood?"

"Nothing. He's safe."

"That's what I thought. Well, keep writing, but I think Mamood is you. I don't know who Alfredo is yet. He clearly is some character of you, a warlock, but I don't know yet. Keep writing. Bring me more chapters."

Chapter Six:

"So, they checked in before midnight? How do you know she didn't leave before two?" Mamood was asking.

"Because I watched the security cameras," Alfredo lied. "I saw everyone who left, and she wasn't one of them."

"Why were you watching the security cameras?"

"Because there was something I didn't trust about the guy."

"Well, mon ami, he did not check out until almost three a.m. I don't think you watched the security cameras for that many hours. You had to use the toilet. She could have left."

"I suppose so." Alfredo was not ready to tell Mamood about his digital camera.

"But still," Mamood said, "let's search the hotel. Let's eliminate the possibility that she is here. If she is not here, then she is gone. It's that simple. If she is not here, she is not our problem. If we find her, then we have a problem. Let's eliminate the potential problem, then we have no problem."

"Okay," Alfredo said, glad to have a plan. "If you'll watch the office, I'll search."

"No, mon ami. You seemed kind of stressed out. You stay here and work the office. I will search."

"Okay, yes," Alfredo said.

Alfredo trusted Mamood. And Mamood was right. The search needed a neutral person. Someone who had no investment in the outcome.

An hour later, Mamood came back to the office.

"She is not here, mon ami. I have checked everywhere. She must have left."

"I don't know how," Alfredo said.

Mamood looked at Alfredo.

"Mon ami, there is something you are not telling me. Did you know this woman?"

"No."

"Did she say anything to you?"

"No."

"Then why do you think she was in danger?"

Alfredo hesitated. He wasn't sure what to say. He didn't want to lie to his friend, yet he wanted to communicate that it wasn't just his imagination.

"Well, I told you that I was suspicious of him."

"Yes."

"So, I walked up by their room, and I heard things... sounds that concerned me."

"So, you weren't watching the security cameras the whole time. You left the office?"

"Yes."

"And what did you hear?"

"I heard what sounded like him hitting her."

"Why didn't you tell me this before?"

"I don't know. I thought you might think I was crazy."

"Why would I think that?"

Alfredo didn't have an answer to that. In fact, he was sorry he added this lie to the story. He wondered if Mamood might think he was lying to him.

"Hmmm," Mamood said. "Well, still, the bottom line is that she is not here, and we don't know who she is, so we don't have a problem. Do you agree?"

"Yeah... I agree. Mamood, I'm sorry for dragging you out of bed."

"That's okay, my friend. I think that you are in love with this girl, that's why you have such crazy thoughts. But she is not here. She is gone. Let her go."

But Alfredo could not let go of the girl. The next night, he talked with Eric.

"That guy that Billy asked you to pick up at the hotel for me, can you tell me anything more about him?"

"Whatcha wanna know?"

"Well, did he act nervous or anything?

"No, not particularly. Not that I remember. What's up with him?"

Alfredo had prepared a cover story. "Well, he paid by credit card, and it went through and all, but I'm a little suspicious that it might have been a stolen card, because of the way he was acting."

"No, he didn't say anything. And I didn't watch him too close, cause he was dressed all nice like, I wasn't worried about being jacked."

"Yeah, I remember that too. He did dress nice. Okay, so you took him straight to the San Juan Hotel?"

"Yeah, no, wait, no, made one stop."

"Where?"

"Just briefly, he saw that pay phone at Fifth and Sarantos, and he asked me to pull over, so he could make a call. I told him I'd have to keep the meter running, and he said that was fine. He made a quick call and then got back in, and we headed straight to the San Juan."

"He stopped to use the pay phone?"

"Yeah, I guess he had to make a call."

"Eric, he had a cell phone. I saw him use it just before you pulled up."

"Well, maybe his battery was dead, or he didn't want me to hear his business. Peoples got a right to privacy, you know."

"Yeah, that's true. So, then you took him to the San Juan?"

“Yup.”

“Did you see if he went into the San Juan? I mean, after he got out of your cab, did he go right into the lobby?”

“Hmm, I assume. I was calling dispatch and didn’t pay him no more attention.”

“Okay, Eric. Thanks. I owe you.”

“Anytime, Alfredo.”

Alfredo sat and thought about all this. Using the pay phone made no sense. It’s possible it was his battery, but more possible that he didn’t want Eric to hear him, or even more possible that he didn’t want his call traced. If he killed the girl, if it was a contract job, and he was calling into to say it was done, he might not want that call traced to him.

Alfredo shook his head and looked around. He was thinking crazy. He felt stupid. This was no contract killing. This was some well-heeled businessman and a B&D hooker who was probably well-paid for her time. Somehow, she got out of the hotel without Alfredo knowing about it, and he was getting all freaked out over that and thinking crazy.

Still, it bothered him. He had saved the man’s registration slip “Leon Petroski” was the name on the page, with an address and phone number in Los Angeles. He looked at the page. It wouldn’t hurt to make one more call.

Alfredo called the San Juan Hotel and asked for the reservation desk.

“Hello, is Rick working tonight? Yes? Tell him it’s Alfredo.”

Most hotel managers make it a point to get to know all the other hotel managers in the area. It was a valuable network of information and favors.

“Hello Alfredo, this is Rick. How are you?”

“I am well, Rick, doing well. And you?”

“Same ol’ same ol’, buddy. What can I do you for?

“We had a guy check out of here last night about three a.m. and cab over to your place. A guy named Leon Petroski. Was he a guest? Is he still staying there?”

"Let me check. Petroski, Petroski... no one by that name here this week."

"Really?" Alfredo was dumbfounded. "No one? Rick, that's weird. Were you working last night? Do you remember a guy coming into the lobby around three?"

"No, I was off, Peter was here though. He's here now. Hang on, I'll ask him."

"Tell him it was an older man, heavy-set, well-dressed. He would remember this guy. His hair was thick and almost pure white. Almost glowed it was so white. Around three o'clock."

"Hang on."

Alfredo could feel his head starting to ache. Was the guy visiting someone else there? Did he even go into the hotel? Was he there under a different name?

Rick got back on the line. "Peter says he doesn't remember anyone coming in around three. He said two young guys came back to their room around four, but that's all."

"Maybe the guy was registered under a different name. Does he remember a well-dressed older guy, fat with real white hair staying there?"

"No, I asked him that too. And I checked the registry to jar my memory. We got some older couples but no guy with thick white hair. Did he stiff you?"

"Maybe, I'm not sure yet. Okay, thanks. Call me if anyone remembers seeing him, or if he shows up. Keep this on the down-low, Rick."

"Of course, everything else going okay?"

"Yeah, pretty much. Talk to you later."

"Okay, bye."

This was getting too weird. Alfredo could understand someone using a payphone to keep a conversation private, but why would the guy have Eric take him to the San Juan and then disappear? There were no bars or strip clubs near the San Juan. Alfredo looked at the registration form again. Then he picked up the phone and dialed long distance information. He *gave the operator the name Leon Petroski and spelled it and gave her the address. He was not surprised when no phone listing came up for that address. He got on the computer and put the address into Google Maps. It found an address. He used the Google satellite system to look at the street. It was all warehouses and parking lots, not nice homes where someone with money would live.*

Alfredo knew that hotel regulations forbade him from calling a guest's home number. Several years ago, as a promotion, the hotel had sent "free extra night" gift cards to the homes of frequent guests, and were inundated with irate calls from husbands who did not want their wives to know that they had stayed at the hotel. Since then, hotel staff were forbidden from calling or writing guests.

However, that certainly would not prevent Alfredo from finding a payphone and simply dialing the man's number in Los Angeles, to see if it was a working phone, to see if a man answered, if someone answered. After all, wrong numbers happen every day.

But Alfredo knew, that no matter what the outcome of that call would be, he was stymied. Either the man existed, or he did not, either the girl existed, or she did not, either she was alive or not, but at this point, he was stuck. He could still see her eyes, wide in fear, with the gag across her face. He did not know what to do.

Chapter 14

Paul still was not sure where the story was going. He never outlined his plots, he just wrote. He liked to tell himself that he was giving into the unconscious, dipping into the Shadow, channeling the archetypes, but he also secretly suspected he was simply intellectually lazy. Was this a mystery novel, a cheap detective story? Or was he trying to actually say something about relationships? One thing Paul had tried to do in *The Man Who Mistook his Hemorrhoid for a Clitoris* was to confront the horror of relationships. At least that's how Paul thought about it. He had never been able to handle relationships, any relationship, as anything other than something that had to be manipulated. That's why he had written *The Man Who Mistook his Hemorrhoid for a Clitoris*—he wanted to create a character who was honest about relationships. But then, to Paul's own horror, the protagonist turned out to be not only gay but unable to form any relationship with anyone, male or female. The book was one of the reasons he decided to get into therapy. He had tried several therapists, but they had all just wanted to put him on anti-depressants rather than talk with him. It wasn't until he found his life coach, that he felt he had actually found a therapist who could help him.

His life coach insisted that what she did was not therapy. She was not licensed as a therapist, or a psychotherapist, or a social worker, or a psychologist, or a counselor. She was only listed as a "life coach". He had tried her as a last resort, after trying several different psychologists and psychotherapists. Paul never asked her what "life coach" meant. He just knew the minute he saw her, sitting cross-legged on a pillow on the floor of her apartment, that she was the therapist for him. That day he first walked in, she gestured to a pillow on the floor next to her. He sat down. She looked at him and said nothing for at least thirty seconds. She seemed to be taking him in. Finally she spoke.

"So, tell me, how can I help you?"

No receptionist. No insurance forms to fill out. No survey form of symptoms to fill out.

He looked at her. He looked at the room. The window was open, and he could hear traffic sirens below. He could smell incense burning. He began to cry. It did not faze her. She simply let him cry and said nothing. He began to cry more. She handed him a tissue, and gently waited for him to finish crying. He knew he had come home.

That was two and a half years ago. He saw her once a

week and hoped he would see her once a week forever. She was his lifeline. Even though he got mad at her sometimes, he knew, in his heart of hearts, that she was the only one who really cared about his best interests. It took him months before he could show her the manuscript for *The Man Who Mistook his Hemorrhoid for a Clitoris.* He was so afraid that she would be offended, that she would re-evaluate her opinion of him. But she never reacted negatively towards it or towards him. She never said she liked the book, but she asked him enough questions about the plot that he could tell she had read it closely, and most importantly, she encouraged, no, she *demanded* that he work to get it published.

Sometimes when he was between sessions, he would hold imaginary conversations with her, would ask her questions, or share his fears or frustrations. If he was walking around outdoors, he tried not to talk out loud during these conversations, but if he was at home, he carried on in a normal voice.

"I just don't know where Alfredo is taking me. Does he see the girl again? Does he see the man again? You thought Mamood was the real me. Maybe I should let him talk more. But that's his strength you know, he's quiet and efficient. He's the outsider who blends in. Alfredo's the outsider who can't fit in. The girl is obviously an outsider too. Hell, even Leon's an outsider—he's just got enough money that he can buy his way in."

In his head, the imaginary life coach was asking him about Alfredo's feeling for the girl.

"He does feel strongly for her. Hmm, more than that. He felt a stirring when she walked into the hotel. Maybe Mamood was right, maybe Alfredo's in love with her. But I don't feel like she's coming back into the picture. She's the elusive female, the siren, the mystery, unattainable... I wish I had more clues about her."

Chapter Seven:

Alfredo stood in the empty room 320. It had been three days since the man had checked out. The room had not been rented since. Housekeeping had changed the sheets, vacuumed, cleaned the bathroom, and left the complimentary soaps and shampoos. Alfredo walked over to the desk, pulled out the chair, turned it around to face the bed, and sat down. This was the bed he had seen her in. There was the carved wooden headboard where the ropes that held her wrists were tied. That was the pillow that held her head, a head that was tightly gagged, her mouth held open and soundless by the red ball in the leather gag, a head with two enormous eyes, beautiful eyes, scared eyes.

He got up and walked over to the bed and ran his fingers over the carved wood where the rope was tied. There were no marks, no scratches, no splinters, no evidence that she had ever been there. In fact, other than the image that was in his mind, there was no proof at all that she had been there. Only Leon Petroski had signed the registration form. There were no other witnesses in the lobby when he and the girl arrived. Alfredo had checked past records and Leon Petroski had never been at the hotel before. Eric certainly saw the man, but not the girl. No one at the San Juan had seen the man. They had both turned to smoke and vanished.

Alfredo walked over to the dresser. Did she stand before this very mirror and brush her hair? Did she take off her clothes and neatly fold them before climbing onto the bed? Did she leave her purse on the dresser while he fucked her on the bed? Alfredo felt sick. If he had only seen her leave, if the security camera had only caught the barest glimpse of her running out the side door exit... she could have been crying or she could have been smiling at the money she had made... but if he only had some indication she had left, then she wouldn't haunt him so. It was the not knowing that made him so mad. If he had seen her leave, he wouldn't be thinking about her today. Well, he might be thinking about her, stretched spread eagled and naked, but he wouldn't be worried about her. It was as if Leon Petroski had personally insulted him by making the girl disappear.

But there was nothing more he could do. It was just an unknown. Hotel work is full of unknowns. Alfredo let his eyes follow the line of the side of the dresser. Down on the carpet, lying next to dresser was something. Damn housekeeping, he thought. He bent down and picked it up. A book of matches. He recognized the "SJ" embossed on the cover. These were the matches that the San Juan Hotel used to have available in their restaurant. It had been several years since their restaurant had gone smokeless. Alfredo wondered if they still had these matches available for guests. He remembered watching Leon Petroski light a cigarette while he waited for Eric's cab. Alfredo tried to recall the exact visual image. Did Petroski use a lighter? No, he used a pack of matches to light the cigarette. These matches probably belonged to him. What were the odds? Could a previous guest have left them? This pack of matches looked brand new. He turned it over and looked at the strike pad. Not a scratch. These hadn't ever been used. He opened the pack. He took a sudden intake of air. The fact that all the matches were intact seemed immaterial now. On the inside cover was written a name and a phone number. Sandy 292-3442.

Chapter Eight:

The next day was Alfredo's day off. He went over to the San Juan and spoke to Rick. He asked about the matches and learned that yes, the restaurant and the hotel still carried them. They were in a small tray by the front door, so that guests could take them when they stepped outside to smoke. Rick introduced Alfredo to the maitre d' who ran the restaurant. Alfredo described Leon Petroski and the girl to him, but no, the maitre d' could not recall anyone fitting either description who had dined there in the previous weeks.

Alfredo went back to his apartment and got online. He looked at the number on the pack of matches. "The prefix looks like a cell phone," he thought, "so the reverse phone directory won't list it. But maybe I can still find it." He looked through various bondage websites that promised out-call escorts. The name Sandy was common, but none of the photos were of the girl in the hotel, and he couldn't find the phone number anywhere.

He sat and debated what to do. He could go to a pay phone and call that number. But even if a female answered, even a female named Sandy, he would have no way of knowing whether that female was the same girl at the hotel. In order to establish that, he would have to see her! Which meant that he would have to think up a story when he called that would enable them to meet. That was difficult. What could he say? He thought of simply identifying himself as from the hotel and saying that she had left something behind and somehow had gotten her number... but the details were very difficult. What had she left behind that would be believable? How had he gotten her number? Could he say that Leon had given it to him? No, no. If she was just a bondage hooker, could he schedule an appointment? Could he simply call up and say, "I want to schedule a session with Sandy?" and if the person on the other end acted like this was their regular business and scheduled a session, then he would go to the session. If it was her, well, there would be the double benefit of seeing her and having sex with her. If it wasn't her, there would only be the single benefit of having sex with someone. If the person answering the phone was confused by the "scheduling a session," if they said, "what are you talking about?" or "you must have the wrong number," well, he would be no worse off than now. What if a man answered? He couldn't simply ask for Sandy. And he certainly couldn't try the ploy of something left behind at the hotel. What if she was married? There were just too many ways this phone call could go wrong.

Alfredo tried to slow down and think. "What would Mamood do?" he asked himself. Mamood would calmly analyze every option and then pick the most reasonable one. Alfredo got a pad of paper from his drawer and starting writing.

1.   *the number is a B&D brothel*
    a.   *make appointment w/ Sandy—if no one there by that name, it's a dead end.*
    b.   *make appointment w/ Sandy—if yes, go to appointment, make sure it's her.*

2.   *Someone named Sandy answers*
    a.   *say that Leon asked me to call to make sure she was alright. If she acts like she knows Leon, it's her.*
    b.   *??*

3.   *a man answers*
    a.   *??*

4.   *Someone answers, but there is no Sandy there—that's another dead-end.*

5.   *Someone answers, but says Sandy's not there right now*
    a.   *Leave a message, but what?*
    b.   *Ask to make an "appointment"—but if they act like they don't know what I'm talking about, that's a dead end.*
    c.   *Try and get address.*

Alfredo looked at that last item. If only he had an address, he would watch the place and see if she came or went. That's all he wanted—to make sure she existed and was alive and okay. If he had an address, he could do that without getting involved.

He thought about this for a moment. Maybe he could call, saying he was a legal assistant at some law firm and his boss had yelled at him about mailing some legal papers to Sandy, but he had only given him a phone number... That might work. Alfredo turned to a new sheet of paper and wrote out a script:

"I'm sorry to bother you. My name is Bill Jennings and I'm a paralegal at the law firm of Gottwalls and Smith and my

boss is Jerry Gottwalls, do you know him? No, okay, well he was all mad today because he wanted these papers to go out to someone named Sandy at this number, but Mr. Gottwalls' secretary is out sick today, so he yelled at me to mail these out, but he didn't give me an address, just this envelope. If this is Sandy's phone, can I get an address from you, so I can mail this?"

This might work, thought Alfredo. He read it through a few times. He practiced it out loud, trying to make his voice crack like a young person who was scared might do. Then he grabbed his jacket and the pad of paper and headed out the door. He walked down to the corner, to Simok's corner store. There was a pay phone in the back. Simok knew Alfredo because Alfredo would often stop there after work to buy a bottle of wine.

"Sa-bai-dee Alfredo," Simok said as Alfredo entered the store.

"Sa-bai-dee Simok," Alfredo replied, "how's business?"

"Oh, very bad, very slow."

Simok always complained that business was very bad, yet he had been at that corner for many years and lived in a very expensive condo.

"Oh, I need to make a call," Alfredo said, as if it had just occurred to him. He headed to the back of the store, pulled the paper from his pocket, and dialed the number. His heart was racing. Simok was waiting on some kids at the front of the store.

Alfredo has his script in his hand. He was ready. But he did not anticipate a recorded message. It was a computerized voice. "There is no one available to take your call. Please leave your message at the beep."

He didn't know what to do. He hung up.

"You want wine?" Simok asked him as Alfredo walked to the front of the store.

"Uh, yeah, sure, yeah gimme a bottle."

Simok grabbed Alfredo's usual label and put it in a bag. Alfredo paid him and walked outside into the cool dusk.

"It could be a cell phone," he thought, *"could still be the B&D brothel."* But no matter what it was, Alfredo could not think of a message he could have left. He headed back to his apartment. *"Maybe I've overlooked something,"* he thought. *"After all, I didn't think that I might get voicemail."* As he walked, he thought back through everything that he had done since he found the matchbook. The only thing he hadn't checked was the reverse directory phone book. He had assumed the number was a cell phone number, which would not appear in a reverse directory phone book. It did seem like a cell phone prefix, but like Mamood always said *"leave no stone unturned."*

When he got back to his apartment, he logged onto the hotel's website and then used his password to access security. The hotel paid for a security service that provided several products and one of them was a reverse phone directory. Alfredo typed the phone number in... and to his surprise, an address appeared: 315 Vassar Street. Alfredo stared at it on the screen. He knew the street. Not far away. Not a bad area of town. Shit, he had an address. Now what?

Chapter Nine:

The next day Alfredo had to work. Normally, Alfredo walked to work, but this day he left his apartment early and hailed a cab and asked the cab driver to drive him by 315 Vassar Street. When they got to the address, Alfredo looked out the window. It was just another nice three story gray stone apartment building or condo building like so many others on a nicely manicured block. There was a small coffee shop across the street, and a hair salon next to that. Alfredo paid the driver but told him to wait for five minutes as he just had to deliver something. He got out of the cab and walked carefully across the street, up the eight steps to the entrance and the doorbell panel. There were six buzzers with only last names listed. No Sandy. Not even a first initial of "S". Alfredo picked one name and memorized it—Coleman. He tried the front door. It was, of course, locked. Alfredo turned around and walked back to the cab, got in and asked the driver to take him to the hotel. The cabbie said nothing and drove on.

All day at work, Alfredo worked on various plans. Maybe he could send packages to each tenant at the building, a book, a bland gift, anything, but send it Fed-Ex next-day-before-noon delivery. He could address each one with the first name Sandy as in "Sandy Coleman". Then he could station himself outside and see who signed for, or refused, the package. Or he could go back to phone number and maybe leave a message, something about a package left at the hotel that she needed to pick up. Or he could buy one of those cheap cell phones where you pay for minutes in advance and then leave a fictitious name saying he wanted to schedule an appointment and see what they said when whoever called back. If it wasn't an escort service, he could just hang up and throw the phone away. He even wondered if he could hire a detective.

By the end of the day, he was exhausted. He had no plan, but he did decide that he would go back, maybe sit in the coffee shop across the street and watch the place and see if any more ideas came to him. He had to work the next two days and would not have a day off until Thursday.

Chapter Ten:

That night, Alfredo dreamed of Sandy. He was holding her down on the bed, holding both her wrists in his hands. She seemed to be struggling against him. He was staring into those eyes.

They were naked in bed. He was on top. Her eyes were wide with fear. He looked for her mouth and realized that it was covered with a leather strap. She couldn't speak. Her black hair was splayed out on the pillow. She was staring directly at him. She was terrified.

Alfredo realized he was inside her. He was fucking her. Was this rape? He didn't know, but it felt so good. He couldn't stop. He began fucking her harder and harder. She was wet. He could feel his cock sliding in and out. He heard the slapping of his pelvis against hers, harder and harder, as he pounded away. He wasn't wearing a condom. He felt he was about to cum and squirt sperm juice all inside her.

Alfredo woke up. He was sweating and breathing hard. The sheets were all tangled. He knew he had had a nightmare but couldn't remember what it was about. He sat up in bed and tried to catch his breath. What had he been dreaming about? There was a hotel room. He remembered it as green. There was the smell of sheets, the feel of soft bed covers. There was Sandy... Then it all came back to him, at least the last image. He was fucking her on the bed and she was gagged. Alfredo could not remember any ropes or leather straps. Evidently, he was just holding her hands down, but he did remember not caring that she was terrified, not caring that she did not want to be fucked. He was inside her and was fucking her anyway. In his dream, he simply did not care.

Alfredo sat on the edge of the bed and thought about this. He got up and turned the light on and sat back down. The room seemed small and bleak. He turned the light off and got under the covers. Is that what turned him on about Sandy? The terror in her eyes? The idea of violating her? He wasn't that kind of guy. Yet here he was, just moments ago, pinning her wrists to the bed and fucking her hard, about to come, with her in a leather gag. Alfredo did not think himself capable of rape. This was a disturbing dream. His stomach hurt. He got up and put his bathrobe on and went into the bathroom and found a package of Pepto-Bismol and put two tablets in his mouth and chewed them. Then he went into the kitchen and poured himself a glass of wine. It was just a bad dream, he told himself. Bad dreams happen. He had been obsessing about her and so naturally she would appear in his bad dream. But, he had been enjoying himself and he had to admit that it was rape. He couldn't get the image of her eyes out of his mind.

Chapter Eleven:
Alfredo drew out a map of Sandy's neighborhood. Here was her apartment building, either where she lived or worked. Here was the closest coffee shop. Here was the closest liquor store. Here was the closest grocery store. Here was the closest drug store. Here was the closest fast food restaurant. Whether she lived at, or worked at, the Vassar Street address, she still had to go to out occasionally. Best of all, Alfredo found that there was a bus stop on the same block as Sandy's address. He had planned to find a way to spend time at the grocery store, the drug store, and the fast food restaurant hoping to run into her, but now he had a better plan.
On his next day off, he took a cab to her block. He dressed in the most non-descript clothes he had. He paid the driver and walked to the bus stop. It was 8:00 a.m. There were several people there. Alfredo studied the bus routes. There was an 8:15 bus that ran downtown. He assumed that the people there were waiting for that bus. There was also an 8:30 bus that went to the eastside. And another 8:50 bus downtown. This was good. Alfredo had brought a newspaper. He pretended to read the paper while he stood among the others. But he kept himself positioned so that he could see who might walk into or out of the 315 Vassar Street building. The 8:15 bus came and many people, but not Alfredo, got on. The bus left. Alfredo continued to read the paper, all the while keeping a lookout. The 8:30 bus came. Alfredo let it pass. He found a seat on the bus bench and continued to read the paper. No one would notice him sitting here. He even actually read some of the paper. People showed up for the 8:50 bus. Alfredo gave his bench seat to an old lady. The next bus came, and everyone got on it, except Alfredo. He checked the schedule. The next bus was 9:15. He sat down on the empty bench and

opened the paper again. He considered the virtue of patience. He thought that this is what private investigators must do all the time when they stake out a place. He kept his eye on the Vassar Street building, but no one came or went.

By noon, seven more buses had come and gone. Alfredo was tired. He hailed a cab and went home.

On his next day off, Alfredo did the same thing, except he picked the evening hour. He waited at the bus stop from four until seven p.m. He did see two people come into the Vassar Street building, during those three hours, but neither of them was Sandy

His next day off wasn't for another five days.

Chapter Twelve:

"You seem distracted, my friend," Mamood said to Alfredo.

"I'm just tired, that's all."

"No, mon ami, I think it is more than that. I have watched you for the past few weeks, and you are distracted. Are you seeing some woman?"

"I wish," Alfredo said, "No, I'm telling you, I am just tired. I haven't been sleeping well lately."

"Hmmm, I see." Mamood began whistling softly. Alfredo always hated it when Mamood whistled. It meant he was getting ready to confront him.

"Hey, mon ami, whatever happened to that girl that disappeared from your watch?"

"What do you mean?" Alfredo asked.

"You know, the girl you liked, the one who checked in with that man, the one you called me about."

"I don't know what happened to her, Mamood."

"Did you investigate?"

"A little. But I never found anything."

"Ahh, what did you find?"

"Well, I found that the guy took a cab from here to the San Juan hotel, but was never a guest there, and no

one recognized his description there. And his address in Los Angeles turned out to be bogus, but his credit card did pay for the room. That's basically all I found."

"So, we got paid for the room?"

"Yes."

"But you still obsess about her?"

Alfredo paused at this question, but finally answered. "Yes, Mamood, I do."

"Well, mon ami, I think there is more. Tell me."

It was difficult, but Alfredo told Mamood everything. About the camera, about what he saw, about how he had been spending all his days off at the bus stop, hoping to catch a glimpse of Sandy, how he couldn't get her out of his mind. Mamood listened quietly, and occasionally took notes.

After Alfredo finished, both were quiet. Alfredo felt somehow embarrassed. Mamood seemed deep in thought. Finally, Mamood said,

"Okay, mon ami, let me see what I can do."

Chapter Thirteen:

It was four days later. Alfredo was on duty, but he had the next day off. He had planned to spend the day at the bus stop, as usual. But late in his shift, Alfredo got a call from Mamood.

"Hello, mon ami, how are you?"

"Good, Mamood, how are you?

"I am good. I have some information for you."

"Oh? What is that?"

"Well, at approximately seven o'clock tomorrow night, you should go to the check-out lanes of the QFC grocery store at Third and Victoria. Just go there and wait."

"Okay... and what would I be waiting for?"

"You'd be waiting to see if you recognize anyone."

"I see. Okay, thanks, Mamood."

"No problem, mon ami."

So, the next day, which was a Friday, at six-fifty in the evening, Alfredo arrived at the grocery store at Third and Victoria. Luckily there was a small Starbucks counter inside the store next to the check-out lines. Alfredo bought a paper. He bought a lottery ticket. He bought a Starbucks coffee and sat at a table where he had a good view of the check-out lines and he pretended to look at the paper and sip his coffee. The minutes ticked by. He checked his watch: seven p.m. He turned the pages of the paper and pretended to read while he scanned the faces that walked by. Five minutes past. There was a constant stream of shoppers walking by his table. He finished his coffee. Ten minutes. Alfredo wondered what he was doing here. He felt stupid. He scanned the check-out lanes again. Then he saw her. It was Sandy.

Chapter 15

Paul was stuck. He had written several chapters but now simply had no idea where the story was going. He spent several days trying to write the next chapter, but nothing came. Finally, he emailed what he had written to his life coach and then asked if he could come by to see her.

"I've lost the thread of the story," he told her after he had arrived and sat down. "I was connected to Alfredo as some sort of outsider who witnesses what he thinks is a crime and somehow falls in love with the victim, although she may not be the victim after all, but now that he finds her, I don't know what he's supposed to do."

"How are you connected to Alfredo?" she asked.

"Well, you know, he's me. He's the immigrant, the outsider, the loner. He keeps his head down and does his job and longs for love but lives alone…"

"And you feel like you're Alfredo?"

"Yeah, sure, I mean… look at my life. Yeah, I feel connected to him."

"Hmmm. I always felt you were more like Mamood. But anyway, when did you lose your connection to Alfredo?"

"When he saw Sandy in the grocery story."

"And what do you imagine is going to happen if he reconnects with her?"

"Well, I know this sounds strange, but I think he's going to kill her."

"And how is he going to do that?"

"Well, the image I had was that he would hire her and act out the same bondage sex scenes that Leon Petroski had performed on her but something would go awry and she would die, and then he'd have the problem of having to get rid of the body, the same problem that he mistakenly thought Leon Petroski had. In effect, he would become Leon Petroski."

"And how do you feel about Alfredo, who you say is you, becoming Leon Petroski?"

"I can't do it. Alfredo is not that evil."

"*You're* not that evil."

Paul paused, then finally said, "I don't think so."

His life coach looked at him a while. "Well, I don't think you are, either. But you know, you are *all* the characters you write. I mean, they are *parts* of you. You *are* the outsider, whether it's the gay man from your first book or Alfredo. You are also the smart insider, like Mamood. And you are the Leon Petroski. And you are the girl Sandy, who may be evil or may be a victim. But you have parts of anything you write, otherwise you wouldn't be able to write them. If you can't write that Alfredo kills Sandy, then it's because *you* can't kill Sandy. You might be able to dominate her like Leon does, but you are incapable of killing her."

"But I thought about it."

"Yes, you thought about it. But you can't write it. And that's the difference. It's one thing to think about an evil deed. It's another thing to write about it. And it's a totally different thing to actually do it. Just because a person can write about it doesn't mean they can do it. But the fact that you can't even write about it says a lot about you."

Paul sat silent for a moment.

"Let me ask you this," his life coach said, "just to stir the pot. What does Alfredo want?"

Paul answered without hesitation. "He wants love."

"What does Mamood want?"

"He just wants to continue on, work the system, stay unknown. But he has a loyalty to his friends, and Alfredo is his friend."

"What does Sandy want?"

Paul thought about this for a minute. "Well, I do think she wants to be dominated. But she also wants to get out of the sex game... Maybe she enjoys the domination but not the degradation. But I imagine that she's practical. She's doing it mostly for the money. She secretly enjoys the bondage, but she also has a cold edge to her."

"What about the fear that Alfredo saw in her eyes?"

"No, you're right, at that moment, she was genuinely terrified. That's what attracted Alfredo to her."

"Hmmm, so you have Sandy and Alfredo and Mamood... Is Leon going to show back up?"

"I hadn't thought about that..." Paul said. "But he could, he definitely could. I just don't know yet."

"Well, what I think you ought to do, Paul, is to sit down at the computer, and leave your mind in the other room and just type out three different next versions, three different radical versions, of the next chapter as fast as you can. Don't even think as you write, just write. Do this tonight, write three versions and come back to see me tomorrow at one o'clock."

Paul followed her directions. That night he opened a bottle of wine and started writing as fast as he could type. He wrote several pages where Alfredo walks up to Sandy and speaks to her in the store. That felt wrong. He deleted those pages from his computer. He poured himself another glass of wine and started again. He wrote several pages where Sandy sees Alfredo and starts talking to him. That felt even more wrong. He deleted those pages. He poured another glass of wine and started writing again.

Chapter Fourteen:
She walked right past him. She had purchased something small at the express cashier and was stuffing it into her purse when Alfredo first saw her. He thought about standing and walking up to her, but he had no idea what he would say. Besides, it all happened so fast. She made her purchase, stuffed the item into her purse, turned and walked towards him, then past him and out the door. She had her hair pulled back, and was wearing jeans and a simple gray jacket, but he would have recognized those eyes anywhere. But now she was out the door.

Alfredo stood up and walked out the door. He saw her about twenty feet ahead, walking toward Victoria Street. He wasn't sure what he was doing, but it seemed like a good idea to follow her, so he did. He tried to walk nonchalantly, matching her pace so as not to gain on her. She walked down Victoria Street three blocks towards Vassar Street. Alfredo assumed that she was walking home, that she would turn left on Vassar Street and head for her apartment. That would confirm that she lived there. But other than that, what had he gained? Well, at least he knew she was alive, and not a dead body stuffed somewhere in the hotel.

But she did not turn left on Vassar. She kept walking, and Alfredo kept following her. She turned left on a street called McDougal. Alfredo slowed his pace and dropped back another ten feet. After several blocks, she turned again on a street that had no street sign. There were no apartments on this street, just metal shops and warehouse buildings. After two more blocks she turned right and walked across a parking lot and into a one-story gray building with no windows. Alfredo slowed down as he approached the building. What was he supposed to do now? Was this a business? A factory where she worked the night shift? Was she meeting a friend? The building had no sign, not even numbers for an address. But there were five or six cars parked in the parking lot directly in front of the door she had entered. As he approached the building, he saw a car pull into the parking lot. A man and woman got out and entered the building. The man wore a coat and tie. The woman had on tight jeans. They walked arm in arm. Alfredo wondered whether this was an art gallery. He knew he had to go in and find out. He wasn't sure why he had to find out, but he had come this far. He might never see her again. He had to go in.

In times of ambiguity, Alfredo always fell back on a trick he had learned from his father: act like the lost immigrant. Even though Alfredo's English was perfect, he could muster an accent when he needed to. His mind worked out the plan. Walk into the building. It had to be a business. Surely there would be a guard or a receptionist or someone right inside the door. Beg their pardon in broken English and ask for McDougal Street. Alfredo knew how to open his eyes wide and look lost and confused. Thank whoever answered his question with overly grateful expressions and then leave. But not without taking in all that he could see while he smiled and nodded his head when they told him that McDougal Street was just a few blocks east.

Alfredo reached the door. It was metal and heavy. He opened it and stepped inside. The lighting was low. There was a glass counter directly in front of him, with several tables with chairs on the left. A heavy-set woman stood behind the counter. The man and woman who came in before him were sitting at one of the tables filling out some forms. Alfredo stood there trying to figure out what he had walked into. The heavy-set woman came out from behind the counter and smiled at Alfredo as she walked up to him. She looked about forty-five with a rather unattractive face. He saw that she was wearing a leather mini-skirt and a very low-cut blouse and some type of push-up bra that thrust her breasts prominently up. Still, she was smiling warmly at him.

"Hello," she said. "Are you here for the orientation?"

Alfredo didn't know what to say. He looked at the couple at the table. They were still filling out their forms. He decided to play along. He could always play the confused immigrant card and leave if things got sticky.

He used a thick accent. "Jes. Orientation."

"Well, my name is Lorraine. What's yours?"

"Roberto. Roberto Rahula." Alfredo used the name of an old school mate.

"Okay, Roberto, here are some papers to read and some forms to fill out. There are pens at the tables. When you finish filling them out, bring them back to me."

Alfredo took the papers she handed him and went and sat down at one of the tables. He began to read.

The Center for Friends of BDSM

The Center for Friends of BDSM (CFBDSM) is a non-profit 501(c)7 members-only center. We provide a safe environment for our community. We seek to foster a supportive, comfortable, and above-all safe environment for a full range of BDSM and other activities. We welcome all adults, gay, lesbian, straight, transgendered, etc., who seek a friendly safe and accepting place to play, learn, grow, and meet like-minded individuals.

Holy shit, Alfredo thought. He quickly looked through the rest of the papers. There was an application for membership form, a section on "rules and etiquette," a release form and waiver of liability, a description of "events," a page of definitions, a list of membership fees, and a description of the "mandatory orientation" held every Friday evening. Evidently, this is what he had wandered into tonight—the mandatory orientation. But where was Sandy? Did she work here? Alfredo looked up. Another couple had entered, and Lorraine was greeting them and handing them papers. The first couple was still filling out their forms. Alfredo noticed that, aside from Lorraine, no one made eye contact with anyone else.

Another couple walked in. Lorraine greeted them. Alfredo continued reading through the papers.

<u>*Events We Host*</u>

> *We host an event every night of the week and a variety of events all day Saturday and Sunday. Members are welcome to all events, unless gender-excluded. Members may bring guests (21 and older of course) to any event for a fee of $20 per guest per event. All guests must read and sign the consent form.*

> *On Monday nights we host "Introduction to BDSM," a night geared to our newer members. Each Monday we explore different aspects of BDSM, such as ropes and knots, whips, chains, the rack, the X-rack, and after-care. On Tuesdays, we offer a Womyns Only Night, where explore a variety of topics such as orgasm, toys, relationships, and alternative lifestyles. On Wednesday nights we host the Bump, a primarily sex-oriented dance night, for all sexes, genders, and dispositions, with light BDSM and self-pleasure areas. On Thursdays, we have education nights, when our library is open for discussion groups, and on Fridays, we host our new members orientation, followed by our*

pansexual BDSM party. On Saturdays, we have our weekly leather/latex dance mixer from 9 p.m. to 3 a.m., and on most Sundays we do Tantric yoga in the afternoon and a masturbation party in the evening. Every fourth Sunday is men-only dance and sex party with our darkroom and dungeon. See our website for specific descriptions and times.

Alfredo realized that he had to fill out the application form if he wanted to stay, and he had to stay to find out where how Sandy fit into all of this. So, he got out his pen and began to write. He used the name Roberto Rahula and gave the hotel's street address as his address. He completed the waiver of liability form and checked the box that said that he had completely read the BDSM "rules of etiquette" and agreed to abide by them. The membership fee was $50. Luckily, Alfredo had cash on him. He handed Lorraine his money along with his completed paperwork.

The other people had finished their forms as well. Lorraine collected everyone's money, handed them membership cards, and ushered them into the next room.

There was a dozen or so chairs arranged in a circle. Alfredo took a seat and looked around. There were three couples and two other men. At the head of the circle sat a large bearded man who was smiling broadly and greeting everyone warmly. He was obviously in charge of this orientation. As soon as everyone was seated, the large man began to speak to the group.

"My name is Brian Porter and I am one of the staff here at the Center for Friends of BDSM, or as we call it, the Center for Friends, because we are a lot more than just BDSM, and I'll explain that in a minute. But first of all, I want to welcome you here. I know how difficult it is to walk through that door for the first time. When I first came here, thirteen years ago, I spent two months driving up and down the street, not even *daring to come into the parking lot. It takes an enormous amount of courage just to walk in here the first time, but I promise you that it is very easy to come back the second time and the third time. Every week I have new members just like yourselves come up to me after they've here a second or third time and tell me, 'Brian, you were right. We can't believe how scared we were when we first came here, and how much at home we now feel here.' I guarantee you will have that same experience. Now, let me tell you a little of the history of this place."*

Brian was obviously doing his best to try and relax the group. Alfredo looked around at the other people. Each was sitting stiffly. Alfredo had not realized that they were all as scared and tense as he was. There was an older man, about 60 years old, well-dressed, balding in front, his remaining white hair tied in a small pony-tail. Next to him sat an attractive petite woman, about 40 years old. They were obviously together. Brian was talking about how the Center was founded some twenty years previously. Alfredo wondered how couples came to the decision to come to such a place. Did the older man bring his younger wife there because she demanded more variety? Or did he have a lot of money and she came along to appease his interests? Next to them was a paunchy man in a black shirt and a gold chain, sitting by himself. Alfredo thought gold chains had gone out of fashion decades ago. The man had a long drooping mustache and was reading the handout literature intently. Next to him was another couple, younger and casually dressed. The man was skinny. The woman was fat. Alfredo saw a tattoo on her arm. It looked like a tweety bird. Again, Alfredo wondered what communication they had to come to the agreement to come to this place. Next to them was another single man. He was not what one would call pleasant-looking. His face was slightly off, the nostrils just a bit too wide, the eyes offset. His mouth was slightly opened. He was a mouth-breather. To Alfredo's left was another couple, sitting on a low leather couch. Alfredo's chair was somewhat behind them at an angle, so he could not get a good look at their faces. They seemed young, dressed in jeans. Alfredo found himself thinking that they looked normal. Of course, what did that mean? He was here too, wasn't he? Alfredo tuned into what Brian was saying.

"And then we moved to our present location, which we will take a tour of in a few minutes. But first, I want to describe tonight's event. As you know, every Friday is our pansexual BDSM party." Brian pointed toward the large open space behind him. "As you can see, the large play area behind me here has a variety of racks and iron crosses and stocks where partners can be tied. We've arranged the couches and chairs on the perimeter of the room so that there are plenty of places to sit and watch. However, we ask that if you are watching and not participating in a scene, then do not walk across the play area. That will disturb the scene. Walk around. Coffee and soft drinks are available on the left side here. As the rules state, no alcohol is allowed in the center."

Alfredo took a closer look at the room. There were indeed large structures in four or five places on the floor. Some were giant wooden X's with metal rings every couple of feet. Alfredo assumed these would be used to secure ropes. There was one old fashioned pillar, where someone's head and hands could be locked. There were several wooden structures, like giant picture frames, sitting vertical. In other areas there were simply large metal rings mounted into the ceiling. The edge of the open space was lined with large sofas and chairs. There were also two full size metal cages, just large enough to hold one person, at two of the corners of the room.

Brian was still talking. "Each scene has to be reserved by talking with one of our monitors. We have six monitors always on duty at every event, and we can usually accommodate thirty scenes a night. You can tell who the monitors are because they wear a red name tag like the one I'm wearing. Monitors are here to schedule the scenes, to help with supplies, to answer questions, and to make sure that everyone has a good time. Feel free to approach a monitor any time you have a question. The only thing we ask is that if *a monitor is in the play area helping the players in a scene, wait until they are done, and the monitor comes back to the sidelines. Some of you may have already reserved a scene tonight. Just check with any monitor as to when you can begin and what area you'll be in. And always remember, our center's safe word is "safe word." If you are doing a scene and need help or need to stop for any reason, just say "safe word." Someone will immediately be at your side to help you.*

"If you are doing a scene that involves fire play, you must clear that with the monitor in advance. We have a special room for fire play, and you will have two monitors assigned to you. Likewise, any scenes involving cutting or even using knives or sharp instruments must be cleared with a monitor first. And if you are doing a cutting scene, you must use our blood room and provide your own towels and tarps. Let's see, what else? Oh yes, wax play is always fine, but because it involves fire, you must let a monitor know about it in advance. Oh, and I should mention that while most members prefer to use their own whips and straps, we do have a small collection of whips and other devices that you can borrow. See Lorraine about them and be sure to return them afterwards.

"Okay, let's talk about etiquette. Clear communication is an absolute must. If you ask someone to join a scene or to have sex, you must make your intentions as to what will happen absolutely clear. Likewise, if someone asks you, you must make your response absolutely clear. Around here, no means no. If you ask someone to play and they say no, don't take it personal, just move on. And if you are asked to participate in a scene and you don't want to, by all means, just say no. I remember one of my first parties here, and a nice gentleman asked me to have sex with him, and I was trying to be polite and I said something like, 'well not right now, maybe later.' And he kept coming back to me every twenty minutes. Because he was taking me at my word. So, don't try to be nice. You don't have to cushion the blow. We're all adults here. Just say 'no thank you'.

"All sex here should be safe sex. You will notice that there are bowls of condoms and lube sitting on every table. We provide them for you. Use them. On the other hand, it is your responsibility to communicate with your partner and discuss what safe sex means to you. Communicate clearly. I can't say it often enough."

Alfredo looked over at the tables. There were indeed two large clear plastic bowls on each table, one full of condoms and one full of small packages of lubricant. *What have I stumbled into?* he wondered. He glanced around at the other new members. No one seemed really relaxed. Everyone had a fixed stare at Brian except for the man in the black shirt who still seemed obsessed with reading each page of the literature.

Alfredo noticed that other people were starting to quietly drift into the room. Some men were rearranging the wooden racks. One couple came in with two duffle bags and were unpacking them, pulling out long leather straps and short cat o' nine tail whips. Another woman came in dressed in a latex body suit and walked over to the coffee pot. Brian was still talking.

"Nudity and sex are allowed in the play area. However, we ask that if you are just watching a scene that you do not masturbate. We do have special masturbation nights that are described in the handouts, and you can check our website to see when they are. Finally, remember that the sex room, which is located just to the back right of the play area, is partners only. Now we don't limit the number of partners you can take back there, but what I'm saying is that it's off limits for voyeurs. When we do the tour, I'll show it to you, and you'll see it's one big room with three large beds. It's for people or groups who want to have sex out of view of the play room, so we respect their privacy. If you have one or more partners and wish to go back to the sex room, no problem, just check with a monitor to see if a bed is available. Okay, well, if there are no questions, I will take you on a brief tour of the dungeon, the showers, the blood room, the sex room and the play area. Are there any questions?"

Chapter 16

Paul's life coach finished reading the pages he had given her. When she put the pages down, he asked her, "Well, what do you think?"

She laughed. "What do *you* think, Paul?"

"Well, I'm glad to be writing again. I just don't know where it's going."

"You never do. That's how you write. You always get stuck when you try to make the story go one place or another. We talked about that many times on your first book. But when you just let yourself write, the story writes itself. It goes against everything they teach in writing classes, but it seems that, for you, it is the only way you can write. The story emerges from some other part of you."

"Yeah..."

"So, how far ahead can you see the story?"

"I see Sandy coming out to do a scene. Alfredo is going to watch her. I don't know his reaction yet."

"That's good. Probably better if we don't talk about it. So, tell me Paul, what else is going on with your life? Have you gone back to Vagabonds recently?"

"No."

"Have you been taking breaks from writing, walking to the coffee shop, or walking to the grocery store?"

"Yeah."

"And have you been practicing flirting with women during those breaks, just making small talk?"

Paul looked down at his hands. "No, I really haven't. It... it just never seems like there's an opportunity to talk with anyone. I mean, I know it sounds like a cliché, but everyone seems to be a couple. If I go to Starbucks, there's always people sitting there, but they're sitting there with someone else. If there's a woman by herself, she's always got a laptop open and is engrossed in something. There's no way to start a conversation."

"Well, that's true, Paul. Conversations can only be started at transition points, before the other person gets to where they are going and opens up their laptop. If a woman is in front of you in line, ordering coffee, that's when you have to say something. While she's transitioning from here to there. Once she gets there, the walls go up... And you know why the walls go up, Paul?"

"No."

"Because she's just as scared as you. A woman can't just go to Starbucks and sit and drink coffee, unless she's waiting for someone. She would be too vulnerable. She has to look busy. She has to have her protection, her wall up. Just like you do. I think everyone feels exactly the same, scared of opening up. So, we all put up walls, just like you do. Remember that the next time you're in line behind some woman and you're scared of making small talk. She's scared too."

Paul was listening. She continued. "I think that loneliness is such a huge problem today. Everyone wants to be connected, but everyone is scared of opening up and talking, scared of looking like they need people. Maybe they can't open up first, Paul. Maybe it's too scary for them. Maybe it's up to you to open up first. You know, I've said this before, but small talk is supposed to be small. It doesn't matter what you say, you just have to say something, something that acknowledges their existence. They may be standing in line in front of you or behind you, but they feel like they're alone in the world too. If you turn and say something unimportant, like, 'it seems there are lines everywhere', even something that unimportant, you are in fact acknowledging their existence, confirming the fact that they are in line, that they exist at that moment. You have to start somewhere. You shoot yourself in the foot if you don't talk. Keep going to coffee shops and grocery stores. Watch for transition points where someone has ended one activity but hasn't started another. Then just say something that confirms what is going on. Just open the door. That's all we're working on, these small contact moments."

Chapter Fifteen:

Alfredo found a seat on a small leather couch on the edge of the play area. There were about seventy-five people in the room now, mostly couples, and there seemed to be a lot of activity involving unpacking suitcases and dufflebags and moving things around. Alfredo watched a woman in a leather bra and leather mini-skirt and leather boots arrange eight or nine short whips in a very precise pattern on a table near one of the racks. A young Asian man who seemed to be with her had taken off his shirt and was positioning one of the large wooden racks. About ten feet away a man on a ladder was feeding a thick rope through one of the metal rings embedded in the ceiling. He let the rope dangle down to where a slim woman was standing with her arms folded watching him. She wore glasses and had her hair pulled back into a bun. Her blouse was buttoned to the neck. She looked like a prim librarian.

Nearby, at one of the corners of the room a man was locking a woman into one of the full-size metal cages. She only had a bra and panties on and was wearing a leather collar with a metal ring attached to the front of the collar. Alfredo could hear her speak to the man. "Master, can I have a drink of water before you lock the door?" The man looked at her, then removed the padlock from the cage and said, "Yes." She thanked him with her eyes averted and darted out of the cage to the water fountain, took a long drink, and then hurried back to the cage where he was waiting with the door open.

Directly to Alfredo's left was a large wooden device like a giant X, standing straight up and down. Alfredo assumed this was the "iron cross" that Brian had mentioned. An older fat man was attaching ropes to two rings that were mounted on the sides of the X.

Suddenly, Lorraine walked up and sat down beside Alfredo. She was still wearing the same low-cut blouse and mini-skirt, but when she sat down, Alfred realized that she was not wearing any underwear. She sat with her legs slightly apart so that Alfredo could see a brown patch of pubic hair at the top of her heavy thighs. Alfredo tried not to look and focused on her face instead.

"It's Roberto, right?" she asked.

"Jes," Alfredo replied, still using a thick accent.

"Well, Roberto, I just wanted to welcome you here. I know you're going to have a good time. Do you have a partner at home or are you by yourself?"

"By myself."

"Well, you're an attractive man, and I know you're going to make a lot of friends here. Are you a dominant or a submissive?

Alfredo had a sense of what she meant but wasn't exactly sure of how to answer her.

"Well, I don't know jest yet. I am jest... exploring."

"I understand. I'm a submissive. I love being tied up and beaten. Well, you have a good time and remember, my name is Lorraine, and if you have any questions, just let me know."

"Jes, thank you berry much."

As she got up to leave, she leaned forward, placing her hand on Alfredo's knee to push herself up, giving Alfredo a nice view of her breasts while letting him feel the full weight of her body through the hand on his knee as she pushed herself up. Alfredo watched her lumber away.

He looked back at the play area in front of him. The young Asian man had taken off all his clothes. The leather woman was tying him with rope to the metal rings of the wooden frame. The rings were above and out from the height of the man's shoulders. He stood there facing the wooden rack, with his feet apart, looking like a large naked X. The *leather woman had a stern and intense look on her face as she finished tying the knots. Alfredo noticed that the man was getting a slight erection. The woman stepped over to where she had so carefully laid her whips out, and she carefully selected a short cat o' nine tails with a woven leather handle. As she walked back to the naked man she said something to him, and he tensed up slightly. She pushed him forward so that he was leaning into the wooden rack. Then she started gently rubbing his shoulders with the palm of her left hand. That seemed to relax him. Then she took the handle of the whip and started rubbing his back with it. The man's erection started to bob up. The woman took a half step back and brushed the ends of the whip back and forth across the man's shoulders. She did this four or five times. Then she started swinging harder. Alfredo did not think she was swinging hard enough that the whip ends were hurting the man. But then she pulled her arm back and snapped the whip onto the man's back. Alfredo could see the man wince. The woman stepped forward and gently started rubbing the man's back with her open palm again, as if to comfort him. Then she stepped back and hit him hard with the whip again.*

Alfredo noticed that ten feet beyond this scene, the librarian-looking girl had taken off all her clothes. Alfredo thought she looked beautiful. Her brown hair was still pulled back into a bun and she still had her glasses on. Alfredo could see her dark nipples and brown pubic hair between her legs. The man had put the ladder away. He had her put her arms forward and hold her palms together. Then he took one end of the rope that was hanging down from the ceiling and tied a complicated knot around her wrists. Then he grabbed the other end of the rope and started to slowly pull it, hand over hand, which caused the girl's hands to be lifted above her head. When her arms were fully extended over her head, the man put his full weight into pulling the rope down, and the girl was lifted by her arms off the ground. He pulled her about a foot off the floor, and then tied his end of the rope to a ring that seemed to be embedded in the floor. She dangled there, her feet pointed downwards. The man then took a small strap of some kind and tied the girl's feet together. Then he picked up what looked to Alfredo to be a long flat paddle. He walked around to the back of the girl and started hitting her ass with the paddle. The paddle made a loud smack every time it struck her ass.

In fact, Alfredo started noticing that the sound of smacking—the hitting of whips and paddles—was slowly building into a wall of sound. To Alfredo's left, the older fat man had taken off his shirt. There was a younger woman with him. She was naked with very pale white skin. Alfredo noticed that her pubic hair was completely shaved off. The fat man and the naked woman were taking turns whipping a fat naked black woman who had her back to them and was simply holding onto the sides of a large iron cross. The black woman was not tied to it. She was just holding on while being whipped. The naked white woman was laughing and taunting the black woman. Suddenly, the black woman turned and grabbed the white woman's hand and shouted something. The white woman continued to laugh. The fat man grabbed the black woman's hands and turned her back to the iron cross. She once again grabbed the sides of the iron cross and the fat man and the white woman recommenced whipping her. They had a rhythm going where they would alternate blows across the black woman's back and thighs.

Someone put some music on. It was a type of industrial electronic music, mostly just bass percussion. The sound of the whips and paddles seemed to in synch with the music. Alfredo sat transfixed. Around him in the various chairs and sofas, a large crowd was also watching. No one spoke.

Chapter 17

Paul poured another glass of wine and read what he had written. He had no idea where this was going. He had never understood why some people seemed to like to suffer. He thought back to the women he had known who seemed to invite abuse, the ones who were always in bad relationships, in emotionally abusive relationships, even physically abusive relationships, the ones who would come to him crying about their lovers, complaining how *wrong* it was that they were treated that way after all the love they had given to those men. Yet, invariably, so invariably that Paul learned to count on it, no matter how often he would tell them to end the relationship, invariably they would return to the loveless, brutal, abusive men. Paul thought of one woman, Christine, and she was not even living with the man who abused her, and yet she would return day after day to the poison well of the relationship.

He remembered how she would call him late at night, sobbing on the phone.

"I can't take this hurt any more, Paul. I am so done with him, so done," she would exclaim between sobs. "This time he's hurt me like I've never been hurt before. Let me tell you what he did." And she would proceed to tell him, moment by moment, line by line, how he had yelled at her, or hung up on her, or cheated on her, or lied to her, or whatever the pain de jour was. At first, Paul was alarmed and sympathetic. But eventually he caught on. *She* always initiated the phone call to this man. *She* always started the interaction that led to his insult, to his broken promise, to his lie. Christine even admitted proudly to Paul when she lied to the man. She *had to* lie, she told Paul, in order to catch *him* in a lie. Paul realized that oftentimes the man was just reacting, albeit overreacting, to Christine's provocations.

During the first month of these late-night phone calls to Paul, he would try to advise her. He would tell her to simply not call the man, to simply not answer his emails, to simply not go to the poison well. And she would always agree and thank him profusely for being her "best friend" and thank him for listening, and for *caring,* and at the end of every call, she would promise never to call the abuser again. Then of course a few nights later, Paul's phone would ring again, and she'd be on the other end, sobbing into the receiver. Eventually, Christine and this man started getting into physical fights, each slapping the other, or throwing things at each other. At one point, Paul considered the possibility of calling the police, but he could not figure out who was the abuser and who was actually being abused.

Finally, after almost eight months of these late-night soap opera phone calls, she married the guy, and Paul never heard from her again.

Paul thought about Christine for another moment. He shook his head, as if to chide himself for wasting so many evenings listening to her. He wondered if women and men who enjoy being whipped were in otherwise wonderfully romantic sweet caring relationships. Maybe they transfigured and transformed the human need for punishment into these ritualistic beatings. He wondered if Christine had let this man simply beat her naked once a week in front of strangers, whether that would have solved her relationship problems. Maybe she was acting all that out on the phone. Maybe Paul had been her large wooden rack, a sturdy listening post against which she could whimper as she reenacted every stinging insult, the smack of every lie, the scourge of every deceit. Paul didn't know. He made a mental note to do some research on the psychology of BDSM, although he suspected that anything written about it would be wrong, some social work mumbo-jumbo about displacement and sublimation. He suspected that only someone who was involved in it could truly explain it.

Paul looked at the clock. It was only eleven p.m. He had a couple of hours left before his normal bed time. He took another sip of wine and returned his gaze to his computer screen and put his fingers on the keyboard.

Alfredo took another look around the room. Still no sign of Sandy. He assumed that she was still in the building. He would have seen her had she exited out the front door. He recalled that during the "tour", Brian had taken the group to another smaller room, which also had racks and ceiling hooks, and mentioned that this room was used for smaller parties, and that tonight it was being used for a "transmasculine" BDSM party. Alfredo was not sure what "transmasculine" meant. But he got up from the couch and made his way around the perimeter of the play area, through the crowd, to the smaller room.

The entrance had no door, just an opening where a door used to be. A dark curtain hung in the doorway. Alfredo pushed it aside and walked in. This room was darker. Various events were happening in the middle of the room. Alfredo could hear the sound of whips. There were no couches or chairs around the perimeter. Alfredo assumed there simply wasn't room for them in this small area. A crowd of people were standing, encircling the center play area of the room. Alfredo moved along the wall until he found a space in the crowd where he could step up alongside the other voyeurs.

Even though his eyes adjusted to the dimmer light, he could not quite understand what he was seeing. In front of him, tied hand and foot and suspended from the ceiling by a hammock of ropes was what appeared to be an older fat "woman" completely naked. Her arms were extended out and tied above her head. Her mouth was gagged. Her large breasts drooped to either side of her body. Ropes from the ceiling were tied underneath her knees, pulling her knees up and apart. She was spread-legged directly in front of Alfredo. Alfredo stared between her massive thighs. There was public hair and a penis and balls, but below them, above her asshole, was a vagina-like slit. Alfredo stared, trying to make out details in the dim light. Then he looked again at her breasts. They looked like an older woman's breasts. He looked at the dark nipples. Then he noticed that the areolas were misshaped. They didn't look natural, as if they were in the wrong place. Then he realized that they weren't areolas and they weren't nipples. They were tattoos. She had dark areolas and darker nipples tattooed on her breasts.

A large man wearing some type of leather crisscross

straps over his naked torso walked up to the hanging woman. He was carrying a very large dildo in his right hand. Alfredo could see that it glistened with some type of lubricant. The man pulled on the ropes and the woman's whole body turned to the left. The woman's large thigh now blocked Alfredo's view of her genitalia. The man grabbed the woman's left knee to steady her and reached in toward her genitals with the dildo. Alfredo could see the woman wince and arch her head back. From the position of the man's arm, Alfredo knew he had inserted the dildo into the woman, but he could not see into which orifice. Was his dildoing her vagina or her asshole? Was it a real vagina or some type of surgical creation? The man was moving the dildo all the way in and out in a slow rhythmic pace. There was a slight smile on the man's face. Alfredo thought about moving closer to where he could see what orifice was being fucked, but his way was blocked by the crowd, and he was slightly put off by what he had seen. He looked away, over to his right.

There, two women, dressed in jeans and black t-shirts, were each standing on chairs, tying a skinny young man's hands to a rope that hung from the ceiling. When they finished, they stepped off the chairs and admired their handwork. The man looked more like a young boy, with some slight Asian feature about his face, but he had a black beard and mustache and was wearing a leather cap. Like the two women, he also wore a black t-shirt and jeans. His feet were flat on the floor and he was standing on his own weight. The two women had arranged the ceiling rope so that it just stretched the boy fully upright, his arms fully extended above his head, without lifting him at all above the ground.

The two women seemed satisfied with their handiwork. Wordlessly, as if in telepathic communication with each other, they turned their attention to undressing the boy. One of them removed his cap and then stepped back. The other woman pulled a small scissors from her back pocket and started to cut his black t-shirt off him. The boy simply stared straight ahead. When the t-shirt was completely cut, from the neck to the top of each arm and from the armpit down to the side, it simple fell from the boy and landed on the floor. Underneath the t-shirt the boy seemed to be wearing a black cloth tube, like a woman's tube top, that ran from under his arms, across his sternum and down to his waist. It fit tight against his body. The woman put the scissors back in her back pocket, and then taking both hands pulled the tube top down to the boy's waist.

Alfredo saw why the boy wore a tight tube top. Two breasts jumped out. The breasts were small and pointy. The woman then reached down and unbuckled the boy's belt, unzipped the zipper, and gave the pants a tug downward. They fell to his feet. Underneath, the boy was wearing red panties. The woman grabbed them and slowly pulled them down to the boy's feet. Alfredo looked at the thick black female pubic hair and the top outline of a vagina. This boy was a girl, tied there, completely naked except for the black tube top that was now wrapped around her waist like a cummerbund. Alfredo looked at the boy's face. There was the beard, full and thick and black as his/her pubic hair, neatly trimmed. It looked real to Alfredo. But there obviously was a young girl's body. Alfredo felt himself getting strangely excited by this. The girl's body seemed perfectly formed, with pink nipples, a flat stomach, small hips, and that bushy pubic hair.

One of the two women, the one with the scissors, had picked up a small whip from the floor and had stepped behind the "boy". She started to gently flick the ends of the whip across his back. The other woman just continued to watch, her arms folded across her chest, a look of approval on her face. The "boy" stared straight ahead, bracing him/herself for what was to come.

<u>Chapter 18</u>

"This is Susan Gilbert with our weekly show, *The Author's Corner*. And tonight, dear listeners, tonight we are indeed fortunate to have with us in the studio, four young writers whose essays, books, novels, and poems have detailed what some critics are calling the Beaten Generation, a generation of young, professional, outspoken, angry, profane, often pornographic, gay, lesbian, bisexual and transgender men and women."

Paul felt trapped. He *was* trapped. Trapped in a radio studio with an enthusiastic broadcaster and three idiots. He listened while the announcer introduced Wilson Concord, Michael Serrell, Amy Pearson, and, finally, him. Paul looked over to the corner of the studio where Marv was sitting. She was texting furiously on her cellphone, apparently oblivious to the agony that he was feeling. The announcer started asking questions.

"Michael Serrell, you are perhaps the best-known mentor to many young gay activists and professionals. As an openly gay Wall Street broker, you were often cited as a role model in the nineties for your ruthless style of gay group investing, one that forced companies to acknowledge and support gay issues or suffer the wrath of hundreds of well-organized gay stockholders that you had personally selected and trained. Your collection of essays, entitled *Capitalism Doggy-Style*, threw the gauntlet down for gay Wall Street investors. Some people complained that your treatise *Trick Towels and Real Estate* played a part in fueling the real estate bubble by encouraging gay couples to use their disposable incomes to flip as many houses as possible. Finally, your most recent book, *The Bareback Investor*, encourages people to get back into the stock market and take as many risks as they can, even in this volatile market. How do you handle it when people look to you as a spokesperson for a whole new force in gay economics?"

"Well, it hasn't been easy, Susan. But I am here today to say that there is a new voice in gay economics, a voice that may be beaten but isn't afraid to take the reality of gay life and use it as a metaphor and a roadmap for the new gay economy. As you know, my book, *Capitalism Doggy-Style* drew a parallel between the, well I'll be delicate because this is radio, but between the receptive gay male as a byproduct of the old-style capitalism, as the whore of capitalism if you will, and the more dynamic top gay male as the dominator of a new style of capitalism. As I like to say, bulls are tops, and bears are bottoms, but we're all gay and capitalism is here to stay. Either you're a top or a bottom, but either way, you're here to play. In my latest book, *The Bareback Investor*, I show the young novice investor, perhaps home alone doing e-trading on the internet, how to use his unique gay intuitions to uncover good investments."

What a crock of shit, Paul thought to himself. What am I doing here? How did I let Marv rope me into this?

"Well, Michael," the announcer was asking, "how do you respond to the criticism that using gay sex as a model for investment strategies is just metaphorizing?"

"Well, of course it's a metaphor, but that doesn't mean it's not accurate. Breeders, which is our term for straight people, use the same metaphors. When someone asks a breeder 'how'd you do today?' and he says, 'Oh I got screwed royally', he's not talking Sears hardware. He's saying he took it up the ass. Sorry, I probably shouldn't say that on radio, but that's what he means. When he says, 'I came out on top' he literally means it—he had an orgasmic day where he dominated someone else. I'm not creating the metaphor—it already exists. I'm just taking the metaphor and milking it for strategic value. The metaphor is valid. It comes out of our subconscious understanding of human interaction. It's more than a metaphor—it's a subconscious map that we can use to guide our investment strategy. If the stock market is just a symbolic archetype for group sex, then gay sex is a model for how to rip the pants off a good investment and plunder it. All I'm saying to gay men everywhere is: *use* the metaphor."

Paul's thoughts wandered off while Michael Serrell continued to pontificate on gay investment strategies. Paul considered his own investments. He still had some money left in savings. The royalty checks were still coming in, but each month's check was smaller than the last. Marv had told him that he had to get his new book finished within the next three months in order to capitalize on the success of *The Man Who Mistook his Hemorrhoid for a Clitoris.* Marv claimed that the public's memory was very short, and if he waited longer than three months, the public would forget him, and the second book would be harder to sell. To her credit, she had managed to get him a "right of first refusal" contract from his current publisher and an option contract with another publisher. She had tried, so she told him, to get an advance from his current publisher, but they were unwilling to do that. The one thing that bothered Paul was that Marv was totally uninterested in reading any of his chapters. He was convinced that no matter what he wrote, she would try and market it with the same frenetic energy as she did everything else. After all, she had arranged for him to appear on the radio with these three other authors, who had each published many more books than his solitary effort, but she made him promise to plug his second book...a book that he hadn't even finished writing. She even gave him lines to say: "Paul, let me write this down for you so you can memorize it. Tell them that *Zero Hotel* will make your hemorrhoid book seem like foreplay." Paul hated it that she always called *The Man Who Mistook his Hemorrhoid for a Clitoris* his "hemorrhoid book." But he never confronted her on it. He knew that she managed a bevy of writers, and that she had a reputation for getting their books published. Paul wanted to be among that group.

The announcer was now talking to Amy Pearson. "Amy, you've had three books on the New York Times Gay-Lesbian-Bisexual-Transgendered bestseller list. First was *Not With Tom Fudgepacker,* a brutally funny story of a hip Jewish housewife who discovers she's a lesbian and then murders her gay husband. Then there was the very successful *Innocent until Guilty,* the story of two lesbian lawyers who are lovers at night but on opposite sides of a sexual harassment trial during the day. And your latest book has just been published, and it's entitled *The Illesbianati,* and I understand it more of an exposé than a novel. Tell our listeners about your latest book."

Amy leaned forward to the microphone. Paul only wished the radio audience could see the Mohawk haircut and pierced eyebrows.

"I'd love to Susan. The Illesbianati is an actual society that has existed since before Christianity ever came into being. The Illesbianati originated on the Isle of Lesbos during the time of the ancient Greeks. However, because of the male-dominated society that existed then, and still exists now, the Illesbianati had to wield their power in secret. When Christianity came along, the Illesbianati saw their chance to extend their influence. In my book, I document how the Illesbianati founded the Catholic Church, and to this day controls the Vatican and the selection of Popes. One of the things that attracted me to the Illesbianati was their fantastic sense of humor. It was the Illesbianati's idea, for example, that catholic priests be celibate. It was also the Illesbianati's brilliant idea to create the concept of a convent, which the world thinks of as a place where devote nuns engage in endless prayers covered from head to toe in heavy robes. In fact, the opposite is true. Most convents have complete nudity behind the high walls. Convents are the Illesbianati's biggest recruiting tool. There, young nubile women engage in almost constant lesbian sex. I've seen this myself, at many convents."

"Fascinating. I know our readers will be eager to read this book."

Paul was working hard to keep his face muscles fixed in as neutral and as natural position as he could. The announcer was moving on.

"Our next two authors have written about the darker side of gay life. Wilson Concord burst upon the scene four years ago with his novel *Backdoor Trucker,* the story of a young truck driver who discovers his sexuality on the road.

He followed that up with *CB Buddy*, a controversial story of a truck driver who befriends a young boy in a wheelchair that he meets on the CB radio, a friendship that leads to tragic consequences for the truck driver. Then there was the romantic novel, *The Rig Stops Here*, the story of a truck driver on the run from the law, who changes his name and finds a job at a truck stop after he meets the short-order cook of his dreams. Most recently, Wilson Concord won this year's coveted Blue Velvet Best Gay Book award for his book, *Fag or Gag—Memoir of a Transgendered Truckstop Prostitute*. Tell me, Wilson, where do you get the inspiration for your stories?"

"Well, as you know Susan, before I was a writer, I used to drive the big rigs for a living. And I still find that, whenever I need inspiration, I can get in my pickup and just drive out of town. Drive for miles, with just the CB radio on. I find that the activity of driving seems to drain all the worries from my head, until my mind seems to open to new ideas. Sometimes I like to drive for days until I get a new idea for a book. Of course, the CB radio is a great help. Everyone always has an interesting story to tell. I especially like stopping at truck stops. Not only do they have the best food, and a place to shower and sleep after a couple of days of driving, but it's there that you can meet the most interesting people. I can spend days at a truck stop and just sit at a table and write about the people I meet there."

Suddenly the announcer had switched over to him and was talking about *The Man Who Mistook his Hemorrhoid for a Clitoris*. Paul couldn't exactly focus on what was being said because a loud buzzing had started in his ears, but he realized that he was being asked a question. He felt panic coming on.

"...and I'll pose the same question to you Paul as I asked Wilson: Where do you get the inspiration to write?"

"Well, to be honest, I don't know. I just write."

Somehow, hearing his own voice calmed him a bit. He went on: "I mean, I think searching for inspiration for a writer is like searching for love. You know how that goes, the more you consciously try and find love, the more elusive it becomes. Writing is like that. So, I guess I would say that I don't look for inspiration in order to write, but rather I just sit and write in order to find inspiration."

"Your book *The Man Who Mistook his Hemorrhoid for a Clitoris* dealt with some very dark themes. Your protagonist seemed almost suicidal at times. Were you trying to make a point about the oppression that gay men experience?

Paul did not like this question, although it made him think that maybe Susan had actually read the book. He decided not to answer the question directly. First of all, it was a stupid question. He certainly was not trying to make a point about gay oppression. Paul had never thought his protagonist was that gay. But secondly, he knew this radio show had a lot of gay listeners, and he didn't want to alienate any of them.

"Well, I would have to let the reader decide that. I would say, though, that everyone deals with dark issues every time they deal with the search for intimacy."

"And I understand you have a second book coming out in a few months. What is it called?"

Paul knew that Marv must have been the source of that question. But he did not know how he could have the book finished and published in a few months.

"The working title is *Zero Hotel.*"

"Tell us about it. Will it delve more into these intimacy issues, and will it be as graphic as your first book?"

Paul managed a little laugh. "Oh yes, I'm afraid it's quite graphic. *Zero Hotel* will make *The Man Who Mistook his Hemorrhoid for a Clitoris* seem like foreplay. But I'd rather not give the plot away right now."

"Well, I'm sure your readers will be looking forward to it. Let me ask Amy Pearson a question on the sexual politics of lesbian writing..."

Paul was glad the questioning was off him. He was

glad he didn't screw up the answers. But he felt an odd mixture of pride and shame that he had used the very quote that Marv had given him. Proud because he wanted to stay in her good graces, but shame that he was selling out to a marketing ploy.

Paul knew that marketing was just part of the business of selling books, but it made him feel like a charlatan to be pretending to be some kind of gay radical, some member of a cutting-edge gay writing league, just in order to sell books. He knew that he probably had sexual issues lurking inside, but who didn't? But what he wrote always surprised him, because they weren't based on his direct experience. He just wrote, and stuff came to him.

Paul looked over at Marv. She smiled at him and gave him a thumbs-up sign. He forced a smile back and waited for the next round of questions.

Chapter Sixteen:

Suddenly Alfredo heard a commotion from the back of the room. Out of a door marked Do Not Enter came two women in white t-shirts who were dragging a third girl across the floor. The girl being grabbed and pulled was shouting "No, No" but the two women pulling her had both her arms and were in control. The girl who was being dragged struggled hard. She had shoulder-length hair that had been dyed several different shades of red, as if someone had taken cans of spray paint to her head. Her hair was flipping back and forth as she resisted the two women. One of the women reached forward and grabbed her hair in a fist and shouted, "Stop resisting!" and pulled her hair violently back so the girl couldn't move her head.

Alfredo's entire body stiffened when he realized that the woman doing the hair pulling was Sandy. He started to take a step forward when he saw two monitors with their red name badges carrying some type of leather bench out to the women. This was not an assault—it was another "scene."

The bench was shaped like a large leather saddle with one end higher than the other. Sandy and the other woman dragged the red-haired girl to the bench and forced her to bend forward over the higher end. Sandy still held the red-haired girl's hair tightly in her fist and forced her head down against the leather of the bench while the other woman pulled a small rope from her pocket and tied the red-haired girl's right hand to the leg of the bench. Then the other woman took the girl's left hand from Sandy and tied it to the left leg of the bench with another short rope. The red-haired girl was now bent in half over the bench, her ass sticking in the air, and both her hands securely tied to the legs of the bench near the floor. Sandy and the other woman stood back to admire their handiwork. It was definitely Sandy, alright. That same black hair. Those same eyes. Alfredo was glad he was standing in a dark corner where he could just stare at her. Sandy and the other woman exchanged a few words. Then Sandy stepped forward, reached around the girl's pelvis to undo the girl's belt and pulled her blue jeans halfway down, exposing her ass and blue panties. Then Sandy straightened up and pulled the girl's panties down. The other woman had obtained two more short pieces of rope and bent down behind the red-haired girl and tied each of her ankles to the back legs of the bench. Because the back of the bench was wider than its front, the effect of tying the girl's legs was to spread her legs. Alfredo could make out her vagina and her asshole.

Sandy then took one step back and undid her own pants and let them drop to the floor. Underneath her pants, over her panties, she was wearing a strap-on black dildo, that was fully erect and sticking straight out. Sandy was taunting the red-haired girl and laughing. The other woman handed Sandy a small tube that looked like toothpaste and Sandy started unscrewing the cap.

"No, no," Alfredo heard the red-haired girl say, "Use my lubricant."

"What?" the other woman said.

*"Use **my** lubricant," the red-haired girl repeated. "I'm*

allergic to other lubes."

"Well," the other woman said snidely, "we should have thought of this earlier, shouldn't we have?"

"Please, use my lubricant. It's in my purse."

Sandy walked away and then returned in a moment with a small jar in her hand. Alfredo could hear Sandy and the other woman talking to each other to taunt the red-haired girl.

"Not very good planning, was it?"

"No, not thinking ahead. 'Use my personal lube.' What does she think this is, a catering service?"

"She thinks we're a catering service, well, my, my. That's going to cost her."

Nonetheless, Alfredo watched as Sandy opened the jar and inserted two fingers into the jar and scooped out some lubricant which she smeared all over the black dildo still sticking out from her pelvis. Then she scooped out another glob, placed the jar on the floor, walked up to the rear of the red-haired girl and reached between her legs. Alfredo could see Sandy sticking her fingers inside the girl's vagina and rubbing the lubricant all around. Then Sandy wiped her hand on the girl's thigh, stepped up right behind her, spread the girl's buttocks apart with her hands, and thrust her own pelvis forward to insert the black dildo into the red-haired girl. The girl cried out. Sandy started fucking her. The other woman stood there laughing.

Chapter 19

Paul looked at the clock. It was almost midnight. There was still a sip of wine left in the glass. He finished it and then reread what he had written. He got up from his computer desk and walked over to his easy chair and sat down. Where was this going? he wondered. Sandy has now turned into a dominant. She must be working there. But maybe not. Maybe she's just into that scene. But what was she doing with Leon Petroski? Was she just consenting to do a "scene" with him? Or did he pay her for it? Is that how she made her living? What does Alfredo do with this new knowledge? Once, Paul had thought about having Alfredo end up having sex with Sandy and accidently killing her. Now, that seemed like less of a possibility. What would happen in real life? Well, Paul thought, in real life nothing really happens. Maybe nothing happens to Alfredo. Maybe it just remains a weird mystery.

Something that had always bothered Paul was a comment his life coach had made about the fact that she thought he was more like Mamood than Alfredo. Maybe Mamood had something to say about all this.

Paul went back to his computer and reread the last few lines.

The girl cried out. Sandy started fucking her. The other woman stood there laughing.

Paul moved his hands to the keyboard.

Sandy had grabbed both sides of the girl's hips and was fucking her hard now. The girl was moaning. Alfredo felt so confused inside. Who was Sandy? Was this the same woman he had seen in the hotel video, the girl with the frightened eyes? Was this the same girl he had spent so much time trying to track down, trying to save? Alfredo felt ill. His head was pounding. He realized he was sweating. He broke his eyes away from the scene in front of him and turned toward the exit. He made his way along the wall and out of the "transmasculine room" and back into the main play room. The sounds of whips and paddles had reached a new volume level, but Alfredo did not look. He made his way through the crowd and out of the front door.

The night air was cool, almost cold, but felt so real. He felt relieved to be outside. The night had turned almost black. It took him a moment to orient himself as to where he was, but he got his bearings. He walked down the street to McDougal Street and turned left and headed to Vassar Street. Once there, he turned on to Victoria Street. Here he was back among well-lit shops and couples walking hand in hand. Although he was still trembling, Alfredo felt that he was back in the normal world again.

Chapter Seventeen:
The next day was Saturday and Alfredo was scheduled to work the night shift as usual. But Mamood had the day off. Alfredo called Mamood and asked if he could buy him dinner a little Ethiopian restaurant that Alfredo knew was Mamood's favorite, and if they could they meet about 2 hours before Alfredo's shift started.

"As long as you are paying, mon ami, I am at your service."

"Thank you, Mamood. I'll see you then."

Alfredo was already waiting at the table when Mamood arrived. He had ordered himself a vodka tonic and for Mamood, a Campari with soda.

"Buenas noches, mon ami."

"Bonsoir, mi amigo."

This had been their traditional greeting for many years, whenever they met over drinks, a greeting of respect for each other's culture. Also, whoever arrived first had to have drinks ready when the other arrived.

"Cheers, mon ami," Mamood said as he raised his glass.

"Cheers, Mamood."

"So, my friend, what causes you such pain that you have to offer to buy dinner for my listening ear? Is it that girl?"

"Yes, I'm afraid so."

"Let us order dinner, and then tell me what is troubling you."

Over dinner, Alfredo told Mamood what he had

happened, how he followed Sandy out of the store, along the streets, into the bondage and discipline club, about how he had joined the club in order to find out more, how he had sat in the dark and watched couples beat each other, and finally, how he had watched Sandy act out some girl's rape fantasy, how confused he was by what he saw, how he didn't know what to do next.

Mamood sat quietly after Alfredo had finished. Finally, he spoke.

"Well, my friend, I will tell you what I think. First, I think this girl Sandy is trouble. I think you need to let her go. You found out she is alive and that what you saw in the hotel was not her being a victim, but her playing a part, playing a role. Woman who play roles are dangerous. In my country, we have a saying. It's hard to translate, but when a man is asking about a certain woman's virtue, asking to find out if she would make a good wife, he will ask something that roughly means 'how is her face?' or 'how many faces does she have?' and if he she gets the reply of 'she has many beautiful faces' it means she cannot be trusted, that she acts differently with different men. Such women make for bad wives. But if he gets the reply of 'her face is kind', it means she is consistently trustworthy in all her interactions, and well, that is good. Such women make good wives. It seems to me that your Sandy has many beautiful faces. So, my first advice is to stop here. Don't go back to that place. Stop thinking about her. She is not your problem anymore. However, my second thought is, I understand the attraction. The problem with women with many beautiful faces is that they are intriguing, fascinating, and alluring because, well, because they are beautiful. Combine that beauty with sexual power, well, that's a combination that most men cannot resist. So, I understand that you may not be able to stop obsessing about her. A woman who is beautiful and has sexual power is a formidable opponent. Most men are helpless against that combination."

One of the reason Alfredo always valued Mamood's opinions is because Mamood had a way of seeing both sides of an issue without judging Alfredo's actions. Even when Alfredo had confessed the secret camera to him, Mamood did not condemn Alfredo's actions or, by implication, his desires.

"Yeah, you're probably right, Mamood. I just wish I could get to know her better."

"I don't think that is possible, mon ami. First of all, you would have to somehow meet her and get to know her. You know, you can't just say, 'Oh hello, I watched you have sex in the hotel and followed you here.' It just doesn't sound right."

Alfredo laughed.

"And second, mon ami, even if you did manage to contrive a meeting and a friendship, I would predict that you still would never get to know her. Beautiful women are like onions—you keep peeling off layer after layer and you never get to the center. It's not their fault. External beauty is a curse. Men start leering after them as soon as they hit puberty, so they learn to lie and deceive in order to handle all those adult advances. You would be better off finding a woman who was beautiful from the inside out... What was that saying you once told me? 'Behind every beautiful woman, there is a man who is sick of her shit.' I always thought that was funny, funny and yet sadly true. It may be your fate to see her again, I don't know. You may not be able to stay away from her, but women like that are, what is that expression here, a 'slippery slope'. If you go back once more to that place, you will go back again and again. My advice would be to try and stay away. Try not to think about her."

"Yeah, you're probably right, Mamood. You're probably right."

After dinner, Alfredo made his way back to the hotel. It was getting dark. The evening was cooler than usual, and he zipped his coat up. He was wrapped in thought and oblivious *to the other people on the sidewalk. He was thinking that he really had become obsessed with Sandy. Mamood was right. When he had to actually describe out loud to Mamood what he had been doing ever since he saw Sandy in the hotel that night, it did sound like a man obsessed. He had been spending all his free time trying to track her down, learn her identity, pinpoint where she lived... hell, he had followed her like a stalker, lied about his identity to get into that club just to watch her. These were the acts of a crazy man. Yet he had to admit that Mamood was also right about why he was so obsessed. It was her beauty. Her eyes, the same eyes that looked so frightened in the hotel camera lens, but that looked so cold and menacing while she fucked that red-hair girl... Alfredo found those eyes so captivating. And that body! Alfredo knew that putting a camera in people's hotel room was wrong, but he had always justified it to himself as compensation for his impoverished love life. "At least I can have this," is what he used to tell himself. But that was before he confessed the camera to Mamood. Now that Mamood knew his secret, he had been too embarrassed to use it again. He had taken it home and put it in a drawer. But he knew he would put it back to use in a second if he could watch Sandy having sex again. There was something about her that overrode his common sense, overrode his history. He had never followed someone, never stalked someone before.*

He got to the hotel, entered through the usual side door, down the hall, into the room marked "Employees Only", hung up his raincoat, and got his vest from the locker. He hoped it would be a quiet night. He really did not feel like talking to people tonight.

<u>Chapter 20</u>

The next morning, Paul slept in late. He had stayed up past three a.m., writing. He woke with a crappy hungover headache. His mood worsened when he went to the refrigerator and discovered there was no coffee. He considered just pouring water through yesterday's coffee grounds but discarded that idea after he examined them in the coffee pot's basket. He washed his face and decided to go out for coffee.

The lunch crowd was just arriving at the Starbucks near his apartment. He knew he looked like hell, so his original plan was to get his coffee to go. But he saw an empty table outside as he walked out, and the day was unusually sunny and warm, so Paul sat down at the table. It was in the sun and that felt nice. His brain was still moving slow. The coffee was good, and it felt good to sit outside.

Paul thought about what Mamood had said to Alfredo about beauty. Mamood seemed to be saying that all beautiful women could not be trusted because their beauty had foisted them into the adult world of sexual politics while they were still children and so they only learned childlike manipulative ways of dealing with those sexual politics. And because they were beautiful, they got away with it. Paul thought of beautiful women he had known. Certainly, they could not have all been manipulative, but he had to admit, they were always unpredictable. At least, *he* had been unable to predict their actions. Paul had always assumed it was his inability to understand them, rather than their way of coping with growing up as objects of beauty.

Paul sipped his coffee and watched the different women coming in and out of Starbucks. Most were with someone else, either male or female, but occasionally one would be walking alone. Paul watched a particularly cute blond walk into the coffee shop. She was tall and slender, with her blond hair falling across her face. She didn't make eye contact with him, but she walked like someone who knew she was being watched, being admired. Paul looked away and thought how tough it must be to always be an object of desire, an object of someone else's attention, to always feel like you were being observed and judged. How different that was from him, and from all the characters in his writing. All the men he wrote about just wanted to be alone, to move unobserved through the world. They yearned for love and human contact, but they could not stand to be in the light. They moved in the dark. And life granted them darkness. His life coach was right when she said they were all parts of him, because that's how he was. Maybe not as extreme as his fictitious men, but it was just a question of degree.

The warm sun seemed to melt his headache. Or perhaps it was the coffee. The blond girl came out of the Starbucks carrying a coffee and a small bag. Paul watched her walk away. He watched her hips, the curve of her buttocks. He imagined the damp and blond pubic hair between her legs. What was wrong with him, he thought, that he always felt so detached, not just from women but from everyone? Why couldn't he start a conversation with a nice blond woman like that, at a Starbucks, on a sunny day? Paul could hear Mamood's voice chuckling in his head, as if to say, "Mon ami, it does not work that way. If you were able to easily connect with women, you would never write a word. It is the fact that you are so inhibited that gives me life. That's what makes you write."

Maybe this second book would help him meet women, Paul thought. Before his first book had been published, he had always assumed that being a published author would mean women would be drawn to him, as if life would be suddenly changed, like winning the lottery. He used to have a particular fantasy of being at a cocktail party, and women whispering when they saw him, "Oh that's the author. Let's go meet him." Of course, it did not happen that way at all. In fact, nothing happened. After *The Man Who Mistook his Hemorrhoid for a Clitoris* was published, everything stayed exactly the same. Initially he did get many strange letters from lonely gay men, some who enclosed pictures of their erect penises. But he threw those letters away. There were no publication parties, people did not seek his autograph in the street, and he heard no women whispering nice things about him in bars. Everything stayed the same. But maybe *Zero Hotel* would be different. Maybe because it was not gay sex... But then again, maybe not. Maybe he would just get weird letters from dominatrixes or submissives. Maybe no matter how many books he published, things would stay exactly the same. That was a depressing thought.

"Well, mon ami, first things first," he heard Mamood's voice in his head. "You have to finish writing your second book before you can get it published." Paul nodded his head, and said to himself, "Yes, Mamood, you are right. You are always right. Let's you and I get back to work."

Chapter Eighteen:

Alfredo had that dream again. He was raping Sandy. This time her hands were tied to the headboard. Her mouth was gagged tight like it always was. Tears were flowing out of her eyes. Alfredo was inside her and raping her hard. With every thrust her body tensed and she squeezed her eyes shut.

Alfredo woke in a sweat. He had a hard erection. The sheets were tangled. He must have been thrashing about. He felt sick. Why did he keep having this same dream? He sat up in bed and put his head in his hands.

Details of the dream came back to him. He had been following Sandy on a dark street. He had run up behind her and struck her on the head with a short metal pipe. He felt the thud of the pipe against her skull. She fell to the sidewalk. Then the scene changed and she was hanging by her hands in the playroom of the Friends of BDSM building. The room was empty except for him and Sandy. She was naked, hanging a few feet off the ground. Her mouth was gagged. There was that terrorized look in her eyes. Alfredo had a short whip in his hands. The leather ends of the whip had pieces of sharp glass woven into the leather. He was whipping her back hard. Her back was covered with blood. Every whip cut her flesh.

The images kept cascading through Alfredo's mind. He stepped around to face Sandy and started whipping her front, cutting into her breasts and shoulders. Her screams were muffled by the gag. He was killing her. Then she was tied to the bed. No blood. Just rape. Hard and brutal. She was wet. He felt each stroke around his cock. It felt good. It felt very good.

Alfredo stood up and almost ran to the bathroom. He turned on the light and splashed water on his face. "What's wrong with me?" he thought. He stood up and looked at himself in the mirror. His eyes were puffy, but he looked like himself. He didn't look like an evil man. He did not look possessed by the devil. He did not look like a rapist.

He walked back into the bedroom and turned on the light. He put on his bathrobe and went into the kitchen. He turned on every light along the way. He poured himself a glass of wine and went back into the bedroom, but he left all the lights on. He propped the pillows up and sat back in the bed with his wine and tried to make sense out of this.

Two weeks had gone by since he'd seen Sandy at the BDSM club, but he'd had the dream three times since then. Some of the locations changed, some of the details were different, but it was always a brutal rape, he was always hurting her, and she was always terrified. But the worst part was, it always felt good. He was always enjoying the rape.

Alfredo sat there in bed, with the lights on, taking gulps of his wine, thinking about this. Staying away from Sandy was just making things worse. He thought about her every day. At work, he was distracted, just going through the motions. One day, he even called in sick, and got Tony to handle his shift. Not seeing her, not knowing more about her seemed to be driving these bad dreams. Maybe if he were to see her again, maybe even talk to her...something... he had to do something to make her real. To get her out of his head. It was driving him crazy. He didn't understand it. He finished his glass of wine and got up and went into the kitchen and poured another.

<u>Chapter 21</u>

"I have no idea where the story is going." Paul was talking to his life coach. "Now Alfredo is starting to have dreams of raping Sandy. I don't know why he's having these dreams. I get the sense he wants to act on them, but that scares me. I sorta identify with Alfredo, you know, I always feel like he's one step ahead of me, but now I don't know where he's going."

"Is Alfredo going to see Sandy again?"

"Oh yes, I'm sure of that."

"How does he feel about her?"

Paul had to think about this for a bit. "Well, he's always been mesmerized by her, seduced by her beauty and her sexuality... but that's not really a feeling because he doesn't know her as a person. She's just an object to him, not an object like a rock, but you know, just a form, an apparition, an image. He's never even talked to her, so he doesn't have any true feelings yet, just desires.

"And how is that like the relationship you have with women?"

Paul felt his cheeks reddened. He hated it when his life coach turned the tables on him like this. She would guide him along on the book, encourage him to talk about the characters, and suddenly turn the tables and make him look at his own life. It always made him defensive.

"Well, you know it's like my life," he said.

"Tell me how."

Paul rolled his eyes. "Well, obviously, I can't get close to women, so I always view them from a distance. I don't know how to talk to them, so I never approach them."

"Hmmmm, you know, Paul, I've never viewed it working quite that way. You see it as *you* not knowing how to talk with *them,* as you lacking some verbal skills, along the lines of patter, you know, of having a good rap or a good opening line. But I see it more as a control issue, as you not letting women talk to you. Most of the time, in real life, Paul, women are the ones who make the first move. We do it subtly and most men aren't aware of it. But I suspect that when a woman tries to talk to you, you shut her out. I suspect you don't stay in the moment and listen and respond to a woman. I suspect you make up some excuse to shut the conversation down before it starts. I don't mean to oversimplify it, but if I were to oversimplify it, I would say that in order to stay in the moment and just talk to a woman, you have to remain vulnerable because you have to reveal yourself, and you don't like to lose control, and in being alone, you're in control."

Paul sat quietly and stared at the floor.

Chapter Nineteen:

It was Alfredo's day off. He felt agitated all day long, waiting for night to come. Finally, when it was dark, he took a cab to the corner of Victoria and McDougal streets. His heart was pounding as he walked the two blocks to the Center for Friends of BDSM Club. Alfredo was not sure what he was going to do. He did not even know if the place was open tonight or even if he would have the nerve to enter. When he got there, he saw several cars parked in the lot. He walked up to the door and tried it. It was unlocked. He walked inside.

There was the same counter he had seen before. There were the same chairs and the small table that held brochures. Lorraine was behind the counter. She smiled as if she recognized him.

"Hello." She said.

"Hello," he replied, as he handed her his membership card. "Can you tell me, please, what event is happening tonight?"

She took his card and ran it through a small scanner. "Well, Roberto," she said, reading his name off a computer screen, "tonight we have a demonstration of fire play. After that, there's a demonstration of rope tying. The fire play demonstration starts in about twenty minutes and costs five dollars. The rope tying demonstration is ten dollars. There's a description of each on the flyers on the table."

"Ah, let me look." Alfredo went over to the table and read the flyers. Evidently, fire play involved teasing your submissive partner with fire. Alfredo was not sure he saw any erotic sense in that. Rope tying involved intricate knots to tie someone up with. Neither event interested him. It looked as if the evening would be a total waste. Alfredo was thinking of what excuse he would give to Lorraine when he glanced up at the bulletin board hanging over the table. There were many cards thumbtacked into the bulletin board. All of them were of a sexual or BDSM nature. The left side were products: Whips for sale. Collars for sale. Cages for sale. On the right side were services: Spankings, Discipline Training, and the like. Alfredo perused the list of services: Spankings for fat women, spankings by fat women, whippings by men, "water sports" training, oral training, anal training... But suddenly Alfredo stopped. There was a card with Sandy's picture on it. It read "dominatrix/submissive training $100/hr". There was a phone number at the bottom of the card. It was a different number than the one he'd found on the matchbook cover. Alfredo grabbed one of the fire play flyers and, keeping his back to Lorraine, quickly wrote Sandy's phone number down. Then he pretended to read the flyer as he turned around and walked back to Lorraine. Some other people had come in and were talking to her. Alfredo walked out into the nighttime.

His heart was pounding as he walked along. He felt as if he were trapped. He wished he hadn't seen her card. It was one thing to watch her on a camera or stand safely in the dark corner of the BDSM club and watch her act out a sex scene. But to actually call her, to actually go meet her, to talk with her... he was not sure he could do this. He would obviously have to pretend that he wanted to be trained in either domination or submission, which means he would have to either let her tie him up or tie her up... let her whip him or whip her... he was not sure he could do this.

By the time he got back to his apartment, he felt as if he might get sick. He sat down and took the fire play flyer out of his coat pocket and placed it on the table in front of him. There was her phone number. Should he call? Could he call? Should he write out a whole script of what to say? What would he say? He felt cold. He got up and went into his tiny kitchen and poured a glass of wine and came back and sat down and stared at the flyer again. He took sips of his wine and tried to imagine the conversation. He couldn't. He tried to imagine meeting her. Those eyes. To be standing in front of her looking into those eyes. He remembered terror in her eyes when Leon Petroski was forcing the butt end of his whip into her vagina. He still could not reconcile that image with the fire he saw in her eyes when she was fucking that girl with the strap-on dildo at the BDSM club. Maybe Mamood was right. He should let it go. Nothing good can come of this. A woman can't possibly do all these things and be right in the head. He should not get involved with her. What Mamood said made such sense. Alfredo felt calmer. He looked at her phone number on the flyer again. Then he looked up at his little apartment. It had two little windows on one wall. On the other wall he had hung a painting of a cathedral that somehow reminded him of his boyhood home. There was the sofa that folded out into his nighttime sleeping bed. There was the bright overhead light, light that lit the room where only he lived, where no lover ever came to visit him. He looked at the four dingy walls. He reached over and picked up the phone. His hands trembled as he dialed. He felt unable to catch his breath. The phone rang. It rang again. It rang a third time. He reached over to push the handset button down to hang up, when a women voice answered.

"Dominatrix Training."

Was it Sandy? He couldn't tell.

"Uh, yes, I uh wanted to make an appointment."

"And you referred you?"

"Referred me?"

"Yes, I don't make appointments unless you are referred." She sounded cold.

"Well, no, no one referred me. I just saw your card tonight at the Friends of BDSM Center."

"Oh, are you a member there?"

"Yes."

"That's different. There's a 10% discount for members. What's your member number?"

"Uh, let me look." Alfredo pulled out his wallet and found his membership card. He read her his membership number.

"Okay, hang on a second."

After about ten seconds she came back.

"Roberto?"

He was shocked he knew his fake name. How secure was his membership information?

"Yes, that's me."

"I see you're a new member at the club."

"Yes, I am. I, I'm just a beginner."

"Okay, for club members, I offer group demonstrations at the club. It's part lecture, part demonstration. We have a special dungeon in the basement for those sessions. We limit the group to 4 people and everyone gets a chance to participate as either a dominant or a submissive. Or, if you prefer, I do private sessions, just one on one, with a two hour minimum"

Alfredo certainly didn't want to be in a group where he would be watched by other people while he did whatever "participation" occurred at those sessions.

"I think I would prefer a private session," he said

"How is next Tuesday at three o'clock for you?"

"No, I have to work then. Do you have anything next Wednesday?"

"I could see you at two o'clock next Wednesday. I take it that you are new to this type of experience."

"Yes, I am."

"Okay, the first session for new players is usually an

introduction to both dominatrix and submission practices."

"Okay."

"It's a two hour session, at one hundred dollars an hour."

"Okay."

"Cash only. No credit cards, no checks."

"Okay."

"Do you have any questions?"

"No, oh wait, where do I come to."

She gave him the address—315 Vassar Street, Apartment B1, the basement apartment.

"Any other questions?"

"Uh, do I need to bring anything?"

"No, I'll tell you what to do when you get there. Any other questions?"

"No."

"Okay, see you Wednesday."

There was a click on the other end. She had hung up. Alfredo hung up his phone and stared into space. Had he just made an appointment with Sandy? Was it in fact Sandy or someone else. Damn. What had he actually done? He suddenly felt dampness under his arms and realized that he was sweating profusely.

Chapter 22

Paul was startled to hear his life coach ask, "What's wrong?" even before he sat down.

"Nothing," Paul said automatically.

His life coach stared at him.

After a moment, she asked again. "What's wrong?"

Paul looked down at his hands. "Well, this seems weird, but I think I'm scared."

"Say more."

"Well, the book has progressed to a point where Alfredo is going to meet Sandy. In the book, he's found an S&M business card with her name and number and he's made an appointment for some type of sexual experience, and he's on his way to see her, and I don't know what he's going to do, and I'm scared that someone is going to get hurt. I know that sounds silly. I shouldn't care about them. It's only a story."

"It's not just a story, Paul. It's your story."

"Yeah I know it's my story. I'm writing it, but I mean, they're just characters, fiction, and it doesn't make any sense that I would be scared of something that I know is fiction."

"No, Paul. When I say it's your story, I mean it's *your* story. It's the story *of your* life. They aren't just fictional characters you are making up. If something scary is building up in the book, it's because something scary is building up in your life. What's going on in the book *is* what's going on in your life."

"But I'm not into S&M," he said.

"Neither is Alfredo. But what you are into is fear, inaction, and desire from a distance. And so is Alfredo. And now Alfredo is putting himself into a position where he will have to come out of his safe place and give up control in order to connect with someone he desires. Which means that, on some psychic level, you are struggling with those same issues."

Paul felt his cheeks burning hot. He hated his life coach when she was direct. He sat without moving, tried to control his breathing, and tried to think of a rebuttal. Finally, he said, "Nothing is happening in my life that's like what's happening in the story."

"Well, that's only true in the sense that there's not a real person acting like Sandy in your life right now. But on a psychic level, Paul, on an emotional level, on a subconscious level, what we've been dealing for months, well in fact, from the beginning, is how you approach life, how you approach women, how you handle the fear of being in a relationship. Some part of your subconscious is trying to integrate something very important right now. And you won't be aware of it until after it's integrated, but we're getting a preview of it in your book. That's the great thing about writing, Paul, and particularly the type of automatic writing that you do. It's like being able to see what normally can't be seen. It's like a portal to the unconscious. Did you bring pages of what you wrote this week?"

"Yes."

"Read them to me."

Chapter Twenty:

Wednesday was several days away. Alfredo's appointment with Sandy seemed unreal, like a dream. It seemed like a distant event until Monday afternoon, when he realized he still didn't have a clue what he was going to do with her. Was he going to let her tie him up? Was he going to tie her up? He just didn't know. He called in sick on Tuesday. He bought two bottles of wine and stayed in his apartment all day. He tried to picture himself holding a whip, flaying at her white buttocks. The whip seemed to rip her skin. She would have screamed but her mouth was gagged. He tried to picture himself being handcuffed to a bed, while she dripped hot wax on him. In that fantasy, he was gagged. But nothing seemed to fit. No image felt right. He felt miserable. He kept returning to the image from the first video he had seen of her. Her eyes. She wasn't faking that. Alfredo knew what he saw in her eyes when Leon Petroski jammed the dildo inside her was terror. But obviously this was her job. How could she do this? Could he do that to her? Could she do that to him? Alfredo felt totally alone and totally confused.

By the time Wednesday noon came, Alfredo was in a total panic. He felt he should just cancel the appointment, but he couldn't bring himself to dial her number. He had a knot in his stomach that would not go away. He managed to eat lunch but had to go to the bathroom several times. He looked at his face in the mirror. His skin looked cold and clammy. Yet despite his panic, he managed, quite deliberately, to go to the bank and withdraw six hundred dollars. He asked for, and received, six hundred-dollar bills. Two bills he folded and placed in his left front pocket. The other four bills he folded over very tightly and placed them in the coin pocket of his right front pants pocket. He knew from the few times he had spent with Cecile that no matter what price was negotiated at the beginning, there was always a higher price to pay at the end.

Somehow, as two o'clock approached, he began the process of heading over to her apartment. He decided to walk. Despite the nausea, he somehow felt detached from his body, as if he was watching himself take each step. His legs felt as heavy as bags of sand, yet they kept making each step on their own. He knew he had to keep walking towards her apartment. He knew that if he stopped even for a second, he would chicken out and turn around. He wanted to see her face to face at last, yet he still did not know why. He arrived at 315 Vassar Street and tried to press the door buzzer for apartment B-1. His finger missed button the first time, slid off the button the second time, but finally connected the third time.

He waited for a reply. His face flushed hot as each second passed. Where was she? Was there no one home? Should he turn and leave now? Should he push the button again? More seconds passed. Then the small speaker crackled as a woman's voice said, "Yes?" He couldn't quite tell if it was the same voice he had talked to on the phone.

"Uh, uh, I have a two o'clock appointment," he stammered.

The door to his left buzzed and he opened it. He walked down a hall past several utility rooms, then down a few steps at the end of the hall and then he found the door marked B-1. His heart was pounding. He wiped his hands on his trousers and knocked lightly. The door opened. Standing before him was not Sandy or any other woman. It was Leon Petroski.

Alfredo felt his heart stop. Could he run? His legs weren't moving. His mind began to race. How could Leon Petroski be here? Was this some kind of set up? Did they know what he was doing?

But before Alfredo could think another thought, he heard Leon say, "You have an appointment?"

"Jes, jes I do." Alfredo used his thickest accent. Maybe Leon wouldn't recognize him.

Leon Petroski was looking at a piece of paper.

"Two o'clock?"

"Jes."

"Roberto?"

"Jes."

"Okay." Leon grabbed several papers from a small table by the door and handed them to Alfredo. "Come with me."

Alfredo stepped inside, careful to avert his gaze from the large man. They walked down the hallway into a large living room.

"Fill out those forms. There's a pen on the table." Alfredo took the papers over to a sofa by the table and sat down and read them. They were more disclaimers, indicating that he was an adult and was there for educational purposes only and wished to be instructed in various artistic forms of bondage and discipline and not there for sexual gratification.

"I'll be right back." Leon Petroski said and walked past Alfredo and disappeared behind one of several doors on the other side of the room. As soon as Leon Petroski was out of sight, Alfredo considered whether he should run out the door. He knew that this would be his last chance to escape. He should run, he knew. But he couldn't. The last thing he felt now was lust. But for some reason, or for something that had no reason, he had to stay. He signed each of the documents "Roberto Rahula" without reading any more of them and walked into the living room and sat down.

A moment later, Leon Petroski came back in.

"Finished?"

"Jes." Alfredo handed him the papers. Leon Petroski towered over him looking at each page, making sure Alfredo had signed.

"Okay," he grunted and folded the papers."The introductory lesson is two hundred dollars."

Alfredo reached in his front pocket and retrieved the two one-hundred-dollar bills he had carefully put there earlier and handed them to Leon Petroski.

Leon took them with another grunt of acceptance and said, "Wait here."

And then Leon Petroski left the room. Alfredo was alone. He looked around. This would be described more like an Elizabethan parlor or sitting room than a living room. Nicely furnished with antiques. Formal landscapes paintings on the wall. A marble bust on a table in the corner. Very impersonal. Even the sofa where Alfredo was sitting was formally uncomfortable the way that antiques are. This all added to the surreal buzzing inside his head. What the hell was he doing here?

But as the minutes went by, Alfredo began to calm down. He took several deep breaths and told himself he simply had to keep his wits about him. He saw a card advertising lessons; he had called and made an appointment; he was simply here for an introductory lesson in an esoteric form of personal art that he had a legal right to pursue. Clearly, Leon Petroski had not recognized him from that night in the hotel so long ago. Surely Sandy would not recognize him. Alfredo had learned years ago that no one ever remembers "the help" in America. Servants are always fungible.

He heard a door open behind him, a different door than the one Leon Petroski had disappeared into. He turned around and looked. Sandy was standing in the doorway, wearing full-length white bathrobe. She was tightening the knot in the front. She looked up at him. She seemed so beautiful. Her short black hair framed her face... and those large eyes... She looked so young and innocent. He felt himself begin to panic again.

"Roberto?"

"Jes."

"Come on in."

Alfredo got up off the sofa and walked into the room. The lighting was soft, but he could clearly see that this room was as sparse and utilitarian as the front room had been ornate. There were no pictures on the wall. In fact, there weren't even any windows in the walls. No furniture except for two wooden chairs in the middle of the room a few feet apart facing each other. Various pieces of rope were strewn on the floor by the chairs. Beyond the chairs was a bed with large metal rings bolted into the headboard and what looked like similar metal rings at the footboard. On the wall to the left was a large wooden X formed out of two beams of wood bolted together. The wooden X also had metal rings bolted in every foot or so, up and down the length of each beam. Next to the chest was a small wooden chest. Other than these objects, the room was empty.

"Have a seat," Sandy said, gesturing to the chairs in the middle of the room. "Make yourself comfortable."

Alfredo sat stiffly in one of the chairs and watched her. She walked over to the bed and took off her long white bathrobe. Underneath she was wearing some type of leather bustier and corset, with leather panties. There were metal studs every few inches on the bustier and corset.

She came over and sat in the chair directly across from him. Alfredo had never been this close to her. He looked at her face, her white skin, her black hair. He saw the black mascara and a mole above her left eye. He wanted to see the color of her eyes but there was not enough light. He realized she was talking to him.

"The introductory session is a two-hour session. I'm not going to ask you what experience or training you've had in S&M because it's not relevant. All new slaves must take the introductory session no matter what training they've had. The purpose of the introductory session is for me to make an initial determination of whether you will eventually be a slave or a master. For the first hour you will be my slave. You will not speak unless spoken to. You will listen to everything I say. You will submit to everything I do. Do you understand?"

"Jes."

"The most important thing to remember about any master-slave relationship or any bondage relationship is that it's about trust. We can allow ourselves to be masters or slaves, we can allow ourselves to be tied up, to totally give up control because we trust our partner totally. It's that trust that allows us to put ourselves totally in the other person's hands, allows them to whip us, to abuse us, to penetrate us, because we know that the partner is never going to violate us. The master-slave relationship is a sacred relationship built on absolute devotion to the other person. To submit to the pain of the whip is not pain at all. It's an act of surrender to the other person. And that's what makes it so pleasurable. It has nothing to do with pain. Slaves don't want to be tied up and whipped because they want pain—they do it because they want total surrender. And total surrender can only happen when there is total trust. It's an act of faith. So, for the first hour of this introductory lesson, your only job is to trust me, to surrender to me. That's the only thing that you are to focus on—trusting me. And to accomplish that, you have to listen to every single thing I say, and follow every command, or else you will be punished. Do you understand, slave?"

"Jes."

"Good. Take off your shirt. I'm going to tie you up."

Alfredo unbuttoned his shirt and removed it and let it fall to the floor. Sandy stood up, stepped behind him, picked a short piece of rope from the floor, grabbed both his wrists and with a quick motion secured them tightly together behind his back. Then she tied both ends of the rope to different rails of the chair so that he could not move his arms in any direction. Then she came around in front of him and took another piece of rope and tied his ankles to the front legs of the chair. Finally, she took another piece of rope and quickly looped it around his chest and torso and around the back of the chair three or four times and tied a knot directly in front of his chest.

Sandy walked around him inspecting the ropes. Alfredo was completely immobilized. He was amazed at how fast she *had done that. The ropes were tight but not hurting him. He felt, for the first time that day, a moment of peace come upon him, like a wave it washed over him. He felt himself relaxing into the chair. He realized that his breathing was slow and easy. He realized that... he felt comfortable.*

She came around the front and sat down in her chair and looked at him. "How do you feel, slave?"

Alfredo looked at her and paused. He had a sense that nothing bad was going to happen to him. So, he said, "Safe... I feel safe."

Sandy's eyebrows went up. "Really?"

She reached out and slapped him hard across the cheek. The sound of the slap surprised Alfredo, and it stung. Although he knew that she had not actually hurt him, it still made him angry. He turned his head back and glared at her.

"You didn't have to do that, Sandy."

"I'll do whatever I ..." she blurted but stopped short and stared at him. "How do you know my name?"

Alfredo felt his heart instantly begin to pound fast. "I, I, well, it was on your card."

She glared at him. "No, it's not. Tell me the truth. How do you know my name?"

Alfredo decided to stick to his quick lie. "At the Center, where I first saw your card. Someone had handwritten Sandy on it. I just assumed that was your name."

She reached out and slapped him across the face again, but this time it was much harder and much more painful.

"You're lying," she shouted. "I go there every day. There's nothing written on my card. Who are you and how do you know my name?"

Alfredo pulled on the ropes with his arms, but he was locked in tight. He looked down at the floor. He was caught. "You came to my hotel."

"What?!"

"I work at this hotel. You and Leon Petroski came there about two months ago and rented a room. I thought

you were in danger. Then you disappeared, and I thought he had killed you. I tried to find you. Then, I saw you a couple of weeks ago at that bondage center, and then I saw your card."

She stared at him and said nothing. Then suddenly, she stepped behind him and started to quickly untie the ropes that bound him. He could feel her hurrying. As she was untying the knots she leaned her head right next to his ear and whispered, "You need to get out of here!" There was a sense of fear in her voice.

Suddenly Alfredo understood. How could he be so stupid? He looked at the walls, and then up at the light fixture in the ceiling. There it was, in the middle of the light fixture, where the metal attached to the ceiling, the small hole that meant that there was a camera aimed straight at him.

Sandy pulled the ropes off him and tossed them to the floor. Alfredo stood up, feeling suddenly cold. Sandy reached down and grabbed his shirt from the floor and threw it at him. "Get out of here now!" she hissed.

Suddenly the door burst open and Leon Petroski was standing there.

<u>Chapter 23</u>

Paul's shoulders ached from hunching over the keyboard. He felt a headache coming on from staring at the small computer screen for hours. He realized that he had not typed a new sentence for at least ten minutes. He got up, stretched, and went into the kitchen. It was almost one o'clock in the morning. There was some wine left in the bottle that on the counter. He poured himself another glass.

His life coach had said that it all would become clear to him the more he wrote. She claimed that if he could just finish the book, that somehow it all would make sense, that he would see how his life and Alfredo's and Mamood's and Leon's and Sandy's were all connected. He hoped she was right, but so far, he was in the dark. He had known women like Sandy of course, beautiful and crazy, usually dramatic or in horrible situations, and almost always flirtatious. But they had always ignored him, preferring to entice and ensnare the bigger men, the sports jocks, the successful men, the lawyers, the doctors. Paul remembered one such woman at college who drove him crazy. She wore outfits to class that seem to mold to her body, and when she walked by him, her scent was exquisite and intoxicating. He always felt like such a loser when she was around. She ended up as a victim in a domestic fight with some professor's assistant who tried to throw her off his balcony one night. The police came and arrested him. The story around campus was that he had caught her having sex with some other guy. He got fired of course. Paul didn't see her around much after that, but he heard that she testified against the guy and then transferred to some other school. But he saw her in a coffee shop about three months later, sitting with some new guy, laughing at something he said. Her clothes were still molded to her body. He still loved the sound of her voice. His feelings for her made no sense to him. Later he heard she went back with the professor's assistant. That was decades ago. Nobody's lives made any sense to him.

He refilled his glass and walked back to his computer.

Chapter Twenty-One:
Leon stood there in the door. His face was red, and he looked very angry. In his right hand was a metal pipe about a foot long.

"Leon, no! He's not the one!" Sandy yelled and moved towards him, but Leon took two steps forward, cocked his right arm back and just as she reached him, he swung the pipe hard and fast across the space in front of him right towards her. Sandy's arms were extended out and the pipe caught her under her right arm, right on her ribcage. There was a loud crack and she went careening over backwards against the side of the room. Alfredo heard her cry out as

the back of her head hit the wall just as her ass hit the floor. Leon didn't even look at her but continued moving toward Alfredo. Alfredo picked up the chair and tried to push it into Leon's middle, using it as a shield. He was able to stop Leon's forward momentum for an instant.

Alfredo yelled out, "ARE YOU FUCKING NUTS? STOP THIS!" but Leon raised the pipe over his head and smashed it down towards where Alfredo's hands were holding the chair. Alfredo pulled his hands back at the last moment. The force of the pipe hitting the chair broke the wooden back as it ripped the chair out of Alfredo's control. Leon cocked the pipe back to his left and swung it across his body towards Alfredo's head, but Alfredo jumped backwards, and the pipe missed his face by inches. Leon then pulled the pipe straight back, moved forward, and thrust it like a dagger toward Alfredo's middle. Alfredo stepped back but not quite far enough. The very tip end of the pipe got him in the sternum and cut into his flesh. It hurt. Leon pulled the pipe back and thrust again, but this time Alfredo was able to deflect it with his left arm and grabbed Leon's forearm. But the momentum of the thrust put Leon closer to Alfred. Alfredo's fist went straight to Leon's face. Alfredo was aiming for his jaw but hit him square in the nose instead.

"Eeeoooh!" Leon yelled. Leon stepped back and grabbed his nose with his left hand. Blood was spurting out between his fingers. Leon looked at his hand in disbelief. Alfredo knew this would be his only opening. He kicked Leon as hard as he could right between his legs. He felt his foot go up deep into Leon's genitals.

Leon screamed and fell to his knees. He still held onto the pipe, but it was clear he wasn't going anywhere.

Alfredo leaned against the wall, trying to catch his breath. It hurt to breathe. He looked down at his chest. Blood was oozing out of a perfect circle in the flesh of his sternum where the pipe had cut him. He wiped the blood away with his hand. The cut was not deep, but his sternum ached. He grabbed his shirt off the floor where he had dropped it and put it on. Blood started to stain the front of his shirt, but he did not care.

Leon was still on his knees but straining to talk, "I'm going to kill you... I'm going to kill you."

"Leon, no."

Alfredo looked over. Sandy was crawling on the floor toward Leon. "Leon, listen to me," she was saying. "He's not the one. That's not him."

Leon moved his head to the side and looked at Sandy.

"What?" he said.

"That's not him."

"Who is he then?" Leon said.

"I don't know, but it's not him. Look at him."

Leon lifted up his head and looked at Alfredo then put his head down.

Sandy had reached Leon and put her arm around him.

"You see darling, it's not him."

Sandy gently pulled the pipe out of Leon's grasp and let it roll away. Leon covered his genitals with both hands and put his head to the floor and moaned while Sandy held him.

"I'm not who?" Alfredo demanded.

"None of your business," Sandy said.

"None of my business? This jerk just tried to kill me! Why are you protecting him?"

Sandy looked at Alfredo. "He's my husband."

"What!! You're married to him. But but..."

"Just get out," she said. "You've done enough damage."

Alfredo was dumbfounded. "I've done damage!!?" he said, "He attacked me!! Who did he think I was?"

"None of your fucking business, asshole," Sandy spit out. "Now get the fuck out of here!"

None of this made any sense, but the sudden shift in her tone scared him. Who were these people? What was he doing here? Alfredo walked quickly out of the room and closed the door behind him. But instead of crossing the living room to go down the hallway to the front door, he paused, *and opened the door that he had seen Leon Petroski go into when Alfredo had first arrived. Alfredo stepped inside that room. He could see many small lights flickering. He found the light switch on the wall and flicked it on. There was a table and several small black and white TV monitor screens. Only one monitor was turned on, and when he looked he saw what he thought he would see: There was the room with Sandy still holding Leon, who was still curled up on the floor. This was the monitoring room where Leon had been watching him and Sandy.*

Below the screen was a VCR. It was still recording. Alfredo hit the stop button and then the eject button. Out came the tape. He reached down and grabbed it.

"Insurance", he thought, as he stepped out of the room, walked down the hall and out of the apartment, down the building hallway and out of the front door to the building.

Outside, the air was cool. His chest throbbed. "I'll give the tape to Mamood and tell him everything that happened," he thought. "If anything happens to me, he can go to the police."

Thinking about Mamood comforted Alfredo as he walked along. "Mamood was right," he thought, "that fucking girl is crazy. They're both crazy."

<u>Chapter 24</u>

Paul read what he had written. "That's it? He just walks away? No insight? No great revelation?"

He reread it. He went into the kitchen and got another glass of wine and came back to the computer and reread it again. He tried to let a different ending come to mind. Nothing came. This was how it ended.

"I have no idea what this fucking means," he thought to himself.

PART 3:   RICARDO'S EPIPHANY

1.

Ricardo drove up Interstate 190 towards Canada. He liked living in the small town of Hamburg. The name reminded him of his life in Europe. He liked the small-town atmosphere and being just a short drive to Buffalo with its quirky arts culture. He liked being near Niagara Falls. He liked walking the shoreline of Lake Erie and being able to see Canada. He often made the ninety minute drive into St. Catharines, Canada. Prostitution was legal in Canada, and Ricardo liked the brothels in St Catharines.

On this particular day, the air was clear. It was summer. The highway was full of tourists either going to Canada for the weekend or returning home from visiting St. Catharines or Toronto. Ricardo kept his left hand on the wheel and sipped at a coffee.

Both his books had been published, *Monsieur* and *The Book of Paul*, and yet he had managed to avoid having his identity known. He wrote under a pseudonym. He never did book signings. He had done a few radio interviews over the phone, when his publisher insisted, but he was adamant about not doing any in-person interviews or appearances. Ricardo valued his privacy.

Monsieur had sold well, mostly due to some lucky publicity breaks. *The Book of Paul* took some heat from the BDSM community and had not sold as well, but Ricardo did not care. He had only written the books for himself anyway. He was glad they were published, but fame as a "published author" held no interest for him. He wrote only to understand himself. The character Monsieur was a part of Ricardo, as well the character of Paul. Ricardo had always believed that if he let them out on paper, he would somehow achieve some peace. He was already planning his third novel, *100 Brothels You Must Visit Before You Die.*

As traffic began to slow down for the border crossing, Ricardo retrieved a Cialis pill from his pocket and swallowed it. Then he eased the car in the line of cars that was forming to clear Canadian customs. He had his passport and driver's license in hand. Eventually, a young border crossing officer made his way to Ricardo's car, and Ricardo put on his best tourism face.

"What brings you to Canada today, sir?"

"Just visiting for the day."

"Staying overnight?"

"No."

"Will you be seeing any family or friends here?"

"No."

"What will you be doing today?"

"I'm going to the Inner Harbor festival for the day."

Ricardo always made it a point to research what festival or events were happening in St. Catharine's on any particular weekend he traveled there. The Inner Harbor festival was a small music and crafts fair happening that weekend. Ricardo had no intention of going there, but it was always good to have a cover story.

The official handed Ricardo's passport back to him. "Alright sir, have a good visit."

"Thank you. I'm sure I will."

Ricardo drove on through the border crossing and made his way into downtown St. Catharines. He parked the car in the same lot he always used and walked about two blocks to where he knew there were some payphones by a small café. He already had plenty of Canadian money from his last visit. He dialed the number that he knew by heart.

"Can I help you?"

"Yes, I'd like to make an appointment with Haley for

a one-hour session."

"Okay, let me check...Yes, Haley is here today. What time did you want your appointment?"

"Well, I'm about ten minutes away. How about two-thirty?"

"Okay, we can do that. What is your name?"

"Ricardo."

"Okay, Ricardo, we have you down for an appointment with Haley at two-thirty. Do you need our address?"

"No, I know where you are."

"Okay, thank you."

"Thank you."

Ricardo hung up and started walking. He could feel his heart pounding. Even though prostitution was technically legal in Canada, brothels were not, and Ricardo was very circumspect. He never used his cell phone to call the brothel. He never called from the States. He knew he was being paranoid, but he also knew that U.S. laws prohibited travel to another country for sex, and he knew that cell phone conversations were not protected from government surveillance. He wasn't a lawyer for nothing.

So, he always used a Canadian payphone to arrange his appointments. He always paid in cash, never with a credit card. He never used his last name.

A few minutes later, he arrived at the block where the brothel was located. It was a busy city street with lots of shops. One of the businesses was a gay bathhouse. Ricardo had been there once before, when he had traveled all the way to St. Catharines only to find the brothel had no one available. He needed release, and the bathhouse was there. Ricardo was bi-sexual, although he detested that term. He thought the label was stupid and wrong. As far as he was concerned, he was just sexual, nothing more.

The brothel had no identifying marks other than a sign saying, "private residence". Ricardo walked up the steps and pressed the buzzer. The door was made of steel. In a moment the hostess opened the door and said, "Do you have an appointment?"

"Yes," said Ricardo, "at two-thirty with Haley."

The hostess opened the door wider and let him into the waiting room.

"She'll be right down."

"I need to use the restroom."

"It's right here to the right."

"Yes, thank you."

Ricardo peed and checked out his appearance in the mirror. He was fifty-six, but looked a few years younger. He looked at the color of his shirt and jacket. He needed to buy more stylish clothes, but also thought that his older styled clothes made him more non-descript. He washed his hands and stepped out of the restroom. Haley was waiting for him.

"Hello, Ricardo, good to see you."

"Hello, Haley."

She led him into a large room off the waiting room and closed the door.

"One hour?"

"Yes."

"That will be one hundred eighty dollars."

Ricardo handed the money over. "I have to turn this in. I'll be right back. Make yourself comfortable", she said, gesturing to the bed.

Ricardo took off his clothes and piled them on the floor. He unstrapped a velcro strap that he wore around his knee, because his knee often hurt him if he walked long distances. He was slipping off his underwear when Haley walked back in.

"How have you been?" she asked.

"Good" Ricardo said, "Better now that I'm here."

"Do you want me naked now?"

"Yes."

Haley was a skinny girl, blond with pale skin, maybe about nineteen or twenty, with slightly buck teeth and small pointy breasts. She was wearing a lacy peach-colored bra and panties. She slipped out of them. She didn't have to explain her rules to Ricardo. Ricardo knew them. No fingers, no anal, always wear a condom, be gentle with her breasts. She got onto the bed and slipped into Ricardo's arms. They began to kiss.

The reason Ricardo always asked for Haley was because she was the only prostitute that he had ever been with who liked to kiss. No deep kisses. No tongue. But kisses nonetheless. Real kisses. Lingering kisses. Ricardo liked her kisses. He ran his hand over her skinny ass. She hugged his shoulders. They kept making little kisses for a while.

"What did you want to do?" she finally asked.

"I liked cuddling with you."

"I like cuddling too. We got plenty of time."

Ricardo bent his head down and gently kissed her nipples. She had small aureoles with short blunt nipples. Ricardo liked those too. The only thing that Ricardo would change about Haley was that she shaved her pubic hair. It did make her look child-like, but Ricardo preferred hairy pussies. Haley's pussy did not have thick lips—it was more like a slit, which added to the child-like look.

Haley was rubbing her hands gently over Ricardo's cock. He began to get hard. Thank God for Cialis, he thought.

They kissed more. Ricardo gently ran his hands over her legs, along her inner thigh and over her pussy, up her belly and over her breasts. She ran one hand along his side and over his ass and fondled his cock with the other hand.

"Do you want oral?" she asked.

"Actually, I think I want to be inside you now." Ricardo said.

"Okay." She answered and reached over to the nightstand and grabbed a condom. She opened the packet and rolled it on his cock. Then she grabbed a small tube of lubricant and opened it and spread that on his condom-covered cock.

"Do you want me to be on top?" she asked.

"Yes." Ricardo said.

She eased his cock up inside her and began to slowly rock up and down.

"We've got plenty of time, Ricardo." She said. "I don't want to rush you."

"We're doing fine, Haley. This is good."

Ricardo had always loved brothels, when they were run well. Most of the time, the prostitutes were kind and sweet to Ricardo. He thought that it was insane that the U.S. made them illegal. He needed love, and for the reasons he set forth in *Monsieur*, he was incapable of finding it anywhere else. He didn't like the term prostitute, nor the term sex worker. For some reason, he didn't mind the term hooker. But he thought of them all as lovers, rather than paid sexual partners. He liked that the communication was direct. He liked that he didn't have to pretend to be someone he was not. He liked that he felt loved by them. He liked that he could leave when he was done.

Ricardo had been married before, and he knew the downside of married life: you always had to take another person into account when you made any plans. Want to stay late at work? Better let the wife know. Want to have a drink with a friend? Better check with the wife. Want to visit the strip club? What will your wife think? Want to go to a gay bathhouse? Are you insane? Better keep that to yourself. Want to fuck someone else? Better get a divorce lawyer.

Even the simple things, like what restaurant to eat at, were distorted when you were married or dating someone. Of course, Ricardo also recognized and appreciated that being married or dating meant that you had someone to talk with at the restaurant, someone to make plans with, someone to go on vacation with, someone who might care for you beyond the hundred and eighty dollar brothel fee. But all in all, when he compared married life with brothels, brothels still won out. At least there was sex. In all his relationships, dating or marriage, the sex tended to diminish somewhere between six months and a year of the relationship. Ricardo liked sex. He wanted sex. He needed sex. It didn't have to be every day. Two to three times a month was fine. But it had to be good. Haley, like many other hookers he'd been with, was good at making it seem passionate. Haley would moan as she rode Ricardo, as if she were consumed by passion. Ricardo appreciated this. He always tipped her well.

Ricardo had been seeing Haley for almost eight months. He would make the drive to Canada at least once a month to fuck Haley. In some ways, he felt he loved her. He felt that he clicked with her; that his body fit hers; that they got along well together. After the lovemaking was over, they would cuddle, and she would tell him of her life, of her difficulties with her roommates or what she did when she wasn't whoring. But he knew his relationship with her was totally illusional. He didn't want to think that she charmed plenty of other middle-aged men, but he knew she did. In one way, that was another benefit of the brothel. It prevented him from getting too involved, from falling in love with a sex worker. Ricardo knew that Haley didn't cum with him, yet she moaned as if she did, as she probably did with all her other clients. The reality of the brothel world helped to protect Ricardo from getting too involved with the women there. He appreciated the psychological benefits of the brothel. It had evolved over centuries to fill a specific need and did so with economic and psychological efficiency that was better than any other business model ever created.

2.

Ricardo had been married twice. No children. Sometimes he thought he had been lucky—lucky enough to have been married to two very interesting women, and lucky enough to have divorced them before time and age turned them old and bitter. Time adds a bitterness to most things, he believed. And he felt sorry for women, who seemed to bear the brunt of time more than men. He remembered the French saying that the ideal age of a woman for a man was half the man's age plus eleven; which meant that Ricardo, who was fifty-six, would be looking for a woman about thirty-nine years old. But that also meant that a woman who was Ricardo's age would have to settle for a man ninety years old. Nothing about aging was fair, but it was more unfair to women.

Ricardo's first marriage lasted ten years; his second lasted eight years. He no longer knew where his first wife was, but wherever she was, he was pretty sure she still hated him deeply. He cheated on her—had an affair with a married woman with whom he thought he was in love. He made the classic mistake, the classic *fatal* mistake, of telling his wife. She had fought the divorce and it took two years to get it done. By that time, of course, he and his new love had split up.

He met his second wife a few years later. That marriage had lasted eight years. One day she announced she was leaving. He just said okay. They got divorced thirty-five days later. He never asked her why they got divorced, but he was glad they did, and he believed she was too.

It was after his second divorce that Ricardo had what he called his epiphany. It came to him one morning while he was lying in bed, half-awake, during those endless early mornings right after a divorce when the first thought that greets the waking mind and sticks in the throat each and every morning is "You just got divorced. You're alone. She's gone. You're on your own." It was a Saturday morning and he didn't have to go to work, and he just lay there in the bed, looking at ceiling, walls and windows of the bedroom, the room in the condo where she no longer lived, knowing that as soon as the condo sold, he would have to move and find a new place to live. He was simply letting his thoughts drift when the epiphany came to him, out of the blue, almost like a vision. "I'm an idiot," he thought. "I am just an idiot, a biological idiot. I am no different than the drooling village dullard who thinks he understands life. I have no more control over what happens to me than a mosquito that flies around looking for food, thinking he is choosing his path, when in fact he's being blown about by winds he is unaware of, and will eventually be gassed by bug spray or squashed by some hand of a creature he has no concept of. All my dreams of success and achievement are illusion. I know nothing. I have no idea why or how I got married or why I just got divorced. I have control over nothing. There is simply no point in trying to control what happens to me because I simply don't have the mental capability to understand anything. Things just happen. Everything I have ever achieved just *happened* to me. I didn't really accomplish them. They just happened to me. And none of them mean anything to me."

He thought about this for days, for weeks, for months. Eventually, that epiphany changed his life and livelihood. He had been living in New York City, working as a lawyer for a large personal injury law firm. He hated his job. He hated the hugeness of the city and the constant noise. He hated the humidity of summer and the icy winters. The only reason he lived there was because he had met his second wife there and she wanted to live there to be near her family. After his divorce, he assumed he would just throw his energy into his job, move up in status at the law firm, and try and make partner. However, these were activities that held no interest for him. He hated the practice of law, the endless court appearances, the complaining clients, the arrogant law partners, and the constant pressure to make billable hours. The only thing he ever enjoyed, besides sex, was writing. With both of his wives, whenever they were away or had gone to bed early without him, whenever the evening was late, and he'd had a glass of wine, he would find himself writing down poems or just short lines. He never understood why he did this, and he never shared what he wrote with either wife or with anyone else. But he enjoyed this solitary activity and he'd saved the poems for years in an encrypted computer file. He never intended to do anything with them. But with his newfound idiocy, he realized that since nothing he did in life actually had the intended effect, that he might as well write, since it was the only thing that he found meaningful in and of itself.

"If I am an idiot and will never amount to anything, then at least I should live in a place that is beautiful and do what I enjoy doing," was his thought. So, he moved to the other side of the state, to the small town of Hamburg. He left his past behind him. He took a job in a small law firm that only did probate law.

When he moved to Hamburg, he didn't know that prostitution was legal in Canada, but he found out soon enough. Idiot's luck, he told himself.

3.

Ricardo did not really care for probate work. The pay was less than what a brand new lawyer just out of law school would make, but it paid the bills, and there was very little stress to the job. People die and almost always leave a financial mess behind them. Someone has to clean it up. He had great job security. But the reason he took the job—the most important thing about the job—was that it was nine-to-five, so he had time to write.

Ricardo stepped into the new job like an old pair of shoes. He spent his evenings drinking and writing. He had been at the job three years now. It had been almost two years since *Monsieur* had been published, and at least eight months since *The Book of Paul* had come out. He had been thinking about a third book for a number of months, a book about brothels. The project made him restless. He wondered: how can I write about brothels without experiencing them all? He knew the question was rhetorical. He knew that the idea of writing a book entitled *100 Brothels You Must Visit Before You Die* was simply an excuse for him to visit brothels. But vacations and weekend trips would not be enough. Since the United States was so repressed about sex, Ricardo needed a way to spend a lot of time in more progressive countries. Countries where prostitution was legal. He started to research jobs overseas. He looked at international law firms.

He looked at U.N. jobs. He looked at the Peace Corps. After several weeks doing online research, he realized that the ideal job was the Foreign Service. A Foreign Service Officer spends one to two years at an embassy, rotating to a different country on every assignment. It was the ideal way to research brothels, assuming you didn't get assigned to Iraq or some danger post. Getting to be a Foreign Service Officer was a rather complicated process, involving exams and many interviews, and often took over a year to be accepted. But the Foreign Service needed lawyers. Ricardo decided to apply.

4.

    Ricardo had a series of calls from his accountant, Harold Glass. Harold was more than just an accountant—he was Ricardo's buffer and alibi. Both *Monsieur* and *The Book of Paul* had been written under a pseudonym. Only Harold knew the author was Ricardo. Ricardo's contract with the publisher specifically channeled all money and contacts through Harold.

    Harold called Ricardo to relay that the publisher had called Harold. They were going to do a third printing of *Monsieur* and *The Book of Paul* in a single set, tying both books together with an introduction by some editor that Ricardo had never heard of. Ricardo was glad for the third printing but told Harold to ask for approval of the introduction. Harold called back within the hour. The publisher had agreed. Harold mentioned that the publisher had asked him about a trilogy. Ricardo told Harold of his idea for *100 Brothels You Must Visit Before You Die* and told Harold to pass that on to the publisher. Harold called back within ten minutes and said that the publisher seemed excited and wanted to be kept posted on its development. "Tell them I'll keep them posted," Ricardo said. But he thought to himself *as soon as I figure out how I'm going to write it.*

5.

Ricardo hadn't dated anyone (in the traditional dating sense) in over five years. Not since his epiphany. However, once or twice a month he would meet Martina at a restaurant for dinner. Ricardo thought he could be in love with Martina, but he knew for certain she was not in love with him. Shortly after he had met her a year ago, he realized that, for whatever reason, he was not her type, that she liked him but was not attracted to him, and that she was never going to be interested in him in a romantic way. But he enjoyed her company. She was bright and pretty, and they seemed to get along, so he talked with her about this and proposed that they be friends, and over time they had evolved a ritual of trying different restaurants in town, places too fancy to go to alone, places that they hadn't been to yet. On this particular evening, they were dining at a newly opened "small plates" restaurant.

"I think I've finally figured out this free will thing", Ricardo was saying to Martina.

"Yes?"

"I think free will is like poetry. I believe in poetry. It exists. But most of the people you meet are not poets. Free will is like that. It exists, but most people don't have it."

Martina laughed. "Do you have it?"

"I'd like to think I do, but then again, I'd like to think I am a poet and a lot of my poetry sucks."

Ricardo wasn't sure if Martina viewed their monthly dinners as an excuse for a nice meal at an expensive restaurant without having the risk of some date making a move for her, or as a nice excuse for time to spend with him. But either way, he always looked forward to them. Most of the time they commiserated with each other about the lack of relationships. Martina dated a fair amount, but none of her relationships endured. Since Ricardo didn't date at all, they always had much to talk about. Martina had just ended a six month relationship with a younger man named Sam.

"I've got to get better at trusting my instinct," she was saying.

"What do you mean?" Ricardo asked.

"Well, with Sam, I had all the clues very early on. He didn't have his own car. He could make good money doing freelance computer stuff, but he only worked enough to get by. The rest of the time he spent with his volleyball team. He was bright, but he was always taking the easy way. Remember when it was my birthday and he took me to the all-you-can-eat buffet because he had those discount tickets?"

"I remember that." Ricardo had actually thought it was very funny.

"But when it was his birthday and I told him I'd take him out, he wanted to go to that expensive place on Second Avenue, because he knew I had offered to pay. He never saw the balance in a relationship. It was always just about him. Aside from his volleyball team, he never invested his energy outside of himself."

"Well, Martina, he seemed to have the qualities that you always go for. He was athletic, into sports, bright, very charismatic... from what you told me, he was a real charmer."

"I know, that's what I mean. If I had been listening to my instincts early on, I wouldn't have been so taken by his bullshit stories."

Perhaps, Ricardo thought, but perhaps not. We are all deluded by love, he thought. Tricked by attraction. We see nothing. Ricardo did think that it was possible to identify bad choices in partners earlier, but that knowledge didn't seem to stop the bad choices from occurring. One of the reasons he decided to patronize brothels rather than venture into the dating scene came out of his idiocy epiphany. He realized that when he used to select a dating partner, he almost always picked the crazy ones, the "interesting" ones with tons of emotional baggage, the ones with an agenda, the ones with a history of stalking. He liked their stories; he loved their sexual energy. But, eventually, he always paid for it on the cross. But, he also discovered that when he went to a brothel, he always picked the sweet ones, the kind hookers who took care of him, and he always left happy. Brothels were simply a better investment of his time, money, and his emotions.

Other times, if there were no brothels available or money was low, he would go to the gay bathhouses. Those were riskier ventures, but Ricardo was very careful.

He never told Martina about his bathhouse experiences, of course. She did know that he was bisexual, but that's all she knew. And she had confessed, once in a carefully phrased moment, that she had slept with women on occasion too. Ricardo suspected that most women either had, or would, if given the chance. He believed that humans were basically extremely sexual creatures, and given the right setting, people would do almost any sexual act.

He had tried to explore that issue in *Monsieur* and, to some extent, in *The Book of Paul.* Martina didn't know about those books either. She knew that Ricardo liked to write, for he would send her poems and occasional short stories. But Ricardo didn't think she intuited the range of his behaviors or his particular excesses. -

Ricardo knew that Monsieur, Paul, Alfredo, Mamood, and the life coach were all parts of him. They were all elements from his unconscious life, parts of his personality. Sometimes he felt like Monsieur, sometimes like Paul, and most often like the life coach. Ricardo could walk down the street, pass a porn shop and feel like Monsieur, see some beautiful woman and feel like Paul, and then stop for a cup of coffee and sit and watch people hustle by in their important errands and constricted destinies and feel like the life coach wanting to ease their pain.

Both *Monsieur* and *The Book of Paul* wrote themselves. Ricardo felt that he simply gave those characters full control of the keyboard and let them write. Monsieur was probably gayer than Monsieur himself even acknowledged. Paul was ambivalent towards woman, towards life. Alfredo seemed a hopeless romantic who yearned for a woman's love. Ricardo knew he was all of these things. Not particularly integrated, but still he recognized the pieces. More importantly, since his epiphany, he also realized that he was never going to integrate those pieces. They might integrate on their own, but Ricardo had simply come to accept that these were different and contradictory parts of himself, parts that were in certain ways completely opposed to each other. At different times he longed to run his tongue over a woman's pussy, to dedicate his body to making her body quiver and moan. At other times, he only wanted to feel a man's cock pressing against his. It made no sense to him. But, since his epiphany, he had decided to give into whatever his mood and the situation allowed. Although it made for many solitary nights, all in all, he had to admit that he preferred the lifestyle. To date a woman for any length of time meant becoming involved, at which point the woman would become possessive of his time, or at least unduly inquisitive of where he was and what he was doing. Ricardo supposed, that in the realm of all possibilities, there might be a woman or a couple that would be the perfect fit for his lifestyle, maybe some type of ménage a trois. However, he thought the odds of finding such a couple, where he would like both the man and the woman, where they would both like him, where the three of them could find the perfect blend of love, sex, commitment, and freedom... well, he thought the odds of that were very, very remote. Not impossible but very remote. Hell, it was almost impossible for two people to get along—it had to be harder for three people to manage it. In the meantime, his particular lifestyle of brothels and the occasion bathhouse was the best second choice he could manage. He was not unhappy with it.

"What about you, Ricardo, are you going to start dating again?" Martina was asking.

"I don't know, Martina, I've been wondering about that. I look at Match.com and the other sites, and I just don't think they are for me. I tried to write a profile and I couldn't. I don't want to sell me, and the whole culture of those dating sites is presentation, you know, selling yourself. I read these woman's profiles and I don't think they're real."

"I met Ralph online, and that lasted awhile."

"I never trusted him."

"Yeah, well, I've taken my profile down for a while," Martina admitted.

"I have looked into to this six by six dating thing in Buffalo," Ricardo said. "You know, where you just have dinner with six people, that may be more my speed. And there's those tango dancing classes at the Tarifa Ballroom. Or there's that wine tasting club in Hamburg. Something where I can go do something and not feel like I have to *present* myself. I mean, those dating sites are really just blind dates set up by a computer. What people put in their profiles is not who they are. And even if it were, that's not how people are attracted to each other. You might hate what someone wrote in their profile but really like them in person, or vice versa... I think attraction is like the sense of smell. It's all a chemical thing. You might hate the way a person looks in a photograph, hate their profile, but you meet them in person, and suddenly they smell really nice, and you hear violins, and you suddenly feel attracted to them."

"So, are you going to do that six by six dinner thing?"

"I don't know. I'm thinking about it."

Ricardo knew that he wouldn't do it. He would talk about it for a while, and then later he would find something else to talk about. That's how change really is for most people, he thought. Talk had nothing to do with it. Real change just happens, completely independent of talk or plans. It just happens. People could just as well talk about making the seasons change. They just change, that's all. People have no control over it. They can't mathematically change the odds of Spring coming or Summer leaving. Ricardo remembered how he enjoyed writing about Paul, who thought he could increase his chances of meeting women by breaking his behaviors down to their smallest component. Yet Ricardo knew, from his own experience, that people don't change, no matter how many exercises they went through. That was the one thing that Ricardo felt he was trying to master: and that was the ability to accept that he would not change. Not to regret it, not to bemoan it, but to simply accept it. Change might happen to him. But no change was going to be created because he "willed" it or "created" it.

In one sense, however, Ricardo did think he was dating. He viewed his visits to the brothels as dating. All the same attributes were there. He would call ahead and make arrangements to be there at a specified time. He knew the costs involved. He provided his own transportation. He made sure he was properly bathed and presentable. He was cordial. He was particularly fond of Haley. There was some conversation. He had sex. It all seemed like a date to him.

Ricardo did not consider his dinners with Martina as dates, because there was never the possibility of sex. He wished there was, but it was simply not to be.

6.

"How would you answer if you were stationed in a Muslim country and a native asked you to justify the Iraq Invasion?"

Ricardo was having his first intake interview for the Foreign Service.

"Well," Ricardo replied, "I have to preface my answer to that question with this: Equality is a political right, not a communications right. One of the basic rules in communication is that every interaction is a reflection of the status of the people involved. And that's true for every interaction, even the one you and I are having here today."

Ricardo paused. He had the interviewer's attention. He went on: "In our communication, yours and mine, because of the status of our relationship, you get to ask the questions, and I answer. If I was, as you put it, 'stationed' in a Muslim country, that would mean a position in an embassy, and if a native of that country visits the Embassy, he is there because he wants something. I would be in the position relative to him that you are to me right now. If he is there seeking a visa, and asks me my opinion of the Iraq War, he is not wanting to know my opinion of the Iraq War. He is trying to ask a question so that he can offer *his* opinion to me, or rather, his conception of what he thinks I want to hear from someone seeking a visa. It's probably a conversation that has happened a million times in embassies in Muslim countries. The visa-seeker asks, 'What do you think of the Iraq Invasion?' and the American replies, 'Well, it's a complicated issue' and the visa-seeker then launches into a pro-American speech about how much the troops have liberated Iraq and how much more freedom exist there now despite the insurgency. In that situation, the best answer, if you want to control the communication, is to not reply at all. The question is not what's going on."

Ricardo paused again, for effect. "However, to answer your question, and just to suppose that I am sitting having coffee with a native of that country who is a peer, someone with whom, hypothetically speaking, I don't have a political relationship with, which of course is a purely hypothetical situation since all relationships are political, but for the sake of discussion, I was asked that question and could speak freely, I would tell him this: wars are like earthquakes. They just happen. Pressure builds up in the tectonic plates over a period of decades, and something has to give. There is no right or wrong with earthquakes, only death and destruction.

And the same is true with war. The only thing that matters is the rebuilding process after the earthquake."

The interviewer was looking at him intently. "So... do you have a position on... on whether it was proper for the United States to go to war?"

"From a political viewpoint, the only thing that matters is how to position the rebuilding process to our country's benefit. If our goal is to build an ally who is going to be cooperative with us because they are dependent upon us, then we should take a certain course in the rebuilding. If, on the other hand, our goal is to demonstrate to other countries that we are not engaged in neo-colonialism, then we should take a different course, a more hands-off course, in the rebuilding. That's the only place where a discussion of what's proper can take place. It's meaningless to ask if it was proper to go to war, just as it's meaningless to ask whether it is proper for an earthquake to happen. You and I both lived through the time when the decision to go to war was made. We both watched the news, read the paper. We had what knowledge we had at that time, and it didn't make any difference. Whether it's our own Civil War, the Spanish-American War, or the Iraq War, the real reasons why wars occur are deeper than the rational level. They are not the tips of the icebergs we see. The real reasons build up slowly, sometimes over hundreds of years, and maybe can only be deciphered after blood has been spilled. I don't know how to explain it any other way. Our job, as politicians, as lawyers, as representatives of our country, is to try and create a meaningful structure *after* the war."

The interviewer was writing down notes very fast. Ricardo smiled to himself. He didn't particularly believe what he had said one way or another, but it sounded good.

7.

Ricardo made the drive to Canada, swallowed a Cialis en route, passed through customs, and walked to his nearest payphone and called his favorite brothel. He was eager to see Haley.

"Yes, I'd like to make an appointment to see Haley."

"Oh, I am sorry, Haley isn't here today."

Ricardo had not anticipated this. He had been looking forward to her kisses all week.

"Will she be in later today?"

"No, she's off all day."

Still, he was horny. "Who else might be available today?" he asked.

"Well, we have Angie, Jennifer, and Ashley."

Ricardo had always liked that Rolling Stones song "Angie".

"Okay, could I see Angie in half an hour?"

"I think she might be available then. Would you like her description?"

"Uh, okay, sure."

"Well, she's a recent addition, twenty-eight years old, curvy, with strawberry blond hair, very liberal-minded."

"Okay", Ricardo said. He really didn't care. He wanted to kiss Haley, but he would probably fuck anyone. "Is she available at two-thirty?"

"Yes, and how long are you wanting to schedule?"

Ricardo had brought enough money to spend an hour with Haley. He probably should only buy a half-hour with this unknown girl, but he so wanted to be loved by someone for a substantial amount of time.

"For an hour."

"Okay, what's your name?"

"Ricardo."

"Do you need our address?"

"No."

"Okay, we'll see you at two-thirty."

Ricardo walked to the brothel. It was a beautiful day. St. Catharines was full of tourists. Summer was waning, but the air was warm, the sky was blue, people were happy to be in the streets. Ricardo loved to look at the faces as he walked along. Today he was feeling like Monsieur but full of grace. As Monsieur, he loved observing people. He was going to a brothel. He was going to have sex with a woman who was a stranger to him. He did not even know who she was, but he knew that within the hour, he would have his cock inside her. Maybe she would be as good, or better, than Haley. Life was good.

He had enough time to window shop. He admired the jewelry in one store's window, the men's jackets in another window. He considered stopping for a cup of coffee. Here was a store with incense wafting out the door. Here was a restaurant with couples sitting at tiny tables outside, eating and talking. Ricardo, as Monsieur, felt he loved them all.

He arrived at the brothel, at the non-descript door that said "private residence". He entered and went up the steps he knew well. The madam, who was much younger than Ricardo, recognized him and directed him to a room. He waited there for Angie.

After a few minutes, Angie entered. Ricardo was disappointed but smiled and said hello. Angie was not exactly curvy; she was heavy, with drooping breasts, and a weak chin. When she smiled, Ricardo could see that many of her teeth were brown. She seemed hesitant and unsure of herself. But Ricardo did not feel like he could exactly back out of the deal. He wished he had chosen Jennifer or Ashley, but the wheel of fortune had handed him Angie. He paid her. She left to give the money to the madam and Ricardo began to disrobe. He was on the bed in his boxer shorts when she returned.

"Would you like a massage to start?" she said.

"Yes, but I'm going to take the rest of my clothes off."

"Okay," she said, "I will too."

And she did. Ricardo was right. Her breasts were large, but sagging. She was overweight. She obviously had had a child, because there were stretch marks on the layer of her stomach that hung out. Still, she was naked. Ricardo was laying on his back on the bed. She was sitting on the bed beside him running her hands over his chest, down his legs, over his cock, and back up his chest. It felt good.

"What would you like?" she said.

"Oh, nothing fancy. I'm not fussy."

"You just want to relax?"

"Yes."

He was starting to get hard. He looked at Angie's face. Perhaps she had a troubled life. Perhaps he would find some comfort in her face. But she had a vacant look, like she was thinking of something far away. So, Ricardo began to play with her breasts, and then began to suck on her nipples. The Cialis was working. He was almost fully erect.

"Would you like me to get a condom?" Angie asked.

"Yes."

She got a condom from the side table and put it on Ricardo's cock. Then, without asking, she began to give him a blow job.

With Haley, Ricardo never asked for oral. He knew that the taste of latex was hardly romantic. But since Angie had initiated it, Ricardo stretched out, closed his eyes, and focused on the feeling of her mouth moving up and down on his cock.

Then Angie hoisted herself up on him and inserted his cock into her pussy and began to fuck him.

The rest was rather mechanical. She fucked him. After a while, he came. She got him some warm towels to wipe himself off with. If she had been Haley, he would have laid there and talked with her; he would have used up his hour. But Angie was no Haley. Ricardo gave her a twenty dollar tip and left.

Outside, he checked his watch. Thirty minutes. He'd paid for an hour but was done in thirty minutes. Such were the odds. He was hungry. He headed down the street to a little Persian restaurant he liked.

While he waited for his food, he ordered hot tea and reflected on things:

He had to admit that even though he had not liked Angie, that nonetheless, fucking her had left him with a strange sort of contentment, a post-coital peace, a feeling of floating. He found it strange that he should be experiencing that same euphoric feeling from fucking Angie that he often had after fucking Haley. He did not particularly enjoy fucking Angie. Yet, he was glad he got fucked, and felt good by it.

8.

Ricardo could not afford to go to the brothel too often. However, his insurance plan did cover therapy, and paid for weekly sessions. Ricardo thought this was ironic. If the insurance would pay for the brothels, he wouldn't need to go to therapy. But he was still grateful to be in therapy. Ricardo was never quite sure why he went to therapy, but he considered it a necessity, like food and wine. He had been in therapy almost all his adult life.

He didn't tell his therapist about the brothels, of course.

Today, he was telling his therapist how he had spent a recent weekend, which was... alone. He had gotten up on Saturday, gone to a diner for breakfast, gone back home, putzed around his apartment, made a sandwich for lunch, worked on some letters and some writing, gone out to a bar around five o'clock, come back home, drank some wine, went to sleep, and basically repeated the itinerary the next day. He could not recall talking to anyone all weekend.

"Well, Ricardo," his therapist asked, "what would you change?"

"I don't know, I guess I'm just waiting for something to happen. I'd like to be back in a relationship, but I'm not sure I would do that. I look at Match.com and the other internet dating services, and, well, I just can't do them. I can't fill out the profiles; I can't put the positive spin on it all. I can't pretend that I care about, you know, finding the perfect soul mate and all."

Ricardo had wiggled the first two fingers of each hand at the word "soul mate" to emphasize quotation marks, as if the concept was silly. It wasn't silly to Ricardo, of course. He knew that secretly he yearned for a soul mate, but he was totally averse to the process of the quest.

"So, you wouldn't do online dating?" his therapist asked.

"No... I mean, I tried it once. I managed to write a profile once last year and stick it up there for a few hours, but it all seemed so fake that I took it down the same day. Even so, even for the few hours that it was up, I got inquiries from women. But they were all either scary-looking, or older than me, or crazy-sounding. It was like... well, it was like fishing in polluted waters. Some of the people that responded were hideous."

"So, does that mean you won't try any type of online dating?"

"Yeah. I don't think I can do it."

"If you did find the right woman, what kind of relationship would you want to have with her?"

Ricardo looked out the window. Across the rooftops he could see three birds sitting on a telephone wire. He thought about Haley, he thought about his two wives, he thought about his failed love affairs. He could list a million things he didn't want in a relationship, a million mistakes he had made.

He looked back at his therapist. "I don't know."

But he did think about it as the days went by. What would it matter that he didn't have a way to meet women if he couldn't even envision what kind of relationship he was looking for? He was backed into a corner. Either he was going to stop expecting a "real" relationship with a woman and stick to the brothels or he was going to have to figure out what he wanted in try a potential partner. Either he was in the market or he wasn't. And the problem was, he couldn't decide. Obviously if he refused to go online and if he declined to try a dating service like six by six or any of the speed-dating services that were advertised, then he was unlikely to meet anyone. He would, as his therapist said, have to wait until, by some fluke, someone wandered into his life. And if someone did, what would he want with her?

9.

Ricardo did not like the second Foreign Service interviewer. The man seemed constricted. The interview had dragged on. Plus, all of the topics of the interview were extremely annoying and useless: Ricardo's personal history, his view on international relationships, his view of war, how he would handle various situations, etc. Like any job interview, Ricardo knew he had to play the part, to say what the interviewer wanted to hear. Nonetheless, Ricardo felt an internal irritation building.

"How do you feel about working in a bureaucracy?" the interviewer had asked him.

"Well, every organization is a bureaucracy," Ricardo had answered, "and you need organizations to get this done. The term 'bureaucracy' has taken a bad rap over the years. We simply have no other mechanism to ensure that things are accomplished by employees except by having a bureaucratic system in place that sets forth a clear mission, procedures to carry out that mission, and some way of tracking whether the subordinates have actually followed that procedures. Rogue agents and maverick employees are the stuff of movies. In the real world, there is no progress without bureaucracies."

What a crock of shit, Ricardo thought to himself, but the interviewer was nodding his head and making more notes. This seemed to be the right answer.

10.

Ricardo was talking to his therapist again.
"I feel like I'm getting more and more depressed."

"How so?"

"Well, I work all week, just waiting for the weekend. But then the weekend comes, and I don't do anything. If I don't plan anything in advance, something that I'm locked into doing, then I don't do anything. Then I simply go back to work on Saturday and even on Sunday, because I have nothing else to do. For example, this past weekend, I once again failed to plan any activity. I realized on Friday night that I was getting depressed, so I made myself go to Renegades, that bar I told you about. But I could only stand to stay there about twenty minutes, then I left, and went home."

"What happened at the bar?"

"Nothing. I walked in, chatted with the bouncer, who knows me. I saw a girl who works at the bank I bank at and said hello. The band was bad. I drank one beer and felt uncomfortable, so I left."

"You didn't try and talk to anyone."

"No. I didn't see any opportunity."

"The girl from the bank?"

"Well, she was sitting with five or six of her friends. I did chat with her briefly at the bar while she was getting drinks... I could have gone over to her table and chatted some more, but she's pretty young... well, that's not it. The truth is I can't just go over to a table and start chatting. I get too paralyzed. I sat at a table by myself and drank a beer."

"I thought the point of going to a bar was to meet people."

"Well, obviously, it is... but I can't do that. I... I can only go and hope someone meets me."

"That's more the female role, isn't it?"

Ricardo could feel his eyes narrowing. But he had to agree. "Yeah, maybe."

"Have you ever met anyone at a bar?"

"No, no I don't think I have."

"But you keep going?"

"Yeah."

"It doesn't sound like an effective plan. If your goal is

to meet women, and you've never met women at bars, then it would seem you need to find another plan. I know that would require some planning on your part. What you seem to tell me is that you don't plan, so you end up going to a bar as a last-minute plan, but when you get there, you don't have the resources to make that plan work. So, either you have to develop the skills to talk to women in bars, or you have to meet them somewhere else. And I suspect that finding a different place to meet them would be easier than changing your behavior in bars. So, I would suggest you look at finding a different place or way of meeting women, because the bar thing just isn't working."

11.

On this particular evening, Ricardo ended up at a Buffalo gay bathhouse, mostly by default. Cash was low, and payday was another week away, but he felt the need for intensity and release. He had parked a few blocks away and was walking toward the bathhouse when he passed a movie house. Some new movie was showing and there was a line outside waiting to get in. He looked at the crowd. The people standing in line—couples, of course—all seemed so *young*. They were all smiling, laughing, and talking, all seemingly at once. It made him feel so foreign, as if he was from a different planet. He walked past the line of clean-scrubbed faces standing out on the sidewalk, got to the corner, turned left and continued to the bathhouse.

There were things Ricardo liked about this particular bathhouse. First of all, it was cheap. Ten dollars for a room for four hours. Extra towels were free. There were lockboxes for valuables. The televisions in every room showing both gay and bisexual porn. The showers always had hot water. The hallways were very dark. The steam room was steamy and dark. Ricardo had been to fancier bathhouses in Europe, ones that occupied four or five floors, ones with huge communal hot tubs and dark mazes and dungeons, where hundreds of men would gather every night. But that was Europe. The United States lagged behind. But this place wasn't bad. Ricardo paid his ten dollars, was buzzed through the steel doors inside, and made his way down the hallway to his room. There he disrobed, wrapped a towel around him, locked the door behind him and walked down another hallway to the showers.

Of course, there were things Ricardo didn't like about the bathhouse experience. He noticed that, in recent years, many men had stopped practicing safe sex. That tended to limit his selection of partners and made him ultra-careful about what activities he would engage in. For instance, he would never give a blowjob without first putting a condom on the man. Many men did not like this and would simply move away.

Because of his fastidiousness, Ricardo often did not have sex in the bathhouse, as contradictory as that might seem. He might masturbate someone, or several people, but not find anyone where there was a mutual agreement to continue to orgasm. Ricardo had learned years ago that mutual masturbation in bathhouses functioned more like a greeting. He would sit next to someone in the steam room who was stroking himself, and if Ricardo liked what he saw, he would open his towel and begin to stroke himself. The key was whether the other man would look over and watch Ricardo touch himself. If he did that, then after a few minutes, Ricardo might scoot over close enough for both men to reach each other. And then, without words, he and the other man might reach out and start stroking each other's cock for a few minutes. Ricardo found this activity very erotic. The loved the feel of someone's erect cock in his hands. He loved the feeling of some stranger's hands on his cock. Yet after a few minutes, he or the other man might simply stand up, maybe say thank-you, or just gently touch the other on the shoulder and move on. Occasionally, there might be a mutual attraction, and something might develop.

Sometimes, groups of five or six men might be

standing in a corner, each fondling one another. Eventually one man would drop to his knees and begin sucking another man. The other men would gather closer, watching the blowjob while continuing to masturbate each other. These communal circle-jerks were always done in perfect silence, in some sort of tribal holy trance. As soon as the man who was being blown started moaning and came, the group would, as if governed by a secret signal, all stop and move away from each other. Ricardo remembered one time when he was selected to be the one receiving the blowjob. He was standing up, while some man was on his knees in front of him taking Ricardo's whole cock in his mouth, sucking back and forth on it, while another man was standing beside him with one arm around him rubbing his left nipple, and another man was rubbing his right nipple, and a fourth man was slowly rubbing his ass and gently rubbing the area around his asshole. Ricardo had someone's cock in his left hand and another man's cock in his right hand. It led to a very good orgasm. But those scenes were rare. More often than not, after an hour or more of roaming through the hallways, the steam room, the dark rooms, after some fleeting mutual groping, Ricardo would retire to his room, and masturbate himself to orgasm. Still, Ricardo liked the bathhouses. He liked the quiet atmosphere where the steam continually hissed softly. He liked the utter lack of preening, the lack of language, the naturalness of it all. He liked sitting in a room with naked bodies and there being no problem with looking at the variety of bodies and variety of genitals.

He knew that in those tranquil bathhouse moments he was like Monsieur, just sitting there enjoying the eroticness—the pure eros—of being male. But Ricardo also knew that, like Monsieur and Paul, he was avoiding navigating the world of women. He experienced the world of male-female encounters as ever-so-more problematic. Language was always involved. Communicating status and marital availability was required. Facial expressions had to be aligned. Some sort of interest had to be exhibited. A sense of humor was needed. Layers upon layers of interpretation had to be dealt with. It wore Ricardo out. And the sex... well, Ricardo certainly preferred sex with women, but it was so different than with men. In the first place, the "do I like you?" phase and the sex phase were in the wrong order. Ricardo never knew how he felt about a woman until *after* he had sex with her. Yet in order to get to the sex phase, he had to like them, or find something to like about them, or at least pretend to like them. It was as if women wanted to be treated *as if* he had already had sex with them and still liked them *before* he could have sex with them. And in the second place, once sex started, it had to be completed. The erection had to be maintained. Attention had to be paid to the female. The whole goal often seemed geared toward pleasing her. This was totally different than the bathhouse world, where anyone could stop having sex anytime they wanted and where the whole goal was to please oneself. The whole process with women seemed backwards to Ricardo. In Ricardo's ideal world, he would prefer to have some sex play with a woman first, to find out if he liked her, and then spend time getting to know her. Like with Haley. Ricardo liked having sex with Haley. He would like to get to know her outside the brothel, to be her friend, her lover, and still her client. But this was not the way it worked.

12.

Evidently the Foreign Service intake interview had gone well enough. Ricardo received a letter scheduling his Foreign Service exam in forty-five days. He read the forms carefully. It would be a four-hour computerized exam. There would be twenty other people taking the exam in the same room on that day, all sitting in individualized cubicles with computers provided by the U.S. Department of State. He was not allowed to bring anything. Small calculators, scratch paper and pencils would be provided. Bathroom breaks would occur every forty-five minutes. He would be tested on world geography, international relations, management skills, mathematics, and U.S. culture. Very annoying, Ricardo thought, and marked the exam day down on his calendar.

The first two to four years of any foreign service officer's tour of duty, no matter what their expertise, was embassy work, meaning that they were assigned to the front counter of some particular embassy, where they spent the day processing visas for natives who wanted to travel to the United States, or spent the day handling problems and requests from U.S. citizens in that particular country. Most natives had their visas denied. They simply did not qualify, or their documents were not in order, or worse, their documents were forged. Since 9/11, the State Department had set up special training for Foreign Service officers in detecting counterfeit identity documents. If there was any question, even a suspicion about a document, the application for visa would be denied.

As for Americans in foreign countries who got into trouble, well, there wasn't much that the Embassy could do for them. If they got arrested, the embassy could contact their family and try to intervene, so they didn't get beaten in jail too often. But the embassy's power with the local police was pretty nil. On the other hand, American tourists who simply ran out of money or had medical problems could come to the embassy and actually get some help.

Ricardo knew that embassy work was a crappy job, just a way to make the Foreign Service officer pay his or her dues. But Ricardo had a different agenda. He wasn't interested in a career in the Foreign Service. He just wanted to travel. He had a list of countries he wanted to visit. On the "A" list were Austria, Belgium, Germany, Greece, Hungary, the Netherlands, Switzerland, and Turkey. Those were countries where prostitution was not only legal but regulated, meaning that the brothels were licensed and accepted as part of life. On the "B" list was Denmark, Finland, Iceland, Latvia, and Luxembourg, where prostitution was legal but not regulated. Further down was the "C" list, which contained Armenia, Bulgaria, Cyprus, Czech Republic, Estonia, Italy, Ireland, Poland, Portugal, Slovakia, Spain, and the United Kingdom, where prostitution, although not legal, was not illegal. Brothels there were technically illegal, but often tolerated. Then there were countries like Thailand and India, which were not on any list despite their reputation. Ricardo did not mind patronizing individual women who had made the choice to work in sex, and he didn't mind supporting a small entrepreneurial business such as brothel, but he was bothered by the idea of countries where it seemed that a large number of women were forced into prostitution. He admired Haley who had once told him that she looked at all her employment options and simply decided that working in a brothel was the best choice for her. The money was good and most of the time she enjoyed her job.

On the other hand, Ricardo knew that Foreign Service Officers had very little choice of what countries they were sent to. Assignments were rotated every one to two years. He could be sent somewhere like Bosnia Herzegovina where the penalty for visiting a prostitute was jail.

And it was possible that he might not pass the exam, or the interview, or the background check, and might never get the job. Still, he had to try. He simply could not figure out any other way to gain the experiences that would be necessary to write a book such as *100 Brothels You Must Visit Before You Die.*

13.

Martina had emailed him an article on the six by six dating club from a local newspaper. The article was fairly positive. The cost to join was two-hundred dollars. There was an interview involved where you had to specify the type of partner you were looking for and the times when you were available for dinner. According to the article, the organizers would then invite you to eight dinners over a year-long period where you would be paired with five other people looking for the same type of partner. Obviously two of the others would be male and the other three would be women. Ricardo was skeptical. It sounded to him that the 'pairing-up' meant simply that they sat you at the same table with others in the same age bracket. He wondered: what if he said during the interview that he only wanted to be seated at a table with twenty-year-old women? Would they have any twenty-year-old women in their club that wanted to be seated at a table with men in their fifties? Ricardo doubted it. Not only was there the two hundred dollar sign-up cost, but you still had to pay for your dinner. Assuming these were nice restaurants, it could run to an additional one-hundred dollars. Plus, if he drank at the dinners, he would not want to drive back to Hamburg, so he'd have to pay for a hotel room and stay over. That could be another eighty dollars. Ricardo did the math. If he went to all eight dinners, he would be out sixteen-hundred dollars. That averaged two-hundred a dinner. For that same two-hundred, he could drive over to St. Catharines, have a half-hour fuck with Haley, tip her, and still be able to buy lunch before driving back to Hamburg. On the other hand, if he met someone he liked at the dinners, someone who liked him, there could be a lot of free fucking, and that would change the math. It was a tough decision.

14.

    "So, it sounds like, in doing a cost-benefit analysis," his therapist was saying, "your conclusion is that joining the six by six dating service is not worth the cost. Is that what you're saying?"

    "Well, no, I'm just saying that for an average cost of two-hundred dollars a dinner, I could use that money better in other ways."

    "And what other ways would you use that two-hundred dollars that would facilitate you meeting women?”

“Well, I could go to shows, or museums, or visit more bars.”

Ricardo omitted the brothels.

“But you don’t. You could do all that now, but you don’t. No matter what the cost, a program that introduces you to women is going to have a better chance at success than anything you’ve done to date.”

Ricardo had to agree that his therapist’s logic was correct. But he also knew that he would not join six by six.

15.

Ricardo was lying in bed, drinking coffee. He liked this part of the day the best, when he was first waking up. He had his coffee pot programmed to make coffee right before his alarm would go off. He would get a cup of coffee, sweeten it, and climb back into bed to sip and think about things.

He thought about women. This morning he was thinking about brothels. He thought of the first American one he had ever been to. It was in New Jersey more than two decades ago. This particular one even had the iconic red light on the front door every night. Parking and the entrance, however, were in the back, out of sight. Ricardo had gotten a blow job from girl in a see-through nightie. She told him she was nineteen. She looked nineteen. Ricardo was thirty-four back then. That place had been alright, safe and clean, a rarity among American brothels. The trouble with American brothels, he thought, was that the ones that were affordable were dangerous and the upscale safe ones were simply out of his price range.

There were lots of nice affordable brothels in Europe, of course. And Ricardo had tried many of them. His favorite was the Tokyo Sauna, a massage house in Frankfurt, Germany, that had been there for years, where you could get a straight massage, or for the equivalent of $50 more, get a hand job or get fucked. For some reason, they did not do oral sex there. The massages were erotic in themselves. Ricardo remembered one time he was lying on his stomach with the naked masseuse straddling him, rubbing his butt with her pussy and thighs. He found that massage so erotic that he came, lying on his stomach, and laughed while sperm sputtered out.

He had tried several brothels in Toronto before settling on the one in St. Catharines. Aside from the one negative experience with Angie, all of Ricardo's experiences with Canadian brothels had been very positive. But he had to admit that, in his heart of hearts, he was very lonely. The brothels alleviated the loneliness for a brief while, made him feel *as if* he was loved, but the girls there did not love him. He did not think Haley even knew his last name, even though he had been fucking her once or twice a month for eight months. This was sex, not love. Ricardo yearned for a kind of sexual love he had only experienced once or twice in his life, where he and a lover ached continuously for each other's bodies. Those love affairs never lasted. But while they did, they sucked the marrow from his bones and lit that marrow on fire.

Were those days over? Was he doomed to senior dating services and senior cruises? Was his attempt at joining the Foreign Service laughable, or worse, would they see through his attempt? What if their background check uncovered his two books? Would they figure out he was joining the Foreign Service just to visit brothels? Would they care?

Ricardo thought of his epiphany and reminded himself that he was not in control of these things. He could join six by six and meet no one except lonely old women. Worse, he could join six by six and chicken-out of ever going to any of their dinners. He could not join six by six and meet a future lover in the aisle at Walmart tomorrow. He could take the Foreign Service exam and fail it or be turned down later. Or he could pass it and be assigned to the embassy in Amsterdam and spend his evenings fucking every whore in the red-light district. Or he might be assigned to Greenland

and spend his time measuring glaciers. Whatever happened was out of his control.

16.

Ricardo had never told his therapist about his two published books. Actually, when he thought about it, he kept his therapist in the dark about almost every part of his life. His therapist didn't know about the books, the bathhouses, the brothels, or the Foreign Service. There was no sense in confusing therapeutic issues with history, or preferences, or orientations.

Still, Ricardo often wondered whether his need for privacy, his need for secrecy, actually formed the walls that he went to therapy to try and break. He remembered one session when his therapist asked him, "If you had a magic wand and could change anything, what would you change?" and Ricardo had no answer to give. Actually, the problem was, he had too many answers to give, but all of them would have revealed things that he did not want to reveal to his therapist, things like the fact that he thought of suicide on a daily basis, that he was obsessed with sex, that he loved going to brothels, that he would occasionally go to gay bathhouses, that he drank at least a bottle of wine a night, or that he was constantly depressed.

He wondered, if the therapy session was a microcosm of his life, and if he couldn't even break the silence in that microcosm, how could he hope to break through in his life. The thought depressed him more.

On the other hand, he was able to tell his therapist little bits of his life, and the weekly sessions somehow seemed to help a little.

17.

After he had cum, Haley brought him a warm moist towel to wipe off with. Then she lay down beside him and snuggled close to him. He wrapped his arm around her.

"We still have thirty minutes left," she said, "if you'd like anything special."

"I like lying here with you," Ricardo said, "let's just hang out here."

"Okay."

Next to kissing Haley, Ricardo liked cuddling with her after sex the best. Their bodies fit so well together. He liked the way her head fit into the crook of his arm. He liked her smell. He liked the feel of her skin next to his. He turned his head slightly and kissed her on the forehead.

"Do you ever think about having kids?" he asked.

"Yeah, I do." she said, "Do you think I'd be a good mom?"

"Yes, I do, Haley. I think you'd be a very good mom. I can see you with a little girl, holding her hand, and crossing the street."

"Do you think I'd have a girl?'

"Uh huh. Yeah, I see you with a little blond girl named Sophia. Little Sophia."

"Sophia. That's sweet. You could be the daddy."

"Yeah, Haley, I would like that."

Ricardo reached over and put his hand on her stomach and looked her in the eyes.

"Could you see yourself having a baby with me?" he asked.

"Yeah, I could see that, maybe, you know, if our situations were different."

Ricardo leaned back and let his thoughts drift. He wondered what Haley would look like pregnant. He wondered how he would feel as the father of her child. He wondered if Haley was just saying those things because she was looking for a sugar daddy to take her out of the brothel. She knew what he did for a living and how much he made, because he had told her early on. So she knew he didn't have much money, that he was no sugar daddy, but on the other hand he always was nice to her, always respectful. Once he had even brought her a gift of some silver earrings.

A cynical voice in his head suggested that many of her customers brought her gifts. Ricardo tried to ignore that voice. But it darkened his thoughts. He thought about the age difference.

"I don't know, Haley. I think you so deserve someone who would treat you right, who would be a soul mate for you. I mean, I would treat you right, but I don't think I am the one. There's that age difference, you know."

There was a pause before she said, "But we fit so well together."

"Yes, we do."

Ricardo pulled the sheets up to their chins. It felt so good to lie there with her. At some level Ricardo knew that outside of the brothel the relationship would never work. Not only was there the age difference, and he had talked enough with her to know that they had nothing in common. But, within the four walls of the bedroom, she made him feel like a king. They often talked of running away, or having babies together, or of living together. It was all part of the fantasy, but it was a fantasy he loved.

"Do you think I'm getting fat?" she asked, as she pinched a roll of stomach skin just below her belly button.

"Let me see," Ricardo said, and he reached down and gently ran his fingers over her pussy and then up to where she was squeezing the skin of her belly between her first finger and her thumb.

"Hmmm, no. I would say you were wet, I would say you were lovely, I would say you were beautiful, but I would not say you were getting fat."

She laughed. Ricardo loved her laugh. It always amazed him how women could do that—stay in the absolute moment and laugh with someone even if they didn't really want to be with that person. A man would finish up and move on rather than pretend to laugh with someone he was done with. Ricardo guessed that was the difference between men and women, and he had to admit, it was something he admired in women.

"Let me ask you this, Haley," Ricardo began for the hundredth time. "If I was rich and lived on a tropical island by myself, would you come and live with me?"

She laughed again. "If you were rich, I'd come and live with you anywhere, even in Alaska. We'd be so good together."

Ricardo pulled her closer and kissed her. He loved her mouth, full-lipped and always open. He loved her smell and how it always got all over him.

They kissed and cuddled for a while longer, twenty minutes longer to be exact. Then his time was up, and he got up to get dressed to go. He put his pants on and took a nice tip out of his wallet and placed it on the dresser. As he was putting on his shirt, he asked her a question that he already knew the answer to.

"Tell me again, Haley, how it works if I want to see you outside of here, say for dinner or something."

"Well, you need to schedule it advance of course, and they schedule in three-hour blocks. If it's just for company out, it's one-hundred dollars an hour. If we go back to your place or back here, then the regular rates apply."

"Okay, let me meditate on that. I was thinking it might be nice to just do a dinner out sometime."

"I would like that, Ricardo. Just let me know."

"Okay, let me think about that."

"Okay, while you're finishing getting dressed, I'll make sure the coast is clear."

It was Haley's habit to always let him get dressed while she made sure he would not run into any other clients on the way out. Ricardo finished putting his clothes back on and waited for her.

She returned. "Everything's fine. I'll see you again."

He kissed her. "Thanks for everything."

"Take care, Ricardo."

As he walked out of the bedroom, the hostess was waiting by the front door to let him out.

"Was everything okay?" she asked.

That surprised Ricardo. Usually she never spoke to him except to say goodbye.

"Everything was fine." He said.

"Did you want to schedule some time with Haley outside of here?" she asked.

Ricardo suddenly realized why she was talking to him. Yet he appreciated the smoothness of it. He thought quickly. Did he have three-hundred dollars available in savings? Yes, he thought he did.

"Actually, I do. Do you think she'd be available next Friday or Saturday night for just a dinner out?"

"Friday or Saturday might be difficult. How about three hours early in the evening next Sunday, say between five and eight?

Ricardo thought for a moment, calculating the drive time and traffic patterns.

"Yes, I think that would work. Do I pick her up here?"

"Yes. So, we'll see you at five o'clock next Sunday?"

"Yes... yes, thank you for asking. I'll be here next Sunday at five p.m."

18.

For the whole next week, Ricardo was on a roller coaster of anticipation. He was elated that Haley had made sure the hostess would ask him about scheduling a date. He was depressed that he was being exploited. He was looking forward to sitting with Haley at a restaurant table, being the envy of those other fifty year old men sitting with their fifty year old wives. He felt angry, being conned by a nineteen year old hooker. He felt high, like he was in love. He felt a fool being so old. He thought about Sophia Loren marrying Carlo Ponti, thirty years her senior. He thought of Clint Eastwood, marrying someone twenty-seven years his junior, and happy when she had gotten pregnant. He had erotic fantasies of Haley, pregnant with his child, nursing his child, raising his child at home while he went out into the world to bring home the bacon. He chastised himself for indulging in stupid thoughts. This was simply a business relationship, where he was paying three hundred bucks to enjoy a fantasy that someone so young and beautiful would actually stoop to loving him. "I am such an idiot," he thought. But he also thought, "what the hell, I'm not breaking any laws. It might be fun. And I won't have to worry about getting it up."

He got online and researched restaurants. He narrowed his choices to three that were within walking distance of the brothel. He would let Haley decide which one. One was Italian. Ricardo thought that Haley would like Italian food. She seemed somehow Italian to him, even though she didn't look Italian. But he hoped she would pick the Italian place.

As Sunday approached, Ricardo experienced a nervousness he hadn't felt in years. He wondered what she would wear. He wondered what they would talk about. He examined his face in the mirror. There was some gray in the hair on his head, but his beard had far more white hairs than dark. The hairs on his chin were almost totally white. If this was a blind date, he would have shaved his beard off, to appear younger. But Haley knew what he looked like. As long as he had money his looks didn't matter. Still, his looks bothered him. Even though he could pass for ten years younger than he was, he was still old. He saw it in bars and restaurants. Waitresses would address him as "sir". Women sitting in bars would gather all the visual information they needed in the first glance they took of him and did not look at him again. He was off their radar. Hell, he had been off the radar of anyone he would date for at least a decade. When he walked into a bar or a restaurant, he felt invisible. He could saunter in, sit the bar, order an appetizer and a drink, sit there and eat and drink, and there could be people all around him, packed like sardines, talking and laughing, and he would pay his bill and leave, and he bet that were the police interview all of them later, no one would even remember that he was there. That's just the way it is when you're over fifty, he told himself. A voice in his head said, Hell, just wait till you're over sixty. That thought was depressing, as it was only a few years away. Ricardo wondered why he even kept holding onto the idea that there might be someone out there for him. He knew he should resign himself to prostitutes and bathhouses, that they were the only guarantee of sexual release he was likely to find.

Still, whenever he thought of Haley, he felt his heart soften. He loved her soft skinny body, her adolescent boy hips, her small breasts with the tiny areolas and nipples. Even though he preferred women who did not shave their pubic hair, he loved her little shaved pussy. She would not let him eat her out—house rules, she said, no fingers, no anal, no pussy eating—nonetheless he longed to run his tongue over her labia and her clit. Mostly, he realized, to give her pleasure, to hear her sigh, to moan. If he was rich, if he had the money, he would want her as a companion, a sexual partner. He knew most rich men did this. They kept women (on the side if they were married) to fuck, often they would keep the same woman for decades. Pay her apartment, pay her expenses, slip away from wifey twice a week for fucking. That's true love, Ricardo thought. To spend that much effort in hiding the bookkeeping, hiding the expenses, making excuses, taking showers to wash off the scent of vaginal fluid so wifey wouldn't suspect. That's true love. Or if there was no wifey, just having someone like Haley available twenty-four seven for sex, for dinner. If he was a rich man, Ricardo thought, that's what he'd do. He'd draw up a contract for Haley that laid it all out, set her up in an apartment, pay her overhead, pay her school bills if she wanted to go to school. Maybe set her up in a little job as a receptionist somewhere. It was a total fantasy, but Ricardo liked it. He'd call her up and say, "Haley, come over and I want you to wear that torn pink teddy. And bring the handcuffs." That would be heaven, Ricardo thought. But he knew that was only fantasy. Even on a lawyer's salary, he lived paycheck to paycheck. He would never be rich. It was all he could do to go to St. Catharines twice a month. Taking Haley out to dinner was a fool's journey. The money would be better spent just fucking her. But still, he thought, he was looking forward to it. Dinner with her was a different kind of fucking, a different kind of love-making. It would be, at least he hoped it would be, as intimate in its own way, just the sitting together and talking over food, as intimate as his being inside her.

Most people's lives can be reduced to one or two sentences. Ricardo was no exception. He was just another foolish older man; an aging Lothario; he was Don Quijote yearning for Dulcinea; Quazimodo yearning for Esmeralda; he was Lucius Atherton of Spoon River; he was every man who every made it into middle age... and every man who makes into middle age nurses the same secret desire— to possess some nineteen year old woman. That secret desire may manifest itself in different ways, but it cannot be denied. To those men who cannot act it out, who are married to thick women their own age, women they cannot ever admit they have come to hate, those men manifest it at work, they dominate the secretaries or the customers. God help their daughters. To those men who are not encumbered with wives, they dye their hair and pursue women. To those men who cannot find women, they find men. To those men who cannot find women or men, they generally explode or implode, taking others with them, or taking themselves quietly, unknown, unnoticed. It is the nature of man to require frequent release. If genetics and evolution had a voice, it would disclaim, "it comes with the plumbing". Man, like all drones, was evolutionarily programmed to squirt seed. That was his only purpose. It was, as Ricardo often thought, a barren landscape in which to find meaning.

19.

Sunday arrived. Ricardo made the drive to St. Catharines. He considered going over early in the morning "just to be sure he got there", but decided that this would be too compulsive. He was just being nervous, he told himself. But he arrived downtown thirty minutes early and had a glass of wine at a nearby bar just to calm his nerves.

The sun was coming through the large window by the bar where he was sitting. The warmth of it lulled him. He studied the color of the wine in his glass. Some man behind him was talking about his children, but he couldn't make out the words. He closed his eyes and thought of Haley. Thoughts of Paul and Monsieur were in his head. Why didn't he ever have them meet, he wondered. What would they say to each other? They had so much in common, each living in their isolated worlds. And that would include Alfredo as well, wouldn't it? He lived in his own isolated world too. And Ricardo realized, that would include him too. Monsieur was gay yet fell in love with a woman and was devastated when that love failed. Paul was straight but couldn't fall in love with women. Alfredo could only fall in love with a woman but picked a woman who was into bondage and submission. Ricardo felt he was in love, but knew he felt that way only because he paid a nineteen year old prostitute to act like she was interested in him. We're all idiots, Ricardo thought. The sun was warm. At least this idiot was going to have dinner with a nineteen year old female.

20.

He left the bar and started walking towards the brothel. He stopped at a currency exchange and bought some more Canadian dollars. He counted out three-hundred dollars and folded the bills and put them in his left front pocket. The rest he put in his wallet. He stepped out of the currency exchange and began walking north. He unwrapped a breath mint and put it in his mouth. The afternoon sunlight was a soft yellow. The people around him were a blur.

He arrived at the unmarked brothel door and made his way up the stairs and rang the bell. His heart was pounding. After what seemed like a long time, the door opened. The same hostess he had seen countless times before was there.

"Hello", she said, "Do you have an appointment?"

"Yes, I'm here to pick up Haley for dinner."

The hostess smiled, but Ricardo felt it was perfunctory. "Yes, of course, come in. She'll be down in a minute."

She gestured toward a small couch in the foyer. Ricardo had never noticed the couch before. He sat down and tried to relax. His shoulders and back hurt. He looked around the foyer and wondered how many men had waited here, had walked through that door, had come here to squirt out the sticky seed of life, to feel loved for a minute, and then to leave as anonymously as they had arrived.

He heard the distinctive clickety-clack of high-heel shoes coming down the stairs.

"Hello Ricardo."

Haley was wearing a white turtleneck blouse and tight blue jeans with a rhinestone designed running up the side. Black stiletto heels added three inches to her tiny frame. Ricardo realized he had never seen her dressed.

"You look marvelous, Haley."

She smiled. "Thank you. I'm looking forward to dinner. I'm *starved*. You wanted to go out for about three hours, right?"

"Oh, right." Ricardo reached into his pocket and removed the $300 and handed it to her. He was always impressed how she took care of business so smoothly.

"I'll be right back," she said. Ricardo watched her small ass move as she went back upstairs.

When she came back down the stairs she was wearing a blue jean jacket with rhinestone embroidery on the arms and pockets that matched the jeans. She walked up and took Ricardo's arm.

"Let's go!" She was all smiles.

21.

As they walked down the street, Ricardo told her

about the three restaurants he had researched. She said she was familiar with all three. He asked her to pick the one that was quietest. Ricardo wanted to get to know her better, so he wanted a place where he could hear her. He didn't like to admit it, but he knew that as he had aged, it had become harder for him to filter out background noises. Even a moderately noisy restaurant would make it impossible for him to hear Haley. Luckily, she said the Italian restaurant was pretty quiet. So, they headed there.

One of the things that Ricardo had always liked about Haley was she was never at a loss for words. She could chat for twenty minutes about a cat she had seen just for a moment in the street the day before and make it interesting. It must be a genetic trait in women, Ricardo thought, that they can remember every single tiny detail of every single event and never prioritize which had importance and which could be forgotten. And not only was every detail equally important, it was all connected. The cat that Haley saw in the street reminded her of the cat Brewster she had as a child and that led to a story of how Brewster once bit her on the nose and that led to a story of how she thought her nose was crooked and always wanted to have it fixed. Ricardo, who could barely remember what he had for lunch the day before, was always appreciative to be in the company of a woman who could chat away. It took all the pressure off him. But what made Haley's gift extraordinary was that she didn't just gab on and on mindlessly—she made eye contact with Ricardo and really put effort into communicating with him, so that Ricardo felt drawn into her story, felt that it mattered to her that he was the one she was telling it to, even if the details were all fluff.

At the restaurant, they sat and talked, and ordered appetizers and wine, and talked, and ordered dinner and talked. Or rather, Ricardo would prompt her with a question and Haley would talk. And as she poured out detailed stories, she would reach across the table and stroke his hand.

But some of the details didn't make sense to Ricardo.

She had moved to St. Catharines to get over a bad love affair, someone who she cared about who had cheated on her. But then later she mentioned how she had cheated on him throughout the relationship. And then at another point, she mentioned that he was married. When Ricardo asked her about school, she made only the vaguest mention of classes at some college somewhere and turned the topic around.

"You know what I'd really like to study? Fashion design. I love fashion design. See this jacket? I made it!"

"You sewed all those rhinestone on yourself?" Ricardo asked.

"Well, no. But I designed it. I drew the pattern out and took it to this little Chinese seamstress and she sewed it on. I *love* doing clothes like that. When I was a kid, I used to draw on my clothes all the time. It drove my mother nuts."

"It is very pretty, Haley. I noticed it right away. Where does one go to study fashion design?"

"Oh, you can go to Italy or New York or Los Angeles. There's *tons* of places."

"Have you thought about applying to any of them?"

"Oh, I think about it *all* the time. I'd love to go to school in Italy. That would be so *romantic*."

"Do you think you'd have to learn to speak Italian?"

"Oh no, they have lots of classes in English," she said with certitude.

If there was any awkward moment at dinner, it came when Ricardo asked her a question that he later realized was a stupid question to ask, as there was no answer that he would want to hear.

"Do you like working where you work?"

"Well, I don't mind it. The hours are good. Some of the clients are kinda gross, but I just put my mind somewhere else."

She must have sensed Ricardo felt a sudden worry, for she immediately reached across the table and said, "But not you. I always enjoy being with you. And you seem to like me. At least, you always ask for me. Have you tried any of the other girls in the house? There are several real pretty ones who work there."

"I do like you Haley. I always ask for you. There was one time when you weren't there, and I ended up with someone named Angie."

"Did you like her?"

"No. I like you."

"I don't like her either. She and I roomed together for a few months. We couldn't get along. She always left her stuff lying around the flat. She was such a slob. She doesn't work there anymore."

"What happened to her?"

"She went to work at another house."

"Here in town?"

"Uh huh. I know the lady who runs it. Real control freak. I wouldn't work there."

Ricardo realized that there was a whole economy of brothels in St Catharines and in nearby Toronto, a whole layer of people who worked in the brothels, or who rented to brothels, or provided services to brothels, a whole stratosphere of people whose everyday world contained knowledge of where each brothel was, who worked there, who had gotten recently fired, who had just been hired, how strict the management was, how many trick towels were used in a week, how many condoms ordered, how much lubricant was used, and the driving force behind the existence of so many brothels: how much money was being made and where that money went. Ricardo thought about that for a moment. He wondered how he could work that information into his book *100 Brothels You Must Visit Before You Die*. He wondered if Haley could be a source he could use to describe that whole culture. But he discarded that idea. He didn't want to write an exposé; he wanted to write a travelogue.

After dessert, Haley said, "We have lots of time left. Did you want to go back to the house and use one of the rooms or did you want to walk down to the park and enjoy the evening?"

Ricardo knew that using one of the rooms would entail additional charges. "I like the idea of walking down to the park. We can sit and talk there by the harbor."

"Okay, I'm ready when you are."

Ricardo paid the bill and they left. As they stepped into the street, Haley took his arm again. It felt old fashioned, but Ricardo liked it. He wondered if anyone noticed them as a couple, so he looked at the faces of people as they walked by, but they seemed preoccupied with where they were going. He did not think anyone was paying them any attention.

Haley was talking about her past boyfriend again. "Peter never liked to walk anywhere. He always had to drive. He would drive to the gym to use the exercise machine. That's so *crazy* I would tell him. You'd get twice the exercise if you walked to the gym. But he'd never listen to me."

Ricardo thought about how women always want to talk about their past boyfriends in such excruciating detail. When he was younger he believed that they were trying to let him know what mistakes not to repeat, that they were really trying to help him be a better boyfriend by letting him in on the secret "what not to do" list. But later in life he realized that they were just talking about themselves, and all past boyfriends were past because they had not made the woman the center of their attention. No matter how many ex-boyfriends there were, the bottom line was always the same—they didn't make the woman feel like the center of attention. He wondered if that also explained why women hung onto abusive relationships—because the abuse made them centerstage.

It was a beautiful evening. The park was full of other couples walking and talking or sitting quietly together. Ricardo and Haley found an empty picnic table and sat down beside each other. Ricardo put his arm around her shoulders. He could feel the interplay of warm and cool air as the breeze blew in from the harbor. Down near the boats there was a small stage and a band was playing old rock and roll songs. The music floated up to them. Ricardo looked out across the park at the other couples sitting at benches. He was one of them. Each of them had come to this park on this night at this particular moment to sit with someone they loved. He felt somehow connected to each of them. Somehow, they were all a part of this moment. Ricardo felt at one with the world.

"Do you like my shoes?" Haley stuck her leg out and wiggled her stiletto heel encased foot. The shoes were a golden leather with many straps and tiny black rivets along the leather. The heels were thin and black. Her toenails were painted a bright purple that somehow matched the rhinestones on her jeans.

"They're very nice, Haley."

"I got them in L.A. I flew over there last month and bought ten pairs of shoes."

"You flew to L.A. just to buy shoes?"

"Uh huh. I go to visit my friend Martin. I really love him, but I could never marry him—he's impotent. He just likes to have someone to sleep with, but he never touches me. Sometimes it makes me so *angry* because I really do love him. But he never has time for me. He works for Universal. I met him at the Toronto Film Festival last year. I take him shopping with me and let him help pick out the shoes. He has such good taste; I told him he could be gay."

Ricardo was not sure he wanted to fully understand that arrangement. Martin flies her out to L.A. where he buys her shoes and sleeps in the same bed with her but doesn't fuck her. That just seemed weird.

"Do you have a lot of shoes, Haley?"

"Oh *yes*, I have hundreds. But these are my favorite." She wiggled her foot again. Ricardo didn't care one way or the other about shoes, but he did think her foot was very pretty."

"Yes, they're very pretty."

"I wore them just for you."

"Well, thank you. How long have you known Martin?"

"About three years now. Do you like the nail polish? I did those for you too."

Three years didn't sync up with what she had told him about Peter or her life before the brothel, but Ricardo decided not to pursue that line any further.

"So, do you see yourself doing some kind of fashion work then, in the future?"

"Uh huh. I did some modeling in high school."

"What kind of fashion work do you see yourself doing?"

"I'd like to have my own modeling agency. I'd have several girls work for me who could do catwalk assignments or convention shows or press work."

"I see."

Ricardo wasn't sure if all this modeling talk was a metaphor for the sex trade business. Maybe Haley wanted to open up her own escort service. He changed the subject and asked her if she lived near the brothel.

"Oh no, I live in the same building. The woman who owns the house rents rooms to all the girls, but we almost have to double up with roommates because the rent is so high, but on the other hand we don't pay utilities, and there's no lease to sign."

Ricardo thought to himself, "I bet there's no lease." He thought again about the fact that although prostitution was legal in Canada, running a brothel was not. That's why he always had to hand the money to Haley directly, and never to the woman who answered the door and let him in.

"Who's your roommate now?"

"Her name is Tiffany. She's new there. You'd like her. She's blonde and real beautiful. She works out and has a killer body. You ought to ask to meet her sometime."

That was the second time that evening that Ricardo felt that Haley was suggesting that Ricardo have sex with other women at the brothel. That bothered him.

"Well, you know, Haley, you're the only one I want to

be with."

She leaned into him. "Ahh Ricardo, you're so sweet."

The band down by the harbor was playing an old Lennon/McCartney song "In My Life." For Ricardo, it seemed to fit the moment.

"I love that song," he said.

"Hmm it sounds nice. Who's it by?"

"The Beatles."

"Who?"

"You know, the Beatles - John, Paul, George, and Ringo."

Haley leaned closer into Ricardo.

"Never heard of them," she said.

22.

After Ricardo had walked Haley back to the brothel, through the outside door marked "private residence" and up the long stairs to the metal door entrance, after he told her what a wonderful evening he had had, after he slipped her a fifty-dollar tip, after he had kissed her goodnight, after he asked if she'd like to have dinner with him again, after she said yes she'd *love* that, after she explained that he just had to make the appointment with the hostess, after all that he walked slowly back towards the lot where his car was parked. He did not feel in any type of a hurry to get home. Even though he really had had a good time with Haley, he felt oddly at loose ends. His walk took him back past the same park they had been in an hour earlier. Ricardo walked over to the same picnic table that he and Haley had sat on. He sat down on the same bench and looked around. There were still a few couples in the park, sitting on benches or strolling on the paths. The band that had been playing at the harbor was gone. The last rays of sunset were long gone.

Ricardo looked at the other couples who were still in the park. They were all young. Most of the women seemed attractive, or at least their silhouettes were thin. He imagined them all going home in a while and making love. He wondered how different each of their lovemaking would be. He thought of Haley's body, her hairless pussy, her full open-mouth kisses, the way she would grab his cock and look him straight in the eyes and smile before she climbed on top of him and slid his cock up inside her. He loved that about her. She was wonderful in bed.

But then he thought of how she didn't know who the Beatles were, how she hadn't even been born when the Vietnam War was raging, and how none of her relationships had ever worked out. Worst of all, she couldn't keep her stories of her past consistent to Ricardo for even a few hours. If she was nineteen then she must have started dating Peter when she was fourteen and he was married; and she must have started flying to L.A. to see Martin when she was sixteen; or she was much older than nineteen. Maybe the pieces would have made sense if he had asked enough questions, but Ricardo knew that a person's past should have some kind of consistency, even at first telling. How can you be nineteen and own hundreds of pairs of shoes? Ricardo didn't care if she had shoes, but his fantasy of having a life with her, of living with her, of having her be his girlfriend or wife, that fantasy seemed odd to him now. He had spent so many nights dreaming of living with her, fathering children with her, being her lover, her mentor, her protector, her provider. He felt like a fool for having those thoughts. He was her client, her john, her customer. She was sweet and special, and he felt some type of love for her, but it was the kind of love that a man can only feel for someone who is so close physically but totally unconnected culturally and intellectually. Ricardo knew that, yes, he would still fantasize about winning the lottery and keeping Haley as a mistress. But now the fantasy was more cold-blooded. There would be no love involved, no children. Just sex.

Ricardo looked around. The other couples in the

park seemed like foreign objects. They had what he could never have again—a relationship with someone their own age with the same cultural references. They had youth and the possibility of a future growing old with someone. He had only a few years left and could only look forward to women who would fuck him for money. He lived in a different time zone, a different world, than these silhouetted couples.

He didn't regret taking Haley out to dinner. He enjoyed it. But it opened his eyes. Nothing was resolved. He had not progressed to anywhere. He only had what he had always known—that he did not fit in anywhere.

As he watched the other couples, Ricardo thought of Monsieur. "These are thoughts that Monsieur would have thought," he said to himself. Then he heard Mamood's voice in his head. "Be careful, mon ami. Keep it under control." He thought of Paul's yearning to be loved, to find love with someone. He felt Alfredo's pure carnal desire for Sandy, the same way he desired Haley. But Mamood's advice won the day. Ricardo stood up and walked toward the parking lot where he had left his car.

23.

The next week Ricardo got a phone call from his accountant Harold Glass.

"Ricardo, I had a call from someone claiming to be from the Foreign Service, something about a background check."

"Okay."

"They know I'm your accountant because my name is on your income tax forms. I told them I couldn't talk with them until I had a release from you."

"Okay, well, I did apply for the Foreign Service, and they did say they would do a background check. I didn't think they would do it so soon."

"Well, the problem is, they're wanting to know about your publishing income."

"What? What do you mean? What did they say?"

"Well, they see you declared additional income for the past two years for publishing and they want to know what was published."

"What did you tell them?"

"I told them that I couldn't talk with them until I had a release from you."

"Hmmmm." Ricardo thought for a moment. "Are you supposed to call them back?"

"Yes."

"Well, don't. Don't do anything. If they call you back, just blow them off. Tell them you haven't gotten ahold of me, and if they call again, tell them you're very busy and don't have time for their questions, and if you really get pushed, tell them that you are not authorized to release that information. If you want to really fuck with them, you can tell them that you can't release it for national security reasons."

"Ricardo, I never kid with the government. I can fog them, I can stonewall them, I can refuse them, but I won't taunt them."

Ricardo laughed. "Okay Harold, don't taunt them, just don't play ball with them."

Ricardo hung up the phone. "Fuck," he thought, "that screws that plan." He went to his computer and pulled up his files on the Foreign Service. He knew there was a link that he could access that would automatically withdraw his application. He found the link and pressed "Send". He got an automatic reply within thirty seconds, saying his application had been withdrawn and wishing him luck in his endeavors.

24.

It had been three weeks since his dinner with Haley. Money had been tight, and it had taken him that amount of time to save up enough to see her again. It had been a difficult three weeks. His body ached for hers. He didn't care whether she knew who the Beatles were or not. He just wanted to see her naked, to feel her body press against his, to feel her cool nakedness against his nakedness, to kiss those small nipples, to grasp each cheek of her small butt, to feel her wetness, to be inside her again.

It was a beautiful day for a drive across international borders. Traffic was light. That pleased Ricardo. He passed through customs, parked in his usual lot, and started walking. He was oblivious to the people around him. He found a pay phone near the harbor.

"Can I help you?"

"Yes, I'd like to make an appointment with Haley for a one-hour session."

"I'm sorry. Haley is not here today. We do have Tiffany and Susanna available this afternoon."

Shit, Ricardo thought.

"Will Haley be back tomorrow?"

"No, I'm sorry. She's gone for the weekend."

"Okay... I'll call back next weekend."

"Are you sure you wouldn't want to meet Tiffany or Susanna? They are both very nice."

"No, no thanks. I'll check back next week."

"Okay, thank you for calling."

Ricardo hung up. Now he felt doubly crappy. Crappy for Haley not being here, and crappy for wanting her. He could feel a massive headache starting to swell up.

There was a small coffee house across the street. Ricardo decided to get a cup of coffee, sit down, and try and relax.

When he stepped inside, there was no one occupying any of the tables. He walked up to the counter. A young clerk appeared from the back. She had a pretty face, soft brown hair, and a small nose ring. Ricardo ordered an Americano. Appropriate he thought. An idiotic Americano ordering an Americano. He watched the girl make the drink. She had bigger hips than Haley and a bigger bust. Ricardo felt attracted to her. He guessed she was in her early twenties.

She brought the drink to him. As he paid her, he said, "Not much business today?"

"No, it's been pretty quiet. You're the first customer in an hour. But it gives me time to study."

"Ah, what are you studying?"

"Anthropology. I just work here part time."

"I see. Umm, do you have any of those packets of honey for the coffee?"

"I think so. Let me see."

She bent down to look under the counter. Ricardo was able to look down her blouse. He could see the firm breasts in her bra. I'd love to taste those, he thought.

"Yes." She stood up and handed him some packets. "Here you are, sir."

Ricardo hated the word "sir". It reminded him of his reality. Here he was, trying to grab a titty peek at a girl less than half his age. He was a "sir" to her, just another middle-aged customer.

"Yes, thank you."

He put a large tip in the tip jar and found a table by the window. He sat and sipped his coffee and watched the people walking by, all going to their different destinations, all on a mission. All of them, in one way or another, wanting sex. Either today, or this week, or soon. Even the ones who had sworn it off, the very act of swearing it off meant they wanted it. Some were getting it regularly, some were getting it badly, settling for sex with their wives or husbands or lousy boyfriends or stupid girlfriends. The things we do for just sex, Ricardo thought.

He thought back to his epiphany. That morning so many years ago, when he was lying in bed, when he first realized he was an idiot. Nothing much has changed, he said to himself. You're just as deluded, as stupid, as unaware of the forces that drive you as you ever were. You married because you thought you were in love. You divorced because you thought you weren't. You think you love Haley because she makes you feel good. You are crushed when she's not here. You think she likes you, that she would be your wife if you could afford her. But she's no different than the girl that just gave you coffee. Fucking that girl would make you feel good too. But you're just an old man to her. The only reason

Haley had dinner with you was because you paid her. You paid her! If she really liked you, if money wasn't the point, she would have done something to get together with you outside of the payment schedule. It's not what people do— it's what they don't do that tells you how they really feel. If through some fluke, Haley really wanted to be with you, she would have stepped outside of the payee relationship and said something. But what was it she said when you asked her if she'd like to have dinner again? She said she would love to, that all you had to do was make the appointment with the hostess. It was just a job for her. Just another Americano. Just another fuck. Another blow job. An agreeable fuck, an easy blow job, but just another middle-aged lonely man. Easy pickings.

Ricardo realized it was Mamood voice he was hearing in his head. Mamood had never been wrong.

What would he do now? The foreign service was out. How could he write *100 Brothels You Must Visit Before You Die* ? He would have to find some other easy way to research it. "What do you think I should do, Mamood?"

"Well my friend, you're not going to give up brothels, are you?"

"No."

"They are the only place you get sex, yes?"

"Well there's the bathhouses."

"Well, the brothels are only place you get sex with women, yes?

"Yes."

"And you are not going to give up the brothels?"

"No, no I'm not."

"So, mon ami, do what you need to do. You're no different than anyone else."

"What about my book?"

"Write it. Maybe change the title but write it. You're not going to stop writing, are you?"

"No."

"So, just do what you need to do."

Ricardo finished his coffee, stood up, tossed the paper cup into the trash and walked out of the coffee shop. He walked back to the pay phone and dialed the number.

"Can I help you?"

"Yes, I'd like to make an appointment with Tiffany for an hour."

"Okay, what time would you like your appointment?"

"I can be there in ten minutes."

FIN

ABOUT THE AUTHOR

Robert Rahula was born in Spain to an American father and Spanish mother, but grew up in Virginia on the farm of his paternal grandparents. He returned to Menorca, Spain, in the 1960s to pursue his writing career. These days he travels in Europe, Central and South America for several months a year, giving readings and lectures, and spends the rest of his time writing, dividing his time between Spain and the United States.

Over the past 30 years, Robert has published dozens books of prose and poetry in Spain and in the United States. While he remains relatively undiscovered in the United States, he is revered in Spain as the founder of the "portilla" style of popular Spanish poetry: non-metered fluid verse that deals with love, loss, bisexuality, separateness, and growing older.